Reid reached out and smoothed a silky lock away from Christiane's face. "I could have killed Etienne for what he did to you."

Emboldened by his touch, she placed the palm of her hand against his bearded cheek and felt him stiffen at the contact. "Does my touch offend you?" She couldn't quite control the tremor of hurt.

"Of course not," he denied brusquely.

Before she could lose courage, she lightly brushed his mouth with hers. Though inexperienced in the ways of pleasing a man, she was rewarded when she sensed an immediate response.

He wrapped his fingers around her wrist to halt her advances. "What kind of game are you playing?"

"I want you to make love to me."

"What?" His grip tightened. "I don't think that's wise."

"You do not want me?"

His breath whistled from between clenched teeth. "Countess, I've wanted you since the moment I set eyes on you in Le Cap."

"Then what is stopping you?" she asked.

"This isn't the time—or the place—to do something foolish. Something you'll regret later."

"But you are wrong. The past is dust, the future filled with uncertainty. The present is all we have." Boldly she kissed him again, a kiss filled with longing and tinged with desperation. "Make love to me," she whispered against his lips.

Reid capitulated with a groan, and his mouth slanted over hers, greedily plundering what she so generously offered. . . .

BOOK YOUR PLACE ON OUR WEBSITE AND MAKE THE READING CONNECTION!

We've created a customized website just for our very special readers, where you can get the inside scoop on everything that's going on with Zebra, Pinnacle and Kensington books.

When you come online, you'll have the exciting opportunity to:

- View covers of upcoming books
- Read sample chapters
- Learn about our future publishing schedule (listed by publication month *and author*)
- Find out when your favorite authors will be visiting a city near you
- Search for and order backlist books from our online catalog
- Check out author bios and background information
- Send e-mail to your favorite authors
- Meet the Kensington staff online
- Join us in weekly chats with authors, readers and other guests
- Get writing guidelines
- AND MUCH MORE!

Visit our website at
http://www.zebrabooks.com

BAYOU MAGIC

Elizabeth Turner

Zebra Books
Kensington Publishing Corp.

http://www.zebrabooks.com

ZEBRA BOOKS are published by

Kensington Publishing Corp.
850 Third Avenue
New York, NY 10022

First Printing: October, 1999
10 9 8 7 6 5 4 3 2 1

Printed in the United States of America

For Joan Avery,
a wonderful friend and fellow writer.
This one's for you.
Thanks for being there every word of the way.

Prologue

June, 1790

Spanish justice came swiftly.

"Señor Reid Alexander," the magistrate intoned, scowling at the prisoner from his lofty perch. "I pronounce you guilty of murdering Gaston du Beaupre. By the power vested in me by Charles the Fourth, king of Spain, I hereby sentence you to spend the remainder of your days at hard labor on His Majesty's penal colony on the island of Hispaniola. May God have mercy on your soul."

Two soldiers stepped forward, one on either side of the condemned man, and shoved him toward the side door leading to the prison.

Chained at wrists and ankles like a mad dog, Reid shuffled past the row of spectators. Feeling the object of intense scrutiny, he cast a glance sideways—and found himself gazing into Leon du Beaupre's swarthy face. An unmistakable glitter of triumph lent the Creole's obsidian eyes a malevolent gleam. In less time than it took to blink, Reid's suspicions solidified into certainty. His mind had rebelled at accepting the obvious—the odious. But the truth stared him in the face.

Leon du Beaupre had cold-bloodedly killed Gaston, his own brother!

Fury and loathing propelled Reid over the railing that separated him from his nemesis. Wrapping his manacled hands around du Beaupre's neck, he squeezed the air from the man's throat.

Quickly recovering from their surprise, the jailers sprang into action, beating their hapless prisoner mercilessly until at last, defeated, he released his stranglehold.

"Someday . . . somehow . . ." Reid vowed grimly.

Revenge was his last coherent thought before a blow to the head rendered him senseless.

Chapter One

She'd make a bargain with the devil himself.

Her rash declaration taunted her. Christiane Bouchard Delacroix watched the island of St. Domingue loom closer. Panic rose in her throat, bitter as bile. Her gaze dropped, and she willed her fingers to relax their tight grip on the ship's rail. She stared transfixed at the wedding ring that graced the third finger of her left hand as though seeing it for the first time. The large square-cut ruby framed by diamond baguettes caught fire in the rays of the noon sun. It was an expensive ring, an ostentatious show of wealth— and ownership. Beautiful as it might be, it felt uncommonly heavy, weighing down both her body and spirit.

Worriedly, she gnawed her lower lip. What kind of man was Etienne Delacroix, this husband she had wed by proxy and had yet to meet? What kind of man would welcome a bride, yet deny sanctuary to her only kin?

That question had become a refrain, singing through her mind unceasingly. If she lived to be a hundred, she'd never forget the bleak look in her beloved grandfather's eyes, or the sharp twist of pain in her heart, as they bade each other adieu on the dock at Calais. But the terms of the marriage contract had been specific. She was to come unfettered by relatives.

Only at the last moment, unnoticed, had she slipped a jeweled bracelet into her grandfather's pocket. He had stubbornly refused to accept her offerings, protesting that her jewelry had always belonged to the Bouchard women, going back many generations—a family tradition he refused to break. Christiane had consoled herself with the knowledge that the sale of the bracelet would bring enough money for her grandfather's safe passage to America, a land far from spying and thieving servants who cunningly plotted their demise.

Tears had streamed down her face unchecked as she watched him walk away and out of her life. His once proud carriage was bowed, but not broken. Jean-Claude Bouchard, Comte de Varennes, her seemingly invincible grandfather, was old and frail.

And all alone.

"We should be ready to dock in less than an hour, Countess."

Lost in reverie, Christiane had failed to hear Judson Heath, captain of the merchant vessel *Marianne*, approach the bow. "How many times must I remind you, *Capitaine*, that I am no longer a countess?" she asked, giving the grizzled seaman an affectionate smile.

"Nonsense!" he scoffed. "It's plain to see you're a countess born and bred. Nothing can ever change that."

"Since my marriage to Monsieur Delacroix, I, too, am a citizen, no different from anyone else." All traces of her smile vanished. "Since the revolution, it is no longer safe—or prudent—to consider oneself a member of the aristocracy."

"Surely, Countess, no one would wish to harm a young woman as lovely, or as charming, as yourself?"

She gave a small, philosophical shrug. "In a time of great unrest, people react in unpredictable ways."

Taking off his cap, Judson Heath scratched his head. "Reckon you're right, but one thing I do know. That new husband of yours is going to be delighted to see the prize he won for himself. You're a jewel any crown would be worthy of."

Her smile returned. "And you, *mon capitaine*, are as gallant as any of the nobles in King Louis's court."

"Who, me? I'm nothing but an old sea dog," he protested as a dull red blush spread under his weathered skin. "Having your delightful company aboard my ship has been a rare pleasure."

"You have been very kind to me, *Capitaine. Merci.*"

"We expect to dock within the hour," he said, clearing his throat. "I assume your husband will be at the Cap to welcome you?"

"*Oui,*" she murmured. She was saved from elaborating further when the seaman was hailed by the ship's first mate. Excusing himself, Captain Heath hurried off to attend to duties. In truth, Christiane had no idea what to expect when the ship docked. Etienne's letter had been rather vague, stating only that she would be met at the pier, then transported by carriage to Belle Terre.

A mild breeze tugged at her skirt and teased the plume of her hat. Shading her eyes against the glare of sun that shimmered off waters an impossible shade of blue, Christiane studied the island that was to become her home. Whitewashed buildings hugged the shoreline and dotted the craggy hillside. Flowers grew in riotous profusion. Even from a distance, she could see their bright splashes of red, pink, yellow, and white. Pretty as a painting, the lush green isle dozed under the tropical sky.

Resolutely squaring her shoulders, she gazed toward St. Domingue with an odd mixture of anticipation and trepidation.

An hour later Christiane stood on a wharf teeming with activity. Unique blends of the scents of coffee beans and exotic spices filled the air. Through the loud babble of voices, she was able to identify French, English, and Spanish being spoken, as well as the musical dialect of the island.

Slaves, naked except for dirty strips of cloth tied about their hips, toiled loading and unloading heavy crates. Their dark skin glistened with sweat, and many of them bore marks of previous beatings. Christiane flinched as a shouted order from a brutal taskmaster was punctuated by the sharp crack of a whip.

Mon Dieu, what have I agreed to? she wondered. This beautiful island, which had looked like paradise from a distance, seemed more like hell, brimming with violence and misery and—she shuddered—indifference.

Deliberately, she turned her back on the scene. Where was her bridegroom? What was keeping him? Surely he hadn't gone through all the trouble of sending for her only to abandon her on the dock in this godforsaken place.

From the shade of her silk parasol, she anxiously scanned the crowd. One man in particular, whom she judged to be nearing thirty, captured her attention. Tall and broad-shouldered, he stood half a head above the rest. Tawny, sun-streaked hair was worn long and tied at his nape with a leather thong. His face was arresting with high cheekbones, a slightly crooked nose, and a strong jaw with a shallow cleft in his chin. His deeply bronzed skin and muscular physique attested to long hours of physical labor under a tropical sun. Though not classically handsome, he possessed a rugged appeal that Christiane knew many women would find attractive.

But it was more than the man's physical appearance that intrigued her. It was his demeanor. Fascinated, she studied him unabashedly. He radiated supreme self-confidence, that certain brand of arrogance that springs from the knowledge you can handle yourself in any situation. She guessed him to be the sort who would not let obstacles stand in his way. Perhaps because she was plagued with uncertainty, or perhaps because she was simply a woman, she found this quality compelling.

Narrowing his eyes, the man frowned thoughtfully at the throng on the dock, then settled his gaze upon her.

Could it be? Her hand fluttered to her throat to still the suddenly accelerated beat of her heart. Caught like a rabbit in a snare, she stood frozen as he cut through the crowd toward her.

"Christiane Delacroix?" he asked without ceremony.

"Oui, m'sieur." His voice, she noted, was a pleasing baritone.

"Your husband instructed me to bring you to him."

Of course, this man was not Etienne. How foolish she had been to imagine otherwise. She should have realized immediately from his manner of dress. The loose-fitting collarless shirt was the type worn by tradesmen and shopkeepers, not wealthy landowners.

Before she could gather her wits to respond, Captain

Heath materialized at her side. A suspicious scowl replaced his usually affable expression. "Who do you think you are, sir, to accost this lady?"

"You must be Captain Judson Heath of the *Marianne,*" the stranger replied, nonplussed by the blunt remark. "I assure you, I am not here to accost Madame Delacroix, but to escort her safely to Belle Terre."

"Who are you? Why didn't my husband come himself?" Christiane demanded, piqued that her bridegroom had sent an emissary in his stead. If her new husband was incapable of extending this simple courtesy, she dreaded to think what might lie ahead.

"Reid Alexander, overseer at Belle Terre. At your service, madame." He made a short, mocking bow. "As for the reason your husband didn't choose to welcome you personally, you had best ask him."

Christiane was subjected to the full force of steely gray eyes, appraising, cataloging every detail of her appearance. She returned the look haughtily, refusing to quail under this stranger's cold assessment. She was, after all, a countess, member of one of the noblest families in Provence.

"Not here to welcome his bride!" Captain Heath sputtered. "Never heard of such nonsense in all my born days. This is no way to treat a lady, and a bona fide countess to boot."

Christiane smiled fondly at the crusty old man's staunch protests on her behalf. Raising on tiptoe, she brushed a kiss on his wrinkled cheek. *"Adieu, Capitaine."*

"Good-bye, child." Captain Heath cleared his throat and clasped her small hand in his. "May good fortune follow you always." Then, turning away, he lumbered down the wharf.

Reid gestured impatiently at the brass-bound trunk resting at her feet. "Unless we want to arrive at Belle Terre after nightfall, we should get started. The rest of your baggage can be delivered later."

"There is no other luggage, m'sieur," Christiane replied stiffly. She hated confessing to this cold, aloof stranger that all her worldly possessions were in a single trunk. That she had fled under cover of night like a common thief with only the possessions that could be squeezed into one piece of luggage.

Reid picked up the trunk and hoisted it onto the back of a carriage waiting nearby. Remembering how she and her grandfather had struggled, Christiane marveled at the ease with which he lifted the unwieldy piece. As he reached out to secure it in place, the folds of his loose-fitting shirt lifted to reveal a pistol tucked neatly into the waistband of his pants. She gaped at the weapon in surprise. Was St. Domingue so dangerous that she needed an armed guard? Who—or what—was to be feared? Man? Or beast?

She vowed to be wary of both until she learned the answer.

The luggage safely stowed, Reid assisted her into the carriage, then climbed into the other side and picked up the reins. The matched chestnuts slowly picked their way through the traffic of the dock. Christiane cast a sidelong glance at her companion and found his attention focused on navigating through the tangled maze of carts, carriages, and wooden crates stacked shoulder-high.

They had nearly cleared the dock area when a sound like the sharp report of a rifle rang out, startling her. The noise was followed by a cry of pain. Turning her head, Christiane saw a burly man raise a black-handled whip and viciously slash the back of a slave straining under a cart weighted with bulging burlap sacks.

"You lazy, no good son of Satan," he bellowed. "Move!"

Instinctively Christiane reached out and clutched Reid's sleeve. "Can't you stop this senseless beating?"

Reid merely lifted a brow and looked askance at the fingers gripping his shirt. Christiane's gaze followed his and, embarrassed, she quickly released her hold. She glanced up in time to see the slave renew his grip on the cart and plod forward. As he passed, she got a clear view of the unfortunate man's face. His expression showed neither pain nor resignation, but rather thinly veiled defiance. In spite of the day's heat, a chill chased down her spine.

Reid flicked the reins, and the carriage broke free from the chaos of the wharf. "If you're to remain on St. Domingue, Countess, you'll quickly grow accustomed to such sights."

"Never," she avowed, shaking her head. "In my country, people revolted because they had no bread. Much blood has already been shed. Citizens of St. Domingue would be wise to heed their example."

Reid glanced at her profile curiously. This girl, scarcely more than eighteen or nineteen, knew firsthand what happened when people tired of oppression. Circumstances must have been dire, indeed, to make her flee her homeland for a proxy marriage with a monster like Etienne Delacroix.

Monster or not, his employer possessed impeccable taste. His bride was a rare beauty, with hair the color of a moonless night and eyes equally as dark and mysterious. Her features were finely sculpted and delicate with a small, straight nose, and a mouth that hinted of sensuality. Her skin was flawless ivory, tinged with the palest peach. Everything about her screamed of refinement. Undoubtedly accustomed to being waited on hand and foot by an army of servants since birth, she never had to wonder where her next meal was coming from. Her background and his were as different as day from night.

Pity Delacroix didn't have an ounce of common sense. This was not the time to take a wife. Only a fool would bring a woman to an island teetering on the brink of disaster. But the girl's fate was no concern of his. Reid slapped the reins, urging the horses to a smarter pace. With any luck, he'd be halfway to New Orleans before trouble broke out.

Soon they left the sweltering heat of Le Cap Francois behind. The road, little more than a rutted track, wound up the thickly wooded mountainside. The air became cooler, sweetened with the scent of pine and exotic-looking flora.

Christiane peeked at the enigmatic overseer from beneath a screen of lashes. For the first time she noticed the small crescent-shaped scar that marred one cheekbone. It resembled the imprint of a signet ring. His nose, too, looked as though it had been broken a time or two in a brawl. She would bet her last sou that Reid Alexander had given his opponent as good as he got.

She shifted restlessly on the seat. "Have you worked for my husband very long?" she ventured at last.

"Long enough."

"Tell me, what is Belle Terre like?"

A lengthy silence followed her question.

"Beautiful," he finally replied, keeping his eyes on the road, "but it lacks warmth."

"And my husband," she persisted. "Does he, too, lack warmth?"

Reid's face remained impassive. "I wouldn't know."

"*Au contraire,* I think you do. What is he like? Does he laugh or frown? Is he patient or quick to anger? Generous or miserly?"

"I am not at liberty to discuss my employer. Your questions will be answered soon enough."

She cocked her head to one side, a teasing glint in her dark eyes. "Are you always so reluctant to engage in conversation, m'sieur, or is it me you object to?"

He shot her an exasperated glance. "Are you always this relentless?"

"Always," she said, laughing for the first time in weeks.

The exchange eased the tension between them. Under her constant probing, Reid relaxed his guard and shared what he knew about the island's history. Two hours later, they rounded a bend in the road and crossed a narrow bridge over a babbling stream.

"I need to water the horses," Reid announced as he pulled the carriage to a halt. "If you want to walk upstream a bit, you'll find a waterfall that is much admired."

Christiane needed no further urging. Holding up her skirts, she gingerly made her way along the creekbed, stopping occasionally to inspect a fern here or a flower there. In the background she could hear the muted tumble of falling water. Gradually the stream widened into a shallow pool. Beautiful yellow flowers with petals the size of her hand drooped from the branches of a nearby bush. Bending down, she picked one of the blooms and, smiling, inhaled its spicy fragrance. Her smile vanished when she raised her head and found herself staring at two lovers entwined in an embrace. Intuitively, she stepped backward.

Alerted by the slight movement, the couple broke apart guiltily. For a brief span of time, Christiane and the couple looked at each other in mute astonishment. A myriad of small details etched themselves in Christiane's mind. A fretwork of scars crisscrossing a powerful torso. Fear in the woman's dark eyes. A wicked-looking blade tucked into a red sash.

At a barked command from her companion, the woman disappeared into the thick foliage. Black eyes alight with malice, the man withdrew the knife from around his waist, and, pointing it toward Christiane, advanced toward her.

Christiane whirled and fled. The flowering shrubs she had admired only moments ago became her enemies as their spiny branches grabbed at her gown, impeding her flight. The ground was uneven, the long grass slippery. The air sawed painfully in and out of her lungs. She could no longer tell if the pounding she heard was that of her pursuer or the thudding of her own heart. Her foot caught in a vine and she tripped, sprawling headlong.

"M'sieur Alexander," she cried. "Help!"

Reid ran toward her. He hauled her upright, peering anxiously into her face. "What is it? What happened? Are you all right?"

Blinking up at him, she tried to catch her breath. She resisted the urge to burrow into his chest for comfort and reassurance. "A man," she said, gasping. "By the waterfall . . . he had a knife . . . big knife."

His expression grim, Reid withdrew the pistol. Placing himself between her and the waterfall, he kept the gun leveled in the direction she had just come from. "Just stay calm. Let's make our way back to the carriage as quickly as possible."

"Aren't you going after him?" Christiane's voice rose in indignation. She wouldn't have thought Reid Alexander the sort to run from a fight. Not with the battered face of a pugilist.

"Don't make me your knight in shining armor," he all but snarled at her. "I'm no one's hero."

Neither spoke again until they reached Belle Terre.

* * *

The setting sun gilded the magnificent stone structure in a rosy glow. Entranced, Christiane gazed at the simple beauty of the house. The rectangular building rose three stories high. The lower level was entered through a series of arches and, she surmised, probably used in part for staff and storerooms. Broad steps of hewn stone led to an elegant portico on the main floor. Caught up in admiration, she failed to notice the small knot of people gathered at the far end of the house.

The carriage wheels crunched on the shell drive as they rolled to a stop. Reid swung down and quickly came around to help her alight. Christiane immediately sensed a dozen pairs of eyes trained in her direction. She glanced their way, a tentative smile forming as she prepared to greet the staff of her new household.

The small cluster of servants parted to reveal a crumpled form on the ground. Flesh hung from the victim's back in shreds. Bright splotches of blood like the decaying petals of a rose surrounded the spot where he lay.

All traces of color slowly drained from Christiane's face. A buzzing started in her ears while a wave of dizziness swept over her, leaving her weak. Only Reid's hand firmly at her waist kept her from swaying.

"Ah, there you are, Alexander." A figure holding a bull-whip separated itself from the macabre tableau. "I expected you an hour ago. What took you so long?"

Reid shrugged. "There were the usual delays in the Cap."

Christiane waited with steadily mounting dread as the slender, fashionably dressed gentleman with patrician features advanced toward them. Dieu, she prayed. *Please . . . don't let this brute be my husband.*

"You know I don't like to soil my hands with these matters." The man carelessly tossed the whip aside. "Discipline is your job. Not mine."

"I offered to remain at Belle Terre while you went to the Cap," Reid reminded him equably.

"And let you supervise the unpacking of delicate Venetian porcelain?" he scoffed. "Do you take me for a fool?"

His arrogance confirmed Christiane's worst fear. This cruel man was indeed Etienne Delacroix, owner of this lovely house—and her bridegroom. During the long sea voyage to St. Domingue, her practical nature had warned her not to expect overmuch from this proxy marriage. But in her heart of hearts, she had hoped, if not to love, in time to develop a fondness for the man to whom she had pledged herself. Instead, all she felt was repugnance.

Reid nodded at the inert form on the ground. "What did Hector do to deserve a flogging?"

"Clumsy bastard. He nearly dropped an entire shipment of figurines that I ordered from Italy months ago." Etienne fastidiously blotted perspiration from his upper lip with a snowy linen square. "Fortunately nothing was broken, or I would have had to kill him."

At a subtle hand signal from their master, two young blacks stepped forward and, grabbing the arms of the unconscious man, dragged him away. The others in the small group quickly dispersed.

Turning his attention to Christiane, Etienne smiled and sketched a small bow. "To erase any doubt, madame, I am Etienne Delacroix, your husband."

Christiane found herself mesmerized by the palest blue eyes she had ever seen. Eyes cold and cunning. Evil like the devil himself.

Taking her icy hand, he raised it to his lips. "Welcome to Belle Terre."

Chapter Two

Etienne, his mouth pursed tightly, studied her through narrowed eyes. His pale gaze roamed over her leisurely, critically ... impersonally. Christiane stood rigidly and forced herself to endure the rude appraisal. Reid Alexander, too, had subjected her to a thorough scrutiny when they first met, but with a decided difference. His hadn't been impersonal. Reid hadn't been quite able to mask the gleam of masculine interest that had warmed his gray gaze. Whether he approved of her or not, he had viewed her as a woman, not as an object. Etienne Delacroix might as well have been inspecting newly purchased horseflesh. Or his precious porcelain, she thought with a flash of resentment. Surely not a bride. Outraged, she returned his stare.

When his gaze returned to her face, he smiled at her look of indignation. "You'll do, *chérie.*"

"*Merci,* m'sieur," she replied in a choked voice.

Etienne gestured at her gown, indicating with the flick

of a wrist its soiled skirt and torn sleeve. Disapproval formed a vertical line between his brows. "Were the facilities aboard the *Marianne* so inadequate that you couldn't properly attend to your toilette before greeting your husband for the first time?"

A warm flush of color crept across her cheekbones at the insult. Her lips parted for a sharp retort, but Reid interrupted before the angry torrent could escape.

"We had an unexpected encounter along the way," he interjected smoothly. "The countess is fortunate all she has to show for the incident is a torn and muddied gown."

Etienne's attention shifted to Reid. "What happened?"

"As usual, I stopped midway to water the horses. Meanwhile the countess strolled along the stream leading to the waterfall, where she interrupted a lovers' tryst."

"And . . ."

"The man started toward her with a machete, and she fled."

"Did she get a good look at him?" Etienne asked. "Do you think she would recognize him if she saw him again?"

"I remember only that he carried a big knife," Christiane burst out, irritated at being discussed as though she weren't present. "And he wore a red sash tied around his waist."

Her revelation captured both men's attention.

"You didn't mention the sash before. Are you certain?" Reid asked sharply.

"Absolutely." Puzzled, she watched the men exchange frowns.

"A *marron*."

The loathing in Etienne's voice marked the first hint of emotion Christiane had observed in the man she had married. "What is a *marron?*" she asked.

"An escaped slave," Reid explained. "It is rumored

some have banded together. They chose the red sash as their insignia."

"Your job was to protect the countess," Etienne charged, making Reid the target of his wrath. "If you're incapable of a simple assignment, there are others eager to change places with you. Consider the alternative, M'sieur Alexander. I guarantee my hospitality exceeds that which awaits you elsewhere."

Christiane felt the tension mount. Etienne's words carried an implied threat. She glanced at Reid and saw his jaw clench as he fought for control. "If not for Monsieur Alexander's brave intervention, the man would have killed me," she said partly in an attempt to defuse the tension, partly to afford Reid time to regain a degree of equanimity. Just as, she realized belatedly, he had done for her moments ago.

"So you find him brave, do you?" Etienne lifted a brow, sliding his gaze thoughtfully between his bride and his overseer.

"Very," Christiane lied valiantly, purposely omitting the fact that at the time of the incident she had all but accused Reid of cowardice.

"You are indeed naive, chérie. For the present, I won't disillusion your pretty fantasies. No doubt you have led a sheltered existence on your grandfather's estate, and can't be expected to be an astute judge of character."

"Really?" The pompous fool! The man's condescending attitude set her teeth on edge. She longed to wipe the smug look from his patrician features. "I beg to differ, m'sieur, but once we become better acquainted you'll learn that I am quite a good judge of character. Grandfather always claimed I was better than most."

Etienne flicked an invisible speck of lint from the sleeve of his jacket. "Its been my observation that many of the elderly often suffer a deplorable infirmity of the mind."

"*Pardonnez-moi?*" Was this lout actually questioning her grandfather's mental capacity? Christiane couldn't believe her ears.

Etienne favored her with a bland smile. "Men your grandfather's age often become fanciful and can't be relied on for their opinions."

"That is absurd," she declared hotly. "My grandfather's mind is saber sharp. You insult him by your ignorance."

As soon as the words were out of her mouth, she realized her error. She watched in dismay as mottled color flooded her husband's fair complexion, and his hands balled into fists. *Mon Dieu,* would he strike her? she wondered. Surely she wasn't expected to remain silent while unfounded charges were made against her grandfather?

Once again Reid intervened on her behalf. "The countess's unwavering loyalty to her grandfather is commendable. Loyalty is a quality you greatly admire, isn't it, M'sieur Delacroix?"

With visible effort, Etienne reined in his anger. His heightened color ebbed slowly. "My wife must learn that she now owes allegiance to me," he said, his tone clipped, harsh. "Her first—and only—obligation is to me."

"Loyalty is something that must be earned, not demanded," she countered.

"We'll see," Etienne returned coldly. Turning away, he snapped his fingers.

At the crisp command, a woman stepped from one of the arches lining the lower level of the great house. She wore a dress of plain blue cotton trimmed with a prim white collar and cuffs and covered by a voluminous starched apron. Her hair was hidden beneath a kerchief tied turban style. Tall and exotic, with skin the color of darkly brewed coffee, she moved toward them with a regal bearing.

"Yes, master?" she asked in the same patois Christiane had first heard at the dock at Le Cap Francois.

"This is Hera," he said to Christiane in way of introduction. "She'll act as your maid here at Belle Terre."

"I had hoped to select . . ."

"Hera," he said, cutting her off as though she had never spoken. "Show Madame to her room."

"Yes, master," the woman repeated softly, careful to keep her eyes downcast.

"We'll meet in the library promptly at eight o'clock for sherry. Don't be late. I don't like to be kept waiting." With this pronouncement, Christiane was summarily dismissed.

As she turned to follow Hera, she glimpsed an indecipherable expression on Reid Alexander's face before he quickly schooled his features. Was it a warning? Concern? Or grudging admiration? It had disappeared too quickly to tell.

The servant led the way up wide stone steps to a broad terrace and into the house itself. The great staircase hall set the tone of dignity and restrained elegance. Christiane, feeling dwarfed by the hall's massive proportions, gazed about in awe and admiration. Twin pilasters flanked the two principal entrances. A screened print of tropical birds and bamboo stalks on golden yellow cotton decorated the walls. Crystal chandeliers hung from the ceiling at each end of the hall. A mahogany gaming table with a colorful arrangement of flowers stood to the right of the doorway. To the left, a Queen Anne drop leaf table was flanked by side chairs upholstered in bronze velvet. A family portrait of a man and a boy hung above the table.

Christiane walked forward for a closer view. From the lad's disconcerting pale-eyed stare, she knew instantly that the boy in the painting and her husband were one and the same. Even as a child, Etienne had possessed a stern, unsmiling mouth and a cold, unemotional mien.

The tall case clock in one corner chimed the hour.

"This way, madame," Hera prompted.

Picking up her skirts, Christiane followed Hera up the winding staircase. She had the vague impression of a spacious hallway containing side tables, corner cupboard, and yet another tall case clock. Sconces and gilt-framed mirrors were interspersed along the walls. A quick survey revealed six rooms opening off the main hallway. Hera waited patiently outside one of the doors. She stepped aside and motioned for Christiane to enter.

A sigh of pure pleasure escaped Christiane as she gazed about the beautifully appointed room. No matter how much she disliked her new husband, she couldn't fault his excellent taste. The room was lovely, with its walls covered in striped white silk and the draperies and bed hangings of heavy rose brocade bordered in ivory. An Oriental rug in tones of rose, ivory, and moss green spread across the gleaming floor.

She stepped farther into the generously proportioned bedroom. A Queen Anne–style chest richly inlaid with satinwood stood to the left of the entrance. A mahogany armoire occupied the space on the opposite side. Other items in the room included a carved pedestal tea table and chairs, a dressing table with a bench upholstered in needlepoint, and a slant-front desk also with inlay.

A wide four-poster bed with ornately carved posts and headboard dominated the room. She shied away from it, not wanting to dwell on what would take place there later that evening: a rite of passage that would change her forever, an act that would transform the innocent girl into an experienced woman.

Instead Christiane concentrated on the two oval por-
traits above the tea table. From the painting in the downstairs hall, she recognized the man as Etienne's father. The
woman, she assumed, was his mother. Etienne, it appeared,
had inherited his mother's narrow, unsmiling face and
glacial blue eyes. She couldn't help wondering if he had
inherited her disposition as well.

"Madame died last year," Hera volunteered.

"There is a strong physical resemblance between mother
and son. Were they alike in other ways as well?"

"*Oui,* madame."

"I see," Christiane murmured. The maid's confirmation
left her feeling oddly deflated. Although curious, she was
reluctant to press for more details. Past experience had
taught her some questions were best left unanswered.

Hera smoothed an imaginary wrinkle from the bed-
spread and gave Christiane a sly look. "Shortly after she
die, m'sieur began to look for a suitable mistress for Belle
Terre."

Christiane sighed. Fate, it seemed, decreed she be the
mistress of a great plantation. Most women would be
thrilled with the prospect. Why couldn't she summon even
the slightest bit of enthusiasm?

If it was simply to entertain his guests and manage his
household, surely there must be a number of women on
the island who could perform the task with equal competence. Her gaze darted to the four-poster bed. With a
blinding flash of insight, she realized there was one significant difference between herself and the eligible daughters
on St. Domingue. Etienne Delacroix wanted more than
just a mistress for his home. Like many wealthy, influential
men, men driven by ambition and brimming with arrogance, he dreamed of siring a dynasty.

But not just any woman would do.

The untitled daughter of a fellow planter would not fulfill his need for superiority. His rigid standards demanded a bride of impeccable lineage, a bride who shared the bloodline of European royalty. The French revolution afforded him a rare opportunity, a way to kill two birds with one stone. A proxy bride would provide both a mistress for Belle Terre and an aristocrat mother for his progeny. With the situation in France escalating, many of the nobility were seeking ways to flee the country. Christiane was no exception. She had met every criterion . . . except one.

Jean-Claude Bouchard, her beloved grandfather.

But that problem had been quickly resolved. When remaining in France was no longer safe, no longer an option, it was Christiane who, overriding her grandfather's indecision, accepted Etienne Delacroix's offer, knowing it meant she would probably never again see her grandfather's dear face. Her sole comfort was knowing they were both safe from the cruel bite of Madame Guillotine.

"Did I say something to trouble you, madame?" Hera asked anxiously.

Engrossed in her dark reverie, she started at the maid's question, having momentarily forgotten she wasn't alone. "No, it wasn't you, Hera. Everything is quite lovely."

"If you are displeased, Master has instructed me to inform him."

"How thoughtful," she replied, seriously doubting Etienne would react kindly to criticism of any sort.

A male servant arrived just then, panting under the weight of her brass-bound trunk. Hera indicated a spot near the foot of the bed, where he deposited it; then the man left without a word. From the hall outside the bedroom, he fired a stealthy glance over his shoulder and disappeared downstairs.

Christiane untied the bow under her chin and removed her bonnet. The servants at Belle Terre were distinctly different from their French counterparts, she mused. Even though French servants might be resentful or envious, they were quite voluble and prone to chatter. The heavy, hostile silence she encountered among the blacks on St. Domingue was one of many things she would have to become accustomed to.

"I will press your gowns and place them in the armoire." Hera busied herself opening the trunk. "When the rest of your luggage come, and you need more room, I get another for you."

"That won't be necessary, Hera," she said quietly. "These are all the garments I was able to bring with me."

To Christiane's relief, Hera let the subject drop and went about the task of unpacking with quick, efficient movements. Christiane stroked the plume of her bonnet, happy to find it hadn't been broken during her helter-skelter flight through the woods. Her gown hadn't fared as well. It was torn and grass-stained, and she doubted whether it could be salvaged. However limited her resources, she found the notion of approaching Etienne for funds to supplement her meager wardrobe particularly loathsome. She would rather suffer the inconvenience.

She glanced up at the sound of shuffling footsteps and watched as a small parade of servants entered carrying a copper tub, steaming buckets of water, and an armful of linen. Under Hera's instructions the tub was positioned behind a silk screen. When all the details had been attended to, the servants departed, closing the door softly behind them and leaving only Hera in attendance. Christiane stepped behind the screen, stripped off her clothing, and lowered herself into the water. As she reached for the bar of French milled soap, the sweet essence of roses nearly overwhelmed her with homesickness.

Closing her eyes against the onslaught, she rested her head against the rim of the tub and recalled a time when life had been simpler. Now each new day was fraught with changes, challenges, danger. She thought of Etienne and the night ahead. Not even the warm bath could erase the sudden coldness she felt.

"Time is fleeting, madame." Hera's worried voice sounded from the other side of the silk screen.

With a supreme effort of will, Christiane shook off the cloud of foreboding, opened her eyes, and began to lather herself. When she finished bathing and stepped from the tub, she accepted the linen square Hera offered her and allowed the maid to assist her.

A night breeze sidled through partially open French doors. Candlelight swayed and draperies bowed to the whim of an unseen maestro. Christiane sat before the dressing table while Hera fussed with her hair. At the sight of her silver engraved brush in the maid's hands, another wave of yearning for familiar surroundings assailed her. Determinedly, she cleared her throat to dislodge the lump there and cast about for something to break the stiff silence.

"My husband," she said at last. "Where does he sleep?"

"His bedroom be on the other side of your sitting room."

Christiane peered into the mirror and saw the sitting room door reflected back at her. That was how he would enter her bedchamber in just a few hours to claim what was rightfully his.

"You a virgin, madame?"

"*Pardonnez-moi?*" Christiane was certain she had misunderstood the woman's question.

"You a virgin?"

A telltale blush stained her cheeks. "Your question is highly improper," she sputtered. "Whether I am or not, it is none of your concern."

"Yes, madame."

A knowing smile flickered across Hera's face. Obviously pleased with the response her question evoked, the servant didn't speak again as her clever fingers coaxed Christiane's dark tresses into a becoming jumble of curls.

Following a timid knock, the door eased open a crack and a young maid poked her head around the corner. "M'sieur Delacroix say you join him in library."

Christiane rose and waited while Hera arranged the skirt of her carmine silk gown in graceful folds. She rapidly assessed her mirrored reflection, hoping Etienne would find no flaw to criticize. The rich hue of the gown suited her complexion and emphasized the healthy gleam of her dark hair and eyes.

Hera stood back, hands on hips, and inspected her handiwork. "Do not worry, madame. M'sieur will be pleased."

The maid's assurance bolstered her flagging confidence. Satisfied she looked her best, Christiane left the bedroom and, following Hera's instructions, went to join her husband in the library downstairs.

She paused at the foot of the stairs to draw a calming breath. Then, raising her chin a notch, she crossed through the hallway to the library. Bookshelves containing leather-bound volumes and select porcelain figurines occupied each side of the double doors. A brass chandelier hung above a carved English gaming table in the center of the room. A gentleman's desk stood under a window where heavy brocade drapes and wooden shutters stood open to catch the night breeze. Two men stood with their backs turned before a drop leaf side table holding a variety of crystal decanters.

Christiane was immediately struck by the contrast. For evening, Etienne wore a lightly powdered wig with side curls, the hair in back tied with a narrow ribbon. He was as resplendent as a court dandy in a cream-and-gold-striped silk coat with embroidered panels and gold breeches. Reid, on the other hand, was plainly attired in a bronze-colored coat piped in black, white linen neckcloth, and snug-fitting black breeches that molded his well-muscled legs. His long, tawny mane was swept back from his arresting features and tied at his nape with a black ribbon. Yet plain or resplendent, there was no doubt which man was most attractive. Reid didn't need the accoutrements of fashion and wealth to bolster his appeal.

Her gaze lingered on the ruggedly handsome overseer. The man exuded a mind-numbing virility. Each time she set eyes on him she felt an unwilling attraction grow stronger. She knew with blinding certainty that if he were the one destined to share the huge four-poster she would feel anticipation . . . not aversion. The realization shocked her.

Banishing her unruly thoughts, she stepped into the room. Both men ceased their conversation and turned at the rustle of silk.

Etienne's gaze traveled over her before he gave a small, almost imperceptible nod of approval. He offered her a glass. "I took the liberty of pouring you a sherry."

"*Merci,*" she said, accepting the drink. "Please, gentlemen, don't let me interrupt. Continue your conversation."

"It was of little consequence," Etienne replied. "There's something I want to give you first." Going to the desk, he opened a drawer, pulled out an oblong case, and presented it to her with a flourish.

She looked at him questioningly. "For me?"

"Go ahead," he urged. "Open it."

Feeling both men watching her reaction, she slowly raised the lid. Inside the box, a ruby pendant surrounded by diamonds nestled on a bed of satin. Matching ruby earrings winked on either side.

"Well . . ."

"They're exquisite," she said softly. "I'm at a loss for words."

"Hera said you'd be wearing red this evening. Your gown, while pretty, is rather plain without jewelry, don't you agree?"

"Some things are beautiful even unadorned." Reid spoke for the first time since Christiane had entered the room.

His remark drew Etienne's amused stare. "Why, Alexander, if I didn't know better I'd say you sounded like a ladies' man. But I do know better, don't I?" he drawled. "A man with your background surely must feel a misfit in civilized drawing rooms."

There it was again, she thought—a dark undercurrent racing under a placid surface. Curious, Christiane let her gaze dart back and forth. Etienne's expression was smug, sardonic. Reid's was more complex. Anger arced like lightning in the gray eyes, then dissipated as quickly as a summer storm.

"Even a man with my . . . unsavory background can recognize beauty when it stares him in the face." Reid raised his glass to Christiane in a mocking salute. "Forgive me, Countess, if the attempt was clumsy. It's been a while since I've been in such esteemed company."

"I am no longer a countess, m'sieur. There is no need to regard me differently than any other woman."

Etienne plucked the necklace from the case. "Turn around, *chérie*. Let me fasten this for you."

Christiane did as he asked, trying not to flinch as the cold metal and the equally cool fingers circled her neck. Their icy touch seemed capable of drawing the very heat from her body.

"Beautiful, don't you agree, Alexander?" Etienne asked, slowly running his hands over her shoulders in a display of possessiveness.

"Yes, very," Reid agreed, giving the necklace a cursory glance. "The stones appear flawless."

Christiane sipped her sherry, grateful for the warmth that trickled down her throat to pool in her stomach. A game with obscure rules was being played out. Etienne was flaunting her, using her as a pawn, to provoke Reid into making a false move. She wondered what power Etienne wielded over him to force him to meekly submit to insults.

She let out an inner sigh of relief when dinner was announced. Etienne's hands fell from her shoulders, and he crooked his elbow. Placing her hand lightly on his arm, she allowed him to lead her into the dining room, all the while conscious of Reid Alexander trailing close behind.

Christiane had expected grandeur in the dining room and was not disappointed. An elaborate chandelier hung over a four-pedastaled banquet table of mahogany banded with satinwood. Ribbandback dining chairs upholstered in celadon green cut velvet surrounded the table. Etienne caught her staring at the towering breakfront cabinet displaying an extensive set of porcelain.

"China Trade porcelain," he explained with a note of pride. "I own fifty place settings."

She looked at the fish-scale borders on the dishes with distaste, but held her opinion in reserve. He held out a chair at one end of the table, then sat down at the opposite end. Reid sat midway between them. The buffet along the rear wall held an assortment of domed dishes. As soon as they were seated, a trio of servants appeared and silently began serving an array of delicacies: snails swimming in butter, tiny hens flavored with cashews, and succulent beef smothered with black mushrooms. Christiane had little appetite but, not wanting to draw attention to herself, tried small portions of them all.

"Scylla, my cook, is the best on the island," Etienne boasted.

Dinner conversation consisted of a series of starts and stops, eventually drifting into talk of fields and crops, gains and losses. Christiane toyed with her food and listened as talk swirled around her.

The meal seemed interminable, but at last Etienne leaned back in his chair and motioned for the plates to be cleared. "The perfect way to end a meal is with cognac and a fine cigar."

The servants exchanged anxious looks. One braver than the rest stepped forward and apologized in a low voice. "Sorry, master. No more cognac."

Etienne patted the pocket of his waistcoat. "And I have the only key to the wine cellar right here. If you'll excuse me . . ." Not waiting for a response, he got up and strolled out of the dining room.

As soon as the servants carted off the remaining dinner dishes, Reid swung to face Christiane with a scowl.

She ignored him, taking a small sip of wine. "I must confess, m'sieur, I was surprised to find you here this evening."

He arched a brow. "Does the notion of dining with the hired help offend you?"

"Not at all." She gave him a sharp glance. "I merely

assumed that since this was my first evening at Belle Terre, my husband and I would dine alone.''

"You **sound eager** to become better acquainted with the man you **married**.''

"*Au contraire!*" She flung her napkin aside. Her lower lip jutted like a recalcitrant child's. "I don't like him!''

Reid leaned forward. "Like him or not, Countess, he's not a man to trifle with. Tweak a tiger's tail once too often, and he'll bare his claws.''

She knew there was truth to his statement, but it galled her to be chastened by a virtual stranger. "What I do is my business. Why do you care?''

He heaved an impatient sigh. "Maybe I like to see a fair fight. You're no contest for a man like him. He'll grind you under his heel like a bug.''

"You know nothing about me.''

"True, but I've worked at Belle Terre for almost a year. During that time, I've never known your husband to forget an insult or overlook a slight. He's a patient man, but he always retaliates.''

She gnawed her lower lip. If Reid had intended to frighten her, he had succeeded. She feared she had already dared more with Etienne than most others were allowed.

And the hour of payment was nearly at hand.

Chapter Three

All bravado deserted her the moment she stepped into the bedroom. Seated at the dressing table, she scarcely recognized the ghostly image reflected back at her. The face in the mirror was almost colorless, with eyes much too large, much too dark—the face of a terrified young woman. She was glad Reid Alexander couldn't see her now. Let him think her foolish, or impulsive, better that than to think her a coward.

Hera hovered behind her. The maid's quick, clever fingers coaxed a long ebony lock to fall artlessly over one bare shoulder. Satisfied at last, she stood back to admire her handiwork. "Madame look pretty, but too pale." Reaching forward, she pinched both of Christiane's cheeks.

"Enough!" Christiane pulled away and surged to her feet.

Ignoring Christiane's outburst, Hera removed the stopper from a cut-glass bottle on the dressing table. Instantly the scent of roses filled the bedchamber. "Hold still," she ordered.

Christiane obeyed and allowed the maid to dab perfume between her breasts and at the wildly hammering pulse at the base of her throat. The smell intensified, became cloying, suffocating. A dull ache was building behind her eyes.

"There, now you ready." Hera replaced the stopper in the perfume bottle and started to straighten the bedchamber.

Christiane crossed the room to stand before the open French doors. A lethargic breeze stirred the curtains. From across the distant mountains, she heard the insistent throbbing of drums. Their sound disturbed her, increased her feeling of unrest, of imminent danger.

"The drums, Hera, what do they mean?"

Hera hesitated for a fraction of a second, then continued to turn down the bedding. "Nothing, madame."

"Nothing?"

Hera shrugged, her face carefully blank. "Drums call *noirs* to meet, to talk, to dance."

"Why this late? It's close to midnight."

"*Grand blancs* forbid so *noirs* gather in secret."

"Ahh . . ." *Grand blancs,* or the powerful white landowners, versus the *noirs,* the blacks—the slaves. That explained much of the animosity she sensed between the two classes.

A gust of wind swept into the room, plastering the thin silk nightdress to Christiane's slender frame. She rubbed her arms to chase the chill.

"You cold, madame?" Hera asked, looking up from her task. "I close the doors."

"No, don't," Christiane protested. The thought of having the doors shut was unappealing. With no air to circulate, the smell of roses would be overpowering. "I prefer the doors open."

"Night wind often feels cool after heat of the day. Especially to those just come to the island."

Christiane barely heard the woman. Primal fears that refused to be banished bubbled to the surface anew. What was keeping Etienne? Why didn't he come and end this ceaseless waiting, wondering, worrying? Was everything a game? Did he enjoy stretching her nerves to the breaking point? Turning away from the French doors, she prowled the room restlessly.

Was this the same gut-wrenching dread that prisoners experienced on the eve of their execution? Or was she guilty of being overly dramatic? It hadn't been an idle boast when she had told Etienne that she considered herself a good judge of character. Her assessments of people were usually correct. Now her instincts screamed a warning. Her bridegroom was a cruel, perhaps evil man, possessing few scruples and no conscience. She meant little to him. She was just another costly possession, a decoration—an item to put on display.

And, her mind reminded her slyly, the potential mother of his children. The thought of bearing a son in his likeness made her shudder.

"A glass of wine might settle Madame's nerves?"

She paused in her pacing and looked over her shoulder. Hera waited patiently, hands folded, for her answer. Christiane was about to refuse, then changed her mind. "Perhaps some wine is exactly what I need."

With a nod, the woman left and returned shortly with a silver tray holding a crystal decanter and two goblets, which she placed on the tea table. She poured wine into one of the glasses and handed it to Christiane. "Drink, madame. You have a difficult night ahead."

Christiane blindly reached for the goblet, took one swallow, then another. *"Merci,"* she said with a faint smile.

Hera didn't return the smile. "Many young girls are afraid and nervous when time comes to surrender their maidenhead."

Christiane gave Hera a sharp look. She wanted to repudiate the maid's charge, but what was the use? She *was* anxious, fearful. Nights in her cabin aboard the *Marianne* had been spent reviewing the few facts she knew of the wedding night, many of them supplied by gossiping servants. All had concurred that with a kind and experienced lover, the pain was fleeting, the pleasure intense. But Christiane suspected that Etienne Delacroix would be neither gentle nor considerate.

She resumed her pacing. "Tell me, Hera," she asked, emboldened by the drink and needing a distraction. "Are you married?"

"Master does not permit *noirs* to marry."

Christiane paused and looked at the woman with renewed interest. "Did he give you a reason why?"

Hera frowned, searching for the unfamiliar term. "He call us . . . b-baranians."

"Barbarians?"

Hera's brow cleared. "Ah, yes, that is the word. Barbarians. He say marriage for *blancs*, or *gens de couleur*—the freed coloreds—but not barbarians."

Christiane silently digested this bit of information. Etienne's whims, it seemed, dominated all those with whom he came into contact. Including Reid? she wondered. She doubted Reid was a man easily controlled. She guessed him to be the sort who liked to guide his own destiny. Yet after observing the byplay between the pair, she sensed that Etienne exerted some unseen power over him, too.

Hera reached into her apron pocket, withdrew a small

packet, and proceeded to sprinkle a handful of dried rose petals over the sheets. Again the scent of roses suffused the room with a sickly sweet odor. Roses, everywhere the scent of roses, overpowering in its intensity. They made her head ache, her stomach queasy. In the past she had always loved their fragrance. How strange, she mused, that in the space of one evening she had come to detest their essence.

"No more, Hera," Christiane pleaded.

"Sorry, madame." Hera plumped the goose-down pillows. "Master give me orders."

"Will you not cease even if I tell you the scent is making me ill?"

The maid shook her head regretfully. "Master get angry if I do not do exactly as he says."

"It is not wise to make the master angry, is it?" Christiane said bitterly. "For you or anyone else?"

Hera's heavy lids lowered to conceal their expression.

"That's all right, Hera. I already know the answer."

"Yes, madame."

Catching sight of her reflection in the mirror, Christiane adjusted the shoulder of her nightdress. "I assume M'sieur Delacroix chose this especially for me to wear tonight."

In other circumstances she would have admired the classic lines, possibly even selected it herself. Pure yet provocative, the gown was designed after the Greek fashion of leaving one shoulder exposed. The gossamer-thin silk sensually draped her slender figure, molding her breasts, outlining her curves, and revealing the rosy tips of her nipples. Hera, probably at Etienne's instruction, had arranged her hair in the Greek manner with narrow white satin ribbons winding through her hair and a single long tendril trailing over her shoulder.

A peremptory knock sounded from the direction of the

sitting room that adjoined Etienne's quarters. Christiane swung around abruptly, sending the wine sloshing from side to side in its goblet. She braced herself, physically and mentally, for the ordeal ahead.

Etienne, dressed in a maroon brocade dressing gown and carrying a polished rosewood box, sauntered into view. He stopped on the threshold and smiled. "You look lovely, *chérie.* But from the description my agent provided, I had no doubt that you would be quite exquisite."

"You had someone check on me?" she asked, aghast. "Spy on me?"

"Of course, you silly girl." He advanced into the bedroom. "Henri knows my taste well and would not dare risk my displeasure."

She watched him warily and fought the urge to retreat. However, it wasn't bravery that prompted her to remain still, but the knowledge that there was nowhere to run.

His smile widened, obviously amused at her naivete. "I'm not so stupid as to bid on a wife with no idea of what I'm getting in return."

She moistened her lips with the tip of her tongue. "You make it sound as though I were an item up for auction."

He carefully set the rosewood box on the dressing table and turned to her, a smug expression on his saturnine features. "That is precisely how I see it."

"I did *not* sell myself." Her hand tightened on the stem of the glass. "Your agent informed me you were in need of a suitable wife. I, in exchange, needed the means to escape the revolution. I entered into a partnership."

"Come, come, *chérie,* let's not mince words. Admit it. You're bought and paid for. I presented you with an offer you couldn't afford to refuse. Therefore the prize went to the highest bidder."

Out of the corner of her eye, Christiane caught Hera's

slight movement. Until now, she had assumed the maid had left the room. Embarrassed that the woman had been privy to a personal conversation, she wanted her out of the room before more disclosures were made. "You may go now, Hera."

The servant started to leave, but froze when Etienne snapped his fingers. Ignoring her, Etienne addressed his next words to Christiane. "Whenever I am present, *chérie*, the servants follow *my* orders. Understand?"

Her cheeks stinging with humiliation, she stubbornly refused to answer.

Quick as a striking cobra, he reached out and caught her chin. Pinching it roughly between thumb and forefinger, he forced her head upward to meet his gaze. "Understand?" he repeated in a soft voice undermined with steel.

"Oui," she replied. She understood—perfectly. The man was a tyrant, an absolute dictator. He demanded total submission and yielded nothing in return. Belle Terre was his domain, and all its inhabitants, including her, were his serfs. They were expected to carry out his bidding, immediately and without question.

"Hera," he said, continuing in the same tone, his pale orbs fastened unblinkingly on Christiane. "You're responsible for informing the household staff that when I'm present they're to follow *my* orders, not those of Madame Delacroix. Any infractions will meet with discipline."

Hera bobbed her head. "Yes, master."

"Go then." Etienne dismissed the woman without sparing her a glance.

Hera quickly left the bedroom, closing the door behind her.

The click of the latch was loud in the ensuing silence. Etienne's tenacious grip bit into Christiane's soft flesh with bruising intensity.

She tried to jerk free, but he held firm. "You could have spared my pride by postponing this conversation until we were alone," she managed to say between gritted teeth.

He laughed pleasantly. "You're right, I could have, but I chose not to. You need to learn, *chérie*, that I do and say as I please in my own home. I thought it wise we establish the rules at the onset of our relationship."

"Still, you have no right to needlessly embarrass me in front of the servants."

He shook his head in wry amusement. "You're wrong, *chérie*. I have every right. I'm your husband—and have the documents to prove it."

A wave of helplessness threatened the underpinnings of her composure. The papers she had signed were legally binding, witnessed and sealed by the proper authorities. And the solemn word of a Bouchard was their bond.

Turning her face first one way, then the other, he examined her feature by feature. "Though he commended you highly, Henri's description didn't do you justice. I'll have to remember to award him a bonus."

"I'm happy I didn't disappoint, m'sieur."

"Quite the contrary. You're an extremely beautiful young woman. But don't expect a constant string of compliments. I don't want to turn your head with flattery." He released her. "Besides, conceited women bore me."

"I'll make a point to avoid conceit."

"Good, see that you do. My agent did mention, however, that you might be a bit too spirited for my taste. I assured him that wouldn't be a problem. Training a wife should be no different than breaking a horse to a saddle. I always enjoy a challenge."

Her dark eyes sparkled with fury. "How dare you treat me like some . . ." Words failed her, and her voice trailed off.

"Whore?" he supplied, smiling when her eyes widened in shock at the vulgarity.

Without thinking, she brought her hand up and swung her arm in a wide arc, intent on retaliation. His reflexes were quicker, though. Catching her wrist before she could land the blow, he twisted her arm behind her back, pulling her forward until her breasts were flattened against his chest.

Pain radiated up her arm, making her breath hitch and bringing the sting of tears to her eyes. "You brute!" She gasped.

"You are a fast learner in obedience, my sweet," he said through clenched teeth. "But if you ever, ever, try that little stunt again, you'll regret it the rest of your life."

As if to emphasize his point and erase any lingering doubt, he increased the pressure on her wrist. The pain intensified, tightening her throat with a sob. Her vision grayed, and she heard the angel talk.

"I have ways of hurting you that you can't begin to imagine," he whispered into her ear as she leaned into him to ease the strain on her arm.

"I learn quickly, m'sieur," she said with a gasp. "I seldom repeat my mistakes."

"Good," he said, releasing her arm. "I'm glad we had this little discussion. Now onto more pleasant tasks." Going to the dressing table, he picked up the rosewood box she had seen him carry in. "I brought you a few trinkets."

She wanted to whimper. Wanted to cradle her arm against her body to soothe the ache. Wanted to massage her wrist, which was already beginning to bruise and swell. But she did none of these things. Instead she accepted the gift he offered.

"Go ahead, my lovely," he prompted. "Open it up and see what's inside."

Christiane cautiously raised the lid. There in a careless jumble on lush black velvet rested a small fortune in dazzling gems. Brooches and bracelets, medallions and rings, small but superbly crafted items filled the box in a myriad of vibrant color. Facets caught in the wavering candlelight, making the jewels glow with a life of their own.

Knowing he closely watched her reaction, she summoned an appropriate reply. "You're most generous, m'sieur."

Pleased with her response, he strolled over to the tea table and helped himself to the goblet of wine that Hera had poured in anticipation. Raising the glass, he drained the contents. "The trinkets belonged to Mother. As my wife and mistress of Belle Terre, you're entitled to wear them as well. It would please me if you wore them whenever we entertain."

"Whatever you wish." She closed the box and replaced it on the dressing table. In the mirror, she saw that Etienne had moved to stand close behind her. The moment she dreaded was at hand.

He set his empty wineglass next to the jewelry box. "I always had a preference for virgins. My agent tells me he has every reason to believe that you are one. I promised to sweeten the purse if he was indeed correct in his assumption. Of course, if he's wrong . . ."

She swallowed a lump of fear and loathing, and cleared her throat. Speech was impossible when he picked up a lock of hair and twisted it round and round his finger.

"You have a very delectable neck, *chérie*. I've been wanting to sample it ever since I walked in the room this evening." Bending his head, he nipped the tender spot at the junction of her neck and shoulder.

She sucked in her breath, a mixture of pain and surprise. Chuckling, he drew her against his chest and ran his hands over her breasts. Their eyes met in the mirror, and he laughed again. "We look like lovers. Pity the mirror lies."

Before she could respond, he grasped her nipple, twisting until he elicited a small whimper of pain. Christiane prayed for endurance, reminding herself that she was the proud descendant of a brave Norman warrior. Surely she could find the courage to withstand this coarse treatment. "I thought lovemaking was supposed to bring pleasure," she said, keeping her voice light, hoping to steer him along a gentler course.

"You are an innocent, aren't you, *chérie?*" he said, kneading her breast. "Pain and pleasure are close bedfellows in the game of love."

Taking her by the shoulders, he turned her to face him. Then, hooking his fingers in her gown, he jerked downward. The delicate silk shredded from neckline to hem with a loud tearing sound. The fabric drifted to her feet with a soft *whoosh*, the lovely Grecian gown now a worthless rag.

His light-colored eyes impaled her, making her feel vulnerable and defenseless—but not defeated. "Do you like what you see, m'sieur?" she asked, braving the tiger's wrath.

"Indeed," he assured her, his voice raspy. His gaze rested on the valley between her perfectly rounded breasts. "Instinct tells me that I'll be giving Henri a nice little reward once this evening is over and your maidenhead stains the sheets."

Unable to tolerate his lascivious ogling a moment longer, Christiane raised her arms to shield herself.

"Don't," Etienne barked. "I want to inspect my newest acquisition."

Hot and cold. Her skin felt scorched by a sudden rush of blood. Inside she was chilled to the marrow. A predatory light gleamed in Etienne's pale orbs, searing, branding. *Time for the devil to collect his due,* an insidious voice whispered in the far recesses of her brain.

"Turn around. Slowly . . ." he ordered.

Christiane knew it was useless to protest. Mutely she complied. Stripped of all dignity, she understood what it must be like for the *noirs.* Only instead of chains, she was bound by the terms of a marriage contract, an act documented by clergy and civil authority—an act as binding as iron and steel. Sight unseen she had pledged herself to this man, a total stranger, openly and willingly declaring vows of fidelity and obedience. *What a fool!*

"Well, done, *chérie.*" His voice had thickened to a throaty growl. "Now to bed with you. And don't bother hiding that tempting little body under the sheets. I want to see you—all of you."

Her heart hammering, she moved toward the bed, feeling as lifeless as a wooden puppet. Climbing into bed, she lay there, waiting for the inevitable invasion. She erased all thoughts, keeping her mind blank.

From the corner of her eye, she watched him approach the bed and unfasten the belt of his dressing gown. She quickly averted her gaze. The mere notion of his pale, naked body filled her with revulsion.

Slipping out of the robe, Etienne casually tossed it aside and climbed into bed. "Look at me, *chérie.* I want to view your expression while we make love."

She angled her head on the pillow so she could see only his torso. Sparse brown hair sprouted from a narrow, bony chest. A light sheen of perspiration pearled his skin, giving it a sickly cast in the flickering candlelight. She refused to look below his waist.

Without further ceremony, he positioned himself over her and began fondling her breasts. His flesh felt clammy against hers. She shrank away in disgust, but he didn't seem to notice. She was thankful that he made no attempt to kiss her.

He buried his head between her breasts, and she felt his tongue lave their soft swell. She poised her hands on his shoulder, about to push him away, when she felt his hand slide between her legs.

"Spread, dammit," he muttered.

His fingers worked spasmodically, rubbing the apex of her thighs. Christiane covered her mouth with the back of her hand and bit down on a knuckle to keep from crying out.

"Open!" he demanded. "How do you expect a man to ride you when you have your legs clamped together like a nun?"

Etienne wedged a knee between her thighs, cursing impatiently at her lack of cooperation. Reaching down, he grabbed his male member, frantically pulling and tugging to make it hard. Still, nothing happened. Perspiration beaded his brow. *Damn!* He couldn't believe this was occurring. He never had trouble mounting a woman. Never.

"Touch me, damn you!" he raged. "Or I'll beat you senseless."

Even at the tentative touch of her fingers, his penis remained limp, useless. He knocked her hand away and renewed his efforts. Sweat trickled down his temples. What was happening to him? He had never experienced problems of this nature. Yet something was wrong, dreadfully wrong.

Positioning himself on top of her, he braced both hands alongside her hips. Spurred on by desperation, he ground his pelvis against hers, hoping . . . hoping. His breathing became labored as his frustration grew.

At last he rolled off of her. "Worthless bitch!" he spat, his patrician features contorted with rage and humiliation. "You have no idea how to pleasure a man."

Turning on his heel, he stalked out of the bedroom, slamming the door behind him.

Christiane lay shaking. The memory of his virulent hatred along with a glimpse of his small, inert sex organ were emblazoned in her mind. Shivering violently, she pulled the bedclothes around her and curled on her side. Gradually the tremors ceased. She stayed awake until almost dawn, pondering the events of the day.

At first she could scarcely believe her good fortune. In spite of his efforts, Etienne had not been able to penetrate her. It was amazing. Even miraculous. Except for a few bruises, she had survived the ordeal virtually unscathed, her maidenhead still intact. Then reality descended like an ominous, dark cloud.

Certainty that he would try again destroyed her tenuous sense of well-being.

Late the next afternoon, Reid found Christiane strolling through the garden, pausing here or there to add a bloom to the wicker basket slung over one arm. All day long he had worked to convince himself he was not the least bit concerned about Delacroix's bride. Her fate was no affair of his. Yet here he stood, clutching a handful of vouchers as a flimsy excuse to visit the great house.

He paused just outside the garden gate to watch her. At a glance she seemed no worse for wear—and as beautiful as ever. In her pink gown and wide-brimmed hat, she looked like a flower waiting to be plucked. *Good Lord!* He brought himself up short. Next the girl would have him spouting poetry. What the devil had gotten into him?

Angry at the wayward bend of his thoughts, he continued up the path and pushed through the gate. Christiane, upon hearing footsteps on the shell walk, stopped and turned toward him.

"Good afternoon, Countess," he greeted her.

"*Bonjour,*" she returned solemnly.

He scowled down at her, searching for telltale signs of the night past. He had heard tales of Delacroix's treatment of women, particularly the bastard's fondness for inflicting pain.

"You are staring, m'sieur. Is something wrong?" The corners of her mouth lifted in the barest hint of a smile. "Do I have dirt on my face?"

Reid found himself wanting to return the impudent grin. She had spirit enough for two women, but would it be enough, he wondered, to sustain her through a marriage conceived in hell? Taking a cue from her playful tone, he crooked a finger under her chin and pretended to inspect her face for imaginary smudges of dirt.

His good humor vanished when he saw the bruise marring the perfection of her jaw. "What is this?" he asked, rubbing his thumb gently over the spot and feeling a tiny lump beneath the skin's surface.

"Nothing."

He let his hand fall away, but still pinned her with his eyes. "I tried to warn you, Countess."

She shrugged off his concern. "Next time I will be more careful not to provoke him."

He admired her directness and the resolve in her doelike eyes, even knowing these qualities placed her in greater peril. Though they had met only the day before, somehow she had managed to find a soft spot within him.

That fact put him on the defensive, and he struck out at her. "You lack the common sense to know when to keep your mouth shut. You also don't have the sense to know when you're well off. Only a crazy person would come to an island teetering on disaster."

She gestured wildly toward the great house. "You think I would be here if I had a choice? That I would have abandoned my grandfather if there had been any other way?" Her voice broke.

Seeing her distress, Reid instantly regretted his harsh words. "I'm sorry, Countess."

"Save your apology, m'sieur," she said, defiantly blinking back tears. "I am a survivor, just as, I suspect, are you."

Reid watched her walk away and disappear through a side entrance. It was a good thing he would soon be leaving Belle Terre for New Orleans. He didn't need to get sidetracked from his mission by a pretty French countess.

And a married one at that.

Chapter Four

Late the following evening, Christiane felt the fine hairs prickle along the nape of her neck. Glancing over her shoulder, she froze, hairbrush poised in midstroke. Etienne stood framed in the sitting room doorway, observing her dispassionately. She swallowed hard and slowly lowered the brush to her lap.

"You startled me, m'sieur. I didn't hear you enter."

"I didn't intend that you should, *chérie*." His bottle-green velvet dressing gown whispered about his ankles as he advanced into the room. His footsteps were muffled by green leather slippers with pointed toes.

Christiane eyed him warily, inwardly girding herself for a repeat performance of the previous night. She placed the brush on the dressing table, rose to her feet, and went to the mahogany tea table. Lifting a goblet from a silver tray, she offered it to him. "Hera poured you a glass of your favorite claret."

"My servants are well trained." He accepted the wine with a slight smile. "They informed me that you brought only a single trunk with you. I thought this a good opportunity to inspect your wardrobe . . . and make certain recommendations."

She bit back a tart reply. Maintaining rigid self-control, she waited as he sauntered to the armoire, flung open the door, and carelessly flipped through its contents.

"A pitiful lot," he concluded with a shake of his head. "I had no idea when I contracted to marry you that you would come to me with only the clothes on your back. Many *gens de couleur* are better dressed." He gave her a sly glance to see what impact his insult had had on her.

A spark of temper flared in her dark eyes but was quickly extinguished. "Circumstances permitted me to bring only a small portion of my belongings. It was imperative that Grandfather and I leave the chateau without alerting the servants to our plan."

"Your meager wardrobe will supply ample fodder for gossip among the planters' wives. God knows those silly women endlessly complain of boredom. The catty bunch will seize any excuse to exercise their idle tongues."

"I hope my limited resources won't cause you undue embarrassment."

He rewarded her thinly veiled sarcasm with a cold look. "I'm tempted to do nothing to remedy your sorry predicament. A lesson in humility would serve you well. You tend to be much too proud and outspoken. I would prefer a more . . . malleable wife."

"I'm sorry if you are disappointed, m'sieur."

"Au contraire." He sipped his wine, then smiled. "You represent a challenge no man could resist."

Absently she toyed with the ribbons at the neckline of her simple batiste nightdress. She had overridden Hera's protests and insisted upon wearing her own nightclothes as a defense against her husband's lascivious gaze. She had been mistaken. She looked as chaste as a nun, yet Etienne's gaze seemed to sear through the fabric. She fought the urge to hug her arms against her chest in an ageless gesture of self-protection.

"Never fear, *ma petite*. I won't let you become an object of ridicule." He closed the armoire and turned to her. "It wouldn't do to have people think I'm miserly with the purse strings. You shall be dressed as befitting the wife of one of the wealthiest men in St. Domingue."

"*Merci*, m'sieur," Christiane murmured, finding it difficult to appear grateful when she really wanted to throw the gifts in his face.

"Damn you!" he swore in irritation. "What will people think if they heard the formal way you address me? My name, as you well know, is Etienne. See that you remember it when others are present."

"Very well . . . Etienne."

Satisfied with her compliance, he continued, "Fortunately, there is an excellent seamstress in Le Cap by the name of Simone du Val. I will send word that you are in need of her services."

"You are most generous, Etienne." He was standing so close now that she had to lift her head in order to meet his gaze. She could feel her blood turn sluggish in her veins, becoming thick and heavy with dread.

He drained his glass and set it aside. "Nervous, *chérie?*"

"Of course not," she lied.

He laughed, not deceived by her denial. Reaching out his hand, he traced the line of her jaw. "Before the night is over, we'll see just how brave you really are. Take off your clothes."

Christiane was unable to control the trembling of her fingers as she tugged at the ribbon fastenings.

"Soon, *chérie,* very soon, there will be no need for false modesty between us. I'll know you . . . intimately."

Her cheeks burned as she was forced to disrobe in front of him. Small details were etched on her brain: the overly sweet smell of rose petals; an evening breeze sighing through the partially opened French doors; the distant beat of drums.

He perused her nakedness slowly, his arctic blue eyes surveying every inch of her body, every niche and swell. He had seen her unclothed the night before, but somehow this time seemed more demeaning. He seemed to delight in seeing her vulnerable, humbling her. She desperately wanted to shield herself against his scrutiny. Her hands clenched into fists at her sides, the nails biting into her palms.

"Now get into bed," he said with a snarl.

She glanced at him apprehensively. His features were drawn into a taut mask, his pale eyes burning, alive with an unholy gleam—a portrait of unadulterated lust. She wanted to turn and flee, and if captured, fight off his advances. But practicality prevailed. He was her husband. Turning slowly, she crossed the room, then climbed into the huge bed.

Christiane fixed her gaze on the ceiling. She tried to make her mind as blank as the plaster overhead, tried to will her body numb, her spirit impervious—and failed miserably. Somehow, last night, not knowing what to expect had made things easier. The memory of Etienne's sweaty body pressing her into the mattress, battering her pelvis as he tried unsuccessfully to gain entrance, refused to be dismissed. Revulsion coursed through her, leaving her body stiff and unyielding.

"Spread your legs like a well-paid whore."

Recognizing the futility of protest, she did as told. He fondled her breasts, his hands soft, his touch cruel. Then he grasped the male organ dangling between his legs, squeezing and pumping to coax life into the limp append-age. Sweat dripped from his brow and dampened the bed linen. Vehemently he cursed his lack of success.

The ordeal seemed to go on forever before it abruptly ceased. A swift look at the enameled clock on the dressing table assured Christiane that minutes—not hours—had elapsed.

The assault was over, the results unchanged. To Chris-tiane's vast relief, in spite of Etienne's best efforts, he was unable to perform the act that would consummate their marriage.

"Emasculating bitch!" Livid with rage, he rolled off her and sprang out of bed. "You dare call yourself a woman. You're no more than a stick of wood, a sliver of ice, incapa-ble of satisfying a man."

Christiane pulled the sheet up under her chin, the crisp linen flimsy protection against the barrage of abuse Etienne was heaping upon her.

"You're totally useless as a woman. A cold, passionless little bitch," he raged, reaching for his robe. "To think of all the money I wasted on you. I could get more pleasure from a marble statue."

Christiane clutched the sheet and let him rave.

He strode across the room, poured a glass of wine, downed it in a single swallow, then poured another. "I should have known better than to bind myself to a prim and proper virgin incapable of pleasing a man. I should have insisted on a trial period to make certain we were compatible. It is too late for that now. The contract has been signed. We're legally bound for as long as we both shall live."

With a sudden violent movement, he hurled the glass across the room, where it shattered against the wall. Christiane flinched at the sound of breaking crystal.

He glared at her over his shoulder. "I'm going to find me a woman, a real woman. Not a stick of wood."

He stormed out. The slamming of her door reverberated through the quiet house.

Christiane lay unmoving, eyes wide, staring at the spot where the glass had struck and watched the red wine slowly trickle down the wall to the floor. She ought to thank Reid Alexander for his warning. The man she had married was not only evil, but deranged.

She heard the tall case clock downstairs chime the hour of midnight. Getting up from the bed, she crossed to a washbasin on a corner stand and vigorously began to scrub Etienne's scent from her body. She wished she could cleanse his memory from her mind as easily. He made her feel dirty.

Tainted.

Exhausted by yet another sleepless night, Christiane slept late the next morning. It had been almost dawn before the drums quieted. Her skull seemed to throb in time to their incessant beat. Late, very late, she had heard Etienne's return. She had held her breath as he climbed the stairs, breathing a sigh of relief when he passed her room without stopping. Still sleep eluded her. It wasn't until daybreak peeked through a slit in the draperies that she had finally fallen into a deep, dreamless void.

"Breakfast, madame."

Christiane raised lids that felt weighted and gritty. She

blinked to clear her vision and saw Hera coming toward her bearing a breakfast tray. "What time is it?" she mumbled.

"You sleep late. It's nearly noon." She set the tray down and threw open the draperies.

Brilliant golden sunshine flooded the room. Christiane winced, and flung one arm over her eyes to shield them from the glare. "Have mercy, Hera. I'm not even awake yet."

"Good strong coffee will wake you."

With a sigh of resignation, Christiane dragged herself into an upright position and allowed Hera to plump the pillows behind her back and position the tray across her lap. Though she didn't normally indulge in a leisurely breakfast in bed, today she'd make an exception. She took a bite of a flaky roll and washed it down with hot, freshly brewed coffee.

Hera had been correct. Christiane was feeling much better by the time she finished her second cup of the delicious brew. "The coffee is excellent. I assume it's grown here on Belle Terre."

"Yes, madame. Everything grow on Belle Terre."

"I'm curious, Hera. How long have you been here?"

The servant shrugged. "Long enough."

At the noncommittal reply, Christiane gave up any attempt to engage the woman in conversation. She took an experimental bite of the exotic-looking fruit on her breakfast tray, sighing with pleasure at finding their sweet, succulent flavor. "The fruit, whatever it's called, is delicious."

"They mango and pineapple."

Christiane glanced up, surprised at the unsolicited information. It wasn't like the woman to volunteer information. "Whatever, they're wonderful."

Hera moved about the room, running a dust cloth lightly over the furniture. "You not sleep good, madame?"

"The drums kept me awake."

"Only drums, madame?"

Frowning, Christiane stared at the woman's back. "You say that as though there should be some other reason for losing sleep."

"No offense, madame." The maid, her face wiped free of expression, began to rearrange the items on the dressing table. Only the alert black eyes betrayed her intense interest. "Sometimes husbands keep brides awake all night."

"What occurs between husbands and wives is private, Hera, not something discussed with servants." Having issued the mild rebuke, Christiane steered the conversation into a more neutral channel. "I think today I will familiarize myself with Belle Terre. Tell me about the household staff."

"Not much to tell, madame."

Christiane ignored the maid's sullen tone. "Let's start with the kitchen. The cook's name is Scylla?"

"M'sieur brag that Scylla is best cook on the island."

"*Oui*, her meals have been excellent," Christiane concurred. "What about the two young maids who serve dinner?"

"They be Maya and Astra."

"Which is the nervous, jittery one?"

"She be Astra."

"Astra," Christiane repeated softly. A pretty name for a pretty young maid. She looked as though she was afraid of her own shadow. Christiane set aside her breakfast tray and threw back the bedclothes. "I think I'll wear the blue dress today, Hera."

As soon as she finished dressing, Christiane excused the servant and set out to explore her new home. She wasn't about to spend another day skulking about like a whipped puppy. Yesterday the only time she had emerged from her room had been for a late-afternoon stroll through the garden—an excursion on which she had encountered Reid Alexander. Belle Terre's overseer had the capability of both infuriating and intriguing her, usually within the space of a heartbeat. In spite of this, she was drawn to the man. She had found a well-meaning heart and unexpected kindness under a tough exterior, traits he tried to keep hidden. And that intrigued her, all the more.

It was time to venture forth, make her presence known. Just because Etienne had issued an edict that the servants were to take orders only from him, she didn't want them to think she was afraid to show herself.

After inspecting each of the guest bedrooms, she made her way downstairs, where she leisurely toured the house, room by room. In the morning room, she ran her hand across the satiny smooth surface of a polished oak serving table. Next she wandered through a carved archway flanked by Grecian-style pilasters into the ballroom. Magnificent brocade panels with exotic scenes of birds and palm trees covered the walls. Ballroom chairs and window seats were upholstered in similar fabric. Elegant and opulent, though a bit ostentatious for her taste, the room was bold testimony of Etienne's wealth.

Turning away from the ballroom, she entered the dining room, where she found a young maid sluggishly polishing silver. "Good morning," Christiane called out in greeting.

"Mornin', madame," the girl muttered, not looking up from her task. Christiane slowly made her way around the room, pausing to admire a painting of boats in a harbor signed by an obscure Dutch artist that hung on the east wall. She was about to leave when a second girl entered carrying an Oriental urn overflowing with brilliant blooms.

"You must be Astra," Christiane said pleasantly.

"Yes, madame." The words came out slurred, almost garbled.

Curious, Christiane waited as the maid carefully centered the arrangement on the dining table. She gasped when the girl presented her profile. One eye was discolored and swollen shut, her lip puffy, the skin split. "Astra, your face!"

The maid clamped her mouth into an obstinate line. Instead of acknowledging Christiane's comment, she fussed with the blooms, refusing even to look at her mistress.

"What happened?" Christiane persisted. "Who did this to you?"

"Do not concern yourself, madame. It was . . . accident."

"Don't lie to me, Astra," Christiane said, recovering her voice. "Who struck you?"

Astra continued to fuss with the flower arrangement, moving a taller stem to the back, a fern to the front. "It was accident," she repeated obstinately.

"Is there anything I can do to help? Perhaps you should lie down and rest. . . ."

The young maid shot her a look of contempt. "You, madame, have done enough to me."

Christiane was stunned by the open hostility in the maid's glance. "Very well, but if you change your mind and decide to tell the truth, I will do what I can to help."

"Astra not change mind."

Knowing there was little she could say or do to change Astra's feelings, Christiane exited the room. What had she done to incur the maid's obvious dislike? Until now they had scarcely spoken. Yet the girl's manner had bordered on insolence. The maid's strange choice of words was also cause for puzzlement. Surely Astra must have meant that

Christiane had done enough *for* her, not *to* her. She dismissed the statement, the phrasing, as being the result of island dialect. She couldn't, however, dismiss the girl's hostility as easily.

Leaving the house, she followed a well-worn path until she came upon a small frame building. Mouthwatering aromas drifted through an open door. Drawn to investigate further, Christiane stepped over the wood sill. The heat struck her like a closed fist, nearly driving her backward with the force. Determined, she stepped inside and looked around with interest. A kettle of broth bubbled over a crackling fire in a giant-size hearth. Iron pots and skillets along with an assortment of utensils hung from hooks on either side. Bundles of herbs were suspended from ceiling beams.

A slender woman with angular features, her dark skin pearled with sweat, stood at a scarred wood table in the center of the room, slicing vegetables. Like the rest of the household staff, she wore a cloth twisted around her head turban-style. She glanced up at Christiane's entrance, her expression revealing neither surprise nor welcome. "Can I help you, madame?"

"You must be Scylla." Christiane gave the woman a smile, but received none in return. The cook continued to regard her through eyes black and bright as ebony— watchful, suspicious eyes. Christiane swallowed back her misgivings and forged ahead. "I wanted to compliment you on your wonderful meals. In my country, your skills would be highly sought after."

"St. Domingue is your country now." Scylla turned her attention back to the scallions she was chopping.

Yes, it was her country now, Christiane acknowledged ruefully. But it was a land she was having a great deal of difficulty adjusting to. Taking out a lace-trimmed handkerchief, she daintily blotted moisture from her temples and wished she were back in France. Except for the murmur of simmering broth and the steady tap of Scylla's knife, the kitchen was quiet, uncomfortably quiet. "What are you preparing?" Christiane asked, searching for a way to sever the awkward silence.

"Master want duckling. He like it served with orange and ginger sauce." Without looking up, Scylla reached for a thick root within hand's reach, whacked off one end, and began chopping it into small pieces. Soon the smell of ginger mingled with the other spices in the steamy air.

"If the duck is like everything else you've prepared, I'm sure it will be excellent."

Scylla shrugged diffidently. "You want different, you ask Master. I take orders only from him—except when old Madame alive." She ceased chopping and gave Christiane a sly look.

"I'm not here to give orders, Scylla," Christiane said quietly. "I only wanted to meet you and tell you that your talents are appreciated."

Christiane left the cookhouse with Scylla's final words echoing through her mind. The woman had in effect told her that Etienne's mother had had authority, while she, Christiane, had none. Indeed, she felt little more than a guest in her own home. Utterly useless. Worthless. Just as Etienne had charged the night before.

Head bent in thought, Christiane strolled farther down a well-trodden path that led away from the great house. Her spirits plummeted. Belle Terre was as lovely as a picture book. She loved the lush vegetation and profusion of exotic flowers. She should be thrilled to find herself in a tropical paradise, far from a country torn by strife. Yet she had never felt more miserable.

St. Domingue was proving to be more prison than paradise. It reminded her of a shiny red apple that was beautiful on the outside, but rotten at the core. It was a country teeming with fear, evil, oppression, hostility, and suspicion. A land where no one smiled, no laughter rang. She wished she had never heard its name, wished she and her grandfather had found some other means of escape rather than a proxy marriage to a wealthy French planter on a faraway isle. She wished—

Her head came up with a snap as she rounded a bend and saw the stables. Her mood shifted from pensive to anticipatory. Poking her head inside, she looked around with interest. Emboldened when she saw no one around, she stepped inside the dark interior. Except for one or two stalls, most were deserted. The brick floor was swept clean and the place smelled, not unpleasantly, of leather and horses. A wave of nostalgia engulfed her. For an instant she was back in France, about to request her favorite mare be saddled for a ride to the neighboring village. She loved the feel of being astride a powerful horse with the wind tugging at her hair and the sun warm on her face.

She wondered if she could find a sidesaddle. Perhaps the "old" Madame, as Scylla had referred to her predecessor, had also possessed a penchant for riding. Her steps quickened as she passed the rows of stalls in the hopes of locating the tack room.

"Looking for something?"

Startled at the unexpected sound of a voice, she brought her hand against her chest to calm the rapid beat of her heart.

Reid Alexander stood at the far end of the stable, arms crossed, his tall figure limned in sunlight. The open door behind him made it impossible to read his expression.

Quickly recovering her composure, she let her hand

drop to her side. "Do you make it a habit to sneak up on people?" she asked irritably.

His wide shoulders moved in a negligent shrug. "Stealth has its merits. I've found it a good way to learn things you might not otherwise be privy to."

"Some things are best kept behind closed doors." People here already knew far more about her than she did about them. She wondered briefly if Hera suspected what had happened—or more precisely, what had failed to happen—in the bedroom. The idea didn't appeal to her.

"Prying eyes are everywhere, Countess. There are few secrets at Belle Terre." He pushed away from the door and sauntered toward her. "What brings you to the stable?"

She stood her ground, though the instinct to retreat was strong. It wasn't that Reid posed a threat of physical danger. The problem lay in the subtle, intangible tug of attraction she felt whenever he was in close proximity. That presented a menace of an entirely different sort. "I-I wondered if perhaps there was a sidesaddle?"

"Did your husband give you permission to ride, Countess?"

He stood close, much to close. She moistened her suddenly dry lips with the tip of her tongue. "I didn't ask."

"Well, you should have."

She gave in to the childish urge to stomp her foot. "I'm tired of everyone telling me what I can and can't do."

"No doubt," he agreed dryly. "You're probably accustomed to issuing orders while everyone jumps through hoops trying to please you."

Christiane felt unaccountably stung by his accusation, but hid her hurt behind a screen of arrogance. "May I ask what you are doing here, m'sieur?" she asked, tilting her chin defiantly. "I thought you were my husband's overseer, not a stable hand."

He cocked a sandy brow. "I see you have forgotten my advice to curb that sassy little tongue of yours."

Christiane shifted her weight from one foot to the other. He was staring at her mouth in a way that seemed all too personal, much too intimate. "*Au contraire,* m'sieur, I gave your advice much consideration. In the future, I will choose my battles with greater care."

"Good, I'm glad to hear there's some sense in that pretty little head of yours." He picked up a well-worn saddle from a nearby bench. "You are aware, aren't you, that unless Delacroix gives his express consent, none of the men will saddle a horse for you?"

Her expression turned bitter. "My husband, so I am discovering, likes to be in complete control."

"In this instance he is justified." He carried the saddle toward a stall at the far end. "The times are unsettled, uncertain. If you were my wife, I'd forbid you to ride anywhere unless I was there to protect you."

"But I am not your wife." Christiane trailed after him, silently admiring how his cotton shirt pulled taut across his muscular back. In spite of herself, she found herself comparing the thin, almost bony physique of Etienne to Reid's more powerful build. She doubted any woman, herself included, would be repulsed by his naked body.

"Are you married, m'sieur?" she asked, shocked at her own brazenness. But, truth was, he intrigued her, and she wanted to know more about him.

He grinned at her over his shoulder. "Ah, Countess, I'm flattered that you ask."

She blew out an impatient breath. Had her motives been that transparent? "I don't give a tinker's damn whether or not you're married. I was only making polite conversation. Evidently that's impossible with someone of your caliber."

Her words wiped the humor from his face. "A man far removed from your social class?"

She regretted her words the instant they were uttered. She had failed to consider how her statement might be construed. "I'm sorry if I offended you," she said, spreading her hands in helpless appeal.

"No offense taken, Countess," he said, his tone clipped. Entering a stall, he threw the saddle over the back of a chestnut gelding. "I'll be the first to admit I haven't had a lot of experience conversing with your kind either."

She stood, gnawing her lower lip, and watched him tighten the cinch.

Exactly what had she meant? she wondered. Reid *was* different from any other man she had ever met. Granted, having spent much of her life on her grandfather's country estate far from the extravagant court of Louis XVI, she didn't know a great many men to compare him with. But even with her limited experience, there were few similarities between Reid and the silk-and-powder elite to whom she was acquainted. Reid was masculine, not dandified; strong, not effete; purposeful, not insouciant. He threw her off balance.

"No, I'm not," he said abruptly.

"*Pardone?*" she replied, having forgotten her original question.

"I'm not married."

"Oh." She was unprepared for the relief she felt at his answer, and in the next instant, appalled at her response. Why should she care? Reid Alexander's marital status was no concern of hers.

"Oh?"

She smiled a bit sheepishly as she groped for something to say next. "I thought it would be nice if there was another woman about. Someone to visit with, perhaps become friends.''

''No wife, no sweethearts.'' Satisfied the cinch was secure, Reid next adjusted the stirrups. ''No attachments of any sort.''

''I see,'' she replied, feeling ill at ease and disliking the sensation. To mask her discomfort, she feigned an indifference she didn't feel. ''Belle Terre is a long way from civilization. It's likely to get lonely. Having another woman nearby would relieve the boredom.''

The gelding shifted restlessly in the stall. Reid ran his hand down the horse's flank to settle him. ''Like to ride, Countess?''

''I used to ride all the time. Seeing the stable made me a little homesick,'' she confessed, relieved he had changed the subject.

''Did you leave family behind?''

Christiane felt as though a band tightened around her chest. She missed her grandfather more each passing day. Instead of lessening, the ache grew worse. She worried about his safety, feared for his health, and, most of all, missed his company. ''No,'' she managed to say past the lump in her throat. ''I left no one in France.''

Reid glanced at her curiously, then continued to stroke the gelding's glossy coat.

Christiane followed his reassuring movements. His hands gave the impression of strength and competence. They were strong hands, well shaped, and with a manly elegance. His long fingers were blunt at the tips, the nails clean and clipped short. The backs of his hands were sprinkled with fine hair of spun gold. Her gaze fastened on his wrists. And her eyes widened in shock.

A two-inch band of scar tissue encircled each wrist.

Reid glanced up and caught her staring. He stared back, his gray eyes cool, remote. "Is there a problem, Countess?"

"N-no, none at all," she stammered, her confused gaze skittering away. She cleared her throat nervously. "I'd better get back to the house." She backed away two steps, then turned and fled, a true coward.

What type of injury caused scars of that sort? she asked herself repeatedly as she hastily retraced her steps. Her usually vivid imagination could supply only one answer. Manacles. Why would Reid Alexander bear scars like those of a common criminal? All her instincts cried that he was an honorable man. But was he? an inner voice persisted.

Reid was the only person she had met since arriving in St. Domingue that she felt comfortable around. Had she been mistaken? Was there no one she could trust on this godforsaken island?

Etienne Delacroix had bidden his lovely bride a polite good night hours ago. He stopped pacing and glared at the door that connected their adjoining sitting rooms. Surely his affliction was only temporary. Once it subsided, he would wait until he was fully aroused, then mount his highborn wife with no more consideration than a stallion in heat.

The little bitch had emasculated him with her fine, ladylike airs, her genteel manners, her needle-sharp tongue. *Dieu,* this marriage had turned into a fiasco. He poured a glass of wine from a decanter on a side table and took a long swallow, barely tasting the costly vintage.

Never had he been lacking where women were concerned. Never! Until she arrived. He resumed pacing. Not even Astra had been able to bring him to arousal. And Astra had been well tutored; she knew every trick in the book. Well, he had let her know in no uncertain terms that he had been displeased with her failure.

A sudden thought made him shudder. What if word spread that he was impotent? The results would be disastrous. Everyone, from the governor down to the lowliest *noir*, would snicker behind his back. He'd be a laughingstock. A joke.

He forced himself to think calmly, rationally, through the wine-induced haze that was beginning to fog his brain. His secret was safe with Astra. The girl knew better than to open her mouth. The fair Christiane was another matter, however. She was spirited, bold even, and tended to be outspoken, impulsive. There was no telling to whom she might blurt the details of his abject humiliation. That left only one solution.

The French bitch had to be silenced.

Marriage to her had been a mistake, a colossal mistake ... but mistakes could be rectified. Especially if one were patient. Etienne flung himself onto a chaise, leaned back, glass in one hand, decanter in the other, and began to plot.

He would bide his time. Act as though nothing were amiss, then strike.

The key would be to act soon, but not too soon. If an unfortunate accident occurred too quickly after her arrival, questions might be raised. Not that he gave a damn, but he didn't relish being the object of gossip. Perhaps it was time for a party, he mused. A ball would provide the perfect vehicle to introduce his bride to the elite of St. Domingue. They would give every appearance of newlywed bliss. Later, after an unfortunate *accident*, he could play the role of bereaved widower.

Chuckling at the prospect, he took a small sip of wine. After suitable time elapsed, he would simply send Henri, his emissary, back to France for another bride. The revolt there was escalating. Surely there were other young women of impeccable lineage eager for a chance to flee.

He clucked his tongue, shaking his head in mock despair. Poor French countess, people would lament. So pretty, so young. Such a tragic, untimely death.

Ah, yes, the possibilities . . .

Chapter Five

Several days later, Etienne strolled into her bedroom early one morning, informed Christiane that she would accompany him on a tour of Belle Terre, then left without another word.

Still groggy with sleep, she pushed herself up on one elbow and stared after him. A grand tour of the plantation would be a welcome respite from an afternoon of doing needlework on a garden bench. The island with its lush foliage and exotic smells fascinated her. Bored and restless, she'd been wanting to explore her new surroundings ever since her arrival. Throwing aside the bedclothes, she swung out of bed and summoned Hera.

All during breakfast, she bombarded the taciturn servant with questions. "How big is Belle Terre?"

"Big, madame, very big."

"What do they grow besides coffee?"

"Everything grow on Belle Terre."

"What lies beyond the mountains?"

Hera shrugged. "Beyond the mountains, more mountains."

"Do coffee beans grow on bushes or trees?"

"Enough, madame." Hera threw up her hands in protest. "You ask the master. He tell you."

Christiane lapsed into silence. The thought of asking Etienne anything was unappealing. She'd rather have her questions go unanswered than have him interpret her interest as encouragement. Since the disastrous second attempt to claim his marital rights, he had left her alone. Each night she lay rigid with apprehension, waiting, wondering, until long after she heard his footsteps continue past her bedroom door.

It was during those long hours that she composed imaginary letters to her grandfather and prayed for his safety. Had fate been kinder to him? Where had he gone after leaving France? He had once talked of the United States. Had that been his final destination? As soon as he contacted her, she would write, reassuring him of her safety and extolling the beauty of St. Domingue, careful to omit any unpleasant details of her new life. Perhaps Reid could be entrusted with the missive on one of his trips to Le Cap. Once there, he would be able to find a trustworthy ship's captain, perhaps even Captain Heath, to deliver the letter to her grandfather.

Promptly at one o'clock, a lacquered phaeton pulled by a sleek team of horses was brought to the main entrance. Etienne, looking every inch the prosperous planter in a charcoal gray double-breasted coat, striped waistcoat, and dove-colored breeches, appeared in the doorway of the morning room just as she finished a light lunch. "Ready, *chérie*?"

Christiane nodded and, accepting his arm, was escorted

out of the house and to the waiting carriage. Etienne helped her into the vehicle, then mounted a magnificent white stallion. The liveried driver gave a practiced flick of the reins, and rolled down the drive and past the stone portals that marked the entrance to Belle Terre. Etienne's stallion obediently trotted alongside.

Adjusting the angle of her parasol, Christiane sat back and simply enjoyed the first outing since her arrival. The phaeton rolled through a forest of tropical oak and lush mahogany dotted here and there with bright splashes of color from jacaranda and poinsettias. After a while, the trees thinned and the land leveled until finally a blanket of green stretched as far as the eye could see. Tall stalks swayed in the breeze, their movement slow and graceful.

"Sugarcane," Etienne announced proudly, making a sweeping gesture with one hand.

"I suspected Belle Terre to be vast, but my imagination didn't do it justice," she murmured appreciatively.

Sensing her approval, Etienne grew expansive. "The climate here is ideal. Almost anything will grow here on St. Domingue. It's considered one of the finest agricultural regions in the new world. And certainly the most prosperous."

"Is sugarcane your only crop?"

"My two principal exports are sugarcane and coffee," he explained. "In the unlikely event that one should fail, I can depend on the other for a source of income."

"That sounds wise."

The driver navigated the carriage down a narrow, rutted track. Christiane noticed that slaves, bared to the waist, moved through the cane fields, their movements slow, almost sluggish in the blazing heat. Sunlight glinted off the broad blades of steel they swung from side to side, the steady thump as regular as a heartbeat.

"Those knives . . ." she began tentatively.

"Machetes," Etienne corrected. "The correct term is machete."

Recalling the lovers' tryst she had interrupted the afternoon of her arrival, Christiane felt a prick of fear. "It's the same type of knife the man at the waterfall had," she said, moistening suddenly dry lips.

He shrugged negligently. "A machete is a common tool on a sugar plantation. I insist that all my men become adept at using them."

She suppressed a shudder. "They make a formidable weapon."

"Not to worry, *ma petite*. The *noirs* are too slow-witted to distinguish a weapon from a tool."

In spite of her husband's nonchalance, Christiane remained skeptical. Although the *noirs* might be uneducated, she doubted they were stupid.

"I'm about to have more land cleared some distance from here. In a week or two, I'll send Alexander to look things over and report back to me. In the meantime, I'll need to appoint someone to supervise. I've got my eye on several *noirs* who show promise, but before I make a definite decision, I need to know how well they follow orders."

The road grew steeper. Gradually Christiane noticed a slight drop in the temperature as the buggy climbed to a higher elevation. Trees with dark, glossy leaves planted in precise rows stood on both sides of the road. Women picked berries and dropped them into huge wicker baskets stationed at intervals. When the baskets were filled to overflowing, the men would heft them to their shoulders and haul them away.

"Coffee from Belle Terre is the best on the island," Etienne boasted.

"It is excellent, m'sieur," Christiane concurred. "I have never tasted better."

"Berries must be handpicked, then carefully sorted. After the beans are dried in the sun, they undergo a second sorting. Only the largest and best are chosen."

"How interesting." And how like Etienne, she thought, to insist on only the best.

"Let's walk through the sorting area." He dismounted, handed the reins to the driver, then helped Christiane alight from the carriage. "Nothing like a surprise inspection to keep everyone on their toes."

The moment her feet touched ground, Christiane stepped back, loath to have him touch her a second longer than necessary. Smoothing the wrinkles from her gown, she shifted her parasol to her other hand to avoid taking his arm, and fell into step next to him. "What happens to the beans after they are sorted?"

"They're placed in burlap sacks, weighed, and transported to the dock at Le Cap to await shipment." He led her down a row of trees and around a corner to an open area where coffee beans were spread on huge sheets of canvas and left to dry in the sun. A short distance away, a half dozen men, as yet unaware of their presence, were methodically measuring beans onto a scale.

Christiane's heart caught with an odd little flutter when she peeked out from the shade of her parasol and spotted Reid. He stood off to one side, casually holding a braided whip against his thigh, head bent in concentration as he supervised entries into a ledger.

In deference to the midday heat, Reid had removed his shirt and wore it tied about his waist. She couldn't help but admire the broad shoulders, the well-defined musculature, the flesh burnished a rich, golden tan. Then he turned, and she saw his back for the first time. Her eyes registered horror at the network of scars that crisscrossed his back—scars like those of slaves who had been punished.

Etienne followed the direction of her gaze. "Something wrong, *chérie*?" he whispered solicitously, making little effort to hide a knowing smirk.

"You want me do that now, m'sieur?" a young man asked Reid.

Before Reid could respond, Etienne pushed forward angrily. "Juno, did my ears deceive me, or did I hear you question an order?"

The group turned as one, their expressions revealing varying degrees of apprehension. Though Etienne hadn't raised his voice, all seemed to know that his soft-spoken tone was more foreboding than a shout.

Reid swung around. "M'sieur Delacroix." He inclined his head in greeting, his expression hooded. His steady gray gaze skimmed Christiane before returning to Etienne. "To what do I owe this unexpected visit?"

"You know I won't tolerate any impertinence from the slaves." Etienne's voice was cold, clipped, emotionless.

"I'm certain Juno meant no disrespect."

"I beg to differ," Etienne said with a snarl. "That's not how it sounded to me."

"Didn' mean nothin'," Juno muttered. He hung his head, but too late to hide the contempt burning in his dark eyes.

"A lowly slave has the audacity to address his master?" Etienne asked in mock disbelief. "I think not."

"Juno was merely attempting to clarify an order when you arrived."

"The man is insolent and needs to be taught a lesson." Etienne snatched the whip from Reid's grasp.

"No, Etienne. Please."

The protest sprang from Christiane of its own volition.

The second the words escaped, Christiane realized her blunder. Without turning her head, she sensed all eyes trained on her. Unwittingly she had become the center of attention. The scene being enacted changed to a tableau of sorts, a moment frozen in time. No one seemed to move; no one seemed to breathe.

Although the sun still beamed brightly in the summer sky, its warmth had been leached from the day. Christiane resisted the urge to wrap her arms around herself to chase the sudden chill.

"You don't think Juno deserves to be punished, *chérie?*"

Etienne's icy blue eyes seemed to drill a hole through her, pinning her to the spot. "I didn't intend to question your authority, m'sieur. Surely the man meant no harm."

His thin mouth curled into a cruel smile. "If I allowed the *noirs* to question orders, soon all of them would follow suit. Anarchy would result."

The handle of her parasol felt slick beneath her palms, and her heart began to race. "But surely there is little danger from such a minor offense."

Reid gestured toward Juno. "Consider, if you will, M'sieur Delacroix, that Juno is one of your best workers."

Etienne raised a pale brow askance as his gaze shifted back and forth between Christiane and Reid. "How is it," he drawled, "that both my wife and my overseer unite against me in defense of this man?"

Christiane's unease escalated. Nervously she moistened her lips as she foundered about for a suitable reply. "I simply expressed my opinion . . ." Her voice trailed off.

"I am only considering what is best for Belle Terre," Reid explained, adopting a conciliatory tone. "Juno often performs the work of two men. This is his first offense."

"Then his first offense shall be his last." Etienne

smacked the handle of the whip across his open palm, the sound magnified in the oppressive stillness.

"Forgive my boldness, m'sieur, but Juno will be of little use if disabled."

"Enough," Etienne snapped, suddenly bored with the debate. He pointed to two *noirs* who watched helplessly. "Seize him!"

The pair reluctantly stepped forward, each grabbing Juno by an arm.

Christiane cast a placating look at Reid. *Can't you do something to stop this?* she cried wordlessly. Reid intercepted her silent plea but turned away, his expression inscrutable. *I'm no one's hero,* he had warned on their first meeting. But somehow she kept forgetting his admonition. Instead she persisted in attributing to him noble and courageous characteristics. When would she learn? she wondered dully.

"Good worker or not," Etienne was saying, "the man needs to be made into an example."

Christiane could see that Reid wasn't going to persist in risking Etienne's wrath. But someone had to stop the situation before it escalated any further. Throwing caution to the wind, she clutched her husband's arm. "Etienne, please, for my sake, let the matter rest."

He stared pointedly at the hand resting on his jacket, then slowly raised his gaze to her face. "You dare challenge my authority, madame?"

"I can't bear to watch such cruelty. The sight of bloodshed makes me violently ill," she improvised. "I'm afraid my weakness will embarrass us both."

Etienne paused, studying her through narrowed eyes, weighing her words. "Very well, *chérie,*" he said at last. "It wouldn't do to have you ill in front of my workers. Even *noirs* gossip."

"Merci," she said, stifling a sigh of relief. The tight coil of tension at the pit of her stomach began to unwind.

Etienne tossed the whip to Reid, who caught it in midair. "No need to soil my hands. This is what I pay you for."

"I'll tend to the matter," Reid replied tonelessly.

"See that you do." Etienne tucked Christiane's hand into the crook of his arm, all the while keeping his gaze fixed on his overseer. "Rumor has it that you are much too lenient with the *noirs.* I want strips of this man's flesh as proof that sufficient punishment was meted out. Deliver them tonight . . . after dinner."

Christiane gasped at her husband's cruel edict. Bile rose in her throat, burning, bitter, and she forced it back. Her ears buzzed; her head spun. She drew in a deep breath, then another.

"Come, *chérie.*"

As Etienne led her away, she cast a final despairing glance over her shoulder. Under Reid's terse directions, Juno was being lashed to a nearby post. She quickened her step, nearly stumbling in her haste to be as far away as possible when the first blow landed on its hapless victim.

She fervently wished that she had never heard the name of St. Domingue.

Christiane merely toyed with her meal. Never far from her mind was the knowledge that at any moment Reid would appear, bearing his macabre offering. Earlier she had pleaded a headache and asked to be excused, but Etienne had refused her request. In spite of the headache powder Hera had administered, the pain behind her eyes persisted.

She cast a surreptitious glance down the long dining room table. Initially she had questioned why such a length was needed to separate two diners, but that had changed. Now she was grateful for the seven feet of polished mahogany that stood between her and the man whose name she bore.

While she felt pensive, depressed, Etienne, on the other hand, seemed almost in a jovial mood. He nodded his approval as Astra ladled a rich, creamy soup into a bowl. "Try the bisque," he urged. "It's excellent."

Rather than argue, Christiane took a spoonful, barely tasting the savory concoction thick with seafood. She dawdled, purposely letting the soup grow cold, then sat back and allowed one of the servants to remove her dish.

"I've been thinking," Etienne mused as Astra served him a generous portion of roast fowl. "The time has come to host a party. A delayed wedding celebration. This will be the perfect opportunity to introduce my bride to the other planters and their wives. Let them see for themselves what a prize I won."

"I'll be happy to help with the arrangements," she offered with alacrity. Thus far Etienne had refused her requests to ride horseback or to supervise the running of the household. Except for reading and needlework, there was little to while away the hours, and time hung heavy.

"Your offer, *chérie*, though generous, is unnecessary." He smiled at her obvious disappointment. "My servants function quite admirably whenever I entertain. I doubt this time will prove an exception."

"Whatever you think best, m'sieur," she muttered. It was on the tip of her tongue to ask why he needed a wife if everything could be managed so conveniently without one, but she caught herself in time. She was there in the capacity of brood mare. Pity his well-laid plans had been thwarted by a higher power. A pity for him, but a blessing for her. The thought of bearing his child filled her with revulsion.

He pulled out a pocket watch and made a production out of checking the time. "I expect Alexander should be here soon." Though he maintained a deceptively bland tone, the avid gleam in his pale eyes betrayed his anticipation.

She pressed a hand against her stomach. "I really don't feel very well."

"Nonsense, you've hardly touched your meal." He speared a morsel and popped it into his mouth. "Try Scylla's specialty, chicken livers stewed in port wine. I guarantee they will bring color to your cheeks."

"No, thank you," she managed. The mere thought of food sent her stomach contents dancing.

"I insist. Astra," he said, turning to address the girl, "give Madame a serving of chicken livers."

Astra stepped forward with a malicious smile and spooned a generous portion of the delicacy onto Christiane's plate.

"Humor me, *chérie;* just try them."

Christiane eyed the food with distaste. Even the smell sent her stomach reeling.

"Be a good girl. If not, I just might refuse to let you leave the table until you've cleaned your plate."

Christiane glanced at her husband. The hard gleam in his eyes contradicted his light banter. She would have to be a fool not to heed his warning. Slicing a small portion, she swallowed without tasting, then cleansed her palate with a swallow of water.

Etienne smiled over the rim of his wineglass, then changed the course of the conversation. "My overseer is an interesting fellow, don't you think, *chérie?*"

She cocked her head to one side, wary. "In what respect?"

"Do you ever wonder why someone who seems so . . . independent works for me? Have you ever asked yourself why Alexander is so willing to do anything—and everything—I ask? No matter how disagreeable?"

Juno's name wasn't mentioned; it didn't have to be. "Yes. I admit I've been curious."

"Have you ever questioned him about his past?"

"No." She listlessly shredded a piece of chicken with her fork. "After all, I hardly know the man. His past is none of my business."

"I couldn't help but notice the way you looked at him this afternoon. You could hardly drag your gaze away. You consider him handsome, don't you?"

Christiane's fork clattered to the table. "Etienne, really . . ."

"There's nothing to be embarrassed about, *chérie.*" His tone was amused. "I'm sure many women find him attractive. In a crude sort of way."

"I'm a married woman," she replied stiffly. "I have every intention of honoring our agreement. Do not think for a moment that I plan a dalliance with another."

"How noble, *chérie.* I didn't mean to question your integrity. You're far too intelligent to risk the consequences of cuckolding me."

A chill snaked down her spine. Where was this conversation leading? She tried not to flinch under his cold-eyed stare.

"Confess, *chérie,* doesn't Reid Alexander pique your interest?" Etienne sipped his wine and continued to regard her steadily.

She lifted her shoulders in a shrug. "Perhaps . . . a little."

"Take this afternoon, for instance. Did you happen to

notice the scars . . . ?" He made a moue. "What do you suppose caused them?"

"I have no idea."

He leaned forward, dropped his voice to a conspiratorial level. "He bears the scars from a whip. Whipping is a punishment reserved for recalcitrant slaves and hardened criminals."

She swallowed hard, her mind rebelling at the thought. "Such punishment, so I've been told, is also meted out for misdemeanors committed at sea. Perhaps M'sieur Alexander was aboard ship and had a falling out with the *capitaine.*"

He laughed softly at her naivete. "Anything is possible, but did you notice how he favors shirts with wide cuffs?"

She nodded, the motion barely perceptible.

"He wears those deliberately to hide the scars around his wrists."

Christiane played with the stem of her wineglass. She had noticed the scars—and wondered.

"Manacles . . ." he whispered.

Her hand jerked in surprise. She grabbed at the wineglass to keep it from toppling, but not before some of its contents stained the pristine white tablecloth. "Are you implying that M'sieur Alexander is a convict?"

He nodded in agreement, then sat back in his chair, pleased at the impact of his revelation. "You're shocked, and for good reason, *chérie.* I'm telling you all this for your own benefit. It would be wise to maintain your distance. While I can control him, you cannot. The man is dangerous."

"What did he do?" Her lips felt stiff, reluctant to form the words, just as her mind was reluctant to accept the fact.

"I'm not one to spread tales." He shrugged, noncommittal. "I only wanted you to be forewarned before an attachment formed."

"What was his crime?" she asked softly.

"Murder."

The single word could have been a stone dropped into a still pool, its ramifications rippling outward, spreading through the numb recesses of her brain. "Murder . . ." She shook her head in disbelief. "But who? Why?"

"I won't go into detail. Suffice it to say he's a murderer, a cold-blooded killer." He snapped his fingers and the servants silently and efficiently began removing dinner dishes.

"M'sieur Alexander . . . ? A convicted murderer?" she murmured, trying to absorb the shocking discovery.

Etienne accepted a short-stemmed goblet of brandy. "When I confronted him, Alexander confessed that he fatally stabbed an innocent man to death after robbing him of his fortune."

Christiane's mind reeled. "Why do you employ such a person to work at Belle Terre?"

"Business." Lounging back in his chair, Etienne sipped brandy. "I decided I could use a man of his caliber, a man totally without scruples, free of morals, to keep the *noirs* in line. He owes me allegiance. If not for me, he'd be rotting in a hellhole of a prison on neighboring Hispaniola. A fate worse than death. At any sign of disobedience on his part, I could notify the authorities and have him hauled off to prison."

Christiane remained silent, stunned by all she had just heard.

"I realize this must be difficult for a woman of your sensibilities to comprehend, but I thought it time you learned the truth."

Difficult couldn't begin to describe how she felt. She had suspected something dark in Reid's past, but nothing of this magnitude. Though she had seen the evidence, the scars, the reticence to talk about himself, she had stubbornly refused to believe the worst. But now she could no longer deny the obvious. Reid Alexander was a convicted murderer, devoid of the heroic attributes she had fancifully tried to bestow. No longer a knight in shining armor, but a common criminal, a cold-blooded killer.

A man without honor.

A man unworthy of trust.

She felt betrayed, duped. A fool. She despised him. And despised herself for wishing otherwise.

Chapter Six

"Ah, Alexander," Etienne crowed in delight as Reid entered the dining room. "I've been expecting you."

Reid swept an assessing glance around the room. Etienne Delacroix occupied one end of the impressive banquet table, his wife the other. Wasted space, Reid reflected, when one could sit next to a beautiful woman. Christiane, as though sensing herself the object of his thoughts, sat taller and stared fixedly ahead, apparently unable to bear the sight of him—a sentiment that would soon intensify. Reid felt a sharp pang of regret, but ruthlessly tamped it down and concentrated on the task at hand.

"Sit." Etienne waved expansively toward a row of empty chairs. "Join me for brandy."

"No, thank you." Reid declined with a shake of his head. "In the future, the *noirs* will think twice before questioning an order."

"Good, good." Etienne held up his empty brandy glass, which Astra hastened to refill.

Reid carefully kept his gaze averted from Christiane. "The man will no longer pose a problem."

Etienne nodded toward the cloth bag dangling from Reid's right hand. "I see you remembered my pound of flesh."

"Unfortunately Juno didn't survive his lesson in obedience." Reid tossed the sack on the table, where it landed with a soft thud.

Christiane clamped her hand over her mouth. With a muffled cry of distress, she raced toward the French doors and out of the dining room.

"Women . . ." Etienne wagged his head in disgust. "Go after her, will you, Alexander? Make sure she doesn't do something as foolish as to fling herself off the balcony. The stains would be impossible to erase."

With a curt nod, Reid hurried after her.

He spotted Christiane at the far end of the terrace, her head lowered over a stone balustrade, heaving her stomach contents onto the shrubs below. His first impulse to retreat, Reid took a tentative step backward. He'd return to Delacroix and report that he couldn't find her.

Yet there was something compelling about this particular damsel in distress. Christiane Delacroix possessed a spirit to match her rare beauty—a spirit that he'd hate to see broken. She was all alone, vulnerable, in need of a protector. Reid felt an uncharacteristic—and totally unexpected—urge to stay, to comfort; urges he hadn't felt in years. Not since his brother, Chase, had died . . .

With a final convulsive shudder, Christiane straightened and relaxed her death grip on the railing. She sucked huge gulps of air like a runner after a marathon. Even in the scant light, Reid could see the greenish cast of her flawless ivory complexion, the beads of perspiration dotting her brow. He stepped forward, wanting to help, but fearful his efforts would be rejected.

She ignored the sound of footsteps crossing the stone terrace, and stared unseeingly ahead. Reid took a linen square from his pocket and wordlessly offered it to her.

Knocking his hand away, she whirled to confront him, dark eyes blazing in her ashen face. "How could you?"

While he hadn't expected gratitude, he wasn't prepared for the degree of her fury. "That's a pretty quick recovery for someone who looked ready to hurl herself over the balcony only moments ago," he said mildly, replacing the handkerchief.

"Don't pretend you don't know I'm talking about Juno."

Reid realized belatedly that his impression about her vulnerability had been mistaken. *He* was the one who needed protection from her wrath. "I only did what had to be done."

"I thought you were a decent human being, but you're not. You're evil . . . just like him."

He wanted to refute her charges, justify his actions, but he couldn't. Instead he placed a hand at her waist. "You're white as chalk. Let me help you to a bench."

"Stop it," she said in a hiss, jerking away. "Don't touch me. Don't ever touch me. Your hands have blood on them."

He stared at her, his expression bleak. There was nothing he could say, nothing he could do, to change her opinion of him. He hardened himself against regret that threatened to undermine his resolve. "Toughen up, Countess. Only the strong survive."

Her chin came up with a snap. "I don't need advice from a man like you."

He held up both hands, palms out. "Just trying to be of service."

"You disgust me." Her voice quavered with disgust, loathing. "As far as I'm concerned, the only service you can perform for me is to stay out of my sight." Picking up her skirts, she quickly crossed the terrace and disappeared through the open French doors.

Reid blew out a long breath. The lady had a temper. Christiane Delacroix had certainly succeeded in putting him in his place. A pretty face, a sharp tongue, and a tender heart. An intriguing combination. A dangerous combination.

Her opinion of him should be of little consequence. Yet the temptation to assure her that he was far different from the cold, unfeeling man she had married had almost overpowered his common sense. And what purpose would that have served? *None*, he answered himself, his mouth curving in a bitter twist, *absolutely none. Let her think the worst.*

Jamming his hands into his pockets, he stared across the craggy mountains that formed a charcoal smudge against an indigo sky. He felt perched on a lit powder keg. He was already far too preoccupied with the French planter's lovely bride. The sooner he left St. Domingue, the better.

He cocked his head to one side, listening. Off in the distance he heard the faint but unmistakable tattoo of drums: the signal that Juno had reached safety. Somewhere, in a glade deep in the wood, *noirs* feasted on a boar who had wandered too near a coffee shed at an inopportune moment. And inside the great house, a cruel, sadistic man gloated over a sack filled with pigskin, waiting to hear gory details.

With a heavy sigh, Reid turned and retraced his steps.

* * *

Efficient as a swarm of bees, the staff of Belle Terre buzzed with preparations for a party. Everyone, that was, except Christiane. In denying her participation, Etienne had found yet another way to humiliate her. Like most young women of her social station, she had been trained since girlhood to manage a large household. By rejecting her offers of assistance, he insulted her abilities, labeling her incompetent, inept. Useless.

Christiane chafed under the enforced inactivity; therefore, it was a welcome relief when Hera ushered a woman into her bedroom one morning shortly after breakfast.

"A visitor, madame," Hera announced, then left the two to stare at each other in frank curiosity.

"I am Simone du Val."

"Bonjour, madame." Christiane was fascinated by the woman who represented a blend of two different cultures. Statuesque and exotic, with skin the rich shade of honey and eyes like amber nuggets, Simone du Val could have been anywhere between thirty and fifty.

"M'sieur Delacroix sent word to Le Cap. He said you are in need of a ball gown," Simone explained, her manner businesslike.

Christiane watched as the woman unloaded items from a large wicker hamper and placed them at the foot of the bed. First came a thick stack of fabric samples in a rainbow of hues, followed by a tin box of pins and a book of fashion illustrations. Next she draped a tape measure around her neck and fixed Christiane with an uncompromising stare. "If I am to clothe you, madame, as befitting the wife of one of the wealthiest men on St. Domingue, you will have to undress."

Christiane dutifully went behind a screen and began to remove her gown.

Simone quickly became impatient. "Come, madame, do not dawdle. There is much to do."

Christiane came out clothed only in her undergarments. "My husband did not mention you were coming."

"Perhaps M'sieur Delacroix wishes to surprise you." Simone patted her smooth chignon. "Now come, stand by the window, where I may see you properly."

Christiane walked to the window and turned first one way, then the other, her chin angled rebelliously at the seamstress's steady stream of commands.

Simone studied her client through narrowed eyes. "Ah, *oui,*" she said, nodding with satisfaction, "very nice. With your dark hair and creamy skin, many colors will look good on you. And with your figure . . ."

For the next half hour, Christiane felt little more than a mannequin. Simone retrieved her tape and meticulously took Christiane's measurements, jotting each one carefully into a small notebook.

At last she snapped the book closed. "A new shipment of silk has just arrived in my shop. There is a special one I have set aside. It will be perfect on you."

Recalling her husband's disparaging remarks about her limited wardrobe, Christiane ventured a question. "Did M'sieur Delacroix specify only one gown?"

"*Oui,* madame. Only a single gown." Simone rolled her measuring tape into a neat ball. "M'sieur said you were to be the finest dressed at the ball. Nothing but the best for his wife."

Christiane found the fact that Etienne had requested only a single gown rather strange. His scathing comments about her meager wardrobe had led her to believe that he intended to replenish her apparel. But who could account for the vagaries of the man's mind?

"You will be the envy of every woman on the island," Simone continued, unaware of her client's sudden lapse into silence.

Christiane gave herself a mental shake. Now that the awkwardness of their initial meeting had worn off, she found herself enjoying the company of another woman. "Are you from St. Domingue, Simone?"

"*Oui*, madame. My husband, André, and I own a shop in Le Cap. He is the tailor for many of the *grand blancs*, including your husband."

"How interesting," Christiane replied, trying to assimilate this into her scant knowledge of the island. She had believed the social structure was split into two distinct factors based on the color of skin. However, there must be a third strata as well, since Simone's skin was neither white or black, but a unique mix of each.

"You are new to the island, madame," Simone replied, surmising Christiane's quandary. "André and I are what is known in St. Domingue as *gens de couleur*, or people of color. Our number is small, our privileges few, and our voice unheard by those in power."

"You state your case with simple elegance, Simone. I, myself, can relate to your plight."

"You, madame?" Simone scoffed, pausing in the act of replacing the samples of fabric to regard Christiane. "How could you possibly pretend to understand our plight?"

Christiane didn't flinch under the woman's open skepticism, but met her look boldly. "In spite of our different backgrounds, we share certain things in common. I, too, have recently experienced what it is like to have few privileges and a voice that is unheard. It diminishes you as a person."

The cynicism slowly faded from Simone's expression as she considered Christiane's words. "Forgive me, madame, if I spoke in haste."

Christiane smiled and extended her hand. "Perhaps we can be friends?"

"Have you gone mad?" Scandalized, Simone studied the outstretched hand. "It is unheard of that a *grand blanc* should be friends with *gens de couleur.*"

Christiane smiled, but lowered her hand. "If that cannot be," she said with a philosophical shrug, "then we can be friends as one woman to another. Now tell me more about yourself."

Simone rolled her eyes in disbelief. "You are a very persistent young woman, madame."

"Guilty as charged." Christiane laughed and motioned for Simone to be seated. Reid Alexander had made the same accusation upon their first meeting, she recalled. Then all traces of humor fled as Christiane resolutely banished Reid from her thoughts. She reminded herself that he was not worthy of a memory, not even a pleasant one. He was a beast, a monster—a man who had brutally beaten a defenseless man to death.

"We are truly alike, madame." Simone perched gingerly on the chair Christiane had indicated. "I have also been called persistent. But it is those who are persistent who succeed."

The next hour passed pleasantly while the two women became better acquainted. Christiane learned that through their shop, Simone and her husband had arrangements with agents in Nantes and Bordeaux to import only the finest fabrics. Along with high quality woolens and cotton from the looms of Europe, they also stocked a wide assortment of silks and brocades from the Orient.

"We produce fashions comparable to those worn on

the streets of Paris," Simone boasted, then glanced self-consciously at the plain, unadorned muslin gown she wore. "Please, madame, do not judge my handiwork by this simple offering."

"There is nothing to apologize for, Simone. The color and cut of your gown are most becoming."

The woman rose and efficiently packed the remaining items into the wicker basket. "You are very kind, madame, but I am well aware that my gown is long out of style. *Gens de couleur*, however, are forbidden to dress in the styles of Europe."

"Surely, as free people, the law entitles you to basic rights and freedoms."

"Ah, you have heard only part of it." Simone made a sweeping gesture. "*Gens de couleur* cannot hold office, or pursue such professions as law, medicine, the priesthood, or teaching, or serve in the militia. We must be off the streets by nine o'clock and are forbidden to occupy the good seats at the theater."

"But that is so unfair."

"As I stated earlier, madame, you are new to the island, a stranger to its ways." Simone's voice grew increasingly bitter as she went on. "A drunken planter can demand the clothes stripped from our backs in the middle of the street if he thinks the cut or cloth of our garments similar to his own."

"Will not the courts hear your grievances?" Christiane asked, appalled at the gross inequality.

"Bah!" Simone snorted derisively. "The courts in St. Domingue are nothing but a farce. No *grand blanc* has ever lost against a *gens de couleur*. If a freed colored strikes a *blanc*, his hand will be cut off. If a *blanc* strikes a freed colored, he *might* receive an insignificant fine."

Christiane listened, heartsick at the recitation of injustices that Simone was subjected to on a daily basis. "It is I who should plead for your forgiveness, Simone. I was presumptuous to think we shared common grievances. My problems are trivial compared with yours."

"You could not know." Reaching out, Simone impulsively squeezed Christiane's hand. "It is I who should thank you for the opportunity to air my grievances. Resentment is harmful if kept locked inside."

"Will you join me for a light repast before you return to Le Cap?" Christiane asked a bit wistfully, eager to forestall the monotony that would descend with Simone's departure.

"Your heart is kind, *chérie,* but I must decline." Simone slung the hamper over her arm and started for the door. "It is against the law for *gens de couleur* to eat at the same table as a *blanc.*"

"Would you reconsider if I request the food be served here in my sitting room?" Christiane persisted, reluctant to part with her new friend. "No one need know that we dined together."

"Oh, no, madame." Simone shook her head emphatically. "That is not wise. Your husband would be furious when he discovered such liberties had been taken beneath his own roof."

"He need never find out. Certainly I won't tell, and I'll ask Hera to be discreet."

"He has ways, madame; he has ways. Never underestimate M'sieur Delacroix. He is not a man to tolerate disobedience." Simone turned at the door, her hand resting on the knob, her face troubled. "Be on your guard, *chérie.* Do not make him your enemy."

With this Simone left, closing the door softly behind her.

Christiane sank onto the edge of the bed, her hands

loosely folded in her lap, and contemplated Simone du Val's advice. The seamstress's final words chimed through her head like a funeral knell.

By agreeing to a marriage by proxy, she had set her romantic fantasies aside and allowed practicality to prevail. But the cost was far more than she had anticipated. Marriage to a wealthy planter had promised security, safety. In time, she had hoped to develop a fondness for the man who would father her children, share her life. Children, home, a garden, a circle of friends. Eventually, she had hoped, these would fill the lonely hours, vacant days, and empty years.

If not affection, she thought she might at least have developed a numbing indifference toward the man to whom she was pledged. But with Etienne Delacroix that, too, was impossible. She could never be indifferent to a man she loathed so intensely.

As intensely as she feared him.

Nervously she twisted the ruby wedding ring around and around. First Reid, now Simone had warned her of danger, but Christiane feared their admonitions came too late. She had already made him a formidable enemy.

Vows or no vows, she knew she couldn't remain in St. Domingue indefinitely. She tugged the costly ring over her knuckle, then slid it back in place. A nebulous plan began to form. Grandfather had promised to write. As soon as she learned his whereabouts, she would find a way to join him. His letter could come any day. Then she would turn her back on this whole dreadful experience and forget she had ever had the misfortune to meet the devil in disguise.

Not even Scylla's superb meal could counteract the unpleasantness of sitting across the table from her husband. Christiane regarded him thoughtfully over her raised glass. On this particular night, Etienne seemed in an uncharacteristically good frame of mind. A self-satisfied smile hovered on his mouth, and his manner seemed less abrasive than usual. She couldn't help but wonder what had wrought the change.

"You seem in exceptionally good spirits this evening, Etienne," she observed, taking a small sip of wine.

"Yes, I suppose I am." He beamed, helping himself to another portion of snails swimming in a buttery sauce. "The plans for the party are progressing nicely, even better than I dared hope. Everyone, it appears, is quite anxious to welcome my bride."

"Then we are preparing for quite a crowd?"

"All the guests have written accepting my invitation. Everyone, of course, except the Rodolphes. Madame Rodolphe, Berthe, is expecting another child any time now." He speared another snail, popped it into his mouth, then blotted his lips fastidiously with a napkin. "Probably another girl. Females are all Ambrose seems capable of creating."

"That must be a trial for M'sieur Rodolphe."

"Of course." He pushed aside his plate and signaled for the next course. "Every man wants a male heir."

Christiane traced the intricate pattern on the handle of her fork with an index finger. Etienne, she knew, was no different from any other man. He, too, wanted a son to carry on tradition at Belle Terre. How much longer was he willing to wait before forcing himself on her again? she wondered.

If Etienne noticed her pensive mood, he ignored it. "I've assigned several women to help Scylla in the kitchen, and others to assist with household chores. A number of guests will spend the night at Belle Terre before returning home."

"Ah, *oui*," she murmured. "I have watched the servants ready the guest rooms."

"I've even invited Reid Alexander to join in the festivities."

"Won't an overseer be out of place at such a grand affair?"

He shrugged. "Several of the planters have daughters who find him intriguing. In spite of his background, he can acquit himself on the dance floor."

"There will be dancing?"

"But of course." He nodded as he began to devour a generous slice of beef. "The musicians are coming from Le Cap. Besides, an extra man at a social function is an asset, don't you agree, *chérie*?"

"I had no idea the party would be quite so elaborate."

"No expense will be spared. Attention to detail makes all the difference, I have learned. Plan for every contingency, every eventuality, and your guests won't be disappointed. They will depart praising your hospitality."

"I'll keep that in mind, m'sieur."

Etienne glanced up in time to see her decline a serving of the succulent roast. "Eat, eat," he ordered. "If you become too thin, Madame du Val's measurements will be inaccurate and your new gown won't fit properly."

"There is no need for alarm. Madame du Val promised she would return for a final fitting the day before the party."

"My friends know my penchant for beauty. What will they think if they find my bride nothing but a bag of bones? Astra," he snapped, "serve Madame a slice of roast." His scowl of disapproval smoothed and he resumed eating after the girl complied by placing a large portion on her mistress's dinner plate.

"Etienne, really," Christiane protested, eyeing the unwanted food. "I am not a hen in a fattening coop."

Her analogy drew a small smile. "You could use a little more flesh on your frame, *chérie,* you are becoming thin. Only the strong survive on St. Domingue. The frail just wither away and . . ." His voice trailed off as he flicked a crumb from the sleeve of his jacket.

"Wither away and . . . ?" she prompted.

"Die." Etienne's wintry blue eyes fastened on her, freezing her in place.

A frisson of fear rippled through her. She moistened her lips, then cleared her throat and forced herself to speak calmly. "I am much stronger than I look, m'sieur. Trust me, I am not frail and helpless."

"The tropical climate can affect newcomers in adverse ways."

"I am adaptable."

He gave her an innocuous smile, but his eyes remained cold. "Time will tell, *chérie.* Time will tell."

Christiane found Etienne's comments all the more ominous because of their blandness. She cut a small morsel of meat she didn't really want and put it in her mouth. The food took on the consistency of clay. Were his words a thinly veiled warning?

She glanced down the length of the table at him. Reasonably attractive, impeccably clad, he appeared every inch the successful and wealthy planter, a man of means and privilege. But underneath the urbane, polished surface, he was corrupt—cruel, conniving, and totally lacking scruples. A man capable of anything. Human life mattered little to him: not that of his slaves, and not hers.

His aristocratic features gave no clue to his thoughts.

What extremes would he resort to? Was he already plotting her demise? Surely not. Yet . . .

The notion was too horrendous even to consider. Determined to be warier in the future, Christiane reached for her wineglass, annoyed to find her hand trembled. She didn't trust Etienne. Couldn't trust Reid. There was nowhere to turn. She had only herself to rely on.

Chapter Seven

The drums started again.

Reid had grown so accustomed to their sound that at first he hardly noticed them. But tonight was different. Tonight they sounded frenetic, insistent. Angry.

He rolled from his cot, pulled on his pants, and followed their beat deeper and deeper into the tropical forest. What called the *noirs* night after night? he wondered as he slipped through the woods. In the beginning, the changes had been so subtle that Reid thought he was imagining things. Then he began to pay closer attention, and found his suspicions well-founded. The *noirs* were slower to respond to orders, whispering among themselves whenever they thought no one was watching. Few met his gaze directly. None were openly defiant, yet he often glimpsed animosity shimmering in their eyes, hostility peeking through cracks in their bland expressions.

Purple clouds trailed across the silver moon like gossamer veils. The drums grew louder as he stealthily crept closer. He wanted to know what was going on. Had to know so he could plan accordingly. He intended to be safe in New Orleans when hell erupted on St. Domingue. The problem was, he wasn't quite ready to leave the island. He still lacked the necessary funds to finance the lifestyle he'd need to infiltrate Creole society. Delacroix had promised a bonus if he drove the *noirs* to clear land in record time. He needed that money.

As Reid drew closer, an orange glow suffused the night sky. The drumbeats quickened, the rhythm hypnotic, compelling. He could hear raised voices, the words unintelligible, the language foreign. Crouching behind a dense cover of bushes, he cautiously edged forward, stopping when he found a vantage point where he had a clear view of the proceedings, but was still a safe distance from detection.

A bizarre scene greeted him. A bonfire blazed in the center of a clearing, its hungry red tongues of flame licking skyward. Dead logs and branches snapped and hissed in the flames. A dazzling display of orange sparks showered the inky sky like a swarm of fireflies on a summer night. A large group of *noirs* in various stages of undress gathered around the fire. Women, bared to the waist, danced and swayed, their movements free, uninhibited. Chants, ancient, pagan, reverberated through the clearing. A voodoo ceremony, Reid realized. He had stumbled upon a voodoo ceremony.

Out of the corner of his eye, Reid detected a motion just to the right of his hiding place. Narrowing his eyes, he peered through the darkness. His gaze focused on a figure clothed in filmy white moving cautiously up the same path he had just taken. For a moment he thought he was seeing a ghostly apparition, a product of his imagination and the voodoo rite. Then his jaw dropped in surprise as recognition dawned.

Christiane!

What the devil brought her out here? Didn't the woman have any sense at all? Apparently not, he concluded grimly, answering his own question. Obviously she couldn't resist the chance to flirt with danger. Didn't she stop to consider what might happen if her presence was discovered? Only the invited, the initiated, were welcome this night.

In spite of his irritation, he found himself observing her closely, fascinated in spite of himself. What was she wearing? A nightdress? Whatever it was, the simple style accentuated her beauty. The faint breeze molded the filmy fabric against her body, subtly outlining each graceful curve. Her midnight dark hair was unbound, forming a mantle of loose curls around her shoulders and down her back. Silky tendrils lifted and fell in the night breeze. She looked pure, innocent, undefiled.

She paused in the shadows, her head tilted to one side, captivated by the scene. Reid swore softly under his breath. Anyone coming along the path would see her. Mobilized by the grim possibility, Reid darted out, clamped one hand over her mouth, hooked an arm around her waist, then dove under the bushes of his hiding place, using his body to cushion the fall.

Stunned, Christiane half sprawled across his chest, staring down at him. Reid watched as amazement registered on her features, then quickly turned to outrage. Just as she opened her mouth to protest her rough treatment, Reid heard a noise from along the path. He effectively silenced her the only way he knew how.

Curving his hand around the back of her head, he forced her mouth to his. His lips moved over hers, intent on smothering an angry harangue before it erupted into a roar. Her lips parted in surprise beneath his, and desire of another kind burst into flame—petal soft and nectar sweet. He devoured her mouth with his. He forgot he was kissing her to ensure her silence, their safety. Forgot everything but her tempting, honeyed mouth.

He delighted in the weight of her body atop his, a perfect match. Soft curves pressed against hard planes. Soft, yielding, feminine. He felt his senses spinning wildly out of control. Suddenly he realized he wanted her, not passive or indifferent, but willing and warm. Angling his mouth, he gentled the kiss, coaxing, cajoling a response from her.

The change in tactics bore instant results. Elated when he felt her hands clutch his shoulders, Reid became bolder and deepened the kiss. Skimming the tip of his tongue over her full bottom lip, he took quick advantage of her shocked gasp to slide his tongue into her mouth. His tongue stroked hers in light, teasing caresses. When she shyly met his advances, Reid's pleasure was almost painful in intensity. He savored her unique taste: sweet with a dash of spice.

Then an ear-shattering cheer rent the night, destroying the moment.

Sobering as a bucket of ice water, the cry abruptly brought Reid to his senses. Christiane stared down at him, her dark brown eyes cloudy with passion, confusion. Her mouth, swollen from his kiss, looked as tempting and succulent as forbidden fruit. Reid ruthlessly clamped down on the desire still humming through his veins. What the hell was he thinking? he wondered contemptuously. He had nearly lost control of the situation. What had begun as an attempt to keep Christiane from being discovered had quickly gotten out of hand. One touch, one taste, and he had instantly become oblivious to everything but her. Disgusted with himself, he set her aside and shifted onto his stomach.

Holding a finger to his mouth for silence, he parted the

bushes in front of them so that they had an unobstructed view of the clearing.

"Watch," he whispered. "Listen."

Christiane wriggled into position alongside him, her expression quizzical.

Side by side, they lay on the ground and watched as the crowd parted and a tall, broomstick thin black man stepped into the circle of firelight.

"Boukman," Reid murmured absently. He recognized the man he had once seen in Le Cap. Part houngan, or voodoo priest, part revolutionist, Boukman was rumored to be visiting various plantations to enlist followers for his cause.

Boukman held out his hand, and a woman with a queenly bearing and dressed in flowing white stepped forward. A wild nimbus of hair framed a familiar face.

"Hera." Christiane's mouth silently formed the word.

As Reid and Christiane watched from the relative safety of their hiding place, Boukman and Hera, voodoo priest and priestess, took their positions near a makeshift altar. A cage containing a huge coiled snake rested atop the altar. Boukman speaking in a language that sounded half African, half French, addressed the crowd. When he finished, all eyes fastened on Hera.

Raising the lid of the cage, she hoisted the serpent high over her head. Her face lifted to the midnight sky, she emitted a long, piercing scream. Christiane reflexively clutched Reid's arm as Hera's body began to writhe, then convulse spasmodically. Words in the same odd language used by Boukman poured from her mouth. Then, spent, she replaced the snake on the altar.

One by one, each of the participants approached the altar and laid down their offerings. Chicken bones tied into the shape of crosses, animal skulls, feathers, scraps of red, white and blue cloth were all added to the pile.

Then the tone changed.

Boukman raised his arms, and the throng fell silent. Dropping all traces of dialect, he addressed the crowd. Eloquently, he informed them of what was happening in France, where people like themselves revolted against their oppressors. In ringing clarity, he assured them the same was possible in St. Domingue.

"The Good Lord hath ordained vengeance. He will give strength to our arms and courage to our hearts. Unite, my brothers. We will conquer. We will rule."

Reid tapped Christiane on the shoulder and motioned that it was time to leave. With Boukman's voice still ringing in her ears, she kept low to the ground and followed as he led the way to Belle Terre.

By the time they reached the gate at the entrance to the garden, a million questions were swarming through Christiane's mind. A glance at Reid's closed expression told her no explanation would be forthcoming unless she pressed for answers. Drawing a deep breath, she took the plunge. "Is there a name for the strange ceremony we just witnessed?"

Reid folded his arms across his chest and regarded her thoughtfully for a long moment before finally answering. "It is called voodoo."

"Voodoo . . ." she repeated softly.

"It's a . . . religion of sorts. Or more precisely, a mixture of religion and superstition. It's based on beliefs the *noirs* brought with them from Africa involving the worship of spirits both animate and inanimate."

Christiane listened with rapt attention, absorbing the information. "Who was that man? Boukman?"

Reid scowled down at her, his jaw tightly clamped.

"Well . . . ?" She prompted, returning the scowl. "Why won't you tell me?"

"You might not like what you hear."

"I want to know," she insisted stubbornly. More than idle curiosity drove her to learn the identity of the thin fanatic who spoke with such passion and zeal. For reasons she couldn't comprehend, she sensed his importance.

"Boukman is a slave. By all accounts, he was a former overseer, or *commandeur,* on a plantation near Limbe."

Christiane remembered the man's exhortations and shivered. "He frightened me."

"And for good reason, Countess. The man is powerful, dangerous."

"And Hera?" She placed her hand on the garden gate, but made no effort to open it. "What is her role in all of this?"

Reid shrugged. "Based on what we just witnessed, she's probably a mambo, or voodoo priestess."

"Tonight was more than just a voodoo ceremony, wasn't it?"

"Boukman has been working to rally the slaves, to convince them to unite against the *blancs.*"

"A revolution . . ." Her grip on the gate tightened. How ironic, she reflected, that she flee one revolution only to find herself embroiled in another.

"It's unlikely he'll succeed. Uprisings have been attempted in the past and the conspirators caught and promptly hanged."

She gave a humorless laugh. His words lent her little reassurance. "You are naive, m'sieur. When a large group of people unite for a single cause, anything is possible."

Reid remained silent, unable to come up with a suitable rejoinder.

"Is my . . ." She started to say *husband,* but couldn't

bring herself to say the word. Instead she rephrased her question. "Are the plantation owners aware of what is happening? Should they be forewarned?"

Reid's mouth twisted in a humorless smile. "The *grand blancs* are an arrogant bunch. They choose to turn a blind eye to what is going on beneath their very noses."

She pushed open the garden gate. "Then they're fools. All of them."

"Countess . . ." he said, halting her before she could disappear down the path and into the house. "Don't breathe a word of what you witnessed tonight. Not to your husband, not to Hera, not to anyone. Your life—our lives—depend on silence."

She glared at him over her shoulder, her eyes snapping with ire. "Do you take me for some silly twit with pudding for brains?"

"You married Delacroix, didn't you?" he fired back, inexplicably angry at her for reasons he didn't want to examine too closely.

She drew in a sharp breath. She felt as though she'd just been slapped. "Touché," she conceded bitterly. "Marrying the devil qualifies me as the biggest fool of all."

"Sorry," he muttered. "I shouldn't have said that."

"No, you shouldn't have," she said, her voice choked by hurt. "You have no right to judge me."

"Nor you me," he retorted.

"It's late. I should go before the servants return."

"Countess . . ."

She was halfway up the path when he called out. The tentative quality in his voice had an unsettling effect on her. It contained a certain wistfulness, a sadness, at odd variance with his strong character. She half turned to find him standing with both hands lightly resting on the garden gate. Clouds played hide-and-seek across the moon's surface, leaving his face swathed in shadow. Even so, she could feel the force of his steady gray gaze.

"Be careful."

"And you, also, m'sieur. *Bonsoir.*" With this, she turned and ran inside.

Careful . . . be careful. Be careful.

The phrase whispered through her mind like wind through the trees. The sights and sounds of the voodoo ritual, vivid and bold, danced in her head. Even in the relative safety of her own bedroom with the door bolted, Christiane didn't feel secure. Always on guard, always alert. She had not felt safe since arriving in St. Domingue. Now after tonight a new worry was added to her growing list. The *noirs'* hatred of the *grand blancs* would soon erupt in violence.

As soon as she learned her grandfather's whereabouts she would leave this island. Until then, she would manage the best she could. Her grandfather had promised to write. And Jean-Claude Bouchard, Comte de Varennes, was a man of his word. Something had to be wrong, dreadfully wrong, or else she would have heard from him already. If she left before she received his letter, she would not know where to find him, and they would never be reunited.

Gradually, toward dawn, tension gave way to fatigue. Barriers relaxed and memories of a kiss filtered through. A pleasant warmth spread over her. Reid's kiss had awakened a hidden yearning, an untapped passion. It made her forget everything, made her lose herself totally. For a brief span of time, she had been transported to a world where only the two of them existed.

When the kiss had ended so abruptly, Reid had seemed completely unaffected, while she, on the other hand, had been rocked off her foundation. Had the incident meant absolutely nothing to him? Had he felt nothing at all?

Dieu. She groaned, filled with self-loathing. She turned on her side and punched her pillow. She ought to be ashamed of herself. Married to one man, lusting after another. And not just an ordinary man, but a man capable of horrendous brutality. What was wrong with her? Had she taken complete leave of her senses?

The day of the grand affair dawned gray and misty, but midday the clouds departed, leaving the sky a bright blue canopy. Extra household help had been recruited for the occasion. Under Hera's watchful eye and sharp tongue, every piece of furniture had been polished to a mirrorlike finish. Vases, urns, and baskets of flowers, artfully arranged, were placed throughout the great house, their sweet aroma perfuming the air. Guest bedrooms had been prepared days in advance for those who lived too far to return home after the festivities. By late afternoon, the house began to fill with chattering guests.

Feeling like a stranger in her own home, Christiane smiled until her jaw ached. The wives of the planters all seemed well acquainted with one another and primed for gossip. While they were polite to Christiane, none were overtly cordial. The women seemed intent on scrutinizing their newest member, their curiosity so blatant she felt like an item on an auction block. The men were kinder. The more wine they consumed, the more freely their compliments flowed. Etienne preened under their extravagant flattery, each syllable of praise an ode to his discerning taste.

At last the preliminaries were over; the hour of the party was at hand.

Hera fussed over arranging Christiane's dark curls in a crown atop her head. Simone du Val had delivered Christiane's ball gown just the day before. Even Etienne, as critical as he was prone to be, could not fault the seamstress's creation.

Hera, careful not to muss her handiwork, raised the gown above Christiane's shoulders and let it fall with a soft swoosh. With each slight movement, tissue silk the color of opals shimmered with subtle hues of rose, apricot, and lavender, making it appear iridescent. "Beautiful," Hera murmured.

"*Merci,*" Christiane said, for she valued the servant's rare compliment far more than the planters' obsequious praise.

"I quite agree." Startled, Christiane glanced behind her. Etienne stood in the doorway of her sitting room, resplendent in a sapphire jacket and breeches and a white satin waistcoat lavishly embroidered with silver. Ruffles of fine Belgian lace cascaded at his neck and over his wrists. For the occasion, he had donned a powdered wig complete with side curls, the hair in back tied with a large black bow. "*Magnifique.*"

Christiane graciously inclined her head to acknowledge the compliment.

"Simone earned a well-deserved bonus." Etienne sauntered into the room. "You'll be the envy of every woman present."

Christiane's feminine intuition told her that she looked her best. The dress accentuated her brunette coloring to full advantage. Excitement and trepidation brought a sparkle to her eyes and a delicate flush to her cheeks.

Snapping his fingers imperiously, Etienne dismissed Hera the instant the last silk-covered button slipped through its loop. Smiling, he presented a polished rosewood box to Christiane with a flourish. "These are the finest of my late mother's collection. I want you to wear them tonight."

Christiane gasped as the lid snapped open. Diamonds twinkled against black velvet.

Etienne chuckled, pleased at her response. "I thought even a countess would be impressed."

"I don't know what to say." Christiane held up the elaborate piece of jewelry. The necklace consisted of a double tier of diamonds from which a large tear-shaped stone nearly the size of a baby's fist hung suspended. Tear-shaped earrings completed the set.

"Turn around," Etienne ordered, still smiling.

Numbly, she did as he asked. The facets caught fire in the candlelight, shooting bright sparks of light.

"This piece was once owned by Catherine de Médicis," he said, draping it around her throat.

She lightly touched the large diamond in the center. "It must be worth a king's ransom."

"It is, *chérie*."

The necklace felt heavy, oppressive. A yoke. A burden. Etienne's hands lingered on her shoulders as he fastened the necklace. An involuntary shiver escaped her at the touch of his long fingers along her collarbone. The action was one of affection for some husbands, but not for hers. Christiane wasn't deceived. Their eyes met in the mirror— and held. His pale eyes were intensified by the sapphire of his jacket, making them even more disconcerting. They were as cold and hard as the diamonds she wore. It took all her determination not to glance away, but, not wanting to concede him the victory, she met his look unflinchingly.

"There are earrings, too." It was Etienne who spoke at last, breaking the stalemate. He indicated the jewel box with a nod of his head. "Go ahead, *chérie*. Put them on."

With trembling fingers, she lifted one of the earrings from its bed and fastened it in place. He continued to watch each movement, his hands resting on her shoulders, fingers splayed across the gentle swell of her breast. She fumbled with the second earring, nearly dropping it.

"Tsk, tsk," he chided. "A wife shouldn't be nervous in her husband's presence."

"If I'm nervous, m'sieur, it is only because we've never entertained your guests before. I'm anxious to make a good impression."

"Ah, yes, of course." His breath fanned her cheek as he leaned forward to inspect her reflection in the mirror. "Exquisite. The diamonds are the perfect touch. None of the guests will be able to take their eyes off you."

"Everyone seems curious about your proxy bride," she prattled, his proximity making her increasingly uneasy. "I don't want to be an embarrassment—or a disappointment."

"Don't fret. Tonight will be perfect; you'll see that you worried for nothing." He dipped his head and suddenly, without warning, nipped her shoulder with his teeth, then grinned in wicked amusement at her choked cry of surprise and outrage. "Don't alarm yourself, *chérie;* I was careful not to leave a mark."

Christiane leaned forward and peered into the mirror. The slightly reddened area on her neck was already beginning to fade, leaving only the memory to linger like a festering sore. Etienne was far too clever—and too devious—to spoil the illusion of perfection he had gone to such lengths to create.

Smiling, he held out his arm. "Come, *ma petite,* we don't want to keep our guests waiting."

With a sigh of resignation, she accepted his arm and allowed him to escort her out of the bedroom.

They stood for a moment at the top of the stairs, surveying the scene below. Guests adorned in silks and satin and glittering with jewels milled about the great hall, awaiting the appearance of their host and hostess. Christiane forced a smile and held her head high. She would give Etienne no cause to fault her performance as mistress of Belle Terre. Chatter dwindled into silence as they slowly made their way down the long, curving stairway.

"Later, *chérie*," Etienne said, dropping his voice so that only she could hear, "after the guests retire, you can properly demonstrate your gratitude for my generosity."

She stumbled and might have tripped except for his firm hold. Her face paled. His words struck fear in her heart. With each night that passed without a conjugal visit, her optimism had mounted. But her hope had been premature. In a matter of hours, while the guests slept soundly, her reprieve would be over.

"Does the thought of my visit fill you with anticipation, *ma petite?*" he asked with mock concern.

"No," she replied in a choked voice. "It feels me with dread."

Instead of becoming angry, he threw back his head and laughed in delight. "Ah, *chérie*, what a pleasure it will be to tame you at last."

Chapter Eight

Christiane fixed a smile on her face and held her head proudly. All eyes were on them as they descended the stairs and took their place at the head of a long receiving line. Soon faces and names blurred, and Christiane felt an ache begin to build behind her eyes.

A sidelong glance at Etienne told her he suffered no such ill effects, but assumed the role of host with ease and familiarity. He played the part of devoted husband so well, in fact, that it worried her. No one watching would ever suspect he was anything other than a gracious host or loving spouse. She couldn't help but wonder what thoughts cavorted through his twisted mind.

"My compliments, Etienne." A tall gentleman in a parrot green jacket elaborately embroidered with a gold silk motif of birds and flowers bowed over Christiane's hand. His hazel eyes were alight with frank admiration. "Your bride enhances your reputation for having an excellent eye for beauty.''

Etienne puffed with pride. "*Merci,* Pierre."

The man boldly locked eyes with Christiane. "If Madame Delacroix will save a dance for me later, my evening will be one to treasure.''

Christiane forced a smile. "The pleasure will be mine, m'sieur.''

The line moved forward. Christiane scanned the crowd for sight of Reid, but as yet, he had not made an appearance. Irritation swiftly followed her initial disappointment at not finding him. She despised him, she reminded herself. Loathed him. Didn't want to see him again—ever.

An attractive brunette in a low-cut gown appraised the diamonds encircling Christiane's neck with a sharp eye and ignored the woman wearing them. "Ohh," she cooed enviously. "What a stunning necklace. If only Marcel were half as generous.''

Etienne preened. "Ah, Patrice, we are alike, are we not, in our fondness for fine jewelry?"

Patrice placed her hand lightly on his arm and batted her lashes. "I hope your wife realizes how fortunate she is to have such a magnanimous husband.''

"My wife has yet to realize a great many things," Etienne replied.

Christiane cringed inwardly and struggled to keep her smile intact.

At last, introductions over, Etienne and Christiane joined the guests in the ballroom. Candlelight set the room aglow. Light was refracted by the crystal prisms of the chandelier. Beeswax tapers burned in wall sconces on either side of the room and in strategically placed candelabra. At a signal from Etienne, a quartet in an alcove played the opening bars from Mozart's *The Marriage of Figaro.*

Etienne turned to Christiane with a courtly bow. "It's customary in St. Domingue for the host and hostess to be the first to dance."

"Then we can't disappoint our guests, can we?"

Christiane placed her hand on Etienne's arm and followed his lead onto the dance floor. Other couples were quick to follow suit and soon the floor was filled with dancers. Etienne executed the intricate pattern of steps and glides, dips and rises of the gavotte with grace and skill. Grateful that the dancing provided an excuse not to talk, Christiane concentrated on the music and dance rather than her partner.

A minuet began. Christiane found herself paired with Pierre of the dashing green coat. He flirted outrageously, and, by the time the dance ended, she was weary of deflecting his sly innuendoes. Next the musicians struck up a sprightlier tune. A succession of partners appeared for a series of country dances that were all the rage in Europe.

When the musicians stopped for a break, servants circulated among the guests with trays of chilled champagne and fruit punch. Before Christiane could slip unnoticed through the French doors onto the terrace, Etienne reappeared at her side.

"Naughty girl," he chided, discerning her intent. "A proper hostess must stay and mingle among her guests." He snatched a glass from a passing servant and pressed it into her hand. "Here, you look tense. Champagne should help."

Placing his hand at the small of her back, Etienne firmly guided her toward a spot where two couples conversed near the entrance of the ballroom. Both of them looked up and smiled as their hosts approached. "You remember the Charbonneaus and Beauvois, don't you, *chérie?*"

"Have pity on the poor girl, Etienne." The younger of the two men spoke in her defense. "There are so many of us, and only one of her. How can your lovely bride possibly remember every name?"

"Merci." Christiane felt an instant liking for the man with the short-cropped brown curls and lively brown eyes.

"I am Francois Charbonneau," he replied. "This beautiful lady," he said, indicating the delicate blond at his side who was showing the early signs of pregnancy, "is my dear wife, Yvette."

A portly man of around fifty with a fine network of purple veins on his bulbous nose tugged at his lapel and tried to suck in his considerable girth. "I am Phillipe Beauvois."

"And I am Nanette Beauvois." A tall woman with angular features and wearing a gown in an unflattering shade of magenta slid her hand into the crook of her husband's arm.

After pleasantries had been exchanged, the talk turned to matters close to the heart of every planter. "Have you cleared more land for planting since our last meeting?" Francois Charbonneau addressed Etienne.

"No, but I plan to shortly. I'm sending my overseer to survey the tract and make a preliminary report. Ah," Etienne exclaimed. "There he is—at last."

Every eye in the small group pivoted in the direction of Etienne's pointed finger. Christiane found Reid, wineglass in hand, standing near the French doors leading onto the terrace. He stood somewhat apart, a loner, segregated from the wealthy French planters by both manner and dress. Garbed in a simple but well-cut coat and breeches of fine black wool with lace-trimmed white neckcloth and stockings, he stood out in the throng of revelers, an elegant black swan surrounded by strutting peacocks.

As though sensing himself the object of scrutiny, Reid glanced their way and acknowledged his employer with a slight nod.

With a thin smile, Etienne draped his arm around Christiane's shoulder, skimming his index finger back and forth along the edge of her gown above the swell of her breast with slow deliberation.

Christiane stiffened. His touch made her skin crawl. Onlookers might interpret this as a display of affection, but Christiane knew better. It was a calculated act, a flagrant display of ownership. *She's mine,* the action clearly shouted, *all mine. You can look, but don't touch.*

Reid observed the byplay, his expression bland, then raised his glass in a silent salute.

Phillipe scowled. "Your overseer's bold as brass. Can't say I care for the man."

"Women don't seem to share your opinion," his wife said with a smug smile. "I can think of several in particular who find him quite intriguing."

"Alexander knows how to maintain control among the *noirs,* and that's all I care about," Etienne said, turning away from the man under discussion, in effect dismissing him.

"Lazy bunch," Phillipe concurred with a knowing shake of his head.

Etienne assumed a martyred expression. "Just last week I had to make an example of one who challenged my authority. I hope the message got through to the others."

Christiane tensed at the mention of the harsh punishment meted out to Juno. Suddenly she couldn't tolerate Etienne's fondling a second longer. She brushed his hand aside and, twisting slightly, angled her body so that she stood somewhat apart from him. His icy blue eyes shot daggers at her, which she ignored.

Phillipe Beauvois replaced his empty champagne glass on the tray of a passing servant in exchange for a full one. "Ah . . . we've been hearing rumors, Delacroix. We were wondering if there might be any truth to them."

"Rumors?"

Christiane was grateful that the subject diverted Etienne's attention away from her. She had no illusions, however, that he would not make her pay later for the rebuff.

Francois and Phillipe exchanged glances. Phillipe gave his friend a slight, almost imperceptible shake of his head. "Let's not bore these ladies with talk of business." Taking Etienne's arm, the two steered him away and out of earshot.

With the men gone, the women closed ranks around Christiane. A handful of others soon joined them until they formed a loose semicircle, all apparently eager to learn more about the new mistress of Belle Terre.

"We've been dying of curiosity," Yvette gushed. "We couldn't wait to meet Etienne's bride. A marriage by proxy. Who would have guessed?"

"We all know Etienne's fondness for beautiful things." Nanette fiddled with a ruffle on her magenta gown. "With all his secrecy, we thought maybe you were too ugly to introduce to the other planters."

"Or too beautiful," Yvette confessed amid a flurry of giggles. "We thought perhaps he wanted to keep you all to himself."

"Yvette, shame on you," Nanette scolded. "Just because you and Francois behave like lovebirds doesn't mean everyone does."

Yvette rested her hand on the slight mound below her waistline. "*Oui*, but we make such beautiful babies."

The women laughed. Christiane managed a feeble smile, feeling like an intruder among this group who seemed to know each other intimately.

"Your gown is magnificent, Christiane. Did you bring it with you from France?"

Christiane recognized the woman asking the question as Patrice, the one who had shown a marked interest in her necklace earlier. "My husband commissioned it through a seamstress from Le Cap."

"Ah, I thought so," Patrice pronounced with smug satisfaction. "Only Simone du Val could do work so fine. Her services are booked months in advance. How did Etienne persuade her?"

"Really, Patrice." Nanette looked upon the younger woman with asperity. "The size of Etienne's bank account could persuade a saint."

"Did you spend time in Le Cap?" Yvette asked eagerly.

"No." Christiane shook her head. "I came directly to Belle Terre."

Patrice snapped open her hand-painted fan and waved it in a desultory fashion. "You must convince Etienne to take you there. If not for Le Cap, we'd go out of our minds with boredom."

"The theater." Yvette sighed. *"Magnifique!* It seats over a thousand people."

"And the shops." A young woman in blue satin clapped her hands together in ecstasy. "There are dozens of them."

"Did you try the leather goods shop I told you about, Nanette?" Patrice asked.

The women quickly became so immersed in exchanging names of their favorite haunts that Christiane felt like screaming. Were these women so steeped in self-indulgence, that little else mattered? Were they only interested in clothes, jewelry, shopping, and entertainment? Didn't they realize how precarious their lifestyle was? Her presence forgotten, she slipped through the French doors, then crossed the terrace, and walked down the steps to the garden.

Torches blazed from iron holders skewered into the ground, their flames dancing in the trade winds. The scent of night blooming jasmine perfumed the air. The distant, muted rumble of voices was punctuated by an occasional tinkle of laughter. The musicians had resumed playing, the notes seeming to float on the evening breeze. Several couples strolled arm in arm, enjoying a moment's respite from the gaiety inside.

Christiane strolled deeper and deeper into the shadowy recesses of the garden. She plucked a blossom from a flowering bush and twirled the stem between her fingers. She didn't understand the people inside. Didn't they know, couldn't they sense the unrest churning just below the placid surface? The undertow of hostility and discontent that threatened to drag them under, drown them?

A small lizard skittered across the garden path in front of her, but she hardly noticed it. The women especially acted as though nothing were more important than which play they would see on their next visit to Le Cap. As though the most pressing problem was which gown to wear, which shop to visit.

The men were little better. Although they might be more mindful of rumors, they were an arrogant bunch, supremely self-confident that wealth, breeding, and the color of their skin made them invincible. St. Domingue reminded her much of France, where the aristocracy resided amid glittering splendor while the masses fought for scraps of bread.

And plotted revenge.

She deliberately turned her deliberation on politics aside. Unbidden, thoughts of Reid slid into the void. He had looked as out of place in the crowded ballroom as she had felt. But then he should feel out of place, she reminded herself angrily. He had no right mingling among civilized people. Vicious, cruel, he was no better than an animal. How had she ever imagined him to be a decent human being? How had she been fooled?

The answer to her questions filled her with self-derision. She had allowed physical attraction to cloud her judgment. Bending her head, she inhaled the sweet essence of the flower she held and tried to find peace amid chaos.

"What is the mistress of Belle Terre doing out here in the dark?" a familiar voice asked from the shadows.

The bloom dropped from her nerveless fingers. Reid's tall, black-clad figure blended with the night. In the dim light even his neckcloth and stockings appeared more pewter than white. Cloaked in deep shadow, he seemed more specter than man. "M'sieur Alexander." She gasped. "I didn't see you. . . ."

The tip of a cheroot glowed red in the darkness. "Do I make you nervous, Countess?"

"You merely startled me."

"Were you expecting someone else, perhaps?" Reid stooped to pick up the flower she had dropped and offered it with a flourish. "I noticed Pierre LeClerc was most attentive."

She snatched the flower from his hand. "M'sieur LeClerc regards all women as potential conquests."

"It's not wise to wander so far from the festivities. You never know who you might meet up with." He drew on his cheroot and blew out a thin stream of smoke.

"What are *you* doing here?"

He shrugged. "Perhaps I don't like crowds."

"I didn't mean here in the garden. I meant at the party."

"The invitation came as a surprise to me as well. Your husband, however, insisted I make an appearance. The *grand blancs* tend to ignore me. They make no secret they consider me their social inferior. Your husband seems to derive a certain satisfaction from their open disdain."

"What possible reason could they have to feel that way?" she mused caustically. "After all, you share so much in common with these cultured, educated people. Now" — she turned to leave—"if you'll excuse me, it's time I return to my duties as hostess."

He caught her arm. "Too good for me, Countess?"

She glared up at him, refusing to be intimidated. "Someone warned me there might be snakes about. I fear they were right."

"So you consider me a snake, do you?" His hold tightened,

"Those are your words, m'sieur, not mine." She tugged her arm but to no avail; his grip was like iron. "At least my husband doesn't masquerade as a civilized man. Even so, his company is preferable to yours."

His eyes narrowed to silver slits. "All decked out in diamonds with your pert little nose in the air, you think I'm lower than the dirt beneath your feet."

Christiane smelled the alcohol on his breath. He had been drinking, but he wasn't inebriated. His gaze was steady, his voice hard-edged, his words crisp, clear.

"Let go of me."

His grip gentled, but still he didn't release her. "You're glowing like a goddamn chandelier with all those diamonds. Everyone has their price. Tell me, Countess, is that your reward for playing the devoted wife in front of St. Domingue's elite?"

"How dare you attack me!" She jerked her arm free, unmindful of the bloom being crushed in her balled fists. "How much of a bonus were you awarded for butchering a helpless man?"

Reaching out, he flicked the diamond dangling from her

earlobe with an index finger. "So innocent, so perfect," he said with a sneer. "Who appointed you judge and jury?"

Christiane drew in a sharp breath, but before she could summon a suitable retort Reid continued.

He jabbed the cheroot angrily in her direction. "Everything in your life has been so easy, so simple. You grew up with an army of servants to cater to your every whim. You don't know what it's like to go hungry. You have never had to beg for coins on a street corner. You've never held someone you love while they died in your arms."

She had been prepared to snub him, to address him as though he were the scum of the earth. Instead she was stunned by the abrupt explosion of fury in someone usually so controlled. Then her surprise dissipated, and her temper kicked in full throttle. "How dare you presume to know me?" she demanded furiously. "Just because you watched a loved one die doesn't mean I don't know the pain of losing someone I hold dear."

Her voice came treacherously close to breaking. Reid took an involuntary step forward and reached out his hand, suddenly compelled to comfort her. She flinched away.

"Don't you dare touch me," she said, her voice low. "Your hands have taken the life of another. Nothing you say can deny the fact that you viciously beat a helpless man to death."

Reid remained stubbornly silent. How could he refute the charge after taking every precaution to make the man's death seem convincing?

"And Juno isn't the only man you killed, is he?" she demanded, her voice throbbing with emotion. "Don't bother to deny it. Etienne told me you also killed a man in Spain and were convicted of the crime."

Reid drew on the cheroot smoldering in his hand. What did it matter what Christiane Delacroix thought of him?

Let her think the worst, it was no concern of his. In a week, two at the most, he would be gone. Out of her life forever.

"Nothing to say in your own defense, m'sieur?" she mocked.

"I've already been tried and found guilty by a magistrate in the court of Charles the Fourth. Why would your verdict be any different?"

She gazed at him expectantly, her lustrous brown eyes brimming with hurt, confusion, and righteous indignation. She looked almost as if, in spite of the damning evidence, she hoped he would refute the charges. Her obstinacy angered him. *Damn!* What was wrong with her? Why couldn't she be like everyone else? He didn't like feeling obligated to live up to her lofty expectations.

"I warned you from the beginning not to mistake me for some storybook hero."

She blinked once, twice, then swallowed. "You're no one's hero, m'sieur. Certainly not mine," she said, her voice choked.

Her reply cut deep. Goaded to wound in return, he lashed out. "I didn't hear any complaints the night I kissed you."

She stared at him, stunned into speechlessness by the brazen truth.

"Keep looking at me like that, Countess"—Reid's voice dropped to a husky baritone—"and I'll have to repeat the experiment."

"You"—she scrambled to collect her wits—"bastard." Picking up her skirts with both hands, she turned and fled up the garden path toward the gaily lit great house.

Motionless, Reid watched her retreat. In her iridescent silk and shimmering diamonds, she glowed as bright and elusive as a moonbeam. But even without imported fabric or glowing jewels, she would shine. He had found her just as beautiful the night of the voodoo ceremony wearing a simple cotton nightdress and with her hair flowing about her shoulders.

Glancing down at the crushed-shell path, he saw what remained of the flower she had held. He picked up one of the petals and, holding it between thumb and forefinger, gently stroked the smooth, delicate surface. Her skin, he mused, had the same velvety texture. A hot jolt of desire coursed through him at the thought. When Christiane had looked up at him with her lips slightly parted and eyes dark as the evening sky, he had been almost overwhelmed by the impulse to crush her in his arms, to lose himself in her sweetness. One look from her could drive him to distraction, send desire coursing through his body. A single touch made him forget that she was a countess, that he was a convict.

Forget she was wed to another.

He let the petal fall from his hand. God, her accusations had hurt like hell. In all fairness, Christiane had given him every opportunity to deny the charges against him. When had the woman sneaked beneath his guard? He had been sorely tempted to confide the truth before his cynical nature had intervened. It was pointless to become more and more involved with a woman he would never see again.

His mouth set in a grim line, he tossed his cheroot aside and ground it beneath his heel. Jamming his hands in his pockets, he strode toward his humble quarters. He'd had enough of the party for one evening. If Delacroix noticed his absence and didn't like it, too bad. His plans to leave St. Domingue were nearly complete. It couldn't be soon enough to suit him.

Chapter Nine

Quiet blanketed the great house. Upstairs the last of the guests had retired for the night, while downstairs servants went about their chores with ghostly efficiency. By sunrise all traces of a grand party would be eradicated.

Christiane's shoulders slumped with dejection. She longed to climb into bed, curl into a ball, and sink into oblivion, but that was impossible. With the party over, her real ordeal was about to begin. At any moment Etienne would stroll through the door of their adjoining sitting rooms and demand his rights as her husband. She sighed. Clothed in a diaphanous gown, another in the classic style Etienne preferred, she felt like a pagan offering about to be sacrificed to a vengeful god.

Hera moved about the bedroom rearranging items on the dressing table, then folded back the bed linens. Next she reached into a small chest, withdrew a glass jar, opened the lid, and scattered a handful of dried petals across the sheets. "Master like the smell of roses."

Instantly the room was filled with a cloying fragrance that seemed even stronger tonight than usual. The sickeningly sweet odor left Christiane curiously light-headed. The bedroom walls seemed to close in around her. Her stomach churning, temples throbbing, she stumbled across the room to the French doors. The latch finally yielded to her frantic efforts, and the doors flew open.

"Something wrong, madame?" Hera asked, giving Christiane a sly look.

Hera's voice seemed to come from a great distance. Christiane inhaled deeply, drawing the crisp night air into her lungs. Gradually her head stopped reeling, her stomach stopped quivering. She felt oddly detached from her surroundings. For a long moment she stared at the jagged mountain ridge etched across the star-strewn sky. A distant part of her mind noted the profound silence. No drumbeats echoed through the crystalline stillness. Somehow their absence seemed equally as disturbing as their presence.

Christiane turned from the French doors in time to see Hera slip a packet from her apron pocket and dump its contents into a decanter of wine sitting on the table. Her eyes widened in disbelief as she took an involuntary step forward. The servant turned with a start.

"Hera!" Christiane exclaimed. "What are you doing?"

Guilt quickly transformed into defiance on the woman's features. "What do it look like?"

Christiane gestured toward the incriminating packet still in the woman's hand. "What did you put in M'sieur Delacroix's wine?"

Hera gave a sullen shrug and carefully replaced the

wrapper in her pocket. "Same thing I put in his wine every night since you come to Belle Terre."

Christiane shook her head in confusion. "I'm not sure I understand. What are you telling me?"

"Girl, you thickheaded?" Hera snorted with contempt. "Why you think M'sieur not sleep with you? Not sleep with no woman?"

Christiane cautiously approached the servant. Gone were all vestiges of a subservient demeanor, replaced by a bold, contemptuous expression. She remembered the voodoo ceremony. Hera, holding a snake high above her head, writhing to a pagan chant. Reid had called Hera a mambo, a voodoo priestess.

With an uncanny knack, Hera read her thoughts. "I know many secrets, many spells, can work much magic," she boasted. "I am powerful among my people."

"You added a potion to M'sieur Delacroix's wine that rendered him impotent?" It was half statement, half question.

"So now you know." Challenge gleamed in Hera's eyes. "What you gonna do?"

"My husband has killed with less cause." Surely the woman knew the risk she had taken. Didn't she care?

"You should thank me, madame." Hera poured a single glass of wine, not the least bit intimidated. "Your husband is not a kind lover. He bring little pleasure, cause much pain."

Christiane's eyes narrowed with sudden suspicion. "How do you know this?"

"Trust me, madame, I know this for fact. Astra know, too. You don't believe, you ask."

"Astra?" Christiane recalled seeing the girl's battered face, her thinly veiled hostility. Yet she had given the girl no cause for such hatred. Or had she? Had Etienne vented his frustration on the young maid? Small wonder she had regarded her with such loathing.

"So, what you do, madame? He be here soon."

No sooner had she finished speaking than the knob rattled on the sitting room door. Christiane frantically reviewed her options. She had to make a decision, and make it quickly.

"You tell?"

For the first time, Christiane detected a quiver of anxiety beneath the servant's bravado. In that instant, her indecision solidified into certainty. Picking up the glass of wine, she went to greet her husband.

"Your favorite, m'sieur." She smiled.

Etienne accepted the offering with a quizzical lift of a sandy brow. "You're in a fine mood, *chérie.*"

"And for good reason, m'sieur." Still smiling, she turned, then poured a second glass of wine and touched her glass to his. "The party was a resounding success."

"Yes," he said, rocking back on his heels. "The evening did go rather well, didn't it?" With a flick of the wrist, he dismissed Hera, who hovered close by.

Hera ducked her head and exited, closing the door quietly behind her.

"I must admit I'm quite pleased." He tipped his glass and drank deeply. "Everyone seemed to enjoy my party tremendously."

She raised her glass and took a small sip, reasoning that if Hera's potion hadn't harmed her before, it wouldn't now. "We'll have to entertain more often."

"If you wish, *chérie,*" he concurred amicably.

"I especially liked Yvette and Francois Charbonneau. They seem devoted to each other."

Etienne grimaced. "A little too devoted, if you ask my

opinion. Francois needs to spend more time attending to sugarcane and less time catering to his wife's every whim."

"The Beauvois also seemed charming. Tell me more about them." She refilled Etienne's partially empty glass.

Etienne settled himself into a chair, crossed his legs, and savored his wine. "Phillipe has lived in St. Domingue more years than he cares to count. His first wife died of yellow fever some years back. He met Nanette while in Paris last year, where he was a delegate to the National Assembly."

"Really?" Christiane perched in a chair opposite him. "Did the delegation accomplish what they intended?"

His expression turned sour. "No. Unfortunately, before the *grand blancs* could enjoy success, their victory was spoiled by an amendment."

"What happened?" she asked, wondering how much wine had to be consumed for the potion to be effective.

"Don't bother your pretty head with politics. The intricacies of government are a man's domain, far too complicated for women to understand." He waved a careless hand. "Did the ladies mention the fine theater in Le Cap?"

"*Oui,* they praised it quite highly." She took another small sip, hoping he would follow her example. "In fact, I hope someday we can attend."

"Absolutely, it's important to be seen there. Even *gens de couleur* are allowed to attend." His expression clouded, then cleared. "Their seating area, of course, is restricted."

Of course, she echoed silently.

Etienne leaned back in his chair, stretched out his legs, and crossed them at the ankles. He made a sweeping gesture with his wineglass, growing more expansive. "The theater in Le Cap seats fifteen hundred. There is an even finer one at Port-au-Prince."

Once again she refilled his partially empty glass and dredged about in her mind for another subject of conversation. The longer he talked, the more he drank; and the more he drank, the less his ability to consummate their marriage.

Getting up from the chair, she walked over to the dressing table and ran her hand almost reverently across the rosewood jewel case containing the lavish diamonds he had given her earlier that evening. "All the guests were in awe of the exquisite necklace and earrings you gave me. Not to mention your largesse."

"My father—and after his death, myself—liked to indulge my mother's fondness for fine jewels."

"The quality of the stones appears excellent."

"My mother would tolerate nothing but the best."

"A trait, so it appears, that she bequeathed to her son."

He drained the remainder of his wine and shook his head when she stepped forward to refill it. Christiane did a quick mental calculation. He must have consumed nearly two glasses of wine since entering her bedroom. She knew the moment she dreaded was at hand and prayed that two glasses would be enough to quell any romantic inclinations.

Etienne approached her much like a hunter tracking his prey. Christiane instinctively retreated until she was pressed against the dressing table and could go no farther. He placed both hands around her neck. For a brief moment, she feared he intended to strangle her.

He slowly began to stroke her throat. "Ever since your arrival at Belle Terre, I've noticed that my overseer finds you attractive."

Her pulse bounded at the thought. She wondered if he noticed its startled leap beneath his fingertips. "You are surely imagining things, m'sieur," she said, her voice thready.

"You underestimate the spell you have woven, *chérie*." He cupped her breast in one hand. "I've seen the way the man watches you. Like a stallion in heat."

With him touching her breast, she found it difficult to concentrate on what he was saying. Nervously she ran her tongue over her lower lip. "From our few conversations together, I doubt that Reid Alexander even likes me."

Etienne chuckled humorlessly at her distress. "Oh, he likes you, all right, but he's smart. He knows the consequences of taking something that doesn't belong to him. He knows you belong to me. I observed the two of you in the garden tonight. Don't ever think about betraying me."

"I would never consider such a thing, m'sieur."

His fingers tightened on the sensitive flesh until she let out a small whimper of pain. "So help me God, if you do I'll kill him with my bare hands and force you to watch."

And she knew, without a doubt, that he'd do just that.

He fumbled with the sash of his dressing gown and the robe fell open, revealing his thin, pallid body.

At the sight of his nakedness, Christiane averted her gaze. She could barely suppress a shudder of revulsion.

Swearing softly, he pulled her against him, grinding his hips suggestively while grunting and thrusting his pelvis. Twin vertical lines furrowed his brows.

She balled her hands into fists at her sides to keep from pushing him away. A distant part of her felt grateful he hadn't ordered her to touch him. The mere notion sickened her.

Small beads of sweat pearled on his forehead. He placed his hands on her hips, holding her steady while he rotated the lower portion of his body against hers. Then his movement ceased abruptly. His face purple with rage, he released her and stepped away.

"Is something wrong, Etienne?" she asked, her mouth dry as dust.

"*Is something wrong?*" he mimicked, his voice harsh. He stalked across the room, retying his sash with quick, agitated motions. "Damn right, something's wrong. You haven't the faintest inkling what it takes to heat a man's blood."

She kept her eyes downcast, staring at her locked fingers, careful to mask her triumph. "I'm sorry, m'sieur, that you find me inadequate."

"Inadequate?" he raged. Whirling, he shot her a look so filled with pure venom that she flinched. Her reaction only inflamed him more. Crossing the room in long strides, he grabbed her by the shoulders and shook her until her head snapped back and forth like a flower on a stem.

"Etienne, please . . ."

"Emasculating bitch!" He drew back his hand and struck her full across the face, the blow sending her sprawling to the floor.

Stars burst across her vision; pain exploded, bringing tears to her eyes. Darkness fluttered along the fringes of her consciousness. Then her vision cleared, and Etienne loomed into focus, his features contorted by hatred and fury.

"Not so proud now, are you?" he hurled at her. "Be sure you stay out of sight until the last of the guests depart." Unmindful of a house full of sleeping people, he stormed out, slamming the door behind him.

After an indeterminable amount of time, Christiane pushed into a sitting position and shakily got to her feet. Her knees too weak to support her weight, she sank down on the bench at her dressing table. She scarcely recognized her own reflection in the mirror. Eyes too large, too lost, peered out from a chalky face surrounded by a wild tumble of dark curls. Her nightgown had been torn, baring one shoulder where the dusky imprints of Etienne's fingers remained. Blood trickled from a split lip, and she tasted its metallic flavor on her tongue. With an unsteady hand, she shoved the hair away from her face and inspected the damage. Her cheek was already starting to mottle in the first stage of an extensive bruise.

No one had ever struck her before. No one had ever made her feel so powerless, so terrified.

Her sole consolation lay in the knowledge that Etienne wouldn't return. Of that she felt certain. Hera's potion had had the desired effect. He would never again subject himself to that humiliation.

But instead of relief, she felt increasing apprehension. The tall case clock in the upstairs hall chimed the hour. She sat unmoving, contemplating, worrying. Etienne had suffered a gross indignity, and placed the blame at her feet. He had just suffered the gravest insult a woman could inflict on a man's pride. She had challenged his virility and won the match. Etienne was not a man to let such an insult pass without exacting retribution. What would he do to avenge his honor? How would he retaliate? When? In all likelihood, his violence would escalate in the months ahead.

A night breeze blew through the partially open door, chilling her. Stumbling across the room, she reached out to close the door. As she did so, the fine hairs along the nape of her neck prickled. She hurriedly shut the door and turned the lock, but not before a presentiment of danger crept over her. An evil presence lurked in the shadows, watching, waiting.

Hatred bubbled through Etienne's veins as he stared up at the closed French doors of his wife's bedroom. Tonight he had made one final attempt to claim what was rightfully his. One final, futile, mortifying attempt. Christiane was his—body and soul—yet the damn woman continued to elude him. He clasped his hands behind his back, head bent, and paced the shelled walk.

Did the bitch expect to live under his roof, eat his food, be showered with clothes and jewels, while flagrantly shunning her marital duties? She was a leech, taking everything in sight, giving nothing in return. Did she think these privileges were hers by divine right?

In the future he would have to guard his temper more carefully. She bruised too easily. It would never do for rumors to fly that he subjected his wife to physical abuse. After all, he had a certain image to maintain. He was urbane, sophisticated, not an uneducated brute of a man.

But he would have the final say. She needed to be disposed of, eliminated like a pesky weed . . . or an uncooperative servant. She wanted to visit the theater, did she? He let out a harsh bark of laughter. Pity she wouldn't live long enough to enjoy a trip to Le Cap.

But she would live long enough to suffer a miserable death.

Malice brightened his pale eyes as he began to devise a plan. He envisioned a painful death. Slow, but not too slow. An agonizing death preceded by a moment of sheer terror. He envisioned her tortured by the realization that death was imminent, that nothing could be done to halt the process.

Soon the emasculating bitch would be dead. Then, and only then, he'd regain his manhood. Smiling, he climbed the steps from the garden to the veranda.

Three days had passed since the party, rainy, gloomy days. Each passing day seemed cut of the same dreary cloth. The inclement weather kept her confined inside the great house. Christiane sorely missed her daily walks in the garden, her visits to the stables. Although she tried to keep herself occupied with needlework and reading, worry about her grandfather's safety continued to plague her. She couldn't understand why she hadn't heard from him. Was he ill? Was he in need? Not knowing his whereabouts made her increasingly anxious.

Time hung heavy on her hands until she feared she would go mad with boredom. Maybe that was Etienne's plan, she thought bitterly, to claim she was crazy, a raving lunatic. Then he could have her locked away and wouldn't have to face her across the dinner table night after night.

Glancing up from her needlework, she peered out the window and noted the sun trying to peek through the clouds. By lunchtime, the warm sun had dried the raindrops dotting the veranda. Her spirits lighter than they had been for days, Christiane slung a wicker basket over her arm and, humming to herself, headed for the garden.

Content among the colorful array of flowers, she wandered up and down the rows, pausing here and there to snip one and add it to her basket. A bright yellow hibiscus caught her fancy, and she bent to inhale the sweet fragrance.

That was how Reid found her. Eyes closed, nose buried in a flower, a smile curving her lips, her profile unsullied and pure. He watched in silence, not wanting to disturb the enchanting picture she presented. He had deliberately detoured through the garden, knowing it to be one of her favorite haunts, foolishly hoping for one final glimpse. At dawn he'd leave to survey a distant plot of land for his employer. When that was finished, he'd have the means necessary to flee St. Domingue. If all went according to plan, he'd be halfway to New Orleans before Etienne Delacroix knew he was missing. But before he left Belle Terre for good, he wanted to see Christiane a final time.

As he continued to watch, she plucked the flower and straightened. His being here made no sense at all. Absolutely none. Yet he couldn't seem to help himself. She held a certain fascination that he couldn't seem to resist. She was as vibrant as the flower she held. If it had been physical beauty alone, he could have resisted, but she possessed inner qualities he found even more intriguing. She was hopelessly inquisitive, always brimming with questions. In addition, she could be maddeningly impertinent, painfully forthright, and unstintingly passionate with her likes and dislikes. And brutally honest.

Just as she had been at their last encounter.

You're no one's hero. Certainly not mine.

Her denunciation still rang in his ears.

A butterfly fluttered through the garden. Christiane's eyes tracked its flight before coming to rest on him. He stared back, slack-jawed, unable to conceal his shock at her ravaged face. An ugly bruise discolored one cheek. Livid shades of purple, green, and yellow despoiled the creamy perfection of her skin. He took an involuntary step closer and noticed that her lush lower lip was cut and swollen. Intense anger coursed through him. Only a monster would do such a thing. He wanted to beat Etienne Delacroix to a bloody pulp.

Drawing closer, he crooked a gentle finger beneath her chin. "Who did this to you?" Although he already knew the answer, he felt compelled to ask.

"It does not concern you." She jerked free. "You are overstepping your bounds even to voice such a question, m'sieur."

She swept past him, her pert nose in the air. With a single glance, she managed to make him feel as small and insignificant as a bug. And, he grudgingly admitted, she was absolutely right. She was a married woman, and he had no right to interfere. No right whatsoever. The realization made him seethe with impotent frustration. He wanted to champion her cause, ride to her defense, become her knight on a charger. His feelings made no sense at all.

He cleared his throat, remembering the purpose of his visit. "I'm going to be leaving at first light tomorrow for L'Artibonite."

"Where you go is of no interest to me." She sat down on one of the wrought-iron benches that lined the pathways, placing the flowers on the ground and arranging her skirts in a graceful semicircle.

Footsteps crunched on the walk leading from the house. Reid followed the direction of Christiane's gaze and watched the servant Astra approach, carrying a basket.

"I bring your sewing, madame," Astra announced, drawing closer.

Christiane's face lit up with appreciation. *"Merci.* How very thoughtful."

Astra gingerly set the sewing basket on the bench alongside her mistress and quickly backed away.

"Astra . . ."

The servant froze in the act of fleeing, trepidation erasing her customary sullen expression. "Yes, madame."

"I just picked some flowers. Would you please take them into the house with you?"

The servant warily eyed the basket of flowers sitting at Christiane's feet, then snatched the handle and scuttled off.

"That was odd," Christiane murmured.

"Quite." Reid frowned absently, watching Astra's hasty departure.

"All this time I thought Astra disliked me; then she does something so considerate, so completely out of character, that it catches me by surprise. I believe she's finally coming around."

Reid placed a foot on the bench, rested an arm across his raised knee, and studied Christiane, committing her lovely but bruised face to memory.

Chin tilted defiantly, she returned his look with dark eyes blazing. "It is rude to stare, m'sieur."

His lips twitched in amusement; then he sobered. "You must learn to curb your unruly tongue. It would appear, Countess, that you have tweaked the tiger's tail once too often. Promise me one thing before I leave?"

She sniffed. "You have no right to ask favors."

"True." He removed his foot and drew himself to his full height. "Even though you owe me nothing, I'd rest easier knowing I had warned you again to be on your guard."

She considered the request, then nodded slowly.

"Then," he said with a brisk nod, "it doesn't seem we have anything more to say to each other."

She stared pointedly at the whip casually tucked into the waistband of his pants, a silent symbol of his authority as overseer. Juno's ghost stood between them. "I wish circumstances had been different, m'sieur, but I can't alter facts to suit my whims."

She was right, of course, but knowing he could never explain the truth, and defuse her hostility, brought a hollow sensation to his chest somewhere in the region of his heart. "Good-bye, Countess."

"*Adieu*, m'sieur." She reached for the sewing basket.

A slight flicker of motion caught his attention as she raised the basket's lid. Driven more by instinct than by conscious thought, he knocked the wicker container to the ground.

She stared aghast at the bright profusion of silk floss

and the linen square she had labored on so diligently, now lying in the dirt. "What on earth . . ." She started to retrieve her needlework.

"No!" he shouted. "Move out of the way!" He grabbed her arm, hauled her to her feet, and shoved her behind him.

"Have you gone mad?" she demanded angrily.

"Stand back," he ordered in a voice that brooked no disobedience.

All his concentration focused on the crumpled square of linen, he withdrew the whip from his waistband in a smooth, unhurried movement. Christiane frowned, her gaze darting between him and the spilled stitchery. Then he heard her gasp of horror as she saw what had captured his attention.

A snake, long and slender, slithered out from beneath the linen, its brilliant bands of red, yellow, and black blending perfectly with the skeins of silken embroidery floss. Sunlight glinting off its shiny scales lent the serpent a polished beauty.

With a practiced flick of his wrist, Reid sent the lash whistling through the air. The head of the snake flew off, expertly severed from the body.

"*Mon Dieu,*" she said softly, one hand pressed against her bloodless lips.

Using the handle of the whip, Reid picked up the still-writhing body of the snake and flung it over a low stone wall. "A coral snake," he explained. "Its bite is invariably fatal. You would have been dead before nightfall."

She sank weakly onto the garden bench, her face white as chalk. "How . . . ? When . . . ?"

"Snakes abound in St. Domingue." He tucked the whip back into place. "They are often where you least expect them."

Christiane shuddered as the meaning of his words crystallized. "Another warning, m'sieur?"

He looked down at her, concern mirrored in his silver gaze. He wanted to touch her, comfort her, but knew his attempt would be rebuffed. "Snakes come in a variety of shapes and sizes."

She ran the tip of her tongue over her lower lip. "You saved my life, m'sieur. How can I repay you?"

Reid was relieved to see some color return to her pale face. "There is one thing you could give me in return."

She clasped her hands together to still their slight tremble. "You have only to ask."

Reid found himself mesmerized by her mouth—soft and temptingly ripe. He yearned to sample its sweetness in a mind-emptying kiss, to elicit her response by slow, pleasurable increments. But he knew better than to ask. He was loath to take what wasn't given freely. "A smile," he said instead.

She shook her head in confusion. "M'sieur . . . ?"

"You have a beautiful smile, Countess, but I haven't seen it for some time. I'd like to see it again before I leave."

"Is my life of so little value that it can be purchased so cheaply?"

"Some things are precious beyond the price of gold or jewels," he replied gallantly.

A smile, tremulous at first, bloomed with increasing confidence. "You have, indeed, taken leave of your senses."

His spirit heavy, Reid turned and left, tortured by the thought of leaving her behind.

Chapter Ten

That night, for the first time in months, the dream returned. Reid tossed and turned on his narrow cot. The sights, sounds, smells. The pain . . .

It was the same. All of it. Once again he was in the Spanish casino.

"One more round, mon ami,*" the Creole wheedled.*

Reid eyed the fortune amassed on the faro table. Tonight's winnings would keep him in style and comfort for a long time.

Or buy a small estate.

The notion wriggled through his mind. Elusive. Captivating.

A third man, fury stamped on his dark, aristocratic features, shoved away from the gaming table. "Haven't you lost enough for one night? Have you lost your mind as well?"

Gaston du Beaupre picked up a heavy goblet and indolently eyed his brother over the rim. "Since when does my baby brother give me orders?"

Reid observed the byplay with interest. The Creoles from New Orleans made an interesting pair. Animosity crackled between them like lightning before a summer storm. He waved a negligent hand over the stacks of paper currency and glittering gold coins. "Lady Luck, mon ami, has deserted you this evening. Perhaps your brother knows best."

Gaston bristled. "I may be temporarily out of money, but I have a deed in my room."

Leon slammed his fist against the table. "Not Briarwood!"

Reid drew on his cheroot, blew out a slow stream of smoke, then raised a brow inquiringly. "Perhaps, du Beaupre, you should listen to your brother. It may be time to cut your losses while you still can."

"Remember, Gaston, the land Briarwood rests on, the money used to build her, was your inheritance." *Leon's words were angry, desperate.*

"Enough!" *Gaston roared.* "No one tells Gaston du Beaupre what he can and cannot do."

Word of a high-stakes game quickly spread throughout the casino. Reid sipped his Madeira and waited while a servant ran to fetch the deed. Drunk or sober, it didn't matter. Faro was strictly a game of chance and with little, if any, latitude for skill or strategy.

When the servant returned with the deed, the dealer shuffled a new deck, cut it, and placed the cards in the dealing box. A heavy silence blanketed the casino. Candles sputtered in wall sconces along the arched perimeter of the room. A thick blue haze of cigar smoke hovered above the table. Turn after turn, cards were exposed until finally only three remained in the box.

Reid stole a look at Gaston and watched a bead of sweat drip from the Creole's brow. He was conscious of Leon, too, who stood to one side, his jaw rigidly clenched, his obsidian eyes glinting.

"Señors, call your bets," *the dealer droned.*

Reid flicked ash from his cigar, his face impassive. All or nothing. Players bet against the house. The case keeper showed that a deuce, a jack, and a king remained to be played. Only the first two cards mattered. The last card in the box, the hoc card, was of no consequence.

Gaston drained his wine. "Jack-king."

"Deuce-king," Reid countered.

With the turn of a handle, Reid won his dream of a lifetime.

But Gaston du Beaupre wasn't a man to give up easily. "Perhaps I can persuade you to give me a chance to recoup my losses over a nightcap in my room," he said, draping his arm across Reid's shoulders as he was about to leave.

Moaning in his sleep, Reid flung his arm across his eyes, his slumber even more troubled than before.

Images shifted, settled.

"That's him." Leon du Beaupre pushed through the soldiers and pointed an accusing finger at Reid.

Roughly jostled from sleep, Reid found himself surrounded by a half dozen men in military uniforms.

"That's the man who murdered my brother."

"What the devil . . . ?" Reid muttered as he was hauled to his feet.

"Silence!"

"I have a right to—"

"Silence!"

One of the soldiers backhanded him across the face. Reid felt blood trickle into his beard from a cut lip. Reacting purely on instinct, he balled his fist and drove it into his attacker's midsection. He had the brief satisfaction of hearing a grunt of pain the instant before the soldiers descended upon him as a single unit.

Reid curled into a tight ball on the floor in an effort to protect himself against the heavy blows of their fists and booted feet.

Leon stood over his prostrate form, gloating. "Murdering scum such as you forfeit all rights."

Pressing a hand against his aching ribs, Reid watched, helpless, frustrated, as his room was torn apart, his belongings rifled.

"Aha!" One of the men waved a thin sheaf of parchment.

Reid stared in mute disbelief at the deed to the Louisiana plantation—and the dark red stain smeared across its surface. A smear that looked suspiciously like blood. But how could that be, he wondered dully, when no stain had been present the night before?

The tallest of the soldiers stepped forward as two others dragged Reid to his feet. "By the power vested in me by the court of Charles the Fourth, sovereign ruler of Spain, you stand accused of the death of Gaston du Beaupre."

"That's a lie. I killed no one." His denial earned Reid another blow, causing blood to spurt anew from a broken nose and mat his neatly trimmed beard.

"And what is this?" Leon du Beaupre bent down near a small oak chest, then straightened.

All eyes turned to stare at the small, engraved silver button the Creole held between his thumb and forefinger.

Leon fixed his dark gaze on Reid. "How do you explain why a button from my brother's jacket—one bearing his initials—a button presumably lost in the struggle for his life—comes to be in your possession?"

A painful kaleidoscope of deprivations and brutalities drifted through his sleep-fogged brain. His body sheened with perspiration, Reid kicked the bedclothes aside. He felt as though he were bobbing like a cork in a churning sea. Finally, sucked into a deeper level of slumber, **he lay** unmoving, his body tense even in sleep.

"A prisoner, eh?"

Reid lay on sun-bleached sand, surrounded by a ring of dark-skinned natives. A tall man with pale, cold eyes, and dressed after the European fashion, stepped forward.

"What was your crime?" the man demanded.

Reid tried to shield his eyes from the sun's glare and discovered he couldn't lift his arm. Turning his head slightly, he learned why. His right wrist was manacled to that of the bloated corpse of a fellow prisoner.

When Reid failed to respond quickly enough, he was nudged none too gently in the ribs with the toe of a boot. "For the last time, convict, what was your crime?"

Reid ran his tongue over dry, cracked lips. His mind was slow to function. The plain, unvarnished truth seemed simpler than fabrication. "Murder," he rasped.

"Excellent." A humorless smile curled the man's thin lips before he turned to the others. "Free him; then bring him to Belle Terre. Leave the corpse to rot."

Reid woke with a start. He sat at the edge of his cot, groggy but awake. To his way of thinking, Satan and a French planter possessed the same face. But he didn't regret the bargain he had made with the devil. The year at Belle Terre had afforded time to plot, time to prepare. Soon he would leave St. Domingue and sail to New Orleans. Once there, he would find Leon du Beaupre, the man who had robbed him of a dream. The man who had condemned him to a hellhole of a prison.

A man who had killed his own brother.

Reid swung his legs out of bed and dressed. As always after one of these dreams, Reid thought of Chase, his own brother. He would have gladly sacrificed his own life to save that of his brother. They had been best friends as well as brothers. If he lived to be a hundred, he could never understand how a man could murder his own flesh and blood.

Turning his back on painful memories, Reid picked up his knapsack and strode out of his quarters into the pre-dawn light.

All in all, it had been a strange day. Christiane had awakened before dawn with a heightened sense of expectation. But nothing out of the ordinary had occurred, and the day droned on like all of the others. Toward late afternoon the household seemed unusually quiet, and Christiane took a long nap. She awoke with a start to find night had already fallen.

She immediately rang for Hera, but when the maid failed to arrive to help her dress for dinner, Christiane became alarmed and went downstairs to investigate. She found Etienne in the dining room, seated at his usual place at the head of the table, a decanter of wine at his elbow. The gleaming expanse of mahogany was absent of its customary table settings of silver, crystal, and china, the sideboard empty of covered dishes waiting to be served.

"Where are the servants?" she asked in puzzlement.

"How the devil should I know?" Etienne said with a snarl.

Christiane's alarm escalated. She knew of Etienne's fondness for wine, but until now she had never actually seen him inebriated. Yet his words were slurred, his face flushed, his usually precisely tied neckcloth askew.

He reached for the decanter and refilled his glass. "Not a soul around. The entire place is as quiet as a tomb."

"What is happening?"

"Everyone has simply vanished into thin air. Pfft," he said, snapping his fingers. He picked up his glass, the movement clumsy, sending wine sloshing over the rim. "I even checked the stables. Every stall is empty. The thieving wretches stole my horses."

"What do you propose we do?"

"*We?*" He stood, picking up the decanter in one hand and the wineglass in the other. "I don't know about you, *chérie,* but I'm not going to do anything."

"You're just going to ignore the situation?" she asked in disbelief. "Act as though nothing is wrong?"

"That's precisely what I intend. Tomorrow morning the *noirs* will come crawling back, mewling like a litter of newborn kittens, begging for mercy." He lurched across the dining room, his gait unsteady. "And should they get it into their heads to try something foolhardy, I'll be ready."

She trailed after him, feeling more and more anxious with each passing minute. "Where are you going?"

"I've a small arsenal of weapons loaded and waiting. If the *noirs* attempt anything rash, they won't live long enough to regret it." In spite of his show of bravado, a flicker in his pale eyes betrayed an underlying fear.

Etienne disappeared into the library, slamming the door behind him. The scrape of a key in the lock resonated in the stillness. Christiane stood frozen in the vast hallway. Not even the chirping of insects disturbed the quiet—a quiet so profound that she could hear the loud thud of her heart against her ribs.

Danger swirled around her, imminent, almost palpable. She could taste it, feel its evil presence. Panic fluttered like bat's wings inside her head. Christiane slowly pivoted.

Her frightened gaze locked on Etienne's youthful portrait hanging above a drop leaf table. His milky blue orbs mocked her growing terror.

The tall case clock in the corner tolled the hour. The pendulum swung back and forth, each stroke a warning: *Danger, run, hide.* Picking up her skirt with both hands, Christiane fled up the stairs and into her bedroom, bolting the door behind her.

Jittery as a cat, she paced back and forth. She tried to rearrange her chaotic thoughts into some semblance of order. This turn of events involved the strange, hypnotic Boukman. She knew this as surely as she knew her own name. Had the voodoo priest finally succeeded in uniting the *noirs* to revolt against the *grand blancs*? A small group of *noirs* would stand no chance of succeeding. Unless . . . She shivered at the possibility.

Unless . . . Boukman had been able to provoke an uprising that would encompass the entire island.

Memories of the voodoo ceremony she had witnessed rushed back. Hera with a python lifted high above her head, dancing with wild abandon. The almost gleeful slaughter of a goat. The crazed expressions of the participants. If the *noirs* revolted, violence would be the order of the day.

A growing sense of urgency goaded her to take action, to do something. But what? Where could she go? Etienne in his present condition would be of little help. Instead of defending what was his, he had barricaded himself behind a locked door while he clung to false delusions. How like him to be arrogant to the bitter end. Etienne consistently turned a blind eye on the *noirs'* discontent, a deaf ear to their troubles.

The ensuing hours crawled by at a snail's pace. Christiane stopped pacing and listened, each sense attuned to danger. Every creak of a floorboard, every gust of wind seemed magnified tenfold. In the distance she could hear the drums. She checked the enameled clock on her dressing table. It was nearly midnight. She cocked her head to one side. Their rhythm changed, a subtle difference, but a difference all the same. She crossed to a window and peered through a crack in the drapes. An orange glow illuminated the night sky. Her fear built anew. The eerie orange light could mean only one thing.

Fire.

Energized by the sight, she sped out of the bedroom and downstairs to warn Etienne. "Etienne," she cried, pounding on the locked library door. "The mountain is on fire. We must flee at once."

"Go away."

His voice sounded distant, surly through the heavy oak. She tried again to make him understand. "The *noirs* are rebelling against the *blancs*. We must help each other. This is not the time to argue."

"I will not be driven from my home."

She shot an anxious glance at the main entrance, half expecting to see an influx of armed men. "Let me in, Etienne. I will help you."

"I've a pistol trained on the door," he shouted angrily. "The first one to enter this room will get a taste of lead." He paused a fraction, then added, "You included, *chérie.*"

He would shoot her, she knew. He'd squeeze the trigger without blinking an eyelash. She thought of the poisonous snake that had been in her sewing basket. With a flash of certainty, she realized its presence had not been accidental. If not for Reid's timely intervention, Etienne's plan would have succeeded.

But this was not the time to dwell on such things. If she wished to survive there was only herself to rely on. Turning away from Etienne and the locked room, she hurried back upstairs. Her mind worked frantically, forming and discarding plans. If she could reach Le Cap, she would be safe. But how would she get there with the horses gone? Her chin set with determination. She'd walk if need be.

But first she needed to gather a few personal items for the journey. And money. She wondered fleetingly if Etienne kept any hidden in the house. She thought of searching his room, but rifling through his belongings filled her with disgust. Midway up the stairs, she paused, her hand on the rail. She had something far more valuable than currency. She had a fortune in jewels.

Her pace quickened as she ran up the remaining stairs. Inside her bedroom she removed a carved teak jewelry box from the bottom of the armoire and opened the lid. Rubies and diamonds winked up at her from their bed of black velvet. Quickly she emptied the contents of the jewelry case into a cloth pouch and pulled the drawstring. The sale of these pretty baubles would keep food on her table and a roof over her head. And more important, the jewels would guarantee her freedom.

Lifting her skirts, she tied the pouch around her waist, then let the skirt drop into place, its fullness concealing the slight bulge. As she flung a light woolen cape of midnight blue over her shoulders, she glanced about the room a final time. The irony of the situation struck her. This was not the first, but the second time circumstances had forced her to leave her possessions behind and flee under cover of darkness. Resolutely squaring her shoulders, she blew out the candle.

She had taken no more than two steps when a sound drew her attention. Hurrying to the window, she parted the drapes and looked out. The glow in the night sky seemed even more brilliant, almost as though the flames causing them had crept closer. She frowned, trying to recall Hera's words. *Beyond the mountains, more mountains.* Fear and uncertainty jostled her fragile confidence. If she hoped to reach Le Cap, she had to cross that rugged terrain.

Then the sound that had drawn her to the window repeated itself—grew louder, more distinct. A noise much like the angry swarm of hornets. As she strained to identify it, the buzzing turned into a babble, and the babble transformed into voices, jubilant and defiant.

A wave of panic surged over her. The *noirs* were marching on Belle Terre. She had tarried too long; now it was too late. Fate had allowed her to escape one reign of terror only to lose her life in another. How unfair. How cruel.

A jarring crash from the front of the house jolted her out of her self-pity. It was followed moments later by the sound of splintering wood. A raucous cheer went up from the throng.

"Come out, m'sieur," a voice singsonged. "We come to visit."

Others took up the chant.

Where was Etienne? she wondered frantically. What was he waiting for? Was he still cowering in the library with his guns trained on the door? Then, as if in answer to her silent questions, she heard his raised voice.

"Damn you to hell. Come in if you dare."

Running across the room, she eased the door open a crack. Etienne stood at the foot of the stairs, his back turned from her, a pistol in either hand. A mob of *noirs* pushed through the splintered entranceway. Some wielded machetes and pruning hooks; others carried blazing pitch torches.

"Savages," Etienne roared. "That's what you are, the whole damn lot of you."

He fired into the crowd. When the smoke cleared, the leader lay crumpled on the floor, blood pumping from a gaping hole in his chest. The others surged forward, heedlessly trampling their fallen comrade.

Etienne stepped backward, tripping and falling on the stairs. His second shot went wild, the ball lodging in the ceiling. Flakes of plaster rained down like falling snow on a turbulent black sea. Undeterred, the *noirs* streamed into the great house with weapons raised.

A tall, heavily muscled *noir* moved toward Etienne. The brilliant red sash knotted about the man's waist served as a vivid contrast against black flesh gleaming in the torchlight. Christiane recognized the sash as similar to the one worn by the man who had threatened her at the waterfall the afternoon she had arrived in St. Domingue. As she watched in horror, he raised his blade and plunged it deep into Etienne's body. Christiane pressed a hand against her mouth to stifle a scream. Etienne lay unmoving in an ever-widening pool of blood as the *noirs* began to roam through the great house, destroying priceless treasures in their wake.

Shaken to the core by the violence, Christiane eased the bedroom door closed. Even above the wild hammering of her heart, she could hear the sound of breaking glass and smashing furniture. Soon, tired of the carnage downstairs, the *noirs* would surge up the stairs.

Instinct propelled her across the room, through the French doors, and across the balcony. She flung one leg over the railing and froze when she looked down. It was a sheer drop to the garden three stories below. A wave of dizziness left her feeling light-headed, her palms clammy.

"Don't stop now. You can do it," a familiar voice urged.

She hazarded a cautious look at the ground. Reid? She had thought him miles away. What was he doing here? Or had sheer terror caused her to imagine him? She blinked and looked again. But he stood, no figment of her imagination, feet firmly planted on the ground directly beneath her bedroom window.

"Catch hold of those vines and ease yourself over the side," he instructed. "Hurry."

She swallowed and drew in a deep breath, grateful that her initial dizziness was subsiding. She gingerly reached for one of the thick vines that covered the rear of the great house and swung her other leg over the edge.

"Don't look at the ground," Reid coached. "Work your way down slowly."

Inch by inch, hand over hand, Christiane lowered herself down the side of the house. Hampered by her long skirts, her feet fought for purchase in the slippery foliage, sometimes finding it, sometimes not.

"Don't worry, Countess; I'll catch you if you fall."

She hung on grimly and continued her slow, painful descent. She had nearly reached the second level when a voice from above almost caused her to lose her grip.

"You stop! Hector not let you get away."

Desperately clinging to the greenery, Christiane shot a frightened glance upward. A face she recognized as belonging to one of the workers in the cane fields glared down at her—a face distorted by intense hatred.

"Hurry, Christiane," Reid urged.

She drew in a shaky breath, then resumed her cautious descent. Infuriated that his prey was about to escape, Hector began hacking at the vines supporting her weight with his machete. Each time the blade connected, she slid another foot. The palms of her hands stung, the skin tender and raw. Yet she hung on gamely. The fact that Hector had to twist his body at an awkward angle in order to slash at the vines bought her precious time.

A second *noir* entered the balcony and, seeing what his fellow slave was trying to do, joined in the attempt.

"Reid, I can't." She sobbed, feeling she was losing her grip.

"Let go," he called. "I'll catch you."

The vines holding her weight were being systematically severed, until only a single tendril kept her from plunging downward.

"Trust me, Christiane. I won't let you get hurt."

Trusting Reid to keep his promise, Christiane let go, squeezed her eyes shut, and took a deep breath. She felt herself falling, falling, falling through space.

She landed solidly amid a flounce of skirts and petticoats and thick, green vines that snaked around her like uncoiled rope. Reid untangled himself from the bottom of the heap. He didn't give her time to catch her breath.

Springing to his feet, he caught her hand. "Time to get out of here."

Torchlight wavered along one side of the house, a sign others were coming. He sprinted through the garden, tore through the open gate, and headed toward the forest beyond, half pulling, half dragging her with him.

Footsteps pounded behind them. Or was it merely the frantic beating of her heart? Christiane couldn't tell, didn't care. Once away from the great house, Reid released her hand and jogged ahead, leading the way through the dense maze of trees and bushes.

Christiane struggled to keep up the pace. She felt a sharp stitch in her side. Her lungs burned with each labored breath. Envisioning herself pursued by an angry, machete-waving horde bent on vengeance, she ran. Bushes reached out prickly branches to snag her skirt. Her hair tumbled loose from its moorings and straggled down her back. Occasionally she paused to free long tendrils caught in low overhanging limbs.

At last she couldn't go another step without collapsing.

"Reid, stop." She panted. "I can't . . ." Bent almost double, she gulped in great drafts of air.

Reid halted a short distance ahead, his head cocked to one side, listening. But the night was still. Their pursuers had apparently given up the chase.

"Five minutes, Countess. We've got to keep moving. Get as far away from here as we can."

"All right," she said in a gasp. "Whatever you think best." When her breathing had returned to a more normal rhythm, she straightened and asked the single question burning in her mind. "What made you come back?"

He scowled into the darkness, avoiding her gaze. "I don't know."

"But I think you do, m'sieur," she persisted. "You aren't the sort who does things for no apparent reason."

"I heard there might be trouble." He folded his arms across his chest, his posture both defensive and belligerent.

"And you came to help?"

He glared at her. "Don't get any fancy notions I came back because of you," he said in a growl. "Your husband owes me money. I came to get what's mine."

"I see." She blew a strand of hair out of her eyes. "And if he refused, what were you going to do? Take it like a common thief?"

He shrugged carelessly. "I've been charged with worse. What's thievery compared with murder?"

She tried to read his expression through the shadows. In spite of what she had witnessed with her own eyes—Juno and the damning pound of flesh—part of her still wanted to believe he was incapable of brutality. She owed her life to him. If Reid hadn't returned when he did—for whatever reason—she might not be alive. She could have been stabbed to death just as Etienne had been. Or worse. At least his death had been mercifully quick. She might not have been as fortunate.

As though capable of reading her thoughts, he said, "By the way, Countess, what did happen to your husband?"

She thought of Etienne lying on the stairs in a pool of blood. "He's dead," she said quietly. "Stabbed . . ."

"Are you sorry?"

She could feel the force of his steady gray scrutiny. "My husband was an evil man. I won't pretend to mourn his passing," she answered honestly.

Her answer seemed to satisfy him. "Let's not waste any more time; we can rest later. The farther we are from Belle Terre, the better."

She trudged after him. "Where are you taking me?"

"The Charbonneau plantation is nearby. You'll be safe there."

"What about you?"

"I'm heading for Le Cap. From there I plan to board a ship bound for New Orleans."

The remainder of the journey passed in silence. Christiane trailed after Reid. In time, her brain ceased to function, though her body continued to plod forward. Reid, on the other hand, seemed unaffected by the arduous trek. At last he climbed a small crest and shielded his eyes. Her numbed mind registered the rosy glow in the eastern sky. Daybreak.

She climbed the rise, stopping beside him, and gazed around in horror. The horizon was rosy, but not from the dawn of a new day. Cane fields, acres and acres of cane fields, had been set ablaze. Thick black smoke choked the air. The wind shifted direction, and through the heavy smoke they could see red tongues of flames lick heavenward.

"The Charbonneaus . . . ?"

Her voice trailed off, the thought too horrible for words.

Chapter Eleven

Fire-blackened stone walls enclosed a heap of smoldering timbers. Tendrils of smoke spiraled through the space a roof had once occupied. Near the rear of the house, Christiane could see persistent red tongues of flames dancing among fallen beams. What had once been the Charbonneaus' palatial home had been reduced to a blackened skeleton.

"Yvette and Francois," she ventured, her voice taut with anxiety. "Do you suppose . . . ?"

Wordlessly, Reid moved toward the burned-out shell of a house. Christiane's eyes swept the scene. Not even the outbuildings had survived the devastation. But the most disturbing fact of all, she realized, was the profound silence that lay over the estate like a funeral pall. Dread churned in the pit of her stomach.

Her fatigue forgotten, she picked up her skirts and

scrambled after him. "Maybe they were warned before-hand and fled."

"Anything is possible." Reid's answer was clipped, terse. "Stay where you are while I check."

Christiane ignored the order and kept close at his heels. "Probably at this very minute, they're making their way toward Le Cap."

Reid swung around, his expression so fierce that it halted her in her tracks. He grabbed her shoulders, his fingers digging into her flesh. "I told you to stay behind," he said in a growl.

A muscle in his jaw bunched as he struggled to control his temper. A day's growth of bearded stubble lent him a dangerous look. At that moment it seemed to Christiane that he could be capable of anything—even murder. "I want to help," she said, grateful her voice didn't quaver and betray her qualms.

"Don't be ridiculous," he snapped. "What could a woman of your background do in such a situation?"

Christiane blinked up at him, unaccountably hurt by his curt assessment.

Reid took quick advantage of her silence. "There's no telling what we might find. It could be more than you're prepared to deal with."

"If they're hurt, they'll need help," she replied with dogged determination.

His hold tightened, bruising. "Hasn't it occurred to you these people may be beyond anyone's help?"

"*Oui,*" she murmured, her voice choked with emotion. "If that is the case, then I can at least offer my prayers."

"Is there no reasoning with you . . . ?" He released her abruptly and started toward the entrance.

Christiane half ran to keep pace with him. As they drew closer, the pungent odor of burned wood grew almost unbearable, causing her nostrils to burn and her eyes to sting. She pressed the hem of her dress against her nose and mouth. Reid followed suit, using the tail of his shirt.

The flames at the back of the house, their fury spent, languished. Charred remnants of what had once been a massive oak door hung drunkenly from warped metal hinges. Using his foot, Reid kicked aside a broad beam that barred the entrance. With a stout branch he had found in the trampled garden, he poked through the debris.

While he was thus occupied, Christiane peered through a blackened aperture where a window had once commanded a sweeping view of the front drive. The possessions of a lifetime had been reduced to ash and rubble. Appalled, she stared at the destruction, knowing in her heart that the same fate had befallen the elegant Belle Terre.

A scrap of bright blue caught her attention. Angling for a better view, she made out the shape of a child's rocking horse that somehow had miraculously escaped the inferno. She thought of the new child the Charbonneaus were expecting and a lump lodged in her throat.

Turning her back on the disturbing sight, she picked her way over fallen timbers and joined Reid.

"Don't come any closer," he barked.

But the warning came too late.

Christiane caught a glimpse of a charred corpse sprawled among the wreckage. What appeared to have once been a knife was lodged between two ribs. The intense heat had curled the metal blade into an obscene shape. Christiane pressed her skirt tighter over her mouth and gagged.

Reid swore softly, then placed an arm around her waist, lending support, and drew her away.

Christiane drew in a shuddering breath. In spite of the balmy temperature of an August morning, she felt chilled to the bone, her skin cold and clammy. Visions of the black, shriveled remains, interspersed with those of a tiny blue rocking horse, swam through her mind. Life was so precious, so very fragile. And it could end in the space of a heartbeat.

The violence seemed so unfair . . . so senseless. Granted, the *noirs* had cause to hate the *blancs*, but why must violence always precede justice?

Reid led her some distance from the house before stopping. "I tried to warn you." He dragged a hand through his tawny, shoulder-length mane. "But you're too headstrong to listen."

She vaguely heard his reprimand through the fog of misery that enveloped her. She wanted to wake up and discover this had all been a bad dream. She wished she were a small child again, curled into a tight little ball in her pretty bedroom with the flowered wallpaper, frightened by a nightmare. That her grandfather would appear, comfort her, and convince her everything would be all right. Assure her that the world was a happy place where no harm befell good people.

Reid gave her a swift shake. "I swear, Countess, if you faint on me, I'll leave you here."

"Brute!" she cried, anger acting as an antidote against the shock immobilizing her. "Take your hands off me."

He heaved a sigh that sounded suspiciously like relief. Releasing her, he regarded her warily. "Are you all right?"

"Of course I'm all right," she snapped, irrationally irritated that he had relinquished his hold so readily. She liked his touch, wanted to lean into it, draw from his strength. She chafed her arms to erase the chill. "I've never fainted in my life. And I'm not about to start today."

He studied her critically for a long moment, then, apparently satisfied, gave a brisk nod. "There's nothing more we can do for the Charbonneaus. Its not wise to linger."

"What do you propose we do now?" She unconsciously repeated the question she had asked Etienne earlier. Reid Alexander owed her nothing, she acknowledged. She was not his responsibility. He could very well abandon her beside the burned shell of this former great house. She smoothed her hand over the small bulge at her waist as another thought struck her. This man was a self-professed murderer. If he suspected she carried a wealth in jewels on her person, he could easily rob her, and there would be nothing she could do to prevent him.

"What now? We need to keep moving." Reid arched a brow. "It's just the two of us, Countess. Unless, of course, if you're not willing to gamble on a man convicted of murder."

She considered her options, her expression sober, then rose to the challenge. "I am willing to take the chance, m'sieur."

A humorless smile flitted across his mouth. "Gambling got me into a lot of trouble once. It might work the same with you."

"Life is a gamble," she reminded him primly. "One has to take risks."

His started down the incline, away from the smoldering ruins. "Remind me, Countess, never to sit across a faro table from you."

"Where are we going?"

"If we can reach Le Cap, we ought to be safe. Once there, I'll entrust you into the bishop's care. You can stay under his protection while you decide what to do."

She resented the way he casually announced his plans, never once stopping to consult or consider that she might have plans of her own. If it hadn't required more effort than she was capable of, she would've informed him of her displeasure.

"We'll be safer off the main road. I know a shortcut through the cane fields."

She followed without further protest, focusing all her energy upon placing one foot ahead of the other. After a while, her body seemed to function independently of her mind, which she carefully kept blank.

Reid's gaze darted right and left. Trouble, he knew, could lurk anywhere, usually when least suspected. A chance encounter with a roving band of rebels could—would—result in death. Judging from everything he had seen, the *noirs* were bent on widespread vengeance. The *grand blancs* would retaliate in kind. The rift between the two ran deep. Slaughter and pillage would be the order of the day. Before order was restored, the soil of St. Domingue would be saturated with the blood of both.

He glanced over his shoulder at Christiane, who doggedly tramped behind. Smudges of grime lay like bruises across one cheek. Her dark hair had come loose of its moorings during their flight and straggled down her back. She moved like a sleepwalker, yet she hadn't uttered a word of complaint. However, in the span of eight hours, she had witnessed the murder of her husband, barely escaped an attack on her life, and spent the night traipsing through a forest, only to come face-to-face with more brutality.

He regretted his harsh accusation about women of her class. He had never meant to hurt her, yet he had seen her eyes widen and cloud with pain. Most women, regardless of social strata, would have been overcome with hysteria after the ordeal she had suffered. But not the countess. The woman constantly amazed him. Beneath the delicate exterior, she possessed a core of steel and the fortitude of a soldier. She had spirit.

His steps lagged as the dense hardwoods began to thin.

Unease pricked the nape of his neck. All his senses sharpened as they drew nearer the cane fields. Something was wrong, drastically wrong.

"Is there a problem?" Christiane asked anxiously.

Ignoring her question, Reid burst through the heavy cover of forest and stood at the perimeter of the cane fields. Thick vortices of smoke rose from fields set ablaze by hatred. "Bastards!"

He dimly heard Christiane's gasp of dismay as she came to stand alongside him. Together they watched in horrified fascination as the dark clouds parted to reveal flashes of flame that seemed to reach heavenward.

"Dieu," she whispered. "Tell me this is not a scene from Dante's *Inferno.*"

"I wish I could, Countess," he murmured. "I wish I could, but it's all too real."

At least they were alive. That thought, and that thought alone, sustained her. She knew many of the *blancs* weren't as fortunate. All she could do for the time being was trust that Reid would guide them to safety.

"How long do you think it will take to reach Le Cap?" She shoved a lock of hair out of her eyes.

Reid, who was ahead of her, waited for her to catch up. "A couple days, maybe three, four at the most."

"Three or four?" she repeated in dismay. The thought was daunting.

Reid's eyes narrowed with speculation as he studied her slow progress. The hem of her skirt caught on a bush and she tugged it free, leaving a scrap of lace clinging to one of its spiny branches. "You're slowing us down, Countess."

She glared at him. "Well, I'd like to see how fast you moved with a skirt and three petticoats."

"Touché." He broke into a grin. "Now take off your petticoats."

She stumbled to a halt, her mouth agape. "What did you say?"

"You heard me," he said equably. "Take off your petticoats. They're hindering our progress."

He was dead serious. She could see it in the no-nonsense set of his mouth, the steely glint in his eyes. "No gentleman would ever be so uncouth as to refer to a lady's undergarments."

"Countess," he said, his voice ripe with ill-concealed exasperation, "what do I have to do to convince you I'm no gentleman?"

"You expect me to disrobe here, in front of you, just like that?" She flung up her hand in a quick gesture of disbelief.

"Yes," he said between gritted teeth. "And unless you need my assistance, I suggest you do it without further delay."

"I don't—"

He cut her off. "We're in the midst of a slave revolt. Haste is paramount. Now, I'll give you two seconds to make up your mind. Either the petticoats go, or I do . . . without you."

"Since you put it that way." She sniffed. Then, assuming a haughty air in direct contrast to her bedraggled state, she ordered, "Turn your back, *s'il vous plaît.*"

Reid rolled his eyes, but did as she asked.

The second his back was turned, she lifted her skirt and tugged at the strings of her petticoats. She smiled to herself; the silly man, it wasn't modesty but practicality that prompted her need for privacy. Let him think she was just a shy little goose too embarrassed to show her ankles. Truth was, she'd run through this cursed island stark naked if that was what it took to survive. But she wasn't about to reveal the pouch she kept tied at her waist.

She wiggled her hips and the undergarments dropped to her feet with a soft *whoosh*. Stepping out of the frothy white circle, she arranged the pleats of her gown to cover the slight bulge at her waist. "There," she announced, reassured that her skirt concealed her treasure. "You may turn around."

Reid faced her with a dark scowl, hands on hips.

She shifted her weight, uneasy under his intent perusal. Had he guessed her secret? "What's wrong?" she asked. "I've done what you asked. Why aren't you satisfied?"

"There's one more item that needs attention."

She watched, puzzled, as he walked toward the heap of discarded petticoats, picked one up, and tore a strip of lace from its hem.

"Now, Countess, you're the one who may turn around."

She eyed the strip of lace with some trepidation. What did he plan to do? she wondered. Was he angry that she had repeatedly challenged his authority? That she constantly questioned his decisions? A series of scenarios flitted through her imagination, none of them pleasant. She had known few men well enough to measure him against, but she was certain that Etienne would never have tolerated such insubordination.

"What's the matter? Do I frighten you?"

"Moi?" She immediately rose to the bait. "Scared? That is preposterous." She presented her back, proud and ramrod stiff.

"We can travel more swiftly if you can see where you're going."

Christiane thought she detected a note of amusement, but before she could comment further he was behind her, his body lightly brushing hers. Heat jolted through her at the contact. Each time, no matter how slight the touch, she felt searing warmth. The urge to touch in return stole over her. How different she felt with this man compared with Etienne, she marveled. For a brief second, she wanted to close her eyes, lean against his hard muscular length. To feel his embrace. To feel safe.

"Your hair keeps falling in your face. You're bound to trip and fall."

With his rich baritone purring in her ear, she stood statue still, content, while he scooped her hair away from her face. His movements were unhurried, leisurely, gentle, almost as though he were committing its texture to memory. Dimly she knew that she should protest, step out of his reach, inform him she was perfectly capable of performing the task herself. The words, however, refused to be uttered. His fingers grazed her neck, and her breath caught.

"Sorry," he murmured as his callused fingers snagged a silky curl.

"Strange, but I don't even remember my hair coming loose." Even to her own ears, her voice sounded softer, dreamier, the voice of a stranger.

"There were more urgent matters at hand."

The soothing timber of his voice lulled her fears. Perhaps it was only fatigue setting in, but his proximity was having a strange effect on her. His nearness was as heady as a bubbling glass of champagne. Just as his kiss had been . . .

She had purposely put all memories of that night aside, labeled them disturbing, confusing, unsettling. Such an acute awareness of someone other than a husband was highly improper. Immoral, even. After all, she was married.

Was married. But no longer. With crushing finality, she realized her nightmare marriage had ended.

Etienne was dead. She had seen him killed, watched as

a blade plunged deeply into him. Stared in horror as scarlet bloomed against pristine white.

"I've never played lady's maid before," Reid mused softly. Catching a fistful of hair, he wound the lace around it. "But I think I might have a natural aptitude for the work."

Her skin tingled wherever his fingers touched. She tried to ignore the havoc he was wreaking on her senses, tried to match his nonchalance with her own. She tried to create an emotional distance, and failed. "A lady's maid must be able to take orders. You, I fear, are more accustomed to issuing commands than following them."

"An astute observation." He stepped back to admire his handiwork. "Pity we'll never learn whether or not I have a calling for domestic service."

She swung around ready with a retort, but he held up his hand to silence her.

His brows drew together as he listened intently, head cocked to one side.

"What is it?" she whispered. Then she, too, heard the faint sound.

"Hurry." He caught her wrist and raced toward a raised bunker of earth ten feet away. He hurtled over a fallen log lying along its crest and pulled Christiane after him. The earth had eroded slightly, forming a concave area, and a profusion of tall grasses shielded them from view.

Christiane opened her mouth, about to protest, but Reid clamped a hand over her mouth, silencing her. The fierce gleam in his gray eyes signaled a warning. She signaled that she understood the need for silence with a small shake of her head, and he removed his hand.

The distant sound grew more distinct. Feet thrashing through underbrush. The buzz of many voices jabbering at once. People were coming their way—a large group of people. A whimper of fear escaped before she could stifle it. Reid reached out and squeezed her shoulder, the small act immensely comforting.

The waiting, the uncertainty, became excruciating. Reid cautiously peered over the top of the bunker. And swore softly.

His muttered oath drew Christiane's attention. She shot him a quizzical glance, then followed the direction of his gaze. Her crumpled petticoats formed a snowy white mound on the woodland floor—mute testimony of their presence. She felt sick with dismay. Their hiding place would soon be discovered, and they would be killed. All because of bother-some petticoats.

Her eyes slid to Reid. Did he share the same feelings of inevitability? The grim determination on his face said otherwise. With burgeoning panic, she divined his intent. "No, don't," she whispered. "It's too dangerous."

"You stay here," he ordered. "Whatever happens to me, don't move."

Reid vaulted over the edge of the bunker and, keeping in a low crouch, ran toward the damning undergarments. Christiane watched with bated breath, her heart thudding in her ears. Reid seemed unmindful of the danger. Never breaking stride, he scooped up the garments, wheeled around, and raced back toward the bunker.

The rumble grew louder, the dialect of the *noirs* unmistakable. Any moment a band of them could appear and converge upon Reid. "Hurry, hurry, hurry." She repeated the incantation in her head, willing him speed.

He disappeared over the lip of the bunker just as the leader emerged from the trees carrying a standard topped by a severed head. The sightless eyes seemed to stare back at her. The remainder of the mob swarmed behind, brandishing an assortment of grisly trophies.

Shielding her from the sight, Reid pressed them both against the inner belly of the shallow shelter so tightly they were almost one with the earth. His unshaven cheek rested against her smoother one, and Christiane drew courage from his nearness. She caught hold of his hand and clung to it. As they waited for the horde to pass, the babble turned into individual voices. Jubilant, defiant, boastful.

"Master, he be sorry."

"Madame not so fine now. We show her."

"Did you see it burn? Did you see it turn to smoke?"

The ground reverberated beneath the feet of dozens of angry men. Clumps of dirt rained down on Christiane and Reid, knocked loose by those passing within inches of their hiding place. She offered up a fervent prayer that their presence would go undetected.

For a long time after the voices trailed into silence and the thunder of footsteps faded, Reid and Christiane remained huddled where they were. At last Reid straightened and cautiously looked around. Satisfied the danger had passed, he climbed to his feet and held out his hand to Christiane. "It's safe."

Dazed, she rose on legs that felt as wobbly as a newborn foal's. Everything was quiet again, serene. Shivering with reaction, she wrapped her arms around herself. Except for the trampled woodland floor, it might have all been a dream.

Then her gaze fell on the petticoat crumpled in the dirt. She raised her eyes to Reid. "That took much courage. Surely if the *noirs* had found my petticoat, they would have searched for its owner."

"Don't equate bravery with stupidity, Countess."

"You risked your life. Why do you belittle the effort?" she asked, puzzled by his tone.

"Don't attempt to glorify what I just did. If anything had happened to us, the blame would have been mine."

She was having trouble following his logic. Perhaps it was due to fatigue, perhaps the aftermath of violence, but his words made no sense. Neither did the urge to reach out and smooth the lines of tension that bracketed his mouth. "Surely you can't assume responsibility for this madness that has overtaken the island."

"No, I can't, but ..." Bending down, he swept the offending tangle of linen from the ground and held it in his fist. "But this *is* my fault."

"You retrieved it before any harm was done. I never would have been able to react so quickly."

"*I* was the one who left it behind." He shook it for emphasis. "My carelessness nearly cost us our lives. So don't you dare tell me I'm brave."

"You demand too much of yourself. I said you were brave ... not perfect." Suddenly she yawned and cast a longing glance at the shallow bunker. It looked as inviting as a feather bed.

Reid intercepted her look, and his anger dissipated. "The danger has passed. I don't think they'll be back this way. Why don't you try to catch a couple hours of sleep while I keep watch?"

"But what about you?" She unsuccessfully tried to stifle another yawn. "Don't you need to rest as well?"

He shrugged. "Later, perhaps. I've grown accustomed to functioning with very little sleep."

"Very well." Too weary to argue, she sank down on the ground, curled into a ball, and was asleep within seconds.

Reid sank down beside her and pulled up his knees. He rubbed his bleary eyes, then wearily leaned his head back. They had days of perilous journey ahead of them, each mile fraught with danger. He needed to keep his wits sharp, alert, not make any more foolish blunders. He cast a sidelong glance at Christiane. He envied her. She slept the deep, untroubled sleep of the young and innocent. Had he ever been so young, so innocent? he wondered. Or had he been born a cynic?

Why had he returned to Belle Terre? Reid pinched the bridge of his nose between thumb and forefinger to ease the dull ache. True, Etienne Delacroix had promised him a bonus, but the reason went beyond that. He had overheard the *noirs* talking, and surmised there was going to be a revolt. Whatever happened to Delacroix, the man had brought on himself, but his pretty French wife was another matter entirely. Christiane had done nothing to deserve their vengeance.

Next to him, she stirred in her sleep. Even with a dirty face and a soiled gown, she was the most winsome creature he had ever met. Reaching over, he spread the petticoat over her sleeping form and tucked it around her shoulders. She brought out protective urges that he thought had died with Chase. Perhaps those urges were partly responsible for his return to Belle Terre. All he knew was that she made him feel good about himself, better than he had felt in years. Such faith shouldn't go unrewarded.

Yet he had nearly betrayed her blind trust. It was his fault they had almost been discovered by a roving band of *noirs* bent on violence. Careless, lax, he berated himself. Instead of being alert to danger, he had been playing with her hair like a lovesick schoolboy.

He had assumed the responsibility of leading them to safety. Once at Le Cap, his obligation would end. He would go his way. And she hers. It was unlikely their paths would ever cross. They belonged to two different worlds. She was a countess, a member of the French nobility, while he was considered a common criminal. An escaped convict. If the authorities ever learned that he had survived he would be immediately shipped to a penal colony. His shoulders sagged with fatigue. Yes, he reminded himself, he and the countess were worlds apart. It would be wise not to lose sight of that in the future.

Chapter Twelve

"If my calculations are correct, this path will soon intersect the road."

"Wouldn't it be easier to follow the road instead of struggling through all this?" Christiane indicated the dense forest with a wave of her hand.

"Definitely easier." Reid wiped sweat from his brow. "But not safer."

She slapped at a pesky mosquito. At that particular moment, she would have welcomed a less arduous trek rather than the one Reid had chosen for them. Where the road wound around obstacles, they forged straight ahead, climbing boulders, wading through streams, and traipsing through dense underbrush.

"It's already late afternoon. Let's not waste any more daylight." Reid extended a hand to help her over an outcropping of rocks.

Christiane caught hold and scrambled after him, barely

noticing the small green lizard that slithered over the toe of her shoe. In a relatively short period, she had lost all sense of direction, all track of time, and grown accustomed to a variety of slimy reptiles. According to Reid's calculations, this was only the second day of their journey, but to her it seemed merely a continuation of the first. One day blended with the next.

Reid reached the top of an embankment and waited for Christiane to catch her breath. In front of them, a narrow dirt road snaked its way toward Le Cap. Christiane stared at it longingly. No rocks to climb, no streams to ford, its uncluttered thoroughfare beckoned.

Reid followed the direction of her gaze and seemed to divine her thoughts. "Until something, or someone, better comes along, Countess, I'm your best way out."

He started down the grassy slope, Christiane clattering at his heels. They were about to cross when a ragged band of Europeans emerged from a bend in the road. They seemed to materialize out of thin air, their sudden appearance like a ghostly apparition—refugees fleeing untold horrors with only the clothes on their backs and the few items they could carry. No one spoke, not even when they spotted the two figures standing at the edge of the road. With clothes torn and tattered, their expressions dazed and dull, the motley little group straggled down the road.

Christiane watched them pass. Some faces looked vaguely familiar, and she was filled with the sad realization that they had once been the bejeweled and satin-clad guests at Etienne's grand party. She knew in their eyes she must appear an equally pitiful sight.

Then she recognized a familiar figure.

"Yvette?" Christiane had trouble reconciling the vacuous young woman with the pretty, vivacious Yvette Charbonneau she had once met.

Yvette stumbled to a halt and looked at her blankly. She hugged a porcelain doll wearing a dirty white dress to her breast.

"Yvette," Christiane said softly, her voice filled with sympathy. She smoothed lank strands of blond hair from the woman's startlingly pale face. "Do you remember me, *ma chère?* I'm Christiane Delacroix. We met not long ago at Belle Terre."

Yvette continued to stare at her with no hint of recognition.

A woman, her brown hair liberally threaded with gray, stopped and placed a comforting arm around Yvette's shoulders. "We found her wandering near the river." She lowered her voice to a whisper. "Poor thing, her mind is gone."

"It's a miracle she managed to escape," Reid commented.

"Francois?" Yvette asked in a small voice. Clutching the doll tighter to her chest, she glanced around, her expression hopeful.

"Come with me, *ma chère.*" The woman gently tugged on Yvette's arm. "Sadie will take care of you."

Christiane's eyes welled with tears as she watched the two women walk away, the younger of the two leaning heavily on the older one.

"Are you coming with us, madame, or are you staying with him?"

The terse question jolted Christiane out of her apathy. She looked into small, dark eyes deeply set in the narrow face of a stranger who had approached.

"Better make up your mind," the man's companion added. "No telling how far behind those murdering bastards are."

"I know a route through the mountains," Reid said. "Why don't you come with us instead?"

"Follow you?" the first man said with a sneer. "Why should we trust a man such as yourself?"

Reid's hands bunched, then relaxed as he fought to ignore the insult. "This road is likely to be crawling with rebels waiting to prey on those fleeing toward Le Cap."

The man spat in the dust. "I wouldn't trust someone with your reputation with a loaf of bread. If the lady," he continued, nodding toward Christiane, "has any sense at all, she won't either."

"You're welcome to join our party, madame," the second man said as the group turned and resumed the long walk to Le Cap.

The decision was hers. Singly and in twos and threes, the motley group of refugees straggled past. Most were too intent on their personal misery to spare the pair at the roadside more than a passing glance. Their expressions revealed varying degrees of shock, horror.

And fear.

Even so, they were more fortunate than many. At least these people had escaped with their lives. She thought of Etienne sprawled on the staircase, a knife protruding from his body. Of Francois Charbonneau's burned corpse.

"Well . . ." Reid growled.

His voice startled her out of her reverie. "Well what, m'sieur?"

"If you're going with them, you'd better make up your mind."

"If I am slowing you down, I am sorry. I do not mean to."

He scowled down at her, his face hard and unsmiling. "If I am a burden—"

"Damn!" He exhaled sharply. "Don't you realize I'm giving you a chance to be with those of your own class?"

"But you said it wasn't safe on the main road," she reminded him with infuriating logic.

"It isn't."

"Then I don't understand why you're trying to get rid of me."

"I'm not trying to get rid of you." He raked an impatient hand through his hair. "I merely thought you might feel . . . safer, more comfortable . . . among a group of your own kind rather than with a convicted murderer."

"I feel safe with you."

His gray eyes drilled into hers, seeming to search her soul. "All right," he said, his voice gruff. "Let's not waste time."

He stepped off the road and disappeared into the woods. She did likewise, all the while pondering the strange expression that had flitted across his features when she had told him that she felt safe with him: confusion, surprise, and some softer, deeper emotion she couldn't identify.

"We'll keep parallel to the road for a short distance, then cross it one last time, and veer due north."

"Very well." Christiane trailed behind, keeping a sharp lookout for snakes. After finding the one in her sewing basket, she had developed a strong aversion. She jumped over a fallen log and felt the pouch of jewels bounce against her hip. She had considered the gems as her security. Security? She nearly laughed aloud at the thought. What good were diamonds and rubies? Indeed, what good was all the money in the world when there was nothing to buy?

Money and jewels couldn't buy a crust of bread. Couldn't buy a hot bath. Couldn't buy safety.

She snagged a handful of wild grapes and popped them into her mouth. They eased, but didn't erase, the hunger. She reminded herself to be grateful for the small comforts such as fruit and water. It was senseless to fuss. Reid must be just as hungry as she.

And he never once complained. She studied him carefully, and found evidence of strain beginning to show. There were smudges of fatigue beneath his eyes, and the lines of his face seemed more deeply etched. His fine gray eyes were never still, but constantly alert for danger. She noted the way he bunched his shoulders and rolled his neck to release tension. On those occasions, she had been sorely tempted to massage away his aches. But something always held her back.

As she tramped along behind him, she became acutely aware of the way his broad shoulders tapered to a trim waist and narrow hips. In deference to the heat of the day, Reid had removed his shirt and tied it around his waist. The smooth perfection of bronzed flesh was spoiled by a network of raised scars.

Her thoughts scattered, drifted. Mentally her fingertips traced each scar; then she followed their path with a trail of kisses. The notion shocked her. Forgetting to watch her footing, she tripped over a gnarled root and nearly fell headlong, but caught herself in time.

Reid turned and studied her flushed face. "Having second thoughts about coming with me, Countess?"

"Non," she snapped, irritated at herself for finding him even more attractive viewed from the front. At some point during their flight, the leather thong used to hold his hair back had been lost. Several days' growth of beard added a rugged appeal. Sun-streaked, shaggy locks that formed

an unruly tangle around his shoulders reminded her of
a lion's mane. Indeed, the man himself resembled the
predatory jungle creature: lean, hungry, dangerous—an
animal waiting to be tamed.

"The waterfall is directly ahead. We'll stop there to rest."

Twenty minutes later they were greeted by the sound of
rushing water. Energized by the thought of cold, refreshing
springwater, Christiane picked up her skirt and ran ahead.
Sinking down beside the rushing stream, she cupped her
hands and drank deeply. Finally, her thirst slaked, she sat
back on her haunches and closed her eyes. If she tried,
she could pretend the bloody revolt had never happened.
The sun felt warm on her uplifted face. The scent of flowers
filled the glade like an exotic perfume. It was peaceful
here. Serene. The cathedrallike silence was broken only
by the sound of rushing water.

"Reid . . . ?" she began tentatively.

When no answer was forthcoming, her eyes flew open
and sought his. One glance at his taut features sent an
arrow of fear through her heart. Reluctantly dragging her
gaze from his, she followed the direction of his stare.

A *noir*, tall, muscular, a strip of red cloth knotted around
his hips, stood partially hidden by brush on the opposite
bank of the stream. He held what appeared to be a rusty
knife carelessly in his right hand. With dawning compre-
hension, Christiane realized it wasn't rust on the blade,
but dried blood.

Her mouth dry with fear, Christiane remained frozen
in place, powerless to move. At any moment she fully
expected to find a horde of *noirs* descending with raised
machetes. Seconds ticked by; still neither man moved a
muscle. Silence spun a sticky web of fear and suspicion.

Slowly her initial terror began to wane, and her brain
began to function. She warily climbed to her feet. There

was something disturbingly familiar about the *noir*. Her gaze traveled over his thickly muscled torso to a face cast in mutinous lines—a face she had seen once before. A scene flashed through her mind, vivid, chilling.

"Juno." A mere whisper of sound escaped her bloodless lips.

The warrior lowered his eyelids fractionally in acknowledgment. She swallowed, the sound loud in the stillness. Her gaze skittered nervously to Reid. His steady gray eyes were fixed on Juno, his bland expression not betraying his thoughts. *Like a gambler in a high stakes game.*

"W-we thought you were dead," she stammered.

Juno's unblinking stare never wavered. "That is what you were supposed to think."

"It can't be." She pressed a hand against her midsection. Her stomach clenched in her revulsion at the memory of a burlap sack casually tossed on the dining room table, the pound of flesh Etienne had demanded as proof of punishment.

"As you see, madame, I am alive and well."

She edged closer to Reid. Surely Juno was about to retaliate for the brutal treatment. And his anger would be justified. He would raise his arm and use the machete to slice them to shreds as proficiently as he did the stalks of sugarcane. What she didn't understand was why Reid just stood quietly waiting. Was he frightened? Or simply resigned to his fate? Her mind stumbled trying to find a logical cause for this stalemate.

"So, Juno." Reid spoke at last, his voice calm. "Have you reached a decision?"

Footsteps could be heard crashing through the brush behind the spot where Juno stood. A muted babble of voices grew louder. Christiane unconsciously clutched Reid's arm.

"Hide there." Juno pointed at a mound of rocks next to the waterfall. He turned to leave, then swung back, his hooded gaze locking on Reid. "At last, my friend, the debt is paid."

Reid grabbed Christiane around the waist and propelled her toward the tumbled pile of rocks that Juno had indicated. He slipped through a narrow opening into a space barely big enough for two and pulled her in after him. From a distance they heard Juno's raised voice command the *noirs* to follow him. Christiane crouched into a tight ball, her hands over her ears to block out the sounds of the *noirs* passing within yards of their hiding place. The nightmare was happening all over again. She was only dimly conscious of Reid's comforting arm around her quaking shoulders.

Long after the sound of thrashing footsteps and the jumble of voices faded, Reid and Christiane remained in their hiding place. When he was certain all danger had passed, Reid withdrew his arm from around her, rested his head against a boulder, and closed his eyes. Christiane huddled next to him, her knees drawn to her chest, more shaken than she cared to admit. For the second time in two days, they had had a narrow escape with death. Sleepless nights and harrowing days were beginning to exact their toll. Her nerves felt raw, exposed.

Drawing a long, shuddering breath, she asked the question foremost in her mind. "What did Juno mean, 'the debt is paid'?"

Reid gave a weary shrug. "What difference does it make? It isn't important."

"*Au contraire,* it does matter."

"The debt is paid." Opening his eyes a slit, he turned his head slightly and regarded her with a challenging gleam. "What don't you understand?"

"What debt?" Reid's obvious reluctance to answer a simple question was making her angry. She wanted to grab him and shake him.

"Can't you just forget it? I told you it doesn't matter." He pinched the bridge of his nose between thumb and forefinger.

She shoved a handful of hair out of her eyes. "I disagree. Why did Juno let us escape unharmed?"

"Damn!" Now Reid was the one who sounded angry. "If you aren't the most persistent woman I've ever met."

"Why did he call you 'friend'?"

"Because . . ." Reid blew out an impatient breath. "I saved his life; he spared ours. Therefore the debt is paid."

Christiane digested this in silence. His answer served only to dredge up more questions. When? How? "B-but I saw . . ."

"You saw nothing," he snapped. "Only a sack of pigskin."

She shifted position so that she sat facing him in the confined space. "Then"—she shook her head to clear the confusion—"you didn't punish Juno as Etienne ordered."

"No." Reid climbed to his feet and brushed the dirt from his pants. "Juno didn't deserve that kind of treatment. None of the *noirs* did."

Christiane felt an overwhelming surge of relief. Her instincts about Reid had been correct. He was too decent a man to inflict cruel, unjust punishment, incapable of beating a helpless man to death.

"So . . . you let him go."

Reid nodded curtly.

"But what if Etienne had learned the truth?" Christiane stared up at him, her dark eyes huge, trying to absorb what she had just learned.

"I'm a gambler by trade. Odds were in my favor."

"He would have had you whipped as an example to the others," she said in a voice barely above a whisper. "The strips of flesh could have been yours."

"It was the chance I took. As you can see, I'm still intact." He held out his hand and pulled her to her feet.

She was struck by the realization that she had done him a grave disservice and, remembering all the cruel and hurtful things she had said, felt ashamed. He had risked his life for another and been repaid with comments meant to wound. She moistened her bottom lip with the tip of her tongue. "I owe you an apology. You performed a very brave and noble—"

"Save it, Countess," he snapped. Turning away, he squeezed through the narrow opening of the rocky shelter, then looked around. Satisfied they were alone, he motioned for Christiane to join him. "Let's go."

Reid stepped into the water and waded across the stream. Slipping off her shoes, she hitched up her skirts and followed his example. Upon reaching the opposite bank, she balanced on one foot while trying to wedge her dripping foot into her shoe. "When do you think we'll reach Le Cap?"

"With luck by dusk tomorrow." Reid didn't wait but began to pick his way along the trampled route Juno and his followers had taken. Christiane hurried to keep pace.

They traveled the next mile in silence. Reid suddenly slowed and held up a warning hand. "If my calculations are correct, we're about to cross the road again, then take the shortcut across the hills."

He led the way, with Christiane close behind. Overhead the sun was beginning to dip below the level of the trees, bathing the landscape in mellow hues of green and gold, reminiscent of sunlight streaming through the stained-glass windows of a cathedral. Everything appeared serene, peaceful. The only sound to be heard was that of the breeze gently soughing through the branches.

Through the thinning trees, the road stretched before them like a dark brown ribbon. Reid approached cautiously, straining to listen, looking first to the right, then to the left, then started to cross. Christiane followed suit.

Midway across the rutted track, she spied a small object lying to one side of the road. Something about it struck a familiar chord. She slowly approached the item, trepidation growing with each halting step, vaguely aware that Reid was watching with a frown. Stooping to pick up the object in question, she stared at it in mute recognition.

"Well," Reid prompted tersely. "What is it?"

"A doll," she replied dully. "Yvette's doll." She ran trembling fingers over its matted yellow hair and recoiled when they came away sticky. Crimson stains mingled with the grime on the doll's once-pretty lace dress, its delicate porcelain features smashed beyond recognition.

Reid approached and took the doll from her unresisting fingers. Dread gnawed in his gut. He knew with certainty what he would find on the road ahead. He cast an uneasy glance at Christiane. Her distress was etched on her delicate features. Her face was white as chalk, her eyes enormous dark pools. How much more could she be subjected to before she cracked under the strain? he wondered grimly.

Putting his arm around her shoulders, he led her to a tree stump and urged her down. "Wait here while I investigate."

She wrapped her arms around herself and began to rock slowly back and forth.

Reid hated to leave her like that, but knew he must. He didn't have to go far before he discovered what he feared he would. Men and women alike, no one had been spared the slaughter. Their dismembered bodies had been left to rot along the roadside.

Grim faced, he realized that he couldn't afford the time for a decent burial. It was imperative he and Christiane put as much distance between themselves and the road as possible. He gently laid the doll with the broken face and bloodstained yellow hair beside what remained of Yvette Charbonneau. Though he didn't consider himself a religious man, he offered up a small prayer for the victims.

Regretfully, he turned his back on the dead and hurried back to the living. He found Christiane in the gathering dusk, sitting exactly as he had left her.

She looked up at his return. "Did you find them?"

"Yes."

The single word—and all its implications—reverberated in the encroaching twilight.

When she made no reply, he hunkered down in front of her and took her hands in his. They felt cold as ice, the bones as fragile as a bird's. "There was little anyone could do."

"All those people," she murmured dazedly. "All those lives . . ."

"Try not to think of them," he urged, chafing her hands to restore warmth. "We need to concentrate on reaching Le Cap alive."

"Alive . . . ?" She blinked once, twice; then her gaze became focused. "Are we going to make it, Reid? Tell me the truth; don't lie to me."

He squeezed her hands between his, trying to impart a confidence that was at best shaky. "Of course we're going to make it."

She leaned toward him, her expression intent. "Say it one more time, Reid. I need to hear it again."

"We're survivors, Christiane, you and I," he said with

growing assurance. He reached out and gently ran the backs of his fingers along her cheek and jaw. "We're going to make it."

They walked until it was too dark to see where they were going. Entirely by chance, they stumbled upon a shallow cave, barely more than a minor indentation in the rocky hillside, its entrance protected by a thick fringe of tall poinsettias that had grown to the height of small trees.

"We won't find better shelter," Reid announced. He left and returned minutes later with an armful of ferns, which he spread on the ground. "Not exactly a down mattress, but it's better than a dirt floor."

Christiane sank down onto the ferns and gratefully accepted the banana and handful of figs he offered. Reid lowered himself to the ground and stretched out beside her, resting his weight on one elbow. She ate slowly, mechanically, barely tasting the food. She was achingly aware of his presence next to her. Close, but not touching. Shrouded in utter darkness, she felt as though she were in a tomb. She shivered, recalling their near brush with death.

Poor Yvette. What a horrible fate. Christiane had envied the young woman's life. She would have changed places with her in a heartbeat. A loving husband, children, a beautiful home, wealth—she had seemed to have it all. And now it had all been swept away.

What would it feel like to know a lover's tender touch? she wondered despairingly. Or to bear a child? Would she perish on this godforsaken island having only experienced Etienne's hateful advances? What if Etienne's cruel accusations had been correct? Maybe she was incapable of ever pleasing a man. She cast a sidelong glance at the man next

to her. Was she woman enough for a man such as Reid?
Somehow she sensed he would be a gentle, considerate
lover, not one who derived perverted pleasure from
inflicting pain.

Many thoughts had tumbled through her mind while
she had waited by the roadside for Reid to return. There
were still so many things she hadn't done, hadn't experienced. She didn't want to die until she had lived life to
its fullest.

But life was fragile.

And often brief.

"Are you all right, Countess?" Reid asked softly, sensing
her morose mood.

"Reid . . ." She moved closer.

"Hmm . . ."

"Don't call me 'Countess.' My name is Christiane."

"Very well . . . Christiane." He reached out and
smoothed a silky lock away from her face. "I noticed that
the bruise on your cheek is quickly fading. I could have
killed Etienne for what he did to you."

Emboldened by his touch, she placed the palm of her
hand against his bearded cheek and felt him stiffen at the
contact. "Does my touch offend you?" She couldn't quite
control the tremor of hurt.

"Of course not," he denied brusquely.

"*Bon.*" Before she could lose courage, she lightly
brushed his mouth with hers. Though inexperienced in
the ways of pleasing a man, she was rewarded when she
sensed an immediate response.

He wrapped his fingers around her wrist to halt her
advances. "What kind of game are you playing?"

"I want you to make love to me."

"What?" His grip tightened. "I don't think that's wise."

"You do not want me?"

His breath whistled from between clenched teeth. "Countess, I've wanted you since the moment I set eyes on you in Le Cap."

"Then what is stopping you?" she asked, hurt and confused by his refusal.

"This isn't the time—or the place—to do something foolish. Something you'll regret later."

"But you are wrong, m'sieur. The past is dust, the future filled with uncertainty. The present is all we have." Boldly she kissed him again, a kiss filled with longing and tinged with desperation. "Make love to me, *s'il te plaît*," she whispered against his lips.

Reid capitulated with a groan, grabbing a fistful of her hair and rolling her beneath him. His mouth slanted over hers, greedily plundering what she so generously offered. He couldn't think above the blood roaring in his ears. He trailed a line of kisses down the slender column of her neck and felt the frantic beat of her pulse at the hollow of her throat.

In the gray light filtering into the cave, he could see the swell of her breasts above the edge of her bodice, pale and inviting, tempting him to caress the plump globes, taste their sweetness. He fumbled with the fastenings of her gown, wanting to be rid of any unnecessary barriers between them. Sensing his urgency, she worked to unbutton his trousers. He bit back a groan at the exquisite torture whenever her dainty hand encountered his throbbing, engorged manhood.

Their clothes lay in an untidy heap. Reid slid his body down the length of hers. Christiane closed her eyes and moved against him, the gesture innocent yet sensual, an intoxicating combination. Unable to resist, he cupped her breast and found it fit his hand perfectly. He rubbed his thumb against its nipple, felt it tighten in response, and heard her sharply indrawn breath. Bending his head, he drew the tightly furled bud into his mouth and flicked it with his tongue. Christiane wove her fingers through his hair, holding fast, and arched against him.

His entire body quivered, taut as a bowstring, as he fought to slow the desire coursing through him. This was insanity. He should stop before it was too late.

As though sensing the campaign he waged against his baser instincts, she wrapped her legs around his waist. *"Non,"* she pleaded. "I need you. Make me forget everything but you. Make me feel loved."

His battle hopelessly lost, he slipped his hand between her thighs and found the inner petals guarding her femininity dewy with anticipation. With one long finger, he mercilessly teased the small nub of her sex until she writhed beneath him in mindless pleasure. He led her toward a shuddering climax; then, positioning himself between her legs, he thrust into her.

Hot, slick, tight. Incredibly tight. Heaven, he thought. Perspiration beaded his brow. He had discovered heaven. He thrust again, firmer, deeper, and was met with an obstacle. His eyes widened in disbelief. "How . . . ?"

But Christiane was lost in a sensory haze that no words could penetrate. Every fiber of her being was attuned to the new sensations rippling through her. Of their own accord, her hips began to move to an ancient rhythm. She felt wondrously, gloriously alive. Her legs locked around his waist, imprisoning him, begging for more. She was dimly aware that he was about to withdraw, but at her small whimper of protest, he resumed with a deep, masterful stroke that ruptured the membrane guarding her vault.

Her nails bit into his flesh as a sharp pain splintered through her. He paused, waiting for the discomfort to subside, then resumed the rhythm. Wave after wave of pleasure built, cresting higher and higher, until they reached their pinnacle, hurtling her toward an unexplored shore. Her arms around his shoulders, she clung to him as he shuddered and emptied himself.

Afterward, she lay with her head resting trustingly against his shoulder, savoring the intimacy of this elemental act. Reid pressed a light kiss to the damp curl along her temple. "I have to admit, Countess," he murmured. "You gave me quite a start to realize you were still a virgin."

"Etienne tried, but could not," she confided. "He claimed I was cold, passionless, incapable of pleasing a man. Do you agree?"

Reid let out a hoot of laughter. "Countess, any greater display of passion would have set the woods ablaze."

Christiane fell asleep, wearing nothing but a smile and a mantle of contentment.

Chapter Thirteen

Christiane slowly drifted toward wakefulness. Her spirit felt lighter than air, as though, untethered from a heavy ballast, it was free to soar skyward. Lazily she lingered in this pleasant realm, floating on lulling currents of contentment. With a soft sigh, she rolled onto her side and curled into a ball. Her body squirmed as it sought a more comfortable position on the hard surface beneath her.

Something sharp jabbed her in the ribs. The mild discomfort tore at the fragile sense of well-being and intruded into her blissful haze. She rolled back onto her back and stretched. She realized she was naked except for Reid's coarsely woven shirt. Strange, she didn't even remember slipping into it. Memories of the previous night seeped into her sleep-fogged mind. Memories of passionate kisses and intimate caresses. Memories of inviting Reid's final invasion.

And her unbridled response.

She bit back a groan, fully awake now. Inviting? No, she hadn't merely invited. She had begged, cajoled, coerced. She had wanted him in the most basic of ways. Desire had outweighed reason. Shame flooded through her. What had possessed her to be so brazen, so bold? In the bright light of day, it was hard to reconcile the fear and desperation that had goaded her actions.

But though it shamed her, deep in her heart she didn't regret what had transpired between them. How could she, when her experience with Reid had been as wonderful as that with Etienne had been terrible? Reid had made her feel beautiful, desirable, and awakened slumbering passion. If she survived this hellish place and lived to be a hundred, she would always treasure the night she became a woman.

Everything was so quiet. Where was Reid anyway? Turning her head to the side, she peeked out from beneath partially closed eyelids. Reid stood, his back turned, sorting through the pile of discarded clothing. While she watched unobserved, he shook the wrinkles from her gown, folded it neatly, and set it down. Picking up her chemise, he repeated the process. She noticed he held the undergarment a bit longer than the gown, running his callused fingers over the soft batiste. Her skin prickled in reaction, and she could almost feel the caress of his blunt-tipped fingers on her bare flesh.

As he scooped up her underskirt, a small pouch dropped to the ground with a soft thud. Her jewels. Christiane's heart seemed to cease beating. Reid bent to retrieve it, and for a long moment stood as though mentally weighing the contents of the chamois bag. He shot her a quick glance over his shoulder, but she pretended to be asleep, and he turned his attention back to the contents of the pouch.

Christiane felt overwhelmed with helplessness and frustration. He held all her worldly possessions in the palm of his hand. She wanted to jump up, snatch the jewels, and disappear, but realizing the futility, did none of these things. She was no physical match against his strength. He could easily rob her, then desert her. And there was little she could do to prevent it. She had little choice but to wait and see what he would do.

While she continued to watch, Reid loosened the drawstring of the bag and spilled the contents into his cupped palm. He tipped his hand slightly. Rubies and diamonds, fire and ice, sparkled in the early morning rays. Did he realize he held a small fortune? she wondered. Enough wealth to buy his way off this wretched island and to keep him in comfort for a long time to come. If he decided to steal the jewels and leave, there was little chance she would survive without his help. And if she did manage to reach Le Cap unscathed, what then? With a revolt to quell, the authorities had more pressing matters to attend to than pursuing a common thief.

A tight knot of anxiety coiled in her chest, making breathing difficult. Then, to her utter amazement, he poured the jewels back into their cloth pouch and pulled the drawstring tight. She watched, weak with relief, as he tucked the bag among her clothing. She kept her eyes squeezed shut when he swung toward her. Her body tensed as he hovered over her.

"Countess." She felt him shake her shoulder. "Time to get a move on if you want to reach Le Cap by dinnertime."

She opened her eyes, and he filled her vision. With difficulty, she restrained the urge to reach up and stroke the strong jaw nearly hidden beneath several days' growth of facial hair the color of old gold. He was so close she could see the tiny specks of black and white in his clear gray eyes—eyes that seemed to be searching her face, trying to read her thoughts, to see into her mind, almost as though he were looking for reassurance of some sort.

Clearing her throat in an attempt to break the spell that seemed to hold her in its thrall, she adopted a brisk tone. "If you will kindly provide me a modicum of privacy, I'll get dressed."

He shoved her clothes at her and rose to his feet. She snatched them from him and held them against her breast like a shield. "Turn your back, *s'il te plaît.*"

"Isn't your modesty a bit misplaced?" he asked, but grudgingly complied.

She frowned, not sure whether to take umbrage at his remark, or if he was simply teasing. "A proper gentleman," she informed him stiffly, "never refers to the night he has just spent in a lady's boudoir."

"Really?" This time there could be no mistaking the underlying current of amusement in his voice.

"Really," she retorted. His cavalier attitude infuriated her. She quickly scrambled to her feet.

"Tell me, Countess, how is it you are so well versed in bedroom etiquette when until last night you were still a virgin?"

She slipped out of his shirt, wadded it into a ball, and threw it at his head. It missed, hitting his shoulder and sliding to the ground. "There are some things a woman knows without being told."

Chuckling, he picked up his shirt and tied it around his waist. "You, in my humble opinion, excel in doing certain things with very little instruction."

Her cheeks burned at the implication. Though embarrassed, she was secretly pleased by his remark. After Etienne's blistering criticism of her femininity, she felt vindicated. She dressed hurriedly, pulling the gown over her head before she realized she needed his assistance with the fastenings. Marching over to Reid, she lifted her hair out of the way and presented her back.

She tensed as his fingers slowly worked their way down the row of tiny buttons. Her skin felt singed whenever he brushed against the thin cotton chemise that provided a flimsy barrier between them. Images from the previous night flooded her mind: erotic images, images of two naked bodies straining to become one. Need began to build within her. Need to touch, feel, revel in their joining. She fought the insidious longing. It made her weak when she wanted to be strong.

The instant the task was finished, she stepped away. "Let's go, shall we? As far as I'm concerned, we can't reach Le Cap soon enough to suit me."

He studied her through narrowed eyes, then turned and slipped from the cave into the open. "Believe me, Countess," he muttered, "I'm as eager as you to part company."

Neither spoke again as they neared the end of their journey.

They reached the outskirts of Le Cap at three o'clock that afternoon. Reid and Christiane joined the steady procession of refugees clogging the road and streaming toward the city gates—homeless, penniless, helpless. Christiane smoothed her hand over her skirt and felt the reassuring bulge beneath.

"Mon Dieu," she said, lowering her voice. "These people are unaccustomed to hardship. They'll have a difficult time ahead."

"Even so," Reid replied, "they are the fortunate ones."

"Oui," she murmured, remembering Yvette and the

tragedy that had befallen the small group she had traveled with.

"What about you, Countess? Do you also consider yourself among the fortunate?"

"Most assuredly," she answered without hesitation. "We have been blessed. Not only did we escape with our lives, but we've been given a chance to start anew, mend our mistakes."

"Amen," Reid muttered.

Le Cap Francois was a far different city from the picturesque, bustling seaport Christiane recalled from her arrival in St. Domingue. It was now a city preparing for siege. Men dressed in the red and blue uniforms of the militia supervised the construction of palisades and the digging of ditches. The sound of shovels striking rocky soil and the steady tattoo of hammers filled the air.

As they filed through the gates, she noticed that all shops and businesses had been boarded shut. Even more ominous were the tight-lipped, grim expressions worn by everyone they met. Reid put his arm around her shoulder and tried to steer her down a side street. She resisted his efforts, her feet stumbling to a halt before a newly erected scaffold where the limp figure of a *noir* swung from a gallows. A pike upon which a severed head had been impaled stood next to the scaffold, the unseeing eyes a warning to others—eyes filled with untold terror.

"This way," Reid urged, and this time she didn't resist.

She drew a shuddering breath to calm jittery nerves. "Where are you taking me?"

"I'll leave you in the bishop's care. He'll see that you're taken care of until you decide what you want to do."

"What about you, Reid? What are you going to do now?"

"Worried about me, Countess?" He gripped her elbow and guided her around an abandoned cart.

"Blame it on curiosity." Now that the moment of parting was close at hand, though loath to admit it, she hated to sever all ties.

After passing a stockade containing a dozen or so *noirs* chained and under heavy guard, they turned onto a side street. Several blocks down, a church spire poked an accusing finger at the azure sky. Christiane automatically raked her fingers through her hair in a futile attempt to bring some semblance of order to the unruly mass. Her gown, she knew, was hopelessly torn and soiled, unfit for even a cleaning rag.

What would the bishop think when he saw her? Her gaze slid to Reid. Would the bishop find it odd that she was accompanied by a man other than her husband? Would he guess the two had been lovers? If so, should she confess her sin and beg God's forgiveness? She had been taught it was wrong to share a bed with a man out of wedlock. Yet it didn't feel wrong, didn't feel sinful.

Reid's steps lengthened and she had to run to keep up with him. He stopped before a neat whitewashed house next to the church, pushed open the gate, and stalked down the narrow brick path. He bounded up the porch steps and pounded on the door. When no one answered, he pounded harder. The sound reverberated in the quiet.

Christiane glanced around curiously. The house, in spite of the gay profusion of pink and purple bougainvillea trailing from the porch, gave the impression of being unoccupied. The shutters were closed and bolted. There was no sound of footsteps from within hurrying to greet them.

"Let's go around the back," Reid said impatiently.

Christiane trailed after him as he rounded the corner of the house and nearly collided with a small, stooped figure with skin tanned and creased like well-worn leather. The old man peered at them through eyes clouded by milky white cataracts. "If you seek the bishop, you are too late. He sailed with the tide at daybreak."

"Gone? You're sure?"

"Positive, m'sieur," the man replied with a vigorous nod. "I carried his bags to the wharf myself."

Reid drew his hand through his hair and swore softly under his breath as he watched the bent figure shuffle away.

Christiane tugged on her lower lip. It was clear that Reid was eager to be rid of her and impatient to be off. "If you're worried about me, please don't be. You have seen me safely to Le Cap. I am no longer your responsibility."

He whirled on her angrily. "What am I supposed to do? Abandon you on the doorstep of an empty house?"

"I will manage, m'sieur."

He crossed his arms over his chest and regarded her with a raised brow. "Brave words, Countess, but just how do you intend to *manage?*"

Imitating his manner, she folded her arms across her chest and regarded him with a mutinous expression. "I will be fine. I no longer require your help."

"Is that right?" he asked, his voice rife with exasperation. "Do you know anyone here in Le Cap?"

"No, but . . ." She stalled, her mind working feverishly.

He rubbed his bristled jaw as he weighed options. "Maybe the governor—"

"Simone!" The seamstress's name popped out. At Reid's look of puzzlement, Christiane hurried to explain. "Simone du Val asked me to stop by her shop whenever I visited Le Cap."

Reid resisted the urge to roll his eyes at her naivete. "By all accounts, Madame du Val is a shrewd woman. She merely meant for you to visit her shop when you were in town to conduct business, not pay her a social call."

"Non." She shook her head stubbornly. "Simone won't turn me away."

"The woman is *gens de couleur,*" he said, trying to reason with her. "In all likelihood, she regards you as the enemy."

"She will not turn me away."

Reid recognized the stubborn set of her chin and knew it was pointless to argue. "Very well. I'll take you there. Then you will learn for yourself what kind of friend she is."

Simone du Val's shop was set back slightly from the main thoroughfare, which ran through the center of town. Colorful flowers spilled over clay pots set on either side of the entrance. A neatly lettered sign swung from a post. Shutters painted a bright blue were drawn tight, just as they had been at the bishop's house.

Reid's knock went unanswered. At his I-told-you-so look, Christiane edged around him and took matters into her own hands. "Simone, if you are in there, please open," she said as she rapped on the wood.

"I tried to tell you, but you wouldn't listen."

Christiane renewed her efforts. "Simone? It is I, Christiane Delacroix."

The door opened a crack and Simone's amber eyes peeked through the slit. "Go away, madame. The shop is closed."

"Simone, please." Christiane wedged the toe of her shoe into the narrow opening. "I need your help, as one friend to another."

A long pause followed. Then the door opened wide enough to admit her. Christiane turned, expecting Reid to follow, but he had already left. She scanned the street in time to see his broad back disappear around a corner. A lump the size of a fist rose in her throat. After everything they had shared, he had simply walked out of her life without a word of good-bye. Without so much as a backward glance. Already she was forgotten.

"Hurry, madame," Simone urged.

Blinking back tears, Christiane stepped inside.

"You should not be here."

Christiane stood uncertainly in the center of the small but tidy shop and tried to ignore the woman's blatant hostility. Porcelain dolls dressed in the current European fashions lined several shelves. Bolts of rich brocade, plush velvet, and shimmering silk were stacked on a low counter. Two Queen Anne–style armchairs were arranged around a small table set with a bone china tea set. A curtain shirred on a rod separated the shop from the living quarters beyond.

Her inspection of the shop completed, Christiane had no choice but to meet the woman's unyielding gaze. "I had no other place to go."

"What were you thinking? You cannot stay here."

"I hoped we had established the beginnings of a friendship." Christiane managed to summon a rueful smile. "I see now that I was mistaken."

"There can be no friendship between a *gens de couleur* and a *grand blanc*. I tried to explain this when we first met. I thought you understood."

"The color of our skin does not matter to me. I seek your help as one woman to another."

"I should not have to remind you, madame, that these are troubled times. It is hard to know who is enemy, who is friend."

"Look into your heart, Simone." Christiane took a tentative step closer, her hand outstretched. "If you came to me for help, you know I would give it."

Simone stared at the hand, her tiger eyes bright with suspicion and doubt. "Very well," she agreed with obvious reluctance. "I will help you if I can, but you cannot remain here."

"Merci," Christiane hid her relief behind a polite smile.

While Simone disappeared into the living quarters to prepare a light meal, Christiane removed a diamond earring from the pouch at her waist. Over tea and a bowl of hearty soup thick with seafood, Christiane outlined her plans. When Simone continued to look skeptical, Christiane placed the diamond in the center of the table with slow deliberation.

Simone picked up the earring, examining it carefully. A cunning smile curved her lips as the stone caught the fading rays of the sun. "I will be happy to accommodate your needs, madame."

The two women looked up as a man entered the shop. His light brown eyes stared at Christiane. "What is she doing here?" he demanded.

"André, that is no way to treat our guest," Simone chided gently. "Madame Delacroix is determined to leave St. Domingue and has asked our help."

"Why should we endanger our safety for hers?"

"Because"—she held up the earring between thumb and forefinger for his inspection—"madame has made the risk worthwhile."

André personally escorted Christiane to the wharf. She had undergone a dramatic transformation since Reid had abandoned her on the du Vals' doorstep. A hot bath had done wonders to restore her morale. Under Simone's ministrations, her hair had been drawn away from her face and skillfully arranged into a cluster of shiny curls beneath a plumed bonnet with a pleated brim. The fashionable traveling gown of russet trimmed with ecru lace was one of several that had been hastily altered to fit her petite frame. A number of other gowns, along with a modest assortment of toiletry items, were packed in a small brass-bound trunk.

"The captain of the *Sea Witch* didn't know about the revolt when he sailed into port." André set the trunk down with a grunt. "Some of his crew were impressed by the local militia, so he has a couple of unoccupied cabins."

"André . . . ?" A small frown formed on her brow. "Try to convince Simone to leave St. Domingue. It isn't safe here . . . for anyone."

"Maybe, maybe not," he mumbled, then turned away and disappeared into the night. His guarded expression had given no clue as to whether or not he would heed her advice.

With a sigh, Christiane looked around. Desperation hung in the air like a heavy fog. The wharf that had been teeming with activity the day of her arrival was virtually deserted. Sacks of coffee beans rested on pallets the height of a man's shoulders, but no one loaded them aboard. Though she had scant knowledge of ships, the *Sea Witch* seemed unimpressive, with its peeling paint and untidy piles of rope. Far different from the *Marianne* and Captain Heath's sharp eye.

Swallowing her trepidation, she entered the dockside tavern where the *Sea Witch*'s captain was conducting business. The barkeep never looked up at her entry. "Have a seat. Cap'n will be right with you," he barked in a gravelly voice.

Christiane perched on a rough-hewn bench along one wall. As her eyes slowly adjusted to the dim light, she made out rows of empty tables. The air was redolent with the smell of spilled ale and stale smoke.

The door at the far end of the taproom opened and a

grizzled head poked out. "Right this way, madame. I got one cabin left, so let me hear your best offer."

Christiane rose and made her way across the sticky floor, hoping, praying, that she could convince the man to accept her as a passenger.

"Captain Ian MacGregor." The man stuck out a meaty, blunt-fingered hand. "At your service, madame, that is"— he gave a wheezing laugh—"if the price is right."

She forced a smile. "I can be very persuasive, *Capitaine*."

"Well, the gentleman inside volunteered to work as one of my crew in addition to paying his passage, but I'm still open to negotiation. Can you better that?" He stepped aside and motioned for her to enter the private dining room, where a single candle sputtering on the table provided the only light. She stared in amazement at the other occupant of the room. Reid stared back, equally stunned.

"No telling when another ship will drop anchor in this cursed place. Naturally, the cost of passage increases with demand," the captain continued. "Nothing personal, you understand, but a man has to look out for his own."

"That's all the money I have." Reid tossed a handful of gold coins onto the table.

Captain MacGregor eyed the coins with a greedy gleam and rubbed his unshaven chin. "Well, I don't know. . . ."

"I have something of considerable value." Christiane spoke for the first time since entering the room.

The attention of both men shifted to her. She tugged off doeskin gloves and extended her hand toward the candlelight. Ian MacGregor's attention was drawn to the huge ruby ring like a moth to flame. He swallowed audibly.

Strolling over to the table, she picked up the coins one by one. "My ring is worth far more than this paltry sum, don't you agree, *Capitaine*?" she asked with a sweet smile.

The captain scratched his head, his eyes still glued on the ruby. "Well, I . . . ah . . ."

She disregarded Reid's choked outrage and kept her eyes fastened on the captain's ruddy face. "You could live quite comfortably on what the stone alone will bring."

He broke into a wide smile. "Well, madame, it looks like you just booked passage in my last stateroom."

A chair scraped the planked floor as Reid surged to his feet. He glared at Christiane, his gray eyes glinting like twin dueling pistols. Nonplussed, Christiane took his hand, placed the coins in his palm, and closed his fingers over them. "No need to get so upset, *mon cher*. It is only a piece of jewelry. There is a time to be sentimental, and a time to be practical. *N'est-ce pas?*"

Ian MacGregor scratched his head, perplexed. "You two know one another?"

"Know one another?" Christiane laughed. "But of course. This man is my husband."

Chapter Fourteen

"Why?"

Reid's question exploded the moment they were alone in the cabin.

"Why not?" Christiane turned away in order to hide her amusement. The stupefaction on his face when she had made her announcement had been well worth the price of a ruby.

Reid paced the narrow confines like a caged lion. "What on God's good earth prompted you to let the captain think I was your husband?"

"Will pretending to be Etienne Delacroix be all that difficult?" She carefully removed her bonnet and placed it on the bunk. "I understand the voyage to New Orleans is relatively short. Once there we will go our separate ways. We will never have to see each other again."

"That is what I thought would happen once I left you on the du Vals' doorstep."

She shrugged. "Fate, so it seems, decreed otherwise."

He stopped pacing and grabbed her shoulders. A muscle bunched in his jaw as he struggled to control his agitation. "Dammit! Can't you just answer my question?"

She gave him an impertinent smile not the least cowed by his anger. "It's really quite simple."

"Countess," he said between gritted teeth, "where you're concerned, nothing is simple."

"That is only because you insist on complicating things." Poor Reid, she thought with a stirring of sympathy. He looked so frustrated, so befuddled. She resisted the urge to smooth the frown from his forehead.

"Are you going to tell me, or do I have to shake the truth out of you?"

"Very well," she acquiesced with a pout. "If you insist."

"I insist." He released her shoulders, stepped back, and folded his arms across his chest.

"What was it Juno said when he found our hiding place?" Her brow knitted in concentration, then cleared. "Ah, now I remember. He said 'the debt is paid.' "

"What the hell are you talking about? What debt? You don't owe me anything."

"*Au contraire.*" Her dark eyes snapped with ire. "I happen to value my life highly. If not for you, I would probably be dead by now. Even if I had managed to flee from Belle Terre, there is no way I could have found my way to Le Cap without your help. Not for one minute do I believe that story about Etienne owing you money." She jabbed a finger at him for emphasis. "Why did you *really* come back?"

He stared down at her, his mouth a grim slash in his bearded face. When she didn't flinch under his threatening scowl, he relented with a sigh. "I came back because I was worried about you," he admitted grudgingly. "Whatever happened to your husband he brought upon himself. You were different, an innocent who had accidentally stumbled into a viper's pit. You didn't deserve to get bitten.''

"Ah, m'sieur, like it or not, you *are* my knight in shining armor.''

"A solitary lapse, Countess. I doubt if there will be a recurrence.''

"But you are mistaken.'' She reached into her pocket and withdrew the pouch of jewels. "You have already had a relapse.''

"I don't know what you're talking about.''

"You found these when you thought I was asleep. It would have been a simple matter to steal them, then disappear.''

He regarded the bag of gems with a rueful lift of one brow. "Don't give me too much credit, Countess; the thought crossed my mind.''

"Even heroes are human, m'sieur.'' She tucked the jewelry back into its hiding place. "The fact remains that you did neither, and I am grateful. For those reasons, I was indebted to you. Offering to share my cabin was a small price to pay in return.''

He cleared his throat, studied the floor. "I don't know what to say.''

"There is no more to say,'' she stated matter-of-factly. "You need only to pretend to be my husband. A simple charade. When we reach New Orleans, our paths will part, and we will go our separate ways.''

A slow grin traveled across his bearded countenance. "Countess, you are one stubborn, determined lady. I pity anything—or anyone—who gets in your way.''

"You make me sound like a tyrant.'' She should feel insulted by his description of her, but instead she felt herself responding to the warmth of his smile.

A simple charade? What could be easier, Christiane wondered, than pretending to be the wife of Reid Alexander? The difficult part would be bidding him good-bye.

Reid stood alone at the rail. Occasionally a feeble ray of moonlight speared through an opening in the dark, boiling clouds. A brisk wind churned the waves and puffed the sails. Hurricane weather, Captain MacGregor had called it. Only the heartiest of passengers, he had predicted, would venture out of their cabins during this voyage. The rough seas, however, seemed to have little effect on him—or on Christiane.

He shook his head, recalling the scene that had sent him scurrying on deck. The cabin was small, with the bed occupying most of the space. He had been preparing to sleep on the floor when Christiane, ever practical, had decreed otherwise. Seeing his dilemma, she had given brief consideration to the matter, then scooted to one side of the bunk.

"You may sleep here if you like." Raising up on one elbow, she patted the mattress invitingly.

Reid looked at her for a long moment, weighing her invitation and its possible consequences.

"You cannot sleep standing up," she pointed out reasonably. "And there is no other place."

"Always the practical one, aren't you?" he asked with a mixture of chagrin and admiration.

She smiled. "I try to be sensible."

"Always?"

"Always," she returned primly.

He stood at the foot of the bed, a faint smile playing around his mouth. "I can recall one notable exception, Countess."

A becoming blush stained her cheeks. "Do not harbor any false notions. I am willing to share sleeping space. . . nothing more."

There it was; she had laid down the gauntlet, spelled out the terms. He had never really hoped for a repeat of their lovemaking, yet he felt an inexplicable disappointment.

"Well, m'sieur. . . ? Are you willing to accept my terms?"

The softly issued challenge fluttered between them like an invisible red flag.

"Sleeping space. . . nothing more," he agreed slowly, knowing the herculean effort it would require.

"*Bon.*" With a satisfied yawn, Christiane snuggled into the covers and closed her eyes.

He stared down at her. Hair so dark and glossy it appeared nearly black rippled over the pillow. Her skin brought to mind delicate ivory china adorned with roses. But in spite of her seeming fragility, she was a bubbling cauldron of fire and passion, wondrously responsive to every touch, each caress. Though she refused to share more than a bed, the devil tempted him to test her resolve, to slip between the sheets and mold her soft, pliant body against his, to sample her sweet nectar. Desire shot through him, swift, and sharp. Reid drew a ragged breath; then, turning away, he had left the cabin to come up on deck.

Legs spread, Reid braced against the roll of the ship and stared out to sea. Best not to let a doe-eyed vixen distract him from his purpose. In the weeks to come, he would need all his wits about him if he wished to succeed in proving his innocence and regaining the plantation he had won, then lost. First he needed to devise a plan to locate Leon du Beaupre. That should be the easy part. Once du Beaupre was found, he needed to concoct a clever scheme to get the man to confess to the murder of his brother. And along with a clever scheme, it would require luck and a prayer. Obtaining proof Leon had murdered Gaston would be next to impossible.

He clasped his hands behind his back and wandered toward the bow of the ship. Perhaps it was foolish to go to New Orleans, to confront the man who had accused him of murder and sent him to prison. It would have been wiser—more sensible—to sail to the opposite corner of the globe, where there was little chance of ever meeting Leon du Beaupre. Reid knew he risked being recognized and returned to prison. He recalled Christiane's comment about fleeing one revolution only to land in another. Would he meet a similar fate? Would he escape one prison only to find himself incarcerated in another?

But it was a gamble he had willingly undertaken. Something within him refused to allow him to change course. He felt compelled to seek not only revenge but justice. Try as he might, he couldn't fathom why one brother would kill another.

Reid breathed in the salty tang of the sea, savoring the roll of the ship beneath his feet. He had been on a ship only once before, chained like a mad dog to a fellow prisoner on a journey marked by misery and despair. Salvation had came disguised as a violent storm. After the boat splintered like kindling, he and a fellow convict had clung to a piece of driftwood for nearly twenty-four hours. The tides carried them away from Hispaniola toward the neighboring shore of St. Domingue. Along the way, the other prisoner had lost his will to live and died before reaching shore. Reid himself had been more dead than alive when discovered on a beach by Etienne Delacroix.

What irony! Reid nearly laughed out loud. Now here he was pretending to *be* Etienne Delacroix. And with the man's wife, no less, as an accomplice in the charade!

Remembering Christiane, he wondered if she was fast asleep. He waited another half hour for good measure, then made his way down the companionway and returned to the cabin they shared as man and wife. It amazed him that until last night she had still been a virgin. Amazed and. . . delighted him. She had generously offered herself to him, a priceless, unique gift.

But why hadn't Delacroix claimed the prize himself? he wondered as he undressed and slipped into bed next to her. Christiane sighed in her sleep, her body unconsciously curving against his, seeking his warmth. Exhaustion fled. Reid's body was wide awake now and clamoring for surcease. He gritted his teeth, locked his hands behind his head, and stared at the ceiling.

"Bonjour."

Reid swore softly as he nicked his jaw with the razor the captain had supplied.

She clucked her tongue reprovingly. "Are you always in such bad humor in the morning? Or only when you shave?"

"No, just when I cut myself with a dull razor," Reid retorted, looking at her over his shoulder.

"Don't stop on my account." She plumped her pillow, rested it against the hull behind the bed, and leaned back to watch. Indeed, she found the ritual quite fascinating. Or maybe it was seeing Reid wearing only a strip of linen around his waist that captured her attention. "This is a new experience for me."

"I'm glad you find me entertaining."

"I've never watched a man shave. Doesn't all that scraping make your face hurt?"

"Only when I make it bleed." He turned back to the task.

In the small mirror pinned above a washstand, she watched him draw the razor down one cheek, leaving a wide swath in the thick layer of soap. With a series of grimaces, he repeated the process over and over until his scruffy beard gave way to smooth flesh.

"I'm not sure if I prefer you clean shaven or with a beard." She tilted her head to one side and studied him. "The beard made you look . . . disreputable, dangerous. Like a pirate."

"A scurvy pirate . . . ?"

She giggled at his look of outrage. "Scurvy, but nice."

"You seem in especially good humor this morning, Countess." His eyes snagged hers in the small mirror, and held.

"The sea air must agree with me." Her saucy smile faded into seriousness when she examined his face more critically. "The same cannot be said of you, m'sieur. I've seen you look more rested when you spent the night sleeping on the ground."

He grunted an acknowledgment. "The hard ground held fewer distractions than sharing your bed."

"Oh . . . " His answer pleased her, appealing to her vanity. It started a warm glow deep inside, knowing that her nearness disturbed him.

He wiped the remnants of soap from his face, then reached for the small scissors on the washstand and began hacking at his hair.

Christiane gazed in astonishment at the growing mound of tawny locks on the floor. *"Non,* don't!" Flinging aside the bedclothes, Christiane scrambled out of bed and rushed to stop him.

Another lock of hair fell to the floor. "I don't want to appear the same man who left St. Domingue."

The unyielding determination underlying his words

stayed her hand from snatching the scissors. They served as grim reminder that he was an escaped convict trying to avoid recapture. "Who is it that you fear might recognize you?"

"There are certain things I need to accomplish. I can do this better if I am free to move about without fear of detection. Later it will be time enough to make myself known."

He was frightening her. Suddenly the day seemed less promising, less bright. She reached for a beribboned bed jacket and slipped into it. "You aren't going to . . ." Her tongue stuck to the roof of her mouth.

"Kill someone?" He finished the sentence for her. "Is that the word you're searching for, Countess?"

"Oui." It came out in a whisper. She studied him through troubled eyes. "That is precisely what I am asking."

"You're a brave woman to travel with a convicted murderer." He put down the scissors, folded his arms over his chest, and leveled a long look at her. "Or are you just a lady who likes to court trouble?"

Nervously she twisted the pink ribbon of her bed jacket around one finger. She searched for the appropriate answer, finally settling on the truth. "Even though you have admitted killing, I have difficulty reconciling that with the man I have come to know."

"I never said I murdered anyone."

"But you said . . ." She absently tucked a glossy lock of hair behind her ear and tried to remember the exact words of their conversation. "You implied . . ."

"You reached those conclusions all on your own, Countess. I may be guilty of many things, but, rest assured, murder is not one of them."

She let out a shaky sigh, feeling as though the sun had

just come from behind a cloud, and hazarded a smile. "If you tell me you are innocent, then I believe you."

"Why?" he said with a sneer. "Why would you believe me when no one else does?"

"Perhaps because I know you better than most." When he made no reply, she tried to make him understand. "The hell we experienced trying to leave St. Domingue tests a man's character. You are no murderer."

She wanted to weep at the struggle she saw being waged across his rugged features. Had it been so long since anyone had believed him? Was that why he found her declaration of faith so difficult to accept? A band around her chest tightened. She ached for him. It must have been horrible to profess innocence before an unbelieving audience. To be condemned for a heinous act.

To stand alone. Afraid.

Hope and gratitude flared in the ash gray depths of Reid's eyes. He swallowed down emotion, then cleared his throat. "I appreciate your confidence."

"Bon." Her bright smile dispelled the gloom. "I am glad the matter is settled."

He, too, appeared relieved the tension had been defused. Turning around, he picked up the scissors and was about to snip another lock of hair when she stopped him.

"Non." She took the shears from him. "I will do that for you. Sit there," she ordered, pointing to a small wooden bench. When he was slow to comply, she gave him a gentle shove.

He slanted her a dubious look, but didn't object when she pushed him into a chair. "Fashion is very fickle," she mused as the first of many long strands fell to his feet. "I think short hair will soon be in style."

"At the rate you're cutting mine, I could be bald when you finish."

"Some women, I've been told, find bald men quite attractive."

She laughed at his look of alarm.

"Fortunately for you, m'sieur, I am not one of those women. However, I could be convinced to reverse my opinion." A mischievous twinkle danced in her dark eyes. "I once heard a scullery maid claim that bald men were more virile."

"Virile?" He arched a brow inquiringly. "What does an innocent such as you know about virility?"

She adopted an injured air. "One can learn a great deal from eavesdropping."

"Shame on you, Countess, listening to servants' gossip." He shook his head in mock despair. "Weren't you taught better?"

"Grandfather was very straitlaced and proper. As a child I used to spend a great deal of time around the stables or in the kitchen, where I'd overhear the servants talking. They added a great deal to my education."

He grinned. "I can just picture you as a young girl, your ear plastered to a keyhole."

"I was very discreet." She lopped off another strand, then stood back to inspect her handiwork. He looked handsome with his new, shorter hairstyle. She drew her fingers through his hair, ostensibly checking its length and evenness, but secretly enjoying the texture, his proximity.

He studied her reflection in the mirror. "It's occurred to me that while you know much about me, I know very little about you. I've heard you mention your grandfather, but what about your parents? Are they still alive?"

"They died when I was six," she stated matter-of-factly. "Their carriage overturned after a holiday in Italy."

"I shouldn't have asked," he said, instantly contrite. "Sorry."

"Don't be. It was a long time ago."

"Do you remember much about them?"

"My mother was very beautiful, my father quite dashing." She paused, a slight frown furrowing her brow. "Mother would request that the governess dress me in my frilliest dress, and then show me off at court as though I were a china doll. I even remember meeting the king and queen. And like a toy, when my parents tired of me, I was set aside, dismissed. After their deaths, I went to live with my grandfather. I was very happy with him. He was devoted to me and . . . " Her voice broke.

". . . and you loved him very much."

"Oui."

He looked away, wanting to console but not knowing how. His gaze happened to rest on the dark blond mound of hair scattered about the bench where he sat. He craned his neck for a view in the mirror, but Christiane moved in front of him, deliberately blocking his view.

"Non," she scolded. "No peeking until I am finished."

Reid sighed, resigned to wait to view the results. He found himself thinking about what she had just said. He had tried to draw her out, wanting to know more about her background. Now he regretted that he had. The conversation had made him even more acutely aware of their differences. She had been raised amid luxury, had romped through palaces, while his playground had been the backstreets and alleys of London. Instead of a doting grandfather, he had thrived on the love of a brother—a brother who had taught him everything from tossing dice to sleight of hand, and how to survive in a harsh, unfriendly world.

He shifted restlessly. The cabin suddenly seemed warm, stuffy. Even though Christiane was covered from head to toe, he knew full well that she wore nothing underneath that chaste white nightdress. As she moved about, the soft fabric outlined firm, round breasts, teasing, tantalizing, until he yearned to cup them in the palm of his hand. In his imagination he could feel their fullness, their warmth. He wanted to dip his head and take the berry pink nipple into his mouth, suckle it until it ripened and firmed.

"Many men, such as Etienne, prefer to keep their hair quite short beneath their wigs." Christiane chattered, unaware of Reid's torment. "But the tide of fashion is changing. Some experts predict wigs will soon go out of style."

The faint smell of flowers clung to her, sweet, fresh, beguiling. Reid could envision making love to her on a bed of wildflowers, ribbons of her long, dark hair streaming about them, her slender ivory body kissed by sunlight. He started to cross his legs, then, remembering he wore only a towel, thought better of it. Instead, he drummed his fingertips against the bench. The temperature in the cabin seemed to be inching upward.

"Will you stop fidgeting!" she scolded. "I'm nearly finished." Scissors poised in one hand, lips pursed, she tipped her head from side to side and studied the results. "Hmm . . ."

Reid grew anxious under her scrutiny. "Well? What do you think?"

Her mouth curved into a smile. "I think you look quite handsome."

Good looks were something he used to take for granted. But his physical appearance had altered since Barcelona. Multiple beatings had exacted their toll. His nose was no longer perfect and straight; his body bore an assortment of scars. Even his physique was different, leaner, more muscular. "At one time, women might have considered me handsome, but no longer."

"You think not? You are much too critical." She fussed with his hair, fluffing and brushing. "Men, I have observed, are not always good judges of what appeals to women."

"My face is no longer pretty." Absently he rubbed the small crescent-shaped scar on his cheekbone, the result of a guard's heavy fist. "I doubt if a woman would look at me twice."

"You do women a grave injustice if you think us so petty. Many women admire a man for reasons other than a handsome countenance. A face is much more intriguing when it reveals character." She caught his chin in one hand, and viewed his features with a critical eye. Her thumb lightly stroked the shallow cleft in his chin.

"Does mine show character?"

"Mmm . . ." She pretended to ponder the question.

"Well . . . ?" He raised a brow. "Are you going to tell me or not?"

"*Non,*" she said with a shake of the head and an impish smile. "I don't think so."

"And why not?" He gave her a playful swat on the derriere as she waltzed around him. He was sorely tempted to pull her into his lap and kiss the impudent smile from her lips.

She let out an affronted yelp, then giggled. "I do not like men who strut like peacocks. If I told you that you were handsome, you'd spend all your time admiring yourself in a mirror."

"Is that all you're worried about?"

"*Non,*" she said with a pout. "I do not want every woman trying to steal my husband."

"Husband . . ." he repeated, sobering. His lighthearted

mood fled, replaced by more serious concerns. "I'm not sure we'll be able to pull off this . . . charade."

Picking up a brush, Christiane ran it through her hair. "Why not?" she asked. "It is only for four or five days, until we reach New Orleans."

Reid got up and began prowling the cramped space. "What if someone on the ship knows Etienne? What will we do then?"

"The *capitaine* informed me we were the only passengers taken on at Le Cap. All the others have been on the ship since it set sail from Europe. The *capitaine* knows we are recently married and want privacy. Except for dinner, we will have little contact with others."

He stopped to regard her with admiration. "You have a devious mind, Countess."

"It does not hurt to be prepared." She shrugged off the dubious compliment. "As I told you before, I am a practical woman. Now, aren't you going to look in the mirror?"

Rising from the bench, Reid peered into the mirror above the washstand, gazing at his reflection in amazement. A stranger stared back. The difference in his appearance was dramatic. Short-cropped hair showing a definite inclination to curl formed a bronze cap around his face in a style reminiscent of old Rome.

"Well . . ." Christiane watched anxiously, trying to gauge his reaction. "How do you like your new look?"

He turned his face right, then left, trying to envision it as Leon du Beaupre might remember it from a year ago, comparing the old with the new. Minus the beard and long hair, he might pass muster. Even the loathsome scars and broken nose added a new dimension to his appearance. Similarities existed, yes, but along with them significant differences.

"Do you wish you had had a different barber?"

"No, indeed, Countess." A slow grin spread over his face. "The one I have is quite satisfactory."

More than satisfactory, in fact, he thought as he rubbed his smoothly shaven cheek. A transformation had taken place that far exceeded his expectations. He was a man reborn.

His plan just might work. Jubilant with the results, he scooped an unsuspecting Christiane into his arms and swung her around. She clung to his shoulders, laughing. The laughter slowly died as feelings of another sort clamored for precedence. His eyes held hers captive as he lowered his head. He watched emotion deepen their color until they were almost black. The knowledge that he had this effect on her made him feel both humble and powerful.

His lips settled over hers for a leisurely kiss. He wanted to explore, savor, catalog the tastes and textures that were uniquely hers. With a little purr of contentment, her lips parted, responding to his touch like a flower opening for the sun. The kiss deepened. Time stopped. Two hearts thundered as one.

A knock on the cabin door shattered the moment. "Breakfast," a voice called.

Chapter Fifteen

Christiane hummed to herself as she snipped a piece of thread. Smiling, she smoothed a hand over the plain cotton shirt she had just finished altering. She had cut excess fabric from the hem and used it to make ruffles, which she attached to the cuffs. Reid would be surprised, and she hoped pleased, with the articles of men's clothing the captain had been able to procure. Captain MacGregor had explained that a former crewman had been so eager to jump ship that he had left most of his belongings behind. These would suffice until they reached their destination.

She glanced at the closed door and wished Reid would appear. She hadn't seen him since morning. She blushed at the thought of what might have happened if breakfast hadn't arrived when it did. Though loath to admit it, she missed his company. What sheer and utter foolishness! she chided herself with an impatient shake of her head. In a matter of days they would part, never to see each other again. She needed to put Reid Alexander out of her mind, and concentrate on the task ahead.

The first thing she planned to do was locate her grandfather. After that, she and Grand-père would start fresh. Mechanically she folded the shirt, then sat with it forgotten in her lap. Her thoughts circled back to Reid. She wondered if he also looked forward to a new beginning. What demons propelled him? Why was he so determined to reach New Orleans? He was an enigma; that was his appeal. She had always been fond of puzzles and riddles. He certainly wasn't anyone she'd choose as a lifetime partner. If she ever married again, it would be to someone well established, with a similar background, social standing, and shared interests. Not a self-professed gambler. Not a man with nothing to offer but himself. No—she shook her head—she would definitely not select someone like Reid Alexander if she ever remarried. She was far too practical.

Still, she couldn't quell the tiny quiver of anticipation at the sound of his footsteps in the companionway. Couldn't still the small flutter of excitement at the first sight of him. She rose from the bed where she'd been sewing and crossed the cramped cabin to greet him. His cheeks were ruddy from the wind, and he smelled of the sea, damp wool, and not unpleasantly of musk.

"Did the *capitaine* press you into service?" She resisted the impulse to smooth his rumpled hair.

"No, I offered my services." He shrugged off his jacket. "Several of his crewmen were recruited in St. Domingue to help put down the rebellion, so I lent a hand."

"We're expected for dinner in the *capitaine's* quarters." She held out the shirt she had stitched. "I added a ruffle to the cuffs."

He accepted the shirt, examining the neat, precise

stitches, his eyes warm with appreciation. "Your work is excellent, but you shouldn't have gone to all the trouble."

"The sleeves seemed a trifle short. I thought a ruffle falling over your wrists would help hide the scars."

"Afraid I might embarrass you, Countess?"

"Non." She watched in dismay as the warmth in his eyes turned to frost. "I . . . ah . . . noticed you preferred wide cuffs. I thought the scars about your wrists made you uncomfortable, and hoped you'd feel more at ease if they were concealed."

He searched her face for a hint of insincerity, but finding none, relented. "Sorry if I questioned your motives. I'm not accustomed to such consideration."

Relieved the storm she had expected never materialized, she turned away and began to put away her sewing things. "You took care of me on the journey to Le Cap. It is my turn to take care of you."

"And one more debt is marked 'paid.' "

"Oui. Something like that."

At the sound of splashing water, she resolutely kept her back turned while he stripped off clothes stiff with brine and quickly bathed. She glanced over her shoulder just in time to see him raise the shirt over his head and slip it on. Watching him had a strange effect on her. The air rushed out of her lungs at the sight of his bare torso, each muscle clearly delineated. Her mouth went dry as she followed the wedge of golden hair that tapered into the waist of snug-fitting breeches. She had known for a long time that men admired women's bodies, but until meeting Reid, it had never entered her mind that it could also work in reverse.

"Mind if I borrow your hairbrush?" he asked, already reaching for it.

"Non, of course not."

He put down the brush and turned with an easy grin. "Well, do I meet with your approval?"

She wagged a finger playfully. "If you are fishing for compliments, m'sieur, the smile adds greatly to your appearance. Makes you less fierce, and much more approachable."

His smile faded. "I hope we can be convincing as man and wife. Did the captain happen to mention who will be joining him tonight?"

"He doesn't expect many. The rough water has caused much *mal de mer.*"

"Good." Reid relaxed visibly. "No one must suspect I am anyone other than Etienne Delacroix."

"No one shall, m'sieur." She picked up a light shawl and draped it around her shoulders. "I promise to be a good actress. Of course"—she slanted him a look—"you, too, will have to play your role."

"A loving and devoted husband." He stole a kiss, brash and possessive, then tucked her hand into the crook of his arm. "Come, my little dove. Our audience awaits."

A devilish twinkle livened his usually somber gaze. His lighthearted playfulness delighted her, caught her off guard. *Enchanting.*

With Reid's arm protectively about her waist to steady her, they made their way up the companionway and burst into the captain's quarters on a gust of wind. The door slammed shut behind them. The two occupants in the cabin regarded them with interest.

Captain MacGregor climbed to his feet and lumbered toward them, hand outstretched. He grasped Reid's hand, pumped it vigorously, then slapped him on the back. As he did so, Christiane caught a whiff of spirits on his breath.

"I was ready to send the cabin boy to see what was keeping you two," Captain MacGregor boomed.

"However I tried to dissuade him," a pleasant female voice

offered. "A young couple such as yourselves needs time to enjoy each other's company. Get better acquainted."

Christiane peeked around the captain's ample girth to where an elderly woman in her mid-fifties sat at a long table which was secured to one wall. Gray corkscrew curls framed a plump unlined face with inquisitive blue eyes.

The woman gave her a friendly smile. "The captain has forgotten what it's like to be young and newly married."

Remembering his manners, Ian MacGregor cleared his throat and introduced his guest as Mrs. Frederick Wakefield of New Orleans, Louisiana. "Other than yourselves, Mrs. Wakefield is the only person aboard not indisposed by the rough seas."

"It is a pleasure to meet you, Mrs. Wakefield." Christiane smiled as she slid into the chair Reid held out for her.

The dowager patted the neat bun atop her head. "Call me Polly. All my friends do."

Christiane watched with amusement as Polly Wakefield gave Reid an arch smile as coy as a debutante's and held out her hand.

Reid raised it to his lips. "An honor, madame."

"The honor is mine, M'sieur Delacroix," the woman said, simpering.

Reid tensed for a moment, then recovered. "Friends call me Etienne."

Polly dragged her attention away from Reid and addressed Christiane. "I understand from the captain, my dear, that you and your husband fled that horrible business in St. Domingue."

"*Oui.* My husband and I barely escaped with our lives. Many were not as fortunate." She shuddered, remembering a porcelain doll, its face crushed, its dress bloodstained.

"Terrible thing, that." Ian MacGregor sank heavily into his seat and raised his tankard. "The *Sea Witch* keeps a good supply of rum aboard, but there's some of that fancy French wine for passengers."

Reid picked up the flagon of wine. "Ladies?" When they both nodded their consent, he filled their tankards, then his own.

"You poor child." Polly reached over and patted Christiane's hand. "How terrible to lose everything."

Reid put his arm around Christiane's shoulders. "But we still have each other, and that is all that matters. All else can be replaced."

"Oh, how sweet," Polly cooed, while Christiane shot him a startled look.

"The event, though tragic, taught us to appreciate what is truly important," he elaborated in a somber tone, giving Christiane's shoulders an affectionate squeeze.

She took a quick swallow of wine and nearly choked. He was playing the role of devoted husband with more theatrical flair than she had envisioned.

"It warms my heart to see a young couple so in love. Reminds me of how it used to be with my dearly departed Frederick." Polly dabbed at her eyes with a lace-trimmed, lavender-scented handkerchief.

The door to the captain's quarters swung open and the ship's steward entered with a heavily laden tray. "Ah, dinner," Captain MacGregor exclaimed, rubbing his hands in anticipation.

"Sorry, Cap'n. It ain't nothin' fancy." The steward, a slight, wiry seaman with small black eyes set in a wizened face, set the tray on the table and whipped the covers off dishes. "Seas be too rough for fixin' a proper meal. Cookie's scared o' pots spillin' 'n' gettin' burned."

For Christiane, after she'd spent days existing on fruit and water, the platters of cold meat, smoked fish, cheese, and biscuits spread in front of her looked like a banquet.

Her stomach let out a gurgle of approval loud enough to be heard throughout the cabin. She pressed her hand against her midriff, her cheeks flaming.

The little steward chuckled. "Name's Billy, ma'am. We don't stand much on formality here on the *Sea Witch*, but the food's decent an' the cap'n fair."

Ian MacGregor beamed at the compliment. "Treat the crew well, and they'll treat you well, I always say."

Billy went around the table and offered generous portions to each of the guests. "Not much, but this oughta keep body and soul together until seas are calmer. Lucky fer us, we took on plenty of fresh provisions before we set sail."

Christiane noted that the little steward reserved the choicest pieces for her. She felt alternately grateful and embarrassed by his attention.

"I'll leave ya to enjoy yer dinner," Billy said after making sure nothing more was needed.

Polly waited until appetites had been appeased to begin her questioning. "Forgive my curiosity, Etienne, but I find it odd that you don't have a French accent."

Christiane stabbed a piece of meat with her fork. "He attended school in England."

"I was raised in England by my mother," Reid said simultaneously.

They exchanged guilty glances while Polly looked from one to the other, a confused expression on her face. "What we meant," Christiane explained, recovering, "is that Reid lived with his mother in England where he went to school."

"Ah, yes." Polly nodded thoughtfully. "So that explains it."

Christiane resumed eating, her heart rate returning to normal.

"And what about your father, Etienne? Did he not take an interest in his son?"

Reid shrugged diffidently. "My father was a virtual stranger to me."

"A pity."

"And how is that, madame?"

Christiane listened to the exchange with growing alarm. How naive, how stupid of her and Reid not to have anticipated there might be questions. As it was, they were ill prepared to cope with Polly's avid curiosity.

Polly broke off a piece of bread. "Why, any father would be proud to see the fine man his son has become."

"Thank you," Reid returned.

"I fail to understand how a man can ignore his own child." Polly spread thick, creamy butter over her biscuit and took a dainty bite. "Now take my dear, departed Frederick and myself, for example. We always hoped for a large family, but the good Lord never saw fit to grant our wish. I pray the two of you will be more fortunate. You're such an attractive couple. You'll produce handsome offspring. Are you planning a large family?"

Chrisitiane's cheeks burned. "W-we . . . um . . ."

"I always thought seven a lucky number," Reid interjected smoothly.

"Seven!" Christiane stared at him, her fork poised midway to her lips. Where had this tidbit come from? Had the man gone mad? What nerve! How dare he sit here and discuss the number of children she would bear as calmly as one might discuss the weather?

"Four boys and three girls would be a perfect arrangement," he expounded.

"How wonderful!" Polly beamed her approval. "It's so refreshing to find a man who has given his future family so much thought. Speaks well of his character. You know, don't you dear"—she turned her benevolent gaze on Christiane—"that you're a very fortunate young woman to find such a man."

Christiane made a feeble attempt to return the smile. "Having been an only child, I find the idea of seven children a bit . . . overwhelming."

"If you prefer, love"—Reid smiled at her over the rim of his cup, his eyes dancing with mischief—"we could have four girls and three boys instead."

Christiane waited until Polly was occupied with her meal before shooting him a fulminating look. She could scarcely believe this bizarre conversation. She darted a glance at Captain MacGregor at the head of the table, but saw no help was forthcoming from that quarter. The captain sat slumped in the chair, chin on chest, snoring softly.

"You may discover untold joys in a large family." Reid gave Christiane a bland smile. "Should you prefer an even larger family, my love, I will be only too happy to oblige."

"Oh, my . . ." Polly tittered behind her hand, the girlish gesture at odd variance with her age.

Christiane aimed a kick beneath the table, and felt a certain satisfaction at his grunt of pain when her slippered foot connected with his shin. She glared at him through narrowed eyes, but he grinned back good-naturedly, impervious to her ill humor.

Having missed the byplay, Polly pushed away her plate. "You two seem so well suited. How did you and your husband meet?"

Christiane groaned inwardly. She broke off a piece of cheese and nibbled on it, stalling for time. Meanwhile her mind scrambled frantically for a plausible story. The silence stretched out, with Polly waiting expectantly.

"Go ahead, love," Reid encouraged with a wicked gleam in his silver eyes. "Do tell Polly how we met."

Christiane tapped her foot impatiently. She was going to kill him. The moment they were alone, she was going to kill him. *I handled the last round of questions,* his look seemed to say; *Now it's your turn.* Her imagination invented then rejected various scenarios before settling on the truth. "It was a marriage by proxy."

"A proxy marriage!" Instead of eliciting shock, the announcement had the opposite effect. Polly clapped her hands together in delight. "How wonderfully romantic. I never would have guessed. After watching you together, I thought surely you were a love match."

"I never set eyes on . . . E-Etienne"—she nearly faltered at calling Reid by that name—"until we met in St. Domingue. My husband sent his emissary to France, where the ceremony was conducted before an official. Appropriate documents were signed, and I was given his ring, a family heirloom, to seal the bargain."

"My wife sacrificed her wedding ring to secure our passage out of St. Domingue," Reid explained, intercepting the widow's glance toward Christiane's left hand, now bereft of jewelry. "Never once did she complain."

"Our lives are far more valuable than a pretty piece of colored glass," Christiane added stiffly.

"Absolutely, dear," Polly agreed. Then her affable expression changed to a sterner one. "But you must know that you took a terrible chance marrying a man you had never met. One you knew virtually nothing about. You could have found yourself married to a reprobate instead of a man as devoted and loving as your husband."

Christiane couldn't meet the woman's gaze. She dropped her eyes and shoved her plate away. She thought of Etienne. The widow's description fit him perfectly. What a disaster her marriage to him had been. She felt relieved when it ended, and guilty for feeling relieved. Her guilt was compounded by knowing she had deliberately lied to a sweet elderly lady.

A loud snore erupted from the sleeping captain, so loud it startled him awake. Disoriented, he blinked and squinted at his guests. "Dinner over?"

Polly rose, stifling a yawn. "The sea air makes me sleepy. I'm afraid you young people will have to excuse me."

After bidding their good nights, Christiane suggested they go topside instead of returning to their cabin, and Reid was happy to comply. The sea was too choppy for a turn around the deck, so they lingered at the rail near the bow. Crewmen went about their tasks, adjusting sails and battening hatches, too busy to pay attention to the couple standing at the bow.

Closing her eyes, Christiane lifted her face to the starless sky. She savored the crisp snap of canvas in the wind, the deck heaving beneath her feet, the taste of salt on her lips. "I love it out here."

Reid found himself mesmerized. Her profile was so pure, so perfect, it could be a carved figurehead. But she was too brimming with life, too vibrant, ever to be confused with an effigy. Everything about her screamed energy, vitality. In spite of a privileged background, she had an uncanny ability to appreciate the simpler things of life. She could be as unpredictable as wind and sea, as basic as sun and air. His countess constantly surprised—and delighted.

As he watched, a smile curved her mouth; then a soft chuckle escaped and blossomed into laughter.

"What's so amusing?"

"You." She opened her eyes and turned to him.

"Me? What did I do?"

"You played the besotted bridegroom so well at dinner, Polly is convinced we are a match made in heaven."

The corner of his mouth kicked up in wry amusement.

"My shin will bear the mark of your slipper for days to come."

"Sorry." Her effervescent laughter overrode the muted contrition. "Once I recovered from the shock of finding myself the mother of seven, I was quite in awe of your ingenuity. Particularly the part about having four boys and three girls."

"Or three boys and four girls."

The shared laughter acted as a restorative, a tonic. Reid realized with a start that it had been years since he had indulged in that carefree activity. Until now he had believed the laughter died with Chase. But Christiane Delacroix had revived the lighthearted side he feared he had lost forever. She excelled in bringing out qualities and traits he didn't know existed.

Before they could brace themselves, the *Sea Witch* dove into a deep trough. A formidable wall of water rose in front of them. The sudden motion of the ship threw Christiane against him. Reid caught her to him, preventing her fall. The timbers of the sturdy little ship creaked and groaned, but gradually the vessel began a steady climb upward.

She looked up at him, eyes shining. "Didn't that steal the breath from your body?"

In the dim recesses of his brain, a warning chimed. If he didn't release her immediately, it would be too late. Desire was already clouding reason. He was getting involved deeper and deeper with this woman. That was something he didn't want, didn't need. She distracted him. If he planned to bring down a villain like Leon du Beaupre, he need a clear head.

And if his plan failed, there would be no future at all.

Purposely he set her from him. "The hour is late, the seas rough. I'll take you down below, then offer my help to the crew."

Ignoring the hurt, the confusion, swimming in her eyes, he took her elbow and guided her down the companionway. Damn, he cursed under his breath. Why hadn't he taken what was offered? The former Reid Alexander wouldn't have hesitated. When had all these scruples materialized? Thank goodness the crew was shorthanded. The physical exertion would help take his mind off an enchantress with liquid brown eyes.

Thank goodness for Polly Wakefield, Christiane thought as she readied herself for bed. Dinnertime proved to be the only time she saw Reid. True, they shared the same bunk, but he was usually gone by the time she woke in the morning and stayed on deck late each evening. If not for Polly's cheerful company, the boredom would have been unbearable.

Captain MacGregor had pronounced the foul weather hurricane season. Though the wind hadn't yet reached hurricane proportions, the rough seas, besides incapacitating most passengers, prevented time spent on deck. She put down the hairbrush, climbed into bed, and pulled the covers to her chin against the damp. It was probably a good thing she didn't see much of Reid. He made her feel things she shouldn't feel for a man who wasn't her husband. He distracted her. If she planned to search for her grandfather, she needed to be sensible, practical. To use her head, not an unruly heart.

She rolled onto her side, worries tumbling through her mind. She had no idea where to begin her search for her grandfather. The notion of the once-indomitable Jean-Claude Bouchard, Comte de Varennes, sick and in need, terrified her. Anything could have happened to him since they parted in Calais. She only hoped she wasn't too late.

The cabin door flew open, and Reid entered along with a rush of cold, salty air. In the dim light of the lamp she had left burning, she could see the lines of fatigue in his face, the weary droop of his shoulders. In silence she watched him remove the knit cap one of the crew had lent him, shrug out of his jacket, and toss it aside. He went to the washstand, where he quietly and efficiently bathed.

"You missed dinner tonight," she said softly when he finished. "You must be starving."

He tensed. "I didn't think you'd still be awake."

"There's a plate of food and a tankard of wine waiting on the table."

He cleared his throat and reached for a towel. "That's very thoughtful. Thank you."

She scooted into a sitting position, pulled up her knees, and draped her arms around them. She sensed his dark mood and tried to keep her tone light. "It's the least a wife can do."

He hung the towel on a peg, then crossed the short distance to the small table bolted to the bulkhead and straddled a stool. "If the winds hold strong, we'll reach New Orleans tomorrow."

"Tomorrow . . ." She supposed she should be happy they were going to reach their destination ahead of schedule. Instead she felt a burgeoning sense of loss.

"The weather has proven to be a blessing in disguise," he said, helping himself to a thick slice of cheese.

"That's wonderful. Everyone must be pleased." Why wasn't she happier at the prospect? She had money, independence, youth. Aside from being reunited with her grandfather, what more could she ask for? Yet a curious ache spread throughout her chest in the region of her heart.

An awkward silence engulfed the cabin. Reid quickly

finished his meal, blew out the light, and slipped into the bunk next to her. He shivered as his bare flesh met cool muslin.

"You're cold. Let me warm you." She moved close to share her body warmth.

"This isn't a wise idea, Countess." He tried to inch away, but she placed one arm over his chest to still his efforts and snuggled closer.

"Hush." She laid a finger against his mouth. "You're chilled from your time spent topside. The *capitaine* ought to pay you a crewman's wage."

"He'd probably rather spend the coin on his supply of rum."

"Oui." She gave a rueful laugh. "And if he didn't fall asleep midway through each meal, it would cost him even more."

Reid's chuckle encouraged her to continue. "You have never said exactly what you planned to do in Louisiana."

"I'm going to head north of New Orleans to locate a man by the name of Leon du Beaupre," he replied in a voice hard and cold as a diamond. "The murdering scum killed his own brother, then accused me of the deed."

She gasped. "What happened?"

"I won a plantation outside of New Orleans in a faro game while visiting Barcelona. Leon was furious with his brother, Gaston, for placing its deed on the table. But Gaston was a gambler. He lost on the turn of a card."

"And for that reason you were convicted of murder?" she asked, struggling to understand.

"For that reason . . . and others."

"Tell me," she whispered.

Reid sighed. "I was the last one seen with Gaston alive. The deed to Briarwood was found in my possession the next morning, smeared with blood. And as if there were any lingering doubt about my innocence, a button from the dead man's coat was found in my room. Leon convinced the authorities that when Gaston succeeded in winning back the plantation, I became so enraged that I killed him, then left with the bloodstained deed. I was sentenced to a lifetime of hard labor in a penal colony on Hispaniola."

So that explained the scars, the bitterness. "How did you happen to escape?"

"By chance the prison ship encountered a storm, foundered, and sank. I washed ashore like a piece of driftwood manacled to the corpse of a fellow prisoner. That is how your husband found me."

She traced the ridges of his chest. "I will pray you find this villain and bring him to justice," she murmured.

Absently, he picked up a strand of her hair and ran it through his fingers. "What about yourself, Countess? What are you going to do when we reach Louisiana?"

"I am going to find my grandfather, only I don't know where to begin my search."

"Most ships, or so the crew of the *Sea Witch* have said, dock at major ports along the eastern seaboard. Cities such as New York, Boston, or Baltimore. Perhaps you should start your search there."

"*Oui,*" she agreed with finality. "That is where I shall begin."

"I'm going to miss you, Countess."

A lump lodged in her throat. "I will miss you, too, m'sieur."

He drew her closer, brushed his lips against her hair, skimmed her temple. She raised her face, her eyes fathomless dark pools, and he claimed her mouth for a slow, lingering kiss. He dragged his mouth from hers to nibble a path down her throat, then lightly nip the sensitive junction between her neck and shoulder with his teeth. Her mind emptied.

Lost in a hazy cloud of sensation, she barely felt him slide her nightdress over her shoulders and past her waist. He cupped the fullness of her breast in the palm of his hand, savoring its weight, then moved his thumb across the nipple. She gasped with pleasure as he traced the rosy peak with the tip of his tongue, then drew it into his mouth and sucked. Pleasure rippled through her in ever-widening circles.

"Touching me like that does strange things to me," she managed when she caught her breath.

"Tell me . . ."

"Let me show you."

Christiane surrendered to the temptation to learn his body as intimately as he knew hers. She traced each scar, each hard plane, committing his body to memory. Uneven ridges of flesh interspersed with smooth. She felt his pulse jerk, the heavy pounding of his heart, and felt empowered by the response her touch elicited. Her hand strayed lower, brushed his flat abdomen, and felt taut muscles quiver.

"I'm not sure this is a good idea, Countess," he said between clenched teeth.

"Do not say that," she murmured. She discovered flat male nipples nestled in a thick mat of chest hair. "I do not want to be wise . . . or practical . . . or sensible." Each denouncement was punctuated with a teasing flick of her tongue. She was amazed and delighted at the effect it had on him.

Her inquisitiveness piqued, she allowed her hand to roam lower still, until it encountered the thick shaft of his manhood. Shyly, experimentally, she wrapped her fingers around it and felt it grow harder still beneath her touch.

A small drop of moisture beaded its tip. With a muffled groan, his body grew rigid as he fought for control.

"Enough," he said, flipping her onto her back. "My turn."

He caught her wrists, pinned them above her head, then lavished the same painstaking attention on her. With infinite patience, he kissed and stroked, petted and teased, until she writhed beneath him begging him to end this delicious agony, pleasure so acute it bordered on pain.

Releasing her at last, he spread her thighs and positioned himself between her legs. She was ready, eager. He eased into her, then retreated. Steel encased in velvet. The sensation was exquisite. Explosive. The inner muscles of her pelvis contracted around his shaft, coaxing him deeper, holding him captive.

He moved back and forth, thrusting, retreating, thrusting. Sensations built, strong, fast, powerful. Christiane clutched Reid's shoulders and held fast, trapped between seeking relief from this exquisite torment and wanting it to continue. She felt as though she were hurtling skyward, catapulting into the heavens.

Then the world around her shattered into a million brilliant stars.

Afterward, Christiane drifted back to earth on a current of pure bliss. The memory of Reid calling out her name as he climaxed rang in her heart.

Chapter Sixteen

New Orleans
September, 1791

"Missing your husband, aren't you, dear?" Polly reached across the carriage and patted Christiane's hand.

Christiane gave a guilty start. *"Oui*, madame," she murmured.

She and Reid had bidden each other poignant farewells the night before the *Sea Witch* sailed into the mouth of the Mississippi. That had been over a week ago. Since then she had spent entirely too much time brooding over his departure. She had always prided herself on her practicality, but that quality was being sorely tested. She needed to concentrate on locating her grandfather. Reid needed to find the man who had sent him to prison, to clear his name, to regain lost property. It was time to forge ahead, not sink into the what-could-never-be quagmire. Yet . . .

"You look lovely, but such a sad face." Polly clucked sympathetically. "M'sieur Delacroix will return before you know it. I'm sure he's as anxious as you to complete his business and return to his beautiful bride."

Christiane managed a weak smile. "His business, I am afraid, may take some time. I do not expect to see him any time in the near future." She hated the web of lies, but didn't know how else to account for Reid's absence.

"A night at the opera will perk up your spirits." Polly waved an intricately carved ivory fan.

The carriage slowly wended its way down Calle de Conde, past cafés, coffeehouses, and elegantly appointed gambling houses. Christiane found New Orleans fascinating. Most of the activity centered in Vieux Carré, with its narrow streets laid out in a precise grid pattern. In the brief time she had been here, she had learned many interesting facts. The city had been designed by engineer Adrien de Pauger on a site selected by Jean Baptiste Le Moyne, Sieur de Bienville, son of a wealthy fur trader, during the early days of French rule. Although transferred to Spain by the Treaty of Fontainbleau in 1762, New Orleans remained tenaciously French in spirit and custom.

"There you go again," Polly scolded. "Woolgathering."

"Forgive me if I seem inattentive. I'm still adjusting to the heat and humidity of your city."

Polly waved her fan with more vigor. "After twenty years, I'm still trying to achieve that end. Wait until July and August, when it becomes truly unbearable."

Christiane murmured an appropriate reply. She didn't plan on remaining in New Orleans long enough to find out about their steamy summers. If she didn't locate her grandfather soon, she would search elsewhere. She didn't want to risk a chance encounter with Reid Alexander, and the complications that would ensue. He had made vague references to heading toward a plantation north of the city, but knowing he was still in the vicinity of New Orleans made her uneasy. How would she ever explain his sudden reappearance without arousing further suspicion?

"I'm so pleased you changed your plans and remained in New Orleans even though it is only for a short time." Polly nodded pleasantly to an acquaintance in a passing carriage, then picked up the thread of her conversation. "As I explained when we docked, Governor Miró is welcoming émigrés fleeing the French revolution. Your grandfather very likely could be among them."

"Until I heard that, I was preparing to begin my search in one of the larger seaports along the Atlantic coast."

"I think you are wise to stay in New Orleans. Tomorrow I've arranged a meeting with the mother superior at the Ursuline convent. She has many contacts and is well informed of the happenings in and around the city. Perhaps she can shed some light on his whereabouts."

Christiane gave the older woman a fond smile. "I must admit I'm growing more discouraged each day. There is no record of Grandfather's arrival anywhere. No one seems to have heard of him. I am beginning to think Reid was right when he suggested beginning my search in New York or Boston."

"Reid?" Polly asked with a quizzical frown. "Who is Reid?"

The moment the name slipped, Christiane realized her mistake. Angry color suffused her cheeks at her stupid blunder. Frantically she tried to fabricate a plausible excuse. "When we are alone, Etienne prefers that I call him Reid. That is the name his mother used for him. It wasn't until much later, after inheriting his father's estate, that he assumed the name on his birth record."

Polly nodded knowingly. "My husband and I had pet names for each other, too, when no one was around."

Christiane felt a sharp jab of envy. The Wakefields had shared a bond so strong that not even death could sever it. Once again thoughts of Reid intruded. For a short time they had been friends—and lovers. She wondered if, under different circumstances, they could have forged a link just as unbreakable as the Wakefields'.

"You still miss your husband very much, don't you, Polly?" Christiane asked gently.

The widow's eyes grew suspiciously bright. "Yes, but Frederick wouldn't want me to mourn. He'd want me to enjoy life."

"Have you ever considered remarrying?"

"Heavens, no! I try to keep busy, but it's lonely at times without someone by your side to share life's little absurdities."

Just as it was lonely without Reid. Christiane watched the parade of buildings roll past: small one-story Creole cottages, and other, more elaborate structures with encircling galleries and pretty courtyards, a few adorned with ornate iron grillwork. It made her wonder where Reid was, what he was doing. Who he was with. Irritated to find herself preoccupied with thoughts of him once more, she sternly ordered herself to stop. Unconsciously she squared her shoulders and firmed her jaw.

"Here we are," Polly said in a chirp as they approached a rather plain wooden building near the intersection of Calle de Maine. "This building also doubles as a ballroom. Three years ago a disastrous fire started not far from here. Nearly half the town was in ashes."

The gaiety of the people gathered in front of the ballroom gave no indication that they had ever experienced a hardship of any sort, much less an inferno. Everyone appeared dressed in the height of fashion, clustered in small groups, many animatedly chattering in French. The driver helped them to the banquette, then left after promising to return later.

"We're in for a special treat this evening: *Don Giovanni*, an opera by Wolfgang Amadeus Mozart," Polly explained, then lowered her voice to a whisper. "I knew this would be a popular event. The Spaniards have a perpetual fascination with their legendary lover, Don Juan."

Christiane stifled a groan. She felt caught in a conspiracy. Everywhere she turned she was reminded of love and longing. *Love?* She brought herself up short at the notion. *Preposterous! Impossible!*

Someone brushed against her on the crowded banquette and she glanced up.

"Pardonnez-moi, mademoiselle."

Christiane found herself staring into a pair of bold black eyes set in an incredibly handsome face—handsome, but also arrogant and smug. The man brazenly appraised her, making her feel naked, vulnerable beneath his insolent perusal.

"Shall we go in?" Polly asked, unaware of the man ogling her companion.

"Oui." Christiane turned away, eager to escape the stranger's unsettling black gaze.

Together she and Polly joined the others and found their seats. This was the sort of evening her grandfather would enjoy. Knowing it was futile but doing it anyway, Christiane scanned the audience. She sucked in a sharp breath when she spotted a slightly built elderly gentleman with a shock of silver hair. Then he turned his head, and her fragile bubble of optimism burst.

"What is it, dear?" Polly asked. "You look as though you've just seen a ghost."

Christiane let out a shaky sigh. "That gentleman near the orchestra pit gave me a start. With his back turned, I thought for an instant he might be . . ."

"Never fear, child. If your grandfather is in New Orleans we'll find him."

Christiane smiled at Polly with genuine affection. "You've been so kind. I don't know how I would have managed this past week without you."

"You would have managed even without my help. It gives me great pleasure to be of some assistance. You wouldn't deny that to an old woman, would you?" Polly tapped a finger contemplatively against one plump cheek. "I must say that elderly gentleman you pointed out is most attractive."

Christiane laughed softly, feeling privileged at having glimpsed what her new friend must have been like as a girl. "Grandfather was considered quite dashing in his youth."

"If he resembles that gentleman in the front row, he still is very attractive."

Soon after the music started, Christiane willed her troubles to dissolve and allowed herself to be drawn into the powerful score. Waves of music washed over her, temporarily blocking everything else from her mind.

At intermission, Polly introduced her to some of her acquaintances. While they stood talking, a slender black youth approached with a rose in one hand. He offered it to Christiane with a broad smile. "This for beautiful mam'selle."

"Go ahead, dear," Polly encouraged. "You don't want to offend your admirer."

Christiane reluctantly accepted the bloom. Before she could ask the boy who it was from he had disappeared into the crowd. She stared at the single perfect rose of deep crimson. She used to love roses, but no more. Not since Etienne. Already the sweet scent was having an untoward effect. Memories of Etienne's aborted efforts at lovemaking came back with a rush, filling her with revulsion, leaving her shaken. The rose slipped through her fingers and was accidentally crushed beneath someone's heel.

"Sorry, so sorry." A slight man in his early thirties with thinning brown hair apologized profusely. "Please allow me to buy you another."

"Non, non," she answered hurriedly. "That is not necessary. I do not want another."

When the man left after once more apologizing, Christiane found Polly watching her curiously. "Roses are lovely, but the scent makes me ill," she explained.

Polly nodded. "I noticed you suddenly became pale. If you'd rather leave . . ."

Forcing a smile, Christiane linked her arm through that of her companion. *"Non,* I am feeling much better. Shall we return to our seats?"

The incident with the rose spoiled Christiane's enjoyment of the final act. Though she had nothing concrete to base her suspicions on, she sensed that the rose had been a gift from the dark-eyed man with the bold stare. There was something about the man she didn't like, didn't trust, though she couldn't quite pinpoint the cause.

Then it came to her.

She sat up straighter, her spine rigid. He reminded her of Etienne. Although on the surface the two were as different as night and day, there were subtle similarities. Both possessed the same smug superiority, the same everything-is-mine-for-the-taking attitude. Both had assessed her like a piece of merchandise on the auction block. But while Etienne's gaze had been frigid, this man's burned.

At last the final notes of *Don Giovanni* faded into silence.

Christiane and Polly joined the others filing up the aisle. The street in front of the theater was clogged with carriages. Polly's driver was nowhere in sight, so they contented themselves with waiting along with the rest of the crowd. While they waited, Polly introduced Christiane to more of her friends. Interested in everything and everyone, Christiane found it easy to see why the widow was so popular. People seemed to gravitate toward her.

Now that the sun had set, the temperature had grown cooler. As Christiane stepped back to drape a lacy shawl over her shoulders, her heel caught in the wooden banquette, throwing her off balance.

A firm hand at her elbow steadied her. "Are you all right, mademoiselle?" a deep, melodic, masculine voice asked.

"M'sieur du Beaupre!" Polly exclaimed. "Thank you for saving my new friend from a nasty fall."

"My dear Mrs. Wakefield." A fashionably attired man bent low over the widow's hand.

Christiane recognized him as the one who had boldly assessed her earlier.

"M'sieur du Beaupre," Polly said, giving him a coy smile. "What a pleasant surprise."

A river of revulsion flowed through Christiane as she found herself face-to-face with Reid's nemesis—a man so dastardly he killed his own brother.

"I heard you were spending most of your time at your plantation," Polly chattered, unaware of Christiane's shock.

"You've heard correctly, dear lady. Briarwood has just been completed. I intend to have a housewarming soon. I hope you'll honor me with your presence, and"—he favored Christiane with a smile meant to charm—"bring your beautiful companion with you."

Polly's hand fluttered to her throat. "I'd be delighted to attend, but I can't speak for my friend."

"The lady must be newly arrived in New Orleans. I would not easily forget someone with her enchanting beauty," he said, combining gallantry with charm. "I don't believe we've had the good fortune to meet. I had hoped dear Mrs. Wakefield would supply the necessary introduction."

"Where are my manners?" Polly twittered, then quickly amended the oversight, subtly stressing the word *madame* to indicate Christiane was married and unavailable.

"The pleasure is all mine." Leon brushed warm lips across Christiane's hand. "I must confess, I haven't been able to take my eyes off you all evening. You've cast a spell."

"You, m'sieur, are well versed in the art of flattery." She removed her hand as quickly as possible.

"*Madame* Delacroix . . . ?" He made a moue of regret. "I prayed it would be mademoiselle. How foolish of me."

"Madame Delacroix's husband is away on business," Polly said, a firmness in her tone that hadn't been present earlier. "The poor dear misses him dreadfully."

Leon ignored Polly as though she were no longer present, all his attention on Christiane. "How unfortunate for you, madame. Perhaps, in M'sieur Delacroix's absence, you will permit me to show you our fair city. Many citizens refer to it as 'Beautiful Crescent' because of the way it's situated on the river bend."

"How interesting," Christiane murmured politely. "Your offer is very generous, M'sieur du Beaupre, but . . ."

"Her husband is quite jealous and would take offense." A familiar voice completed her sentence.

Christiane whirled around. The blood drained from her face, leaving her light-headed. Wind roared in her ears, blocking out all other sound. With pupils dilated and fixed, she greedily drank in every detail of Reid's appearance. Dressed conservatively but with simple elegance in a blue-gray jacket, white waistcoat, and black breeches, he looked wonderful—tanned, fit, with rugged appeal shining through a thin guise of sophistication.

Reid placed a hand at her waist. "Surprised, my dove?"

"M'sieur Delacroix!" Polly spoke loudly into the void. "It seems fate has intervened in reuniting two lovers. What a delightful surprise! Your wife was prepared for a lengthy absence."

After giving the widow a tight smile, Reid shifted his attention back to Christiane. From the scowl on his face, he didn't appear happy to see her. "I did not expect to find you still in New Orleans," he said, his tone accusatory. "I thought you would be on your way to New York."

"I thought your business would take longer to conclude," she replied stiffly, beginning to recover from the initial shock.

"What a happy circumstance for both of you." Polly beamed. "How frightfully disappointing if you had returned early only to find your wife no longer in New Orleans."

"*Oui,*" Christiane echoed in a hollow voice. "A frightful disappointment, indeed."

"Devastating," Reid concurred, his tone flat.

His black eyes darting from one to the other, Leon du Beaupré observed the interaction between the couple with keen interest.

Polly smiled with renewed determination. "I tried to convince Christiane you wouldn't stay away longer than necessary. Admit it now, Etienne, you missed her as much as she missed you."

Christiane tapped her fan against the palm of her hand. "My letter informing you of my decision to remain in New Orleans must have missed you."

"Just as mine informing you that my business came to a premature conclusion must have missed you," Reid parried.

Leon cleared his throat to gain their attention.

Belatedly, Christiane realized the men had not been formally introduced. She performed the courtesy quickly, her heart in her throat, praying Leon wouldn't recognize Reid, then deftly drew attention back to herself. "My husband and I recently arrived from St. Domingue, where Etienne owned a magnificent plantation. Alas, we lost everything in the recent slave revolt."

Leon spared Reid barely more than a glance. "My previous offer still stands, madame. Perhaps both you and your husband will visit me soon at Briarwood."

Reid spoke before Christiane could phrase a polite refusal. "My wife and I are pleased to accept your gracious invitation."

"Very well. I shall be looking forward to your visit with great anticipation." His gaze lingering on Christiane, Leon made a short, formal bow, then departed with a smile wreathing his handsome face.

"I daresay"—Polly was the first to speak—"Leon du Beaupre was quite smitten with you, dear. It's fortunate your husband returned when he did. Du Beaupre can be very persistent when he wants something badly. A little too persistent, some claim."

Reid took each woman by an elbow and steered them through the crowd, which was beginning to thin. "What makes you say that, Polly?"

"Quite a rivalry existed between Leon and his older brother, Gaston. Leon resented Gaston because of the plantation Gaston was having built. Leon seemed to think it should be theirs equally, but Gaston refused, insisting the funds were his alone, that he was entitled to them as firstborn. Granted, their father's will was written before Leon's birth, and nearly ten years separated the brothers. Unfortunately their father contracted yellow fever and died without ever changing his will.'' Polly waved as a carriage rounded the corner. "There's my driver now.''

Once they were settled in the conveyance, Christiane retreated into stony silence. Though she had missed Reid more than she cared to admit, his return presented a whole new set of problems. Reid hadn't seemed any happier to see her. Polly Wakefield obviously expected them to behave as husband and wife. The woman would be scandalized if she knew the truth. And Reid's mission would be endangered. What was she supposed to do? Continue the charade?

"From what you just said, the du Beaupre brothers weren't close." Reid flicked a speck of lint from his breeches.

"Quite the contrary." Polly eagerly picked up the story. "Leon and Gaston were constantly feuding. Everyone was surprised to learn they planned a trip to Spain together. Some went so far as to predict that only one would return.''

"Is that right?''

Polly's vigorous nod sent her gray curls bobbing. "No one was really surprised to discover that Gaston had been murdered. The shock came in learning that Leon wasn't responsible.''

The conversation drifted to a variety of topics on the short drive to the house on Calle Real, where Christiane had taken up residence. Polly did the majority of the talking while Reid made an occasional comment. Upon reaching their destination, Reid climbed down first, then wordlessly helped Christiane alight. She could feel the warm imprint of his fingers through the fabric of her gown. The faint scent of sandalwood seemed to cling to him. The moment her feet touched ground, she stepped away, trying to escape the sensual net his nearness always cast.

"Now don't forget," Polly reminded them. "Both of you be ready tomorrow morning at ten o'clock."

Christiane adjusted her lace wrap and avoided looking at Reid. "I doubt my husband will be able to accompany us. In all likelihood, he'll have business matters to conduct."

"Nonsense," Reid replied. "I'll be more than happy to arrange my schedule around yours, *chérie*, but you've neglected to tell me where we're going."

Polly saved Christiane the necessity of answering Reid directly. "To the Ursuline convent. The mother superior may be able to help Christiane locate her dear grandfather, the Comte de Varennes."

"We'll be ready promptly at ten o'clock," Reid answered firmly.

Polly regarded the couple soberly, her sunny smile absent for once. "Life is short, children, with many unexpected twists and turns. Don't waste a precious moment on silly misunderstandings. It's rare to find a soul that mirrors your own." After imparting this final bit of wisdom, she instructed her driver to drive off.

Reid and Christiane stood on the banquette, watching the carriage roll down the street. Christiane felt appropriately chastened by Polly's little speech. Inwardly she shriveled from the mild reprimand delivered with the best of intentions. She hated lying to Polly, hated deceiving someone of whom she had grown inordinately fond. Her own reputation notwithstanding, there was nothing she could do short of confessing the truth, and thereby exposing Reid as a murderer, an escaped prisoner.

Why did Reid have to reappear and complicate her life? Why couldn't he have stayed away? Her temper began to simmer. Turning on her heel, she pushed open the tall gate and marched across the small enclosed courtyard and up the flight of steps to the living quarters on the second floor. The sound of Reid's footsteps told her he followed close behind.

She traversed the narrow gallery that encircled the second story, flung open the door, and stepped inside. She turned on him, dark eyes flashing, hands on hips. "What do you think you're doing? You can't stay here."

He strolled around the drawing room, investigating the neat, tasteful furnishings with interest. "Why not?" he asked affably.

"Why not?" She flung out a hand impatiently. "Because we're not married, you dolt! What will people think?"

He gave a casual shrug. "The question is, Countess, what will they think if we don't?"

She ignored his rebuttal. "This entire situation is preposterous! You are not even supposed to be here. I thought you were going north to . . ." She floundered as the name of the town eluded her.

"Baton Rouge," he supplied, flinging himself into a chair and dangling one long leg over its arm. "And you, *chérie*, were supposed to be on your way to New York or Boston."

Her lower lip jutted mutinously. "Well, I'm not."

"Obviously."

"You can't stay here," she repeated obstinately.

"People will turn a blind eye on a husband and wife who lead separate lives, but not on those who live separately."

As much as it galled her, she was forced to admit he was right. Biting back a scathing remark, she removed her lacy shawl, her movements abrupt, jerky, and tossed it over the back of the settee.

"Have you given any consideration as to how you're going to explain our living apart to your dear friend Polly?

I can see from your expression that you haven't," he continued, pressing his advantage. "And how would that sweet soul react if she learned we shared intimate quarters without benefit of matrimony? All her romantic illusions would be shattered."

Christiane snatched the delicate lace wrap from the settee, crumpled it into a ball, and hurled it at him. "I don't want you here!"

Reid caught it effortlessly in one hand. "I see your aim hasn't improved in my absence." Springing from the chair, he looped the shawl around her shoulders in one smooth, easy motion and pulled her close. "Does having me back in your life make you uneasy, Countess?"

"D-don't be ridiculous," she stammered. She felt imprisoned, mesmerized, by eyes that gleamed like quicksilver and a rich baritone that flowed like honey.

The lacy shawl fluttered to the floor. Capturing her chin with his left hand, he rubbed the pad of his right thumb over her full lower lip. "Afraid I'll take unfair advantage?"

"Of course not." It was becoming increasingly hard to speak, think, breathe.

"Good." He continued the sensual assault on her mouth. "I posed no threat either on St. Domingue or aboard the *Sea Witch*. And," he said with a wicked smile, "if memory serves, you were the one who instigated the lovemaking on St. Domingue."

"No gentleman would remind a lady of such a thing." She shoved him away, but immediately regretted the loss of contact. She wanted to be close. Wanted him to kiss her, hold her. Make love to her. He stirred feelings she didn't want to acknowledge. Inexplicably, this realization both stunned and frightened her.

"Ah, Countess." Reid laughed. "When are you ever going to admit I'm a rogue, not a gentleman?"

"How can you make light of the situation?" she railed, resorting to anger to replace more volatile emotions. She needed to distance herself, rather than succumb to the strong tug of physical attraction. "What did you hope to accomplish by confronting Leon du Beaupre? What if he had recognized you?"

"Would that bother you?" His gaze leisurely traveled over her, beginning with her mouth, then returned to linger on the swell of her breasts enticingly displayed above the daring décolletage of her black silk gown.

"He could have you returned to prison. Or worse, he could have you executed."

The blunt reminder shattered the sensual undertones. Reid circled the room restlessly. "Tonight was as good a time as any to see if du Beaupre would recognize me. My appearance has altered since Barcelona. I need to move in the same social circle in the hope of discovering something that might lend proof of my innocence."

"I once boasted that I'd bargain with the devil himself if it meant saving my life and that of my grandfather. Beware, Reid; the devil will exact a price."

He stopped prowling to stand in front of her, close but not touching. They studied each other warily; then Reid spoke, breaking the tense silence. "If you really and truly believe me, Christiane," he said in a low, somber tone, "you won't interfere when I'm close to proving my innocence."

The request hung heavy between them. An odd sensation filled her chest, making it ache. The feeling was so unfamiliar that at first she didn't recognize it, couldn't call it by name. Then it struck her, staggered her. Simple as blinking. Complex as the universe. The emotion that rocked her being did have a name—and its name was love.

"Well, Countess, what's your answer?" Reid was relentless in his quest. "I saved your life. Here's your chance to save mine."

"Very well," she managed to whisper. "You may stay."

He blew out a pent-up breath, then plunged one hand through his short locks, a gesture Christiane found endearingly familiar. "One word of caution, Countess."

"And that is . . ." she prompted when he appeared reluctant to continue.

"Women often confuse physical attraction with love." Shifting his weight from one leg to the other, he dropped his gaze. "I don't want you to make that mistake. Keep in mind we come from different worlds. I'm a convict—you're a countess. There's no future for us."

Speech was impossible around the lump in her throat, so she simply nodded. Although she knew his reasoning was sound, hearing the words spoken aloud was excruciatingly painful. Where was her usual practicality? Why had it deserted her? When had emotion overwhelmed logic? How had the dictates of her heart overruled those of her head?

Yet in spite of questions, in spite of doubts, reservations, and fears, she deeply loved the man who had dispassionately informed her there could be no future.

Chapter Seventeen

Christiane and Reid were ready and waiting when Polly arrived promptly at ten the next morning. After their discussion the previous night, Reid had left and returned shortly before daybreak with his belongings. In no time at all, he was installed in the small bedroom at the back of the house.

As they climbed into the waiting carriage, both were determined to give Polly the impression that their differences had been reconciled. In spite of their best intentions, the situation seemed awkward. To avoid looking at Reid directly, Christiane adjusted the sheer white fichu tucked into the neckline of her rust-and-black striped gown, then fussed with the ribbons of her leghorn straw bonnet. Reid tugged at his waistcoat.

"Stop fidgeting, my dears." Polly tilted her parasol to block the sun. "I have a feeling the mother superior will be able to help us."

Reid picked up the cue. "Even if we're not successful today it doesn't mean that we won't be tomorrow."

Christiane sighed. "I've been through this numerous times. Each time I think perhaps I will find my grandfather—and each time I leave disappointed. Instead of getting easier, it gets harder and harder."

"Try not to worry; I'm here now. We can search together."

Oddly enough, his words helped. She knew him well enough to detect his sincerity. Experience had taught her that Reid could be depended upon in a crisis. He was rock steady; his resolve never wavered. Maybe he felt he owed her this in return for her cooperation, but whatever the reason, his presence was comforting.

"It's a blessing to have a loved one near in times like these," Polly concurred, beaming at Reid with approval.

The Ursuline convent sat on a large tract of land. Christiane eyed with detachment the imposing three-story structure with dormers parading around a steep gabled roof. The carriage slowed, then turned and passed through a brick porte cochere into a quiet and serene courtyard. An herb garden occupied one end, a rose garden the other.

Polly couldn't resist reciting a bit of history for her guest's benefit. "The convent was spared during the great fire of 1788 thanks to a Negro bucket brigade. They managed to save not only the convent, but the Royal Hospital and the adjoining barracks."

As Reid assisted the women from the carriage, his gaze swept over the stately edifice. "It would have been a grave loss."

"Indeed. The Ursulines are one of New Orleans' greatest assets." Polly smoothed the wrinkles from her lavender skirt. "Following the Natchez massacre, the nuns opened their doors to the orphaned children of the French colonists slaughtered at Fort Rosalie. They are not only responsible for the education of the daughters of plantation owners and city elite, but hold special classes for Negro and Indian girls, instructing them in the care of the silkworm and the making of silk."

Their footsteps rang across the stone courtyard. A little black-habited nun answered the door on the first ring and silently escorted them down a wide hallway. The muffled sound of girls' voices raised in song could be heard through the convent's thick walls. The nun led them through a small antechamber and knocked on a massive oak door.

"Entrez," a voice bid from inside.

Mother Trudeau, a tall, dignified woman, carefully closed a ledger and rose to greet her guests. "Mrs. Wakefield," she greeted Polly warmly. "You're looking wonderfully rested after your long trip."

"Thank you, Mother." Polly clasped the woman's hand. "It was so kind of you to grant us an audience."

"After everything you've done for my students, you have only to ask."

Polly brushed aside the praise with a wave of a dimpled hand. "I had hoped perhaps you could help us locate Jean-Claude Bouchard, Comte de Varennes, the grandfather of my dear friend, Madame Delacroix."

Mother Trudeau shifted her gaze to Christiane, her clear blue eyes kind, but shrewd. "Sit down, *s'il vous plaît.*" She indicated several wooden chairs arranged in a precise row before her desk, then waited until the women were seated. Reid elected to stand slightly behind Christiane. "Now tell me," the nun said gently, "how I may be of service."

Her hands tightly clasped in her lap, Christiane leaned forward in her earnestness, only dimly aware of Reid's hand on her shoulder.

When Christiane's recitation ended, the nun stared contemplatively over steepled fingers. Her heavy brows puckered in a frown. "I vaguely recall one of my colleagues mentioning an elderly gentleman who was quite ill upon his arrival. Unless I'm mistaken, his arrival coincides with the time period you describe."

Christiane gripped the arms of her chair. Only Reid's hand on her shoulder kept her from leaping out of her seat. Questions tumbled out. "Is he here? Do you recall his name? Is he still alive?"

Mother Trudeau's smile was a picture of sympathy and understanding. "No, child, the gentleman is not here, but let me make some inquiries."

"How soon will we know something?" Polly asked.

"This may take a day or two." The nun rose from her chair, signaling that the meeting had been concluded. "I will contact you when I have more information."

Christiane got to her feet as if in a daze. She could scarcely believe it. Finally, after all these months, she was close to being reunited with her grandfather. *"Merci,* Mother Trudeau, *merci."*

"It's a bit early to be thanking me. And, child . . ."

Christiane turned to look at the nun expectantly. *"Oui,* Mother . . . ?"

"Do not set your hopes too high. If the gentleman in question was indeed your grandfather, he was quite ill. In all likelihood he may not have survived."

Christiane swallowed hard, then left the mother superior's office, grateful for Reid's firm arm around her shoulders.

"A prayer to St. Ursula might be in order," Polly murmured. "I'll light a candle."

The occupants lapsed into silence during the short drive to Christiane's home. Polly tried to offer a final bit of advice before leaving Christiane in Reid's care. "Either way, dear, it's best to know the truth rather than harbor false hope. At least your mind will be at peace."

Christiane nodded dully. Everything inside her wanted to scream a denial, insist that her grandfather was alive and well. That he would be found any day, hale and hearty. But the practical, sensible side of her nature knew she must prepare for the worst.

"Please let me know the minute you get word from Mother Trudeau," Polly said as the carriage moved off.

The afternoon and evening stretched interminably. Christiane alternately paced and stared off into space. She made endless laps around the gallery encircling the upper level until Dulcie, a free woman of color that Christiane had hired to cook and clean, planted her ample girth directly in her path.

"You gonna wear a hole in the floor, if'n you don't stop that," Dulcie declared.

Christiane rubbed her arms. "I just can't seem to sit still."

Dulcie planted her feet firmly, arms akimbo. "Well, you gonna sit still long 'nough to eat some supper, else I have Mr. Reid tie you to a chair."

She whirled around at the sound of Reid's deep chuckle coming from just inside the French doors. "I'd have to do it, too. Dulcie's not a woman to trifle with. I wouldn't want to have her angry at me."

"Very well," she muttered through gritted teeth. She marched inside, yanked out a dining room chair, and plopped herself down at the table. "Now, everyone satisfied?"

Dulcie clucked her tongue and shook her head. "Missus, if'n you always like this, I go cook fer someone else. Devil got you today."

Christiane heaved a sigh, and drummed her fingers

against the table. She didn't need anyone to remind her she was cranky and out of sorts. She didn't even like being around herself, but her nerves felt taut as violin strings and ready to snap.

Dulcie bustled out, still muttering under her breath, and returned shortly with a tureen of spicy bouillabaisse and a platter of fresh-baked corn bread. After ladling hearty portions, she left the dining room. "Think it's time fer a visit with the widder woman in Bayou St. John. Get me some gris-gris to ward off evil spirits."

Christiane and Reid exchanged glances. "There's no need for any magic potions, Dulcie," Reid said in a stern voice. "Missus apologizes for being so difficult and promises to eat her dinner. Don't you, Countess?"

She shot him a fulminating look, but obediently picked up her spoon. "Sorry, Dulcie. You don't need gris-gris."

Dulcie pursed her lips and narrowed her eyes. When she saw Christiane spear a piece of crayfish, she gave a nod of satisfaction so vigorous that it sent her tignon wobbling. "See she clean her plate, Mr. Reid."

"Yes, ma'am," Reid said with a broad wink.

When the servant left the room, he broke off a chunk of corn bread. "I like Dulcie. She's not afraid to speak her mind. Far different from those at Belle Terre."

"That's why I hired her," she returned, still in ill humor.

Reid watched her speculatively. She ate with no real appreciation of the tasty dish, nibbling on a crumb of corn bread, selecting only the smallest morsels of shrimp and fish. Was worry about her grandfather the only thing troubling her? He wondered. Or was there something else? Something of even greater magnitude? What if . . . ?

His own appetite suddenly vanished as an unwelcome thought intruded. Could she be pregnant? He began doing a rapid series of calculations, then gave up in frustration.

He had no real notion of the vagaries of a woman's body. Still, it was entirely possible. They had made love not only on St. Domingue, but also several times the last night of their voyage. But it wasn't the notion that she might be carrying his child that chilled him to the marrow. It was the fact that if he didn't prove his innocence, she would have to raise that child alone. His child would forever bear the stigma of having a father who was a convicted murderer.

"Christiane . . . ?" He cleared his throat and broached the subject cautiously. "This ill humor and lack of appetite couldn't be for any reason other than your grandfather, could it?"

She stared at him aghast. "Are you asking . . . ?"

He steeled himself against the tempest brewing in her liquid brown gaze. "Are you by any chance . . . pregnant?"

"Non," she snapped. "I am not pregnant."

Reid breathed a sigh of relief and vowed not to take any more chances in the future, regardless of how tempting the offer. "You're certain, then?"

Her cheeks flamed with color. Flinging the napkin aside, she sprang to her feet, the chair scraping on the wood floor. *"Oui!* Positive." She pointed to the door. "I don't need a nursemaid. Go! Do whatever it is you do. Just leave me alone!"

"Fine!" Reid tossed his napkin down and rose. He didn't need this aggravation. All afternoon he had tried his best to distract her—brought her needlework, a novel, a glass of wine. And this was his thanks? Temperamental, ill-humored, unpredictable! He'd never understand women. Turning on his heel, he stalked out.

Christiane was blinking back tears when Dulcie returned minutes later. She wagged her head as she began to collect the dishes. "Married got teeth," she muttered under her breath, but loud enough to be heard.

Christiane dabbed at her eyes with the corner of a napkin. "For heaven's sake, Dulcie, stop mumbling." She sniffed. "If you've got something to say, come out with it."

"What I means is married life ain't all happy. There be troubles, too, even in good married life."

"You're absolutely right, Dulcie," Christiane concurred heartily. "Married got teeth."

"Your drink, m'sieur."

Leon du Beaupre reached for the glass without looking up. He tapped ash from his cigar into a shallow crystal bowl. The gambling hall was crowded with people testing their luck at a variety of games, but Leon barely noticed the activity swirling around him. For now he was content to sit in a corner, partially hidden from view by a potted fern. Other matters occupied his mind. Earlier that day he had seen a carriage roll past carrying the delectable Christiane Delacroix. She intrigued him, whet his appetite in a way no woman had in years. She was beautiful, yes, but he also sensed she possessed a fiery spirit and passion. She would be a worthy consort for a man with his discerning taste. Briarwood needed a queen. Pity the lady was already taken.

The bourbon traced a heated path down his throat. Leon puffed his cigar. Something odd had transpired between husband and wife at the opera the night before. He had sensed undercurrents beneath overly polite facades. For a couple unexpectedly reunited, their greetings had been strained instead of joyful. There had been no smiles, no outward displays of affection. Odd, he thought. Why wasn't

M'sieur Delacroix happier about seeing his beauteous wife? Perhaps he had one of the exotic quadroons stashed in a little house on Rampart Street.

A round of enthusiastic applause drew his attention to the faro table. He squinted through the haze of smoke and recognized the newcomer as none other than Etienne Delacroix himself.

The dealer shuffled the deck of cards, cut it, and placed it in the dealing box. Delacroix, he noted, wagered like a man who couldn't afford a heavy loss. As he continued to observe, the man lit a thin cheroot and blew out a stream of smoke. Something about the elegantly casual way the French planter held the thin cigar struck a disturbingly familiar chord. Leon's dark brows beetled in a frown. He couldn't dismiss the nagging suspicion their paths had crossed before. But where?

A hazy image formed in his brain. A gambling hall in Barcelona. A man called Reid Alexander. Ridiculous. He raised his glass, drained it, then demanded another. Reid Alexander was rotting in some Spanish hellhole. No way the man could have escaped a penal colony, acquired wealth and a plantation, and wed the enticing Christiane.

He began to feel somewhat calmer now that the effects of the bourbon were kicking in. Yes, the man who called himself Etienne Delacroix did bear a vague resemblance to Reid Alexander. But there were differences as well. This man was broader through the shoulders, thicker through the chest. The features, too, were different. Alexander had been a bit of a dandy in appearance. Delacroix looked tough, rugged, definitely not someone to toy with.

Still, he mused, it never hurt to be cautious. Leon drew deeply on his cigar. He had friends in St. Domingue. He'd simply make a few discreet inquiries.

* * *

The following morning, Christiane rose shortly before dawn and quietly left the house. Reid heard her leave and decided to see where she was headed. Even in the short time he had been in New Orleans, he knew it wasn't safe for an unescorted woman to roam the streets. Robberies were prevalent, and except for a few soldiers who occasionally patrolled, police protection was nonexistent. The city seemed to attract a wealth of gamblers and unsavory characters. Reid nearly laughed aloud. Many who knew his background would describe him in exactly those terms.

Keeping to the shadows, Reid admired the gentle sway of her hips, the trim, straight back, the proud angle of her head. As she turned toward Plaza de Armas, the spire of the Church of St. Louis pointed toward the predawn sky. Christiane's destination finally occurred to him. Even as the realization ran through his mind, she joined the others, mostly older women, who made a practice of attending the first Mass of the day.

Christiane raised the shawl around her shoulders to cover her dark hair, then disappeared inside. Reid thought briefly about returning home, then, on impulse, entered the church and slipped into the back pew. It was dark inside except for the light from tall candles glowing on the center altar and devotionals on either side. The air smelled faintly of melted candle wax and incense.

A priest accompanied by two young servers appeared from the sacristy, and the Mass began. It had been years since Reid had been inside a church. He had been hardly more than a boy when he had foolishly believed God would hear his urgent plea. But if God had heard the frantic prayer to spare his brother's life, He had ignored the request.

While the priest conducted a ceremony centuries old, Reid felt old resentments slip away. Though he didn't understand any words of Latin, he felt a certain peacefulness descend. Although out of practice, he offered a hasty prayer that Christiane's grandfather would be found alive and well. And if not, just as Polly had wished for yesterday, he prayed she would find solace in knowing the truth.

Christiane remained after Mass concluded. Reid waited in the narthex while she lit a candle at a side altar, and knelt, head bowed in prayer. Finished, she left the church and stood on the steps, waiting for her eyes to adjust to the light. The sky overhead was a brilliant collage of vermilion, mauve, and gilt. She stood for a long moment admiring the sight.

"Beautiful, isn't it, Countess?" Reid asked as he joined her.

"You?" She whipped around, startled. "What are you doing here?"

"Tsk, tsk, Madame Delacroix," he chided. "Is that a way to greet your husband?"

Her eyes flashed with ire. "Simpleton," she said in a hiss, looking around to make certain no one was within earshot. "You are *not* my husband. I do not *have* a husband. You took unfair advantage of my generosity, wormed your way back into my life."

He grinned, nonplussed. "Shame on you, Countess. I have it on good authority that God doesn't like shrews."

Her mouth opened, then closed.

He took her elbow before she could protest, pleased he had been able to provoke her. For the time being, at least, the anxiety had vanished. "Perhaps you will be in a better mood after a cup of coffee."

"A shrew! You called me a shrew?" She allowed him to guide her away from the church.

Reid chuckled. "I thought that might get your attention."

"How did you know where to find me?"

"I followed you."

"You not only followed, but actually stayed through Mass. Amazing, truly amazing."

He held a hand to his breast and widened his eyes. "It wounds me, madame, that you find the notion of me in a church so amusing," he said in an offended tone.

Her laughter rippled on the early morning breeze. "Oui, m'sieur, I confess I do find it odd indeed."

"I must admit, I'm more in my element in a gambling hall."

She slanted him a look. "Are you lucky when you gamble?"

"Lucky enough to afford a cup of coffee and a sweet roll."

A vendor near the French Market was selling steaming cups of the strong, chicory-flavored coffee favored by New Orleanians. Reid also purchased two sticky praline pastries. They slowly strolled toward home, sipping coffee and munching on sweet rolls.

"You never said why you followed me."

"It's not safe for a woman to be out alone."

"You feared I might be accosted?"

He shrugged. "Any number of rogues and scalawags roam the streets. The Creoles, so I've heard, call them Kaintocks."

"Kaintocks," she repeated, daintily licking sticky syrup from her finger.

"Mostly keelboatsmen." He smiled at her over the rim of his cup. He could almost see the curiosity clicking inside her head. "Americans who come from such places as Kentucky, Tennessee, Mississippi, and Ohio. A tough, rowdy bunch. Their appetites match the roughness of their trade. After selling their merchandise, they're ready for whiskey, women, and gambling."

"Hmph." She sniffed. "Sounds like the French court."

He gave a loud hoot of laughter at her saucy reply.

Their steps lagged as they neared the house on Calle Real. Reid sensed that Christiane's mood had once more grown pensive. He turned her to face him, his expression one of concern. "If you don't find your grandfather soon, it's likely he's elsewhere. It might be wise if you don't linger in New Orleans. If my identity is uncovered, there will be a great deal of scandal. I don't want you involved."

She smiled sadly. "It's already too late, don't you think, m'sieur?"

There seemed little he could say. Together they silently entered the house.

"Missus." Dulcie rushed up the minute they stepped inside. "Message just come from Ursuline mother." She handed Christiane a sealed envelope.

Christiane accepted it. Her hands trembled as she broke open the seal and read the nun's brief message.

A gentleman meeting the general description of Jean-Claude Bouchard was admitted to Charity Hospital of St. Charles approximately one month ago. He is quite ill and unable to supply any information about himself. The staff, I am told, refers to him only as Jean.

Dazedly Christiane handed the note to Reid. "We must go immediately."

Reid quickly scanned the spidery script, then took charge, instructing Dulcie to take the news to Polly, and request the use of Polly's carriage.

"Have the carriage meet us at the hospital instead," Christiane interrupted. "We'll walk. It'll be quicker this way."

"Yes, missus."

Dulcie started for the door when Christiane stopped her. "As soon as you get back, prepare the spare bedroom for a possible occupant. Make sure the linens are fresh, and start a pot of broth simmering."

"Yes, missus, I do that as fast as these old legs can carry me." Dulcie left at a run to do as she was bidden.

Christiane set off toward the hospital at a brisk pace, Reid at her side. "A charity hospital!" she exclaimed. "*Grand-père* must be mortified. He's always so proud, so fiercely independent."

"Try not to set your hopes too high, Countess," Reid cautioned. "This might not be him."

"Of course it is," she scoffed, but a thin note of hysteria had crept into her voice. "The man's name is Jean. It just has to be him."

"I'd hate to see you hurt."

She fairly flew down the banquette while others scurried to keep out of her path. "If it is Grandfather, I will not leave him at the mercy of strangers. I intend to nurse him myself."

Her feet faltered as they approached the whitewashed rectangular building that resembled an army barracks. She made a hasty sign of the cross and sucked in a deep breath to calm her nerves.

"Steady, Countess." Reid picked up her icy cold hand, brushed a kiss across her knuckles, and tucked it securely into the crook of his arm.

Then, side by side, they walked up the shallow flight of steps and rang the bell.

The bell was answered by an unsmiling black woman with a voluminous white bibbed apron covering a blue muslin gown. Her hair was concealed by a tignon. "Mother Trudeau told us of your inquiry. Dr. de Calabria is expecting you." She ushered them to an office near the end of a long hallway.

A slender man with a trim beard and mustache and wearing black pants, a jacket, and an immaculate white shirt came forward to greet them. "I am Don José de Calabria, physician in charge. You must be Señora Delacroix," he said with a thick Spanish accent. "Mother Trudeau told me to expect your visit."

"*Oui.*" Christiane summoned a weak smile.

Reid shook the doctor's hand. "Mother Trudeau informed us you have a patient fitting the description of my wife's grandfather."

"*Sí.*" He nodded solemnly. "Before I take you to him, I must first warn you that in spite of our finest care, the man in question is quite ill."

Christiane felt her stomach twist. "What exactly is wrong with this gentleman? Just how ill is he?"

The doctor indicated that they should be seated, then sat opposite them behind an ornately carved oak desk. "He arrived approximately a month ago after becoming ill aboard ship."

"He arrived from France?"

"*Sí,* señora." Dr. Calabria folded his hands primly on the polished surface. "Unfortunately we know little about him other than the fact that he hasn't responded favorably to treatment—and, I'm sorry to report, he isn't always coherent."

At Christiane's look of distress, Reid reached over and gently squeezed her hand.

"I am sorry to cause you pain, señora, but you must ready yourself for the ordeal." He stood and gestured toward the door. "Come with me, please. I will take you to him."

Christiane and Reid followed the physician up a flight of steps and through a maze of corridors. Her stomach rebelled at the strong odor of antiseptics and disinfectants that failed to mask even less agreeable smells. Dr. de Calabria entered a ward lined with narrow cots and strode briskly toward the far end. Some patients groaned softly; others stared with the vacant expressions of those who'd given up all hope.

He halted before a small blanket-covered mound, his expression grave. "This is the man known as Jean."

Christiane's heart seemed to rise to her throat, threatening to suffocate her. She stepped closer and eased aside the sheet partially covering the man's face. *"Mon Dieu,"* she whispered. *"Grand-père?"*

Nothing in her wildest imaginings did justice to what she had found. The man on the bed was old and frail, with wasted flesh, sunken eyes, and skin the shade of aged parchment. Hair no longer silver but stark white hung matted and unkempt around a face in which the cheekbones stood out in sharp relief.

"Is this man your grandfather?" Reid asked softly.

With a trembling hand, she reached out and tenderly caressed the man's bearded cheek. *"Oui."* She smiled through her tears. "At last I have found him."

Chapter Eighteen

Jean-Claude Bouchard opened bloodshot eyes and struggled to focus on the face hovering above him.

Christiane cupped his face in the palms of her hands. *"Grand-père,* it is I, Christiane. I have come to take you home."

Don José de Calabria's slight frame grew ramrod stiff. "That is out of the question, sēnora. This man is seriously ill. I refuse to grant permission to remove him from my hospital."

"I don't recall my wife asking your permission, Doctor," Reid said coldly.

"This is absurd," the physician sputtered. "Her grandfather is getting the finest care available. The physicians here at Charity Hospital have studied at the best schools in Cadiz, Madrid, and Barcelona. Nowhere will you find more advanced treatment."

Christiane's resolve began to waver. Perhaps Dr. Calabria

was right. Maybe everything humanly possible was being done by the highly trained staff. Feeling a slight tug on her skirt, she glanced down and found her grandfather's skeletal fingers clenched in the fabric.

"Home, I want . . ." Jean-Claude's eyes closed, his meager store of energy depleted.

She squared her shoulders. The time had come to stop wringing her hands and take control. Her grandfather's life depended on her making a sensible decision. She would not allow this physician with his fancy credentials to intimidate her. She would gather the facts, then do what she thought best for her grandfather's well-being, even if it meant allowing him to remain hospitalized.

She met Dr. Calabria's look squarely. "Precisely what type of treatment are you administering that I can't provide at home?"

"The patient is bled regularly," he replied pompously, folding his arms over his chest. "And each day he receives a carefully monitored dose of arsenic to rid the body of corruption."

"Arsenic?" Christiane repeated, horrified by the notion. "You are slowly poisoning him to death!"

"You are being overly dramatic, sẽnora. We here at Charity Hospital subscribe to the belief that harsh methods provide the quickest recoveries."

"I want my grandfather removed from here at once."

Over the physician's stringent objections, plans were made to transport Jean-Claude Bouchard to Christiane's. When they received word that Polly Wakefield's carriage had arrived, Reid picked up Jean-Claude as effortlessly as he would a small child and carried him from the hospital, depositing his frail body carefully on the seat. During the short drive, Christiane cradled her grandfather's head against her shoulder, crooning reassurances while Reid looked on. Jean Claude moaned softly each time a carriage wheel hit a rut in the road, but his eyes remained closed.

Dulcie ran out to greet them when the carriage pulled into the courtyard. "Missus Wakefield say she sendin' her doctor and a nurse along to help out. Should be here soon, she say."

Christiane made a mental note to thank Polly for anticipating her needs. Once again Reid picked up Jean-Claude and, with Christiane close at his heels, carried him up the stairs to the bedroom Dulcie had prepared.

No sooner was he settled than Polly's personal physician arrived and immediately asked to examine the patient. Unable to sit still, Christiane paced outside the room. Reid silently waited in the shadows.

"Well . . . ?" Christiane asked the doctor the moment he reappeared. "Please tell me he is going to be all right. That I wasn't too late."

"He wouldn't have been able to withstand the type of treatment he was receiving much longer. It's a testament to his strength and determination that he survived as long as he did," he said, his expression grave.

Reid rested his hands on Christiane's shoulders. "Is there anything we can do?"

"The bleeding and arsenic have taken their toll, left him weak, debilitated." The doctor rubbed his hand over his jaw. "Milk will help lessen the effects of the arsenic. Give him liquids to replace those he's lost."

"But he will recover, won't he?" Christiane couldn't suppress the note of anxiety in her voice.

"His body needs time to regain its strength. The next twenty-four hours are crucial. If he makes it beyond, then . . . " He shrugged.

"*Merci*, Doctor."

"More important, Madame Delacroix, the patient has

lost his will to live. That can change now that you're here."
The doctor started toward the stairs, then turned back.
"I'll stop by to see Count Bouchard in the morning. A
nurse will be arriving shortly."

After the doctor left, the house with its drawn shutters
seemed unnaturally dark and still. Christiane bit her lower
lip, her mind churning to assimilate events of that morning. Had she found her grandfather at long last, only to
lose him? Would fate be that unkind? *Grand-père* was only
a pale shadow of the man she remembered. She was
shamed to admit she had scarcely recognized him.

Reid cleared his throat. "If you're anything alike, Countess, your grandfather won't surrender without a struggle.
He'll fight with bravery and determination."

She tried to show appreciation of his understanding,
but, remembering her grandfather's shriveled form, failed
to produce a smile. "I used to think he was the strongest
person in the world, but . . . " Her voice faltered.

"Appearances are often deceiving, Countess."

Something in his tone jarred her from her absorption.
"What do you mean?"

He caught her chin between thumb and forefinger, and
studied her upturned face. "When I first saw you on the
dock at Le Cap, I figured you for a spoiled, self-centered
young woman. You wasted no time showing me I was wrong.
You constantly surprise and amaze me. I've learned you're
compassionate, resourceful. Courageous."

She blinked up at him, momentarily at a loss for a
response. Reid was not one to waste words on idle flattery.
Compliments were sparse, praise hard-won, and each one
a gift.

"Not to mention obstinate and persistent," he added.

"As you've pointed out on numerous occasions," she
replied with a trace of asperity.

The corner of his mouth twitched. "Add that to the fact that you're the most inquisitive woman I've ever encountered."

"The persistence I inherited from my grandfather. I will not allow him to surrender without a fight. I will not," she repeated, her voice low, fierce. A single tear slid down her cheek.

He flicked the tear from her cheek with the pad of his thumb. "Your mettle is being tested. Your grandfather needs you to be strong enough for both of you."

Blinking back moisture from her eyes, she managed a wobbly smile. "Do you know what I thought of you that first day?"

His hands dropped to her waist. He canted his head to one side and raised a brow in inquiry. "No, tell me. What did you think?"

"I envied and resented your self-confidence. Never did I ever dream we'd become friends." Raising up on tiptoe, she impulsively kissed his cheek. "You're a good man, Reid Alexander—and a good friend."

Long after Christiane had disappeared into the sickroom, Reid stood staring after her. Why wasn't he satisfied being only a friend? Why wasn't that enough? Why did he yearn for more? Frustrated, he raked a hand through his shorn locks. He had no room in his life for a pretty French countess. Yet somehow, in spite of his lofty intentions, their lives had become hopelessly entwined. Emotions had sprung up like pesky vines and taken root—emotions difficult to eradicate. If he wasn't vigilant, they would choke his resolve, strangle his determination, thwart his efforts.

Turning on his heel, he clattered down the steps to the

courtyard below. He had nothing to offer any woman, especially a woman such as Christiane Delacroix.

Nothing, he thought grimly, not even himself.

"Christiane . . . ?"

Christiane scarcely heard the reed-thin whisper. She thought it at first was a figment of her imagination. But when the sound was repeated, she glanced up from her needlework and found her grandfather watching her, his eyes heavy-lidded, dull.

Dropping her stitchery, she leaned forward and took his skeletal hand in hers. *"Grand-père?* I am right here."

"Christiane . . . ?"

She wasn't sure if he truly recognized her, or was merely calling her name in delirium. "You are safe now, *Grand-père.* No one is ever going to separate us again."

"Thirsty . . . so thirsty," he rasped in a voice as dry and lifeless as autumn leaves.

She slid an arm around his frail shoulders and, raising his head, pressed a glass to his lips. He took a long swallow, then grimaced.

The reaction was so like her grandfather that Christiane laughed softly. The Jean-Claude Bouchard of her memory never hesitated making his displeasure known. "I remember now that you always disliked milk. But you must drink it all. Dr. Mason says it will counteract the effects of the arsenic they were using to treat you at the hospital."

He drank obediently, then closed his eyes, drained by the effort. Christiane lowered his head gently to the pillow and smoothed the counterpane. "I am going to take good care of you, *Grand-père.* Trust me; soon you will be strong again."

Night fell and still she remained at the bedside. A gust

of wind blew through the partially opened shutters, making the flame atop the candle dance with wild abandon. She rose from the chair, stretched her stiff muscles, then walked across the room to peer through the wooden slats at the unrelenting blackness outside. She had no concept of the time, knowing only that the hour was late. A storm was brewing. Thunder rumbled in the distance. A brisk wind whipped the ferns hanging from baskets along the gallery. She hoped the rain would bring a respite from the unrelenting heat that smothered the city.

She felt as unsettled as the elements. Her grandfather's life hung in the balance. It all seemed so unfair. This was all Etienne's fault. If her grandfather had been allowed to accompany her to St. Domingue, none of this would have happened. Resentment, bitter as acid, burned within her. Etienne had been a cruel, evil man. Even after his death, the innocent suffered the consequences of his perversity.

The door swung open and a large-boned, buxom woman entered, carrying a tray. Unruly curls that had probably been a vivid red in youth but were now faded to a soft strawberry hue peeked from beneath a white mobcap. A liberal sprinkling of freckles and bright blue eyes shaded by pale lashes were the outstanding features in an otherwise plain but pleasant face. Polly had described Rosie O'Banion as strong as an ox, and Christiane agreed with her friend's assessment.

"Now that he's stopped heaving his guts, a good hearty broth is just what the Count's been needin'." Rosie set the tray down. Placing her hands on her ample hips, she studied her patient's slight inert figure, wagging her head in disgust. "Arsenic's a wicked thing. If you ask my opinion, I haven't seen many souls benefit from it. In my experience, most die from the cure instead of from what ails 'em."

Between the two women, they were able to coax some

broth and more sips of milk into their patient before he fell into a deep, untroubled sleep. Rosie plunked herself in a chair in one corner, took out her knitting, and settled in for the night. Soon the steady click of knitting needles filled the room.

Too restless to sit still, Christiane paced back and forth. What dire circumstances had befallen her grandfather since they had parted in Calais? she wondered. The sale of the jeweled bracelet she had given him should have provided enough to live on modestly. From the limited amount of information she had been able to gather, he must have fallen ill aboard ship and been taken directly to Charity Hospital. What money he had in his possession had probably gone to pay for the frequent bleedings and doses of poison that were killing him in slow degrees. Thank goodness she had found him before it was too late.

"Your pacing is wearing my nerves as well as the carpet," Rosie O'Banion complained, not looking up from her knitting. "Go get some rest. You won't be doin' your grandfather any good if I have to nurse you both."

Christiane reluctantly acquiesced after eliciting Rosie O'Banion's promise to call if there was any change in the patient's condition. It would do her grandfather little good if he woke and sensed her worry. Assured he was in capable hands, she left the sickroom, quietly closing the door behind her.

Once in her bedroom, she changed out of her gown into a nightdress of delicate white lawn, its bodice laced with narrow blue ribbon. Afterward she brushed her hair until it swirled around her shoulders and down her back like a mantle of burnished mahogany. Then, still too overwrought for sleep, she stepped through the French doors and onto the gallery. Jagged streaks of lightning raced across the night sky. The smell of an impending storm was in the air. Resting her hands lightly on the gallery railing, she lifted her face to the night sky and closed her eyes. Fitful bursts of wind caught and teased the long tresses of her hair.

"If I owned a ship, I'd have your profile carved as my masthead." Reid's low-timbred baritone came out of the darkness.

"And we'd sail the seven seas together." Christiane smiled dreamily, her eyes still shut. It defied logic, but somehow having him near had a tranquilizing effect on her jangled nerves.

"A pretty picture, but not a realistic one, I'm afraid."

She opened her eyes and turned toward the sound of his voice. He stood next to her at the rail, his open shirt revealing a wedge of bronzed flesh covered with a mat of golden curls. He held a thin cheroot negligently in one hand. His face was an intriguing combination of planes and shadows, its expression hidden, mysterious.

His mouth twisted in a mockery of a smile. "What's wrong, Countess? You look as though you've seen a ghost."

And indeed in her bemused state that was how he seemed. He could have been a fantasy figure conjured by her imagination. She was taken back in time to the night she had followed drumbeats deep into a woods, where she had witnessed a pagan rite. He had silenced her startled outcry with a kiss—a kiss branded in her memory. "I . . . ah . . . thought you had gone out for the evening."

He drew on the cheroot, the tip glowing red in the darkness. "Would you prefer to have me elsewhere?"

"*Non,* of course not," she snapped. His aloofness angered her. It was as though he had purposely retreated behind a barrier of sorts. "I was merely surprised at finding you here."

"It's late. You should be asleep."

She shrugged one slender shoulder. "Too much has happened today."

"Don't you think you should go inside? A storm's about to break."

"You can't order me about like a child," she retorted with an angry shake of her head. "Perhaps you're the one afraid of the storm, m'sieur."

"Don't be ridiculous."

"You might be wise to worry. If you persist in your effort to prove Leon du Beaupre guilty of murder, you could unleash a storm of unimaginable fury. Why not leave New Orleans while you still can?"

"Worried about me, Countess?"

"It is dangerous to remain here." She blew out an impatient breath. "If du Beaupre recognizes you, he'll insist that you be returned to Hispaniola. You are far too intelligent to waste your life on a fool's errand."

"A fool's errand!" he said with a snarl, dropping the cheroot and grinding it beneath his heel. "Is that how you see it?"

"*Oui*, that is precisely what it is." She raised her voice to be heard above the rising wind. "Why do you persist in this madness? Are you any closer to proving your innocence?"

His hand clenched, then unclenched as he struggled for control. "No," he said angrily. "But if there is a way, I'll find it."

"If you had an ounce of sense, you would pack your bags and leave New Orleans at once."

He grabbed her shoulders and pulled her against him. "If I had an ounce of sense, Countess, I'd keep my hands off of you."

His mouth ground against hers for a kiss fueled by anger and driven by frustration. But instead of shrinking from his ruthless assault, she confounded him by answering with a passion equal to his own. Rising on tiptoe, she wound both fists in his shirt and clung to him. The wind whipped her hair about, binding them with silken strands. He could feel every curve and hollow of her body through the thin fabric of her nightclothes.

When she opened her mouth, greedy for his, he let out a primal growl from deep in his throat. Desire rumbled through him, the vibration so intense it left him shaken. His lips devoured hers. His tongue slipped into the honeyed cavern of her mouth, tracking the moist curve of her inner cheek and palate, exploring the sharp, uneven ridges of her teeth, then playfully dueling with hers.

Hot white light arced across an inky sky. A cannon of thunder boomed loudly. Wind lashed branches of the trees into a frenzy. But both Reid and Christiane, enmeshed in a storm of their own making, were impervious to nature's symphony.

Reaching down, Reid cupped her buttocks, lifting her off her feet and holding her against his pulsing manhood. To his delight, instead of being squeamish, she wriggled against him, adjusting her hips for a snugger fit. He felt his shaft grow hard and throb with need. "This is crazy," he managed to say. "We shouldn't—"

"Hush," she whispered. "Don't talk." Taking his head between her hands, she rained kisses over his face, his eyelids, across his cheeks, and down his throat.

His mind reeled. His noble instincts scattered like leaves in a gale. His senses felt saturated with her taste, her smell, her feel.

Wrapping her legs around his waist, Christiane locked her ankles together, holding Reid a willing captive. He ran his hands up the pale, marblelike columns of her thighs.

How could flesh feel cool, yet scorch at the same time? he marveled dimly.

Heavy drops of rain pelted on the tiled roof above and stone courtyard below. Its rapid cadence mingled with the hammering of two hearts. Lightning, wind, and rain— none of the elements could compete with the unleashed passion of the two people entwined on the gallery.

The need to possess was fierce, all encompassing, driving out logic. Blood roared through Reid's veins as he nudged aside the scrap of lace covering her bosom and hungrily drew a pebble-hard nipple into his mouth. He nearly came unhinged when she moaned in pleasure and arched her neck, leaving her throat exposed, vulnerable, her breasts spilling from their confines.

"You deserve better," he murmured.

Her legs tightened about his waist. "Take me," she urged. "Don't make me wait."

Reid felt her hand frantically tug at his waistband and knew he was lost. He didn't want to wait, didn't want to weigh the consequences; he only wanted to sheathe himself in her moist dark velvet vault.

Using the railing to partially support her weight, he kept his hands firmly on her buttocks and plunged into her. She was liquid heat and tight as a glove. Her inner muscles contracted, drawing him deeper, imprisoning him, communicating her need in the most elemental way.

His hips pumped as he drove into her, retreating, then driving again. She clung to him, urging him on, beseeching, offering, taking. Then she climaxed, crying out his name. Moments later, shuddering, he followed suit.

Sated, Christiane went limp in his arms, her head lolling against his chest like a flower on a wilted stem. He pushed aside the damp hair at her temple and pressed a kiss against her brow. The woman in his arms continually amazed him.

Gloriously responsive to his every touch, brimming with fiery passion, tempered with incredible sweetness. He had never known another like her.

And in his heart he knew he never would.

His ragged breathing gradually resumed a more normal rhythm. Slowly a semblance of sanity crept back and Reid became aware of their surroundings, the rain drumming on the roof, the distant rumble of thunder as the storm moved off. For God's sake, he thought with disgust, he had taken her outdoors on the gallery like a stallion in heat. At least the enclosed courtyard and inclement weather had provided privacy from prying eyes. She was a lady . . . a countess . . . and entitled to the comforts of a bed, soft sheets, privacy.

Now she couldn't even raise her head, couldn't look him in the eye. He should have shown more restraint, had more regard for propriety, taken her station into account.

He cleared his throat, prepared for an apology. "That was—"

"*Magnifique!*" She completed the sentence. She lifted a face radiant with triumph, then laughed. "Absolutely *magnifique!*"

Reid's initial surprise gave way to amusement, and he joined in the laughter. All at once he felt happier, more carefree than he had felt in weeks, months. Forever. Still smiling, he kissed the raindrops from her cheeks. "You're all wet," he murmured.

A wicked smile curved her lips. She teasingly bit his earlobe. "Take me inside where we can dry off."

He carried her through the open French doors, kicking them shut with his foot. In a movement as agile as a cat's, she slid down the length of his body. Their eyes locked, darkened, as passion rekindled. Water puddled at their feet unnoticed. Christiane shivered, but the involuntary action had nothing to do with being chilled.

"Here," Reid said as he snagged a towel from the washstand. "Dry yourself before you catch a fever."

It wasn't cold she felt, but sizzling heat. Ignoring the towel he offered, Christiane stripped off her sodden nightdress. Lifting her damp hair from her neck, she presented her back to Reid. "Dry me, *s'il te plaît.*"

"My pleasure, Countess," he said, smiling. With infuriating slowness, he ran the towel down the graceful slope of her spine, traced the gentle flare of her hips and the curve of her buttocks. Dipping his head, he playfully nipped the junction between her neck and shoulder, chuckling at her startled gasp, then soothing the spot with a kiss. "Do I qualify as a lady's maid? Are my services satisfactory?"

She pretended to ponder the question. "Before I decide, m'sieur, I will require further demonstration of your talents."

He banded an arm around her waist and drew her against his bare chest. He proceeded to give the same painstaking attention to drying her breasts and abdomen. When the towel drifted lower still, she caught her lower lip between her teeth to stifle a throaty purr of pleasure that threatened to escape.

Before she could become even more distracted, she snatched the towel from his hands. "Now it is my turn." She waited while he shed the remainder of his clothes, admiring the smooth expanse of muscle and sinew, the broad shoulders and trim waist. She attempted to memorize each line and plane, every scar and ridge. Tried to implant even the smallest details in her brain.

When at last he stood naked in front of her, she took her cue from him. Applying light brushstrokes meant to tease and torment, she explored his magnificent body with the linen cloth. The flat brown nipples nestled in a whorl of golden curls captured her attention. She rubbed them lightly and watched them harden in response. Fascinated, she bent her head and delicately circled the taut peaks with the tip of her tongue.

Reid sucked in a breath. His stomach muscles quivered in his struggle for control, to rein his mounting ardor.

"Do you like that?" she asked, her voice languorous.

"You know I do," he said between gritted teeth. "You seem an expert in slow torture."

Pleased with his answer, she ordered him to turn around. He reluctantly did as she asked, standing with feet firmly planted, a frown on his face. "Does it make you happy to see my scars?"

"Non," she replied softly, gently caressing each place where a whip had taken a cruel bite into his flesh. "But the scars are part of who you are."

He greeted her pronouncement with a harsh bark of laughter. "You are indeed fanciful, Countess, if you think to romanticize something so ugly."

She continued to stroke the healed welts with her finger-tips, then with a series of kisses light as the touch of a butterfly. "Your back tells me you have suffered much, and that in spite of the pain and humiliation, you have grown stronger."

"Enough!" Swinging around, he silenced her with a kiss that left her breathless.

"And what does my kiss tell you?" he asked, dragging his mouth from hers.

She stared up at him, dazed by the whirlwind of sensations he evoked. "That you want me," she replied, her voice husky.

Reid swung her up in his arms and placed her on the bed. Along with desire, she saw questions and uncertainties mirrored in his silver-gray gaze. "I'm not skilled in pretty words. . . ."

She placed her finger to his mouth, forestalling what he was about to say. "I don't want pretty words. Show me what is in your heart."

And he did.

Chapter Nineteen

When Christiane woke the next morning and found Reid gone, she wanted to bury her face in the pillow and weep. How could the previous night have meant so much to her—and so little to him? Did he think she had offered herself so completely only to satisfy a physical urge? Couldn't he sense he possessed her heart as well?

She turned on her side and punched the pillow. How foolish she had been to hope for some sign of affection. Reid Alexander was no callow youth, but a man who guarded his emotions as carefully as a miser his purse strings. Perhaps he was incapable of love, or worse yet, she thought with a groan, maybe she was the problem. After all, she reminded herself, she had virtually thrown herself at him. During the flight through St. Domingue, she had practically begged him to make love to her. And last night . . .

Her cheeks burned at the memory. She had behaved with wanton abandon, no better than a harlot. But then she always did in his arms. Until she met Reid, she had considered herself a sensible, practical young woman. How that had changed! It wasn't only senseless but stupid to love a man who had no more than a fleeting interest in her. But she had only herself to blame. She couldn't fault Reid for taking what was flagrantly offered.

She rolled onto her back, opened her eyes, and discovered that she was still in Reid's bedroom. Buttery-yellow sunlight streamed through the partially opened door. Birds chirped cheerfully from the boughs of a magnolia tree in the courtyard. Curious in spite of herself, Christiane let her gaze roam around the room. Everything appeared neat and orderly, with a few personal items arranged on a chest with military precision. She spotted her nightclothes splayed over the back of a chair instead of in a soggy heap on the floor where she had left them. Swinging her legs out of bed, she dressed quickly, then smoothed the tangles from her hair.

From somewhere in the house she heard a door open and close. Not wanting to be caught creeping out of Reid's bedroom, she slipped through the French doors and skirted around the house using the gallery. She stepped across the threshold of her bedroom just as Dulcie entered from the opposite door with an armload of fresh linens.

Dulcie's eyes went from Christiane to the bed that hadn't been slept in. A knowing grin broke across her broad face. "Mornin'. You sleep well, Dulcie think."

Christiane colored at the woman's words, but she tried to conceal her embarrassment with righteous indignation. "Really, Dulcie, how or where I sleep is no concern of yours."

"No, ma'am, it ain't." She chuckled good-naturedly, not the least offended by Christiane's manner. "I trust m'sieur slept well, too."

"Dulcie . . ." Christiane said, exasperated.

Nonplussed, Dulcie set the linens at the foot of the bed. "I go get coffee. Nice 'n' strong, that wake you up."

Christiane gave a sigh of resignation. Servants in America were nothing like those at Belle Terre, she had quickly discovered. But there was a fundamental difference, she reminded herself. Dulcie was a free woman of color, not a slave. After her experiences on St. Domingue, she wanted no part of slavery. It was a barbaric system, breeding nothing but trouble.

Going to the armoire, she selected one of her prettiest gowns, a soft spring green sprigged with dainty yellow flowers. The bright colors perked up her flagging spirits. She dressed her hair atop her head and wove a yellow satin ribbon through her dark curls. She surveyed her reflection in the mirror critically. She wanted to present a cheerful, optimistic front for her grandfather. Except for a slight pallor, no one would suspect how desperately unhappy she was.

She had just finished her toilette when Dulcie returned with a pot of strong chickory-flavored coffee and sticky pecan rolls still warm from the oven. "Dulcie fatten you up. You too skinny. Need to be strong to have healthy babies."

Christiane nearly dropped the cup she had just picked up. "Babies?"

Dulcie nodded sagely. "You and m'sieur make fine, strapping sons."

Babies? Her knees suddenly weak, Christiane sank to the edge of the bed. *Fine strapping sons.* Dulcie's words whispered through her brain. The thought of cuddling a small infant caused a soft, melting sensation deep inside. The notion of carrying his child tapped a wellspring of maternal feelings, their intensity surprising her. Ruthlessly she tamped them down.

Until now, she hadn't stopped to consider the possibility of a child. How foolhardy. The needs of her body had overwhelmed rational thought. She and Reid had made love numerous times on three separate occasions. Any one of them could have culminated in a pregnancy. And where would that leave her? *Think of the complications.* Her coffee grew cold, untouched. A child deserved the love of both parents, a mother and a father. How unfair to an unborn child—and its father. Reid wanted freedom, not commitment. As much as she loved him, she didn't want him to remain with her based on obligation.

"Hurry now; eat yer breakfast," Dulcie scolded. "Miss O'Banion says yer grandaddy askin' fer you."

Mention of her grandfather snapped Christiane's thoughts back to the present. "Is he all right? He hasn't taken a turn for the worse?"

Dulcie bustled about the room, fussily rearranging the items on the dressing table, opening the blinds. "Lord, child, don't go borrowin' trouble. Trouble find you soon 'nough."

Her heart rate returning to normal, Christiane smiled at her own foolishness. "You're right, Dulcie; thank you for the reminder." She hastily gulped a swallow of coffee and a bite of roll, forestalling a lecture from Dulcie, then hurried out of the bedroom to see how her grandfather fared.

Morning light slanted through wooden shutters to form horizontal gold stripes on the dark pine floorboards. A breeze swept through the partially open door that led onto the gallery smelled freshly laundered after a night's rain. Jean-Claude reclined against a snowy mound of pillows. Although sallow and gaunt, there was an alertness about him that had been lacking at the hospital. Seeing this cheered Christiane as nothing else could have.

"Grand-père." She crossed to his bed, a smile trembling on her lips.

He held out a hand as his eyes filmed with moisture. "When I woke this morning, I thought I must be in heaven and Mademoiselle O'Banion my special red-haired angel."

Bending down, she brushed a kiss across his wrinkled cheek. "You aren't in heaven, but Rosie O'Banion is indeed an angel who has just performed a miracle. You look wonderful."

Out of the corner of her eye, she detected motion in the far corner of the room. "R-Reid," she stammered as he stepped out of the shadows. "I thought you had gone out for the day."

He met her gaze soberly, his mouth grim and unsmiling. "I wanted to check on your grandfather first to see how he was doing."

Seeing him made her heart constrict. She drank in his appearance. He looked fit, trim, and handsome in a gray jacket and striped vest that reflected the color of his eyes. It would have seemed the most natural thing in the world to slide an arm around his waist, exchange an affectionate kiss, feel his solid support. Seeing him unexpectedly drove everything else from her mind, her reaction so potent that even her grandfather's presence faded into the background.

Jean-Claude shifted a quizzical gaze between his grand-daughter and her husband. He cleared his throat noisily to draw their attention. "Who is this Reid you speak of, granddaughter?"

An incriminating blush spread across her cheekbones. Eyes filled with dismay, Christiane scrambled to collect her scattered senses. She had blundered again, addressing

Reid by his given name rather than Etienne. Whenever possible she avoided calling him by that name, with its associated unpleasantness.

Both men were regarding her expectantly, waiting for her answer. At some point she would have to tell her grandfather that Reid wasn't really her husband after all. That the real Etienne Delacroix had perished during the revolt in St. Domingue. That Reid had been his overseer— a man convicted of murder. The small amount of breakfast she had consumed felt heavy in her stomach. Was this the time to tell her grandfather the truth?

Reid, apparently aware of her quandary, started to explain. "Actually my name is—"

"Reid is the name his mother gave him," she said, interrupting. "It was only after his father died and he inherited his estate that Reid assumed the name on his birth record."

She stared across the room at Reid, silently daring him to defy her. They both knew that if she confessed he wasn't her husband, he would have no recourse but to leave the premises immediately. Without the facade of being a French planter from St. Domingue, the opportunity to prove his innocence would be limited. She could afford to wait, to buy him more time. Her grandfather would be furious with her for jeopardizing her reputation with such a scheme. And, she reasoned, his health was still far too precarious to risk any serious emotional upheavals. There would be time enough later for explanations.

Jean-Claude's sharp gaze darted from one to the other. "Ah," he said at last. "I see."

Christiane exhaled a pent-up breath. Ever since girl-hood, her grandfather had possessed an uncanny knack of knowing whenever she told a lie. "Most know him only as Etienne. Only those closest to him call him Reid."

Jean-Claude let his gaze linger on Reid. "It is my hope

that after we become better acquainted, I will be among those to address you as such.''

Reid inclined his head. "That would please me greatly, M'sieur le Comte."

"Bon." Jean-Claude indicated his approval with a weary nod of his head. "The matter is settled."

"If you two will kindly excuse me, I have some business matters that need attention.'' With this, Reid quickly exited the sickroom.

Christiane followed him with her eyes. It had been thoughtful of Reid to show concern about her grandfather's well-being. Once again he had demonstrated his innate kindness and consideration. He constantly refused to recognize his good qualities when, in fact, there were many to admire.

Jean-Claude folded his hands atop the bedclothes. "I have a vague memory of being carried out of that abominable hospital and upstairs to this room. Was Reid the man responsible?''

Christiane perched on the edge of the bed. *"Oui, Grand-père.* Reid insisted upon helping.''

"I thought as much. That husband of yours seems a fine sort. Not at all the monster I imagined.''

"I'm sorry I caused you worry.'' She placed her hand over his.

His expression remained troubled. "I should have forbidden you to marry a man you had never met, knew nothing about, unless I was there to protect you.''

"Our choices were few," she reminded him gently. She longed to confide the entire truth, tell him his fears were well-founded, that Etienne Delacroix was the vilest human being she had ever encountered, but she held her tongue. "We both agreed, *Grand-père,* that a proxy marriage was best. Tell me what happened after we bade farewell at Calais."

A long sigh precipitated a coughing spell. After he settled back onto the pillows, he briefly recounted what had transpired since leaving France. "I must confess that I allowed myself to become overwrought, which contributed to my illness. By the time I reached New Orleans, I was in dire need of medical attention. I was too sick to protest when arrangements were made to bring me directly from the ship to Charity Hospital. A charity hospital . . ." He shook his head sadly. "Can you imagine my profound humiliation?"

"That is all in the past." She smoothed back a lock of silvery white hair from his face. "We have been reunited, and that is all that matters."

"You always were such a joy to me, *ma petite.*" The old man's eyes were suspiciously moist. "When I feared I might never see you again, I lost all interest in living."

"Nothing is ever going to separate us again," she vowed softly. A lump rose in her throat. Her grandfather's near bout with death had wrought a decided change. Emotions formerly held in reserve were now near the surface, threatening to spill over. "Just concentrate on getting well."

While he self-consciously cleared his throat, Rosie O'Banion burst through the bedroom door carrying a breakfast tray. She stood for a moment, head tilted to one side, eyes narrowed, regarding him. "Well, I see the patient has decided to join the living."

"Was there ever any doubt, mademoiselle?" Jean-Claude bristled, blatantly denying his weakened state.

Christiane rose from the bed while the nurse plumped the pillows, then arranged the tray across the patient's lap. Jean-Claude studied its contents with distaste. "Any more milk and I'll moo like a cow," he grumbled.

"Any less milk, and you'll wish ye were a cow." Undeterred by her patient's querulous manner, Rosie shook out a napkin and tucked it beneath the count's chin. "Milk is what the doctor ordered; milk is what ye get."

As she listened to the exchange, Christiane smiled with genuine humor for the first time in days. Already her grandfather was reverting to his old, autocratic ways. But he had met his match in Rosie O'Banion. Christiane made a mental note to thank Polly for recommending the woman.

Polly Wakefield wouldn't take no for an answer. The widow insisted Christiane and Reid join her for a reception being hosted by Governor Esteban Miró honoring a minor dignitary newly arrived from Spain. Christiane attempted to demur, using her grandfather as an excuse, but Polly had been adamant. Her grandfather, she had pointed out, was markedly improved and would be well cared for in Rosie O'Banion's capable hands. She alternately scolded and cajoled until Christiane relented.

Christiane fastened the diamond earrings in place, then critically examined her reflection in the mirror. Dulcie had pulled her hair back from her face and arranged it in a style that accentuated her delicate features. The black satin gown she had selected was elegant in its simplicity, the low cut bodice and narrow waist showing off her figure to full advantage. Her thoughts drifted to the housewarming at Belle Terre and the exquisite gown crafted by Simone du Val. She wondered how the seamstress was faring during the upheaval. Shortly after arriving in Louisiana, she had written to urge Simone and her husband to come to New Orleans. Their services would be in demand,

and they would be safe. Although she hadn't received a reply, she hoped they would heed her advice.

At the sound of carriage wheels crunching in the stone courtyard below, Christiane hurried out to greet her friend. She had promised Polly an introduction to her grandfather. Polly had been eager to meet the French nobleman from the start, but knowing her grandfather's pride, she had judiciously waited until some semblance of his former self had returned.

Polly swept into the drawing room with a rustle of raspberry-colored taffeta. "My dear, you look marvelous," she greeted Christiane effusively. "You'll outshine everyone. No one will pay the least bit of attention to the governor."

"Ah, Polly," Christiane said with a fond smile. "You are too kind."

Polly glanced around expectantly; then her brow wrinkled. "Where is your husband? I had assumed Etienne would be joining us."

"He sends his apologies but had some matters that needed his immediate attention." Christiane had anticipated the question and was ready with a reply. In truth, she had no idea where Reid was or what his plans were. He didn't choose to confide in her. Since that rainy night on the gallery more than a week ago, he had scrupulously avoided any further encounters with her.

"Pity he can't see how lovely you look." Polly was instantly sympathetic to her plight. "Perhaps he'll complete his business and join us later."

"Perhaps," Christiane murmured. She linked her arm through that of the older woman. "I've told Grandfather how instrumental you were in helping to locate him. He's quite anxious to meet you."

"If you're sure this won't be an imposition," Polly twit

tered, patting her silvery curls. "The comte may not be up to receiving guests."

Christiane kept her expression carefully schooled to hide her amusement. Polly's boundless curiosity had made postponing the introduction a difficult task. However, now that the actual moment was at hand, Polly was trying to adopt a studied nonchalance.

Upon reaching her grandfather's room, Christiane pushed open the door and ushered Polly inside. Jean-Claude, attired in a midnight blue silk dressing robe, his silvery white mane neatly trimmed and combed back from his strongly sculpted features, crossed the room to greet them. Though he used a walking cane for additional support, his gait was steady and purposeful.

"*Grand-père*, this is my dear friend Madame Polly Wakefield," Christiane said, performing the introduction simply.

Polly dipped into curtsy. "Comte de Varennes. It is a great honor."

He took her hand, then gallantly pressed it to his lips. "It is I, madame, who is privileged. If not for your assistance, my granddaughter and I might never have been reunited. I am in your debt."

Polly's face pinkened with pleasure. "My only reward comes from knowing you are regaining your health."

"If your search hadn't led to that abominable place, I might not have survived their treatment." He continued to hold Polly's hand in his. "Under Mademoiselle O'Banion's diligent care I grow stronger every day.

"My granddaughter's description failed to do you justice, madame. I shall have to take her to task." Jean-Claude gave Polly a flirtatious smile. "You are much more youthful—and much prettier—than I was led to believe."

"How kind of you to flatter me," Polly replied, her round face flushed and beaming.

"Flattery?" Jean-Claude pretended outrage. "Every word I speak is nothing but the truth."

Christiane watched the exchange in amazement. The couple's interest in each other seemed to eclipse everything else, including her presence. Though her grandfather's face still revealed the ravages of his recent illness, there was a decided twinkle in his dark eyes. Polly positively glowed.

"Then you aren't angry at me for insisting Christiane accompany me tonight? If you prefer that she remain here . . ."

"Nonsense. A change of scenery will do wonders for her. It'll provide an opportunity to speak with someone other than an old man, to wear a pretty gown and jewels. I fear of late I have grown selfish with her company."

"It must be lonely for you." Polly clucked sympathetically. "I would feel honored if you would allow me to introduce you into New Orleans society."

"How kind of you, madame," Jean-Claude said with a warm smile. "I would like that very much; alas, I am still not fully recovered. Perhaps in the meantime you could see fit to visit a temporary invalid."

"Absolutely, M'sieur le Comte." Polly's eagerness shone through her polite reply.

"Bon." Jean-Claude lightly squeezed the widow's hand before releasing it. "I shall look forward to your visits."

"What a charming man!" Polly gushed the minute they were safely out of earshot.

While Polly chattered on and on about Jean-Claude, Christiane listened with half an ear. She knew how fond Reid was of both Polly and her grandfather and wished he'd been there to witness their first meeting. Then she brought herself up short.

In an amazingly brief span of time, Reid had become

such an integral part of her life that she wanted to share even small, everyday occurrences with him. This had to cease. She reminded herself that their relationship had no permanence. Reid didn't want a commitment.

Didn't want her.

By the time they reached the ballroom where the reception was being held, the event was in full swing. Christiane and Polly took their places in the receiving line, where Christiane was duly introduced to the governor and his wife as well as a number of other city officials. Surveying the assembled crowd, Christiane observed that the guest list included an interesting blend of Spaniards, French, and Americans. Most residents, Polly had informed her upon her arrival in New Orleans, considered themselves Creoles or native-born Orleanians of Spanish or French descent.

Waiters in black jackets and stiffly starched shirts circulated among the guests, offering them chilled fruit punch and wine. The room buzzed with animated conversation. Topics seemed as varied as the people themselves, and Christiane caught mention of the revolution in France, a steamboat patent by someone named John Fitch, and a new concerto for pianoforte by Wolfgang Amadeus Mozart.

Polly was quickly accosted by acquaintances and pressed into telling them details of her recent trip abroad. Christiane was listening attentively when she felt someone tap her on the shoulder. Turning, she found herself face-to-face with Leon du Beaupre.

"A woman as beautiful as yourself isn't safe unescorted." His dark eyes smoldered as they lingered on her décolletage.

She forced a polite smile, uncomfortable under the Creole's perusal. "We meet again, M'sieur du Beaupre."

He caught her hand, brushing his lips across the knuckles. "I must beg your forgiveness, Madame Delacroix, for my faulty memory."

"Your memory, m'sieur?" She resisted the urge to snatch her hand free.

"Oui, madame, it failed me miserably." He smiled deep into her eyes. "You are even more beautiful than I remembered."

"Merci, m'sieur." She slid her fingers from his, tempted to wipe off his touch in the folds of her skirt. "You are very kind."

"Not kind, lovely lady. Only truthful." His obsidian gaze roamed over the ballroom. "I haven't seen your husband. Are you alone?"

"Oui. My husband had other matters to attend to and sent his regrets." Under his slightly skeptical stare, Christiane thought the excuse sounded contrived, lame.

"Again?" He arched a black brow. "If I possessed a jewel such as yourself, I wouldn't leave it unguarded."

His bold scrutiny made her want to squirm. She felt as though he were undressing her, stripping her naked. If Reid's assumption was true, and she had no reason to think otherwise, this man had murdered his brother. Thus far Reid's attempts to find proof had been unsuccessful. Then an idea came to her. Perhaps she could help, learn something of value. Du Beaupre was obviously attracted to her. Maybe she could turn his interest to Reid's advantage.

She swept a glance around the ballroom, then gave him a flirtatious smile. "I see no woman under your stalwart protection, m'sieur. Are you not married?"

"I confess, I've been waiting for a woman such as yourself." Even white teeth flashed in a dazzling smile. "No one has captured my interest . . . until now."

Unease slithered through her. She barely knew him, yet she was aware that this man was a master of manipulation. She counseled herself to proceed with caution. She looked around for Polly, but discovered her friend had drifted off.

Leon lifted two glasses of wine from a tray of refreshments. He handed one to her, then raised his in a toast. "To a remarkable lady."

"Remarkable?"

"Since meeting you at the opera, I made some inquiries. I learned you survived not one revolution, but two. That can be accomplished only with bravery and resourcefulness, two traits I admire very much." He watched her, his onyx eyes intent above the rim of his glass.

Christiane took a small sip of wine. "I prefer not to speak of those times, m'sieur. The memories are still too fresh, too painful. I would much rather have you tell about yourself."

Showing little regard for propriety, he drew her along with him toward a balcony overlooking a courtyard. Hoping to discover some little clue that might free Reid from the past, she didn't protest. Giving his life back to him would be her final gift. Then, and only then, would they be truly free.

When they were alone on the balcony, she turned to Leon. "Do you make the city your home, m'sieur?"

Once again perfect white teeth flashed in a swarthy face. "Please call me Leon."

She inclined her head graciously. "Very well. Do you make New Orleans your home, Leon?"

"I have a cottage here in the city. My real home is Briarwood."

"Briarwood," she repeated slowly. "What a lovely name. Tell me more about it."

He rocked back on his heels, his expression smug, self-satisfied. "It's a plantation along the Mississippi, midway between here and Baton Rouge."

"I'm afraid I know little about Louisiana. As yet, I haven't ventured out of New Orleans."

Taking a sip of wine, he gave her an indulgent smile. "You ought to see the bayous. They're like no other place on earth. Beautiful, exotic, teeming with unique wildlife and vegetation. Mysterious and quite lovely."

She studied him curiously. His dark eyes had lost their hard brilliance and taken on a dreamy cast. It made him seem more approachable, almost likable. "These bayous of yours sound quite fascinating."

"They are, but you must find out for yourself. I'm planning a small gathering, just a few close neighbors, to celebrate the completion of Briarwood. I'd be honored if you would accept my invitation to join us."

The invitation had been issued so smoothly that it caught her unprepared. She toyed with her diamond earring. "That is very kind of you, m'sieur, but—"

"Both you and your husband, of course," he amended quickly.

"Of course. We'd be delighted to accept your kind offer, m'sieur." She could scarcely contain her delight. Reid would be thrilled at the prospect of visiting du Beaupre's home. What better place to learn more about the man—and his family? "Why just this morning," she improvised, "my husband expressed an interest in seeing an American plantation."

"And how like you to listen so attentively." Reid stepped out of the ballroom and onto the balcony.

Anticipation danced down her spine at hearing the

smooth, familiar baritone. The mere sound of his voice caused her pulse to quicken. She found herself at once pleased and irritated by his effect on her.

Leon scowled, annoyed at the interruption. With barely a cursory nod to acknowledge Reid's presence, he took Christiane's hand and, bending low, brought it to his lips. "Until we meet again." Then, turning, he sauntered into the ballroom, disappearing into the crowd.

"Did I interrupt?" Reid asked, his voice cold, cutting.

"*Oui*," she retorted. "M'sieur du Beaupre and I were getting better acquainted when you appeared. He had just invited us to Briarwood."

Reid took her arm in a firm grip. "I think it's time we leave."

Perplexed by his behavior, she dug in her heels. "I thought you'd be pleased."

"Well, I'm not," he snapped. A muscle in his jaw bunched ominously. "I'm surprised you're away from your grandfather's side for this long."

She stared at him in wonderment. "Why, Reid Alexander," she drawled, her mouth curving into a slow smile, "I do believe you're jealous."

"That's ridiculous." He cast a quick glance about to make sure no one had overheard the use of his name, then glared down at her. "Leon du Beaupre is a dangerous man. Stay away from him."

Her amusement vanished in the wake of his high-handed manner. "You have no right to give me orders."

"Wrong, Countess." He tightened his grip, forcing her to keep pace as he returned to the ballroom. Dropping his voice so only she could hear, he warned, "Leon du Beaupre is nothing but a two-legged reptile. His venom is every bit as lethal as the snake in your sewing basket. I didn't save you from one only to be bitten by another."

Chapter Twenty

Christiane scanned the courtyard and did a quick mental inventory. Even the weather was cooperating, warm, sunny, but without the stifling heat. Fluffy white clouds floated across a cerulean sky like dollops of clotted cream. Red geraniums blooming in clay pots added to the festive air. Several chairs were grouped around a small table that Reid had carried down earlier. Everything seemed in readiness. At the sound of voices, she plumped a pillow for the final time.

"Watch yer step now," Rosie O'Banion admonished.

Christiane looked up and watched Jean-Claude slowly making his way down the stairs, flanked by Rosie on one side and Reid on the other. A lump rose in her throat at the sight. Each day she could see an improvement in his condition. His recovery was truly remarkable. When she despaired she had lost him forever, he had been given back to her.

"Easy does it now," Rosie continued. "I tried to tell ye this might be too soon, but would ye listen?"

"I'm tired of being cooped up," Jean-Claude complained. "It's high time I get outdoors. Soon I plan to take a stroll, see what this city is like. Etienne, here, has promised to show me the sights."

"When you're stronger, M'sieur le Comte." Reid lightly cupped the older man's elbow as he reached the bottom step. "Then we'll tour the sights together."

Jean-Claude stood for a moment, winded from the unaccustomed exertion, both hands resting on his walking cane. Christiane rushed over in greeting and slid her arm around his waist. "Soon, *Grand-père,* but not today."

"I wanted to pull a chair onto the gallery but no, he insisted on coming outside." Rosie moistened a fingertip, pointed it skyward, then nodded in satisfaction. "At least there's no wind blowin'. Don't want my patient comin' down with lung fever."

"Harumph!" Jean-Claude grunted. "The woman insists on treating me like some feebleminded invalid."

"Shame on her." Christiane nodded agreeably. "Everyone knows you have the constitution of a plowhorse."

She glimpsed the quicksilver amusement lighting Reid's eyes. Between the two of them, they guided Jean-Claude across the uneven paving stones to the table beneath a large magnolia tree. Once the count was seated, Reid stood aside while Christiane and Rosie fussed getting the count comfortably settled.

With a sigh of satisfaction, Jean-Claude sank back against the cushions while Rosie spread a light throw across his lap. "Being away from that sickroom is the best tonic in the world."

Dulcie bustled out with a covered tray. "I brought some of my special molasses cakes to help fatten you up," she said, whisking the napkin aside to reveal a frosty pitcher of lemonade and a plate piled high with pastries.

"*Merci*, madame." Jean-Claude eyed the cakes with interest. "I'll gladly eat or drink anything as long as it's not more milk."

"Ought to be thankful God created cows, if ye ask me," Rosie muttered under her breath.

"No one asked you, madame," Jean-Claude replied acerbically, but tempered his comment by offering his nurse a choice of the cakes.

Just as Dulcie finished pouring lemonade, Polly Wakefield pushed aside the gate that guarded the entrance to the courtyard. Polly paused when she saw the group congregated at the base of the magnolia tree, then broke into a pleased smile when her gaze registered Jean-Claude's presence. "I do hope I'm not disturbing anything," she apologized as she hastened toward them.

"But of course not, madame," Jean-Claude assured her. "Your unexpected visit is as welcome as sunshine after the rain."

At the flowery greeting, Polly colored and her smile widened. "It's such a lovely afternoon, I was out for a drive. I thought perhaps I could persuade Christiane to accompany me to the new milliner's shop just down the street."

Jean-Claude indicated a vacant chair. "Please, dear lady, join us for refreshments."

Polly self-consciously patted a curl in place. "Well, if you're certain I'm not interrupting a family gathering."

"I insist," Jean-Claude stated firmly. "More than insist, actually. I would feel desolate if a pretty lady such as yourself would deprive me of such charming company."

Polly dimpled. "Ah, Count Bouchard, you make me feel young and foolish."

"Young? But of course. Foolish . . . ?" Jean-Claude shook his head. "Never, *ma chère*."

Christiane caught Reid's eye. He had been following the exchange with rapt attention. His lips twitched with suppressed mirth. Christiane bit her lower lip to keep from smiling. The flirtation between her grandfather and dearest friend was a pleasure to observe. Then bemusement turned bittersweet. She envied the fact that they could show their burgeoning affections so openly, so honestly. She wished it could be the same with her and Reid.

The courtyard gate creaked open for the second time to admit a black man of small stature with stooped shoulders and wiry, close-cropped hair, its gray liberally interspersed with silver.

Dulcie narrowed her eyes, glaring at the man suspiciously. "I'll go take care o' him. Don't need no peddlers comin' by this house."

Everyone watched as the housekeeper waddled across the courtyard, then engaged the man in a lively conversation, punctuated by raised voices and flailing arms. But in spite of her best efforts, the man apparently refused to budge. Dulcie turned back, a scowl on her usually affable face.

"Is anything wrong, Dulcie?" Reid asked, stepping forward and taking charge.

"Man say he brung a message for Madame. Won't leave 'till he gives it hisself."

"Did he give you his name? Tell you who sent him?"

"Don't tell me nuthin'." Dulcie sent an indignant look at the man over her shoulder.

Crooking his finger, Reid motioned the unwanted guest nearer. Christiane rose to stand beside him. "I am Madame Delacroix," she said quietly as the man approached. "You have a message for me?"

"Oui, madame." The little man bobbed his head nervously.

"May I ask who you are?" she inquired. "And who sent you?"

"Name's Rollo," he said, shuffling his feet. "I belongs to M'sieur du Beaupre."

"Du Beaupre!" Reid exclaimed in disbelief.

The outburst diverted the servant's attention to Reid. Rollo stared transfixed. The whites of his eyes formed wide rims around dark pupils. He took an involuntary half step backward.

"What's wrong, man?" Reid asked, frowning. "You act as though you've just seen a ghost."

Rollo swallowed once, twice. He tried to speak but no words came out.

"Rollo?" Christiane asked, puzzled at the servant's peculiar behavior. "Is anything wrong?"

"If you're ill, we'll summon a doctor," Polly offered helpfully.

Dulcie rolled her eyes in disgust. "I go gets the man some water."

Rollo seemed to recover his wits. "N-no, don' bother, ma'am. Nothin' wrong."

"Harrumph!" Jean-Claude tapped his walking cane peremptorily. "Out with it, man. What is this important message that had to be hand-delivered?"

Recalling his mission, Rollo dragged his gaze from Reid. He withdrew an envelope from the breast pocket of his jacket and offered it to Christiane with a hand that visibly trembled. "This come from M'sieur Leon."

Sensing Reid's gathering disapproval, Christiane broke the seal and quickly scanned the missive.

"What is it, dear?" Polly voiced the question in everyone's mind.

"An invitation to visit Briarwood." Her gaze locked with Reid's. "It seems M'sieur du Beaupre is hosting a small gathering and wishes us to attend."

"Excellent." Reid's mouth curled into a humorless smile.

Had he gone mad? she wondered. What if du Beaupre recognized him? Until now, the two men had paid each other only cursory attention, but that would change with them in close proximity. Only a crazy person would put himself directly in harm's way. She gave Rollo an apologetic smile. "I'm afraid my husband and I are unable to accept—"

"Nonsense, *ma petite*," Jean-Claude interrupted. "You needn't worry about me. I'll be quite all right in Mademoiselle O'Banion's competent care. Young couples such as yourselves ought to socialize."

"Put your mind at ease, dear," Polly chimed. "I'll gladly volunteer to keep your grandfather company in your absence should he become lonely."

Christiane scrambled frantically to find an excuse. The less time Reid spent near du Beaupre the safer he'd be. She couldn't dismiss Rollo's strange reaction upon seeing Reid. Running the tip of her tongue over her lower lip, she placed her hand on his arm. "My husband has already made other plans. . . ."

"Plans can easily be changed, sweet." Reid placed his hand over hers and gave it a warning squeeze. "Rollo," he said, addressing the slave. "Inform your master that Madame and M'sieur Delacroix accept his generous invitation—with pleasure."

Sick with dismay, she gazed up at Reid, but nothing in his enigmatic expression betrayed his thoughts. What was he thinking? Planning? It was impossible to play with fire and not get burned. Anger and fear warred for dominance.

Didn't the man know it was best to maintain a safe distance until he could prove his innocence? Did he want to rot away in a Spanish penal colony? Didn't he know that believing him innocent but being helpless to prove it would kill her?

Under different circumstances, Christiane might have enjoyed the carriage ride. It was like passing through a verdant green cathedral. The bayous were a unique mix of land and liquid, rampant with luxurious vegetation and abundant wildlife. Mosses, vines, trees, water plants, and ferns grew in profusion. Sluggish waterways were carpeted with a dense green film. Spanish moss hung from the boughs of live oaks like beards growing from old men's chins. She grudgingly admitted Leon's description of the bayous had been apt. The country was indeed beautiful, mysterious, exotic.

And eerie.

Creatures, stealthy and silent, were sensed rather than seen. A ripple in the water, the rustle of a bush, the quivering of a leaf left telltale clues of their presence. Several times Christiane spotted the partially submerged form of an alligator lazing in the water. She spied more sunning on a riverbank.

A swarthy man maneuvered a boat made of hollowed-out cypress through the marsh with a long pole. Upon seeing Reid and Christiane, he gave them a broad smile and a friendly wave as the boat skimmed past. Shrimps and oysters were heaped in the back of the boat, attesting to the man's skill as a fisherman. Christiane assumed he was of the Acadians, or Cajuns, Polly had described, who eked their living from the bayous.

"Cat got your tongue, Countess?"

She sent Reid a scathing look. "I don't know why I let you talk me into this. You're mad to come here."

"Perhaps." He didn't pretend to misunderstand. "However, I'm not left with many choices."

"What do you hope to accomplish? You are only giving du Beaupre a greater opportunity to recognize you as the man he claims killed his brother."

He shrugged off her concern. "It's a risk I have to take."

"Why?" she cried. "You have your freedom. Take it, go somewhere safe."

"I can't." He kept his eyes on the narrow road that snaked its way along the levee.

"Can't?" she challenged. "Or won't?"

He remained stubbornly silent.

"This is just some sort of macabre game that appeals to the gambler in you. But the stakes are too high. You're betting your life. You could lose, Reid, lose everything."

"You don't understand."

"You're right, I don't. Do you?"

How could he explain what he didn't fully comprehend himself? Reid wondered. It was just something he had to do. He didn't need Christiane to remind him that the stakes were high. But he couldn't allow Leon du Beaupre to get away with murder. The man was slimy as the scum floating in the bayou, as stealthy and deadly as the cottonmouths that slithered through its waters. Leon had taken his brother's life, then tried to cheat Reid out of his. Chained like a mad dog, beaten to within an inch of his life, robbed of dignity and his manhood. Then fate, in the form of a storm at sea, had given him a second chance. Why did he risk losing all he had regained?

"It's just something I have to do," Reid muttered more to himself than to Christiane. "I never meant to get you involved."

"I got myself involved," she reminded him.

He shot her a sidelong glance. The countess certainly did have a mind of her own. No one would guess that beneath her cameolike perfection was a core of solid steel. Seeing her as pretty as a picture in her gown the color of ripe apricots sent desire coursing through him. Temper brought a brushstroke of peach across her cheekbones and a wicked sparkle to her dark eyes. His fingers itched to pull the pins from her hair and run them through her silky tresses. He wanted to muss her hair, wrinkle her gown, transform prim into passion. Setting his jaw, he struggled against the impulse.

Instead of lusting after her, he should be trying to convince her to leave New Orleans. Now that her grandfather had sufficiently recovered, there was no reason for her to remain. Any association with him would prove disastrous. He wanted to spare her the humiliation, the pain.

"If you were as sensible as you claim, you'd take your grandfather and leave New Orleans."

"Are you trying to be rid of me?"

"I wouldn't have put it quite that way, but yes. As far as I'm concerned, your presence is only complicating things."

She turned her head away, adjusting her frilly parasol so that he couldn't see her face. "How silly of me. I thought I was being helpful."

There, he had gone and done it. He knew her well enough to recognize the hurt thrumming through her voice. The last thing he wanted to do was cause her distress, but in the long run it might be the kindest thing he could do. "I don't need a woman making demands, looking for commitment. I've traveled alone most of my life. That's the way I like it. There's no room in my life for someone like you."

That at least was the truth, Reid acknowledged bitterly.

She was a member of the French nobility, raised amid wealth and privilege. They came from different worlds—belonged to different worlds. Yet every time he took her in his arms, he wanted to hold fast and never let go.

"Very well." She kept her eyes fixed on the passing greenery, her voice thick with emotion. "Anxiety precipitated Grandfather's illness, and I worry about a relapse. As soon as he's stronger, I'll tell him the truth about you and Etienne. He'll be furious, but I'm sure he'll understand the necessity to settle elsewhere. In the meantime, however, we'll both have to tolerate each other's company awhile longer."

"Agreed." Reid had accomplished what he had set out to do. He had driven the wedge deeper. Why did he feel so hollow inside?

There's no room in my life for someone like you. Reid's rejection echoed through her mind, filling her with despair. She felt as though her heart had been ripped open. Until now she had never imagined words—just words—could cause so much pain. A pain too deep for tears.

They traveled for some time in silence. Christiane retreated into herself, trying to cope with the blow Reid had dealt her, bringing her to her knees. Even the physical cruelty Etienne had subjected her to had not hurt as much. Loving someone made you vulnerable, she realized.

At last pride came to her rescue. She refused to let him see how sorely he had wounded her. "If you can prove Leon killed his brother, will you make Louisiana your home?" Christiane asked, striving to regain some semblance of normality.

"I like it here," he admitted. "I'd consider staying, putting down roots."

In a short period of time, she, too, had grown fond of New Orleans and was eager to put down roots. She had recently fled France, then St. Domingue, and soon would leave Louisiana. Feeling like a perennial guest, she was tired of this nomadic existence. She yearned for permanence, stability—needs Reid would never fulfill.

The ground became firmer, with fewer marshes. Here and there they spotted tracts of land that had been cleared for planting cotton and indigo. Slaves with heavy burlap sacks slung over their shoulders moved through the fields, while an overseer stood watch, whip at the ready.

"If I do remain, I want no part of slavery." His expression grim, Reid surveyed the workers in the fields. "I'd give the men an opportunity to earn their freedom, encourage them to remain for a working wage."

She nodded her approval. "From what I've observed, cruelty and misery foster hatred and resentment. That in turn drives the oppressed to extremes."

Following the directions that had been provided, Reid guided the rented carriage through tall iron gates elaborately scrolled with the letter *B* and down a broad avenue shaded with live oaks. Branches arched and twined overhead to form a canopy so dense that not even the bright Louisiana sunlight could penetrate. Christiane intuitively sat straighter, tension stiffening her spine.

As the plantation came into view, Reid drew the carriage to a halt. Although less imposing than Belle Terre, the house was well proportioned and appealing. Framed at the end of the tunnel of greenery, it appeared stately, with eight sturdy columns supporting a wide gallery. A series of dormers projected from a steepled and gabled roof. Beyond the house, the Mississippi River shimmered in the distance.

Christiane cast a sidelong glance at Reid. Lost in

thought, he seemed unaware of everything but the house in front of him. The raw longing in his expression tugged at her heart. His eyes reminded her of the Atlantic, cold, bleak, unfathomable. "What are you thinking?"

He exhaled a ragged sigh. "This could have—should have—been mine. In my entire life, I never owned anything of substance. Never anything of beauty. Somehow they were always just out of my grasp."

"I wish you would reconsider. I wish you'd turn the carriage around and return to New Orleans before it's too late." Though she realized she belabored the point, she couldn't resist another try.

He slapped the reins and the carriage moved forward. "I'm a gambler, remember?"

Stylishly attired in a burgundy jacket and buff breeches, Leon du Beaupre waited at the foot of the steps to greet them.

"Welcome to Briarwood." He elbowed aside the servant whose duty it was to help guests alight and, placing his hands at Christiane's waist, swung her to the ground. "I feared the trip overland would tire you. But not even the tedious journey could dim your vibrant beauty. The fresh air has brought color to your cheeks and a sparkle to your eyes."

"And as usual, m'sieur, you turn my head with gallant flattery." Ignoring Reid's glower, she smiled flirtatiously at Leon du Beaupre.

Leon's observant gaze went to Reid, who now stood next to the carriage stiff and unsmiling, then back to Christiane's flushed face. With smug satisfaction, he tucked her hand through the crook of his arm and returned her smile. "The same journey by river would have taken a fraction of the time. As my note mentioned, Briarwood does have its own boat dock."

Christiane matched his leisurely pace, leaving Reid to follow. "My husband wanted to view the land."

Leon spared Reid a cursory glance. "The bayous are quite unique, don't you think?"

"Quite," Reid agreed, clasping his hands behind his back. "But I had the impression the bayou hides as much as it reveals."

"Ah, you are perceptive." Leon nodded with approval. "For all their deceptive beauty, the bayous can be treacherous. Poisonous reptiles and alligators abound. One must be ever vigilant."

Christiane tilted her parasol for a better look at the house. "Briarwood is lovely, m'sieur. I particularly admire the magnificent view of the river."

"I'm sure you'll want to freshen up and rest. One of the servants will show you to your room." Leon turned to Reid. "Since you expressed an interest, I've arranged for my overseer to give you a tour of Briarwood. Having owned a plantation in St. Domingue, you must be curious to see how ours compare."

"Indeed," Reid answered with alacrity. "I'm very much interested."

He beckoned to a servant. "Victor, see what M'sieur Delacroix would like in the way of refreshments before his tour."

Victor bowed his head solemnly. "Follow me, m'sieur."

After Reid disappeared behind the servant, Leon directed his attention back to Christiane. "After you've had a chance to freshen up, I'll conduct a personal tour of the house."

"I will enjoy that . . . Leon." She deliberately lingered over his given name, determined to use any weapon in her limited arsenal. His chest visibly expanded upon hearing it. How conceited of him, she thought with disgust, careful to keep her sentiments hidden.

She picked up her skirt and followed a maid up the winding staircase. A breeze from the river wafted through the upper hallway from the double set of doors that opened onto the gallery. She was drawn to the vista beyond. A wide lawn sloped toward a silver-blue ribbon of water that twisted its way to the sea. Huge trees, some cypress, others oaks, dotted the spacious yard. To the right she spied a formal garden with wrought-iron benches strategically placed along the shell walkway. Briarwood seemed to embody gracious hospitality. It was less formidable and more inviting than Belle Terre, and she could easily envision Reid strolling its paths, supervising its crops, and presiding at the head of the table.

As though she had conjured him from her thoughts, she glimpsed his broad shoulders as he accompanied du Beaupre's overseer. The two men had their heads bent, deep in conversation, neither noticing Leon, who stood at the foot of the drive, a calculating smile on his swarthy face.

"Madame, this way," the maid prompted. "I will show you your room."

With a shake of her head, Christiane recalled herself to the present and followed the servant. Leon had provided a guest room befitting royalty. A flower motif was carried out in the draperies and bed hangings of the carved four-poster mahogany bed. The color scheme of pale blue and gold was also evident in the Oriental carpet. A vase of freshly cut blooms on a low chest filled the air with their light, flowery essence.

While waiting for the girl to return with water for bathing, Christiane untied the ribbons of her bonnet as she strolled around the room. Her gaze landed on a small foil-wrapped box resting on the dressing table. A note addressed to her was tucked beneath. Breaking open the seal, she quickly scanned the contents: *A small token of my esteem.*

No signature was affixed to the note, but none was necessary. The gift was from Leon. Slipping off the paper, she opened the box and found a small jeweled brooch. She snapped the box shut. The man was attempting to woo her with expensive jewelry. She shivered. Once again she was struck by Leon's similarity to Etienne.

Chapter
Twenty-one

An hour later Christiane wound her way down the stairs, looking fresh and rested in a lemon yellow gown with tiny silk flowers tucked into her dark curls. Though not eager for an encounter with her host, she didn't want to spend the remainder of the afternoon cowering in her room. If she wanted to help Reid establish his innocence, she needed to use this opportunity to learn everything possible about his adversary. Ideally, she could locate the elusive Rollo and try to engage the man in conversation.

But this wasn't an ideal world.

At her light tread on the steps, Leon du Beaupre stepped into the hallway and watched her descent. Seeing him standing there, handsome, self-assured, and urbane, Christiane found it difficult to reconcile him as anything other than a successful Creole plantation owner. But using words as bitter, angry brushstrokes, Reid had painted quite a different picture. *Evil, cunning, conniving*—Reid had created the portrait of a coldhearted killer.

He took her hand from where it rested on the banister and raised it to his lips. "How did you like my gift, *chérie?*" he murmured in a silky voice.

"It's lovely; however, I can't accept it," she said with a small smile.

He made a moue of regret. "Think of the brooch as a small token of my esteem."

"I fear it would be considered highly inappropriate for a married woman to receive such a token." She carefully extricated her hand from his grasp. "Regardless of the intent."

"I have the perfect solution. Don't tell your husband," he said, brushing aside her misgivings. "Think of it as our little secret."

She tried to disguise her aversion. His suggestion served only to confirm Reid's comments on his unsavory character. "I'm not sure. . . . " she demurred, dropping her gaze.

His black eyes glittering with admiration, he smiled down at her. "Nonsense. All wives, or so I'm told, keep secrets from their husbands."

Raising her head, she studied him. "And husbands," she asked, attempting to keep her tone light, "do they also keep secrets?"

"Absolutely—it is a little game both parties enjoy." He took her arm and led her through the entrance fronting the river. "I thought you might enjoy a stroll through the gardens. I've asked one of the servants to bring refreshments afterward."

Christiane accepted the offer with alacrity. This would be a perfect opportunity to learn more about him. "Has New Orleans always been your home?"

He nodded. "I'm proud to be a Creole, the first generation of my family to be born here."

"Tell me everything," she encouraged as they strolled down the path toward orderly rows of flowers and shrubs. "I want to know all about you."

"There's nothing much to tell. I have led an uneventful life."

"Oh, I beg to differ, m'sieur." Christiane hid her smile. In spite of his deprecatory manner, she sensed he was flattered by her attention. "A successful, sophisticated man such as yourself must surely lead an interesting existence. What was your family like? Did you come from a large family?"

"My family is deceased."

"All of them?" She adopted a sympathetic expression. "I'm so sorry. How lonely it must be for you in such a large house."

"Do not distress yourself, *chérie.*" He laid his hand over hers. "It is a temporary situation, one I soon plan to remedy. All I lack is the perfect woman to grace Briarwood as its mistress."

"There must be many young women eager for the opportunity."

"Unfortunately none of the young Creole women I've met interest me. Now you, on the other hand," he said, lowering his voice, "fascinate me."

She pretended interest in the gardener snipping late-blooming roses. Insects lazily buzzed among the blooms while birds warbled overhead—a peaceful scene in variance with her mounting tension. The Creole was far too bold. Christiane was confounded by the predicament of how to put the man in his place without alienating him completely.

Taking her silence as encouragement, Leon continued.

"My spies inform me that you are a French countess. What lured you from France to a remote island in the Caribbean, and then from the Caribbean to New Orleans?"

He neatly managed to turn the tables, deliberately evasive about revealing personal information while trying to ferret out hers. She gave him a rueful smile. "Both times a revolution is at fault. You need be forewarned, m'sieur: with my history I may infect New Orleans with the need to rebel."

He threw back his head and laughed in delight at her droll comment. "Did you know your husband long before marrying?" he asked after he sobered.

"We met in St. Domingue."

"Did you have a long engagement?"

"Non," she replied softly.

"Personally I have never understood the advantages of a long engagement. When I decide to marry, it'll be as soon as possible after the banns are posted."

"Ours was a marriage by proxy."

"Ah!" He beamed. "That explains it."

She shot him a puzzled glance. "Explains what, m'sieur?"

"I sensed an estrangement, a certain aloofness, between you and Etienne. From the beginning I suspected yours was not a love match."

They slowly retraced their way back toward the house. "Many couples form an attachment over time," she explained to justify her actions. "Marriages are built on other factors, such as mutual respect, common interests, and, in time, children."

"Yes, of course," he agreed easily. "It is that way for many people."

She heaved a sigh of gratitude when she looked up and saw Reid, his tour over, approach from the opposite direction.

"Welcome back, Etienne." Leon's voice took on a hearty tone. "What did you think? Did Briarwood meet your expectations?"

Reid stared pointedly at Christiane's hand tucked into the crook of Leon's arm. "It's a beautiful piece of property," he said as she removed it and took his instead. "I was impressed at how efficiently it seems to run."

"I personally oversee every detail." Leon climbed the steps and indicated his guests be seated around a small table on the wide porch. "It is my understanding that the French planters on St. Domingue leave most decisions to their overseers. I've heard they're more interested in the overall profits rather than the day-to-day running of a large plantation."

Reid sat down, crossed his legs, then flicked an imaginary speck from his pant leg. "You seem remarkably well informed about island ways, yet I don't recall our ever having met in St. Domingue."

"No, I've never been there." With a snap of his fingers, Leon ordered the maid hovering nearby to serve refreshments. "However, I have a good friend, Pierre LeClerc, who lives there. Perhaps you know him?"

At the mention of the familiar name, Christiane clutched her glass of lemonade. Fear knotted her stomach. She recalled meeting Pierre the night of Etienne's party. Had he survived the bloodbath? Did the men correspond? If Leon should question Pierre about Etienne, what would he say?

"Yes, we've met briefly, but I can't claim to be well acquainted," Reid answered calmly.

Christiane took advantage of the slight pause to change the subject. "I was under the impression, M'sieur du Beaupre, that you were hosting a gathering, yet so far there are only my husband and myself. Was I mistaken?"

Leon bit into a dainty fruit tart. "Forgive my man Rollo, *ma chère*, if he gave you false information. Other than yourselves, I expect only my nearest neighbors, the Blanchards, to join us. I prefer small, intimate dinners to large gatherings. They provide a much better opportunity to become acquainted, don't you agree?"

"Oui." Christiane rose, her pastry untouched on her plate. "If you gentlemen will excuse me, I need to change before dinner."

Both men climbed to their feet. "But of course." Leon smiled. "Though it means we will be deprived of your charming company. I hope you two don't mind terribly that I've given you separate rooms." Leon spread his hand in a helpless gesture, but his oily smile betrayed his lack of sincerity. "The guest rooms are quite small, cramped actually. I thought you might be more comfortable if you each had more space."

"How thoughtful of you, m'sieur, to consider our comfort," Christiane replied.

"My late brother, Gaston, designed the house himself," Leon said, his expression darkening. "I don't know what he was thinking to have such small bedrooms. I'm afraid Gaston didn't always exercise good judgment."

Reid helped himself to another tart. "You must have found it difficult to tolerate your brother's foolish mistakes."

Leon nodded curtly. " 'Difficult' scarcely describes my feelings."

"Bonjour, gentlemen." Her spine stiff and straight, Christiane turned and left, aware that both men followed her departure with interest.

* * *

Christiane prepared for dinner slowly. She wasn't eager to continue the verbal sparring match with Leon du Beaupre. She felt out of her league with a man of his caliber. She only prayed that Reid proved himself a worthy adversary.

She lounged back in the tub of rapidly cooling water. Now that she was alone, she felt the lash of Reid's harsh rejection all over again. Once again pride came to the fore. How dare he accuse her of making demands, then carelessly toss her aside? She was a countess, a descendant of French royalty. She refused to grovel like a peasant for his affection.

Picking up a sliver of lavender-scented soap, she thoughtfully lathered a sponge. Reid had deliberately erected an invisible barrier between them, diligently adding brick after brick until it was nearly impossible to scale. Deep in her heart, in spite of his cruel demeanor, she knew he cared. A kernel of hope took root. The blood of Norman warriors flowed through her veins. She would not surrender without a battle. She would not make it easy for him to leave.

Or for him to forget her.

Christiane sighed as a little maid entered carrying her newly pressed gown. "They call me Minnie. Master said I'se to help you dress for dinner."

"*Merci.*" Christiane rose from the tub and accepted the towel the girl offered.

Later, clad only in her chemise and petticoats, she sat before the dressing table while the girl silently fussed with her hair. Christiane gave up trying to engage the girl in conversation. Glancing at Minnie's closed expression in the beveled mirror, she was reminded of Hera. The servants here at Briarwood, she noted, were as sullen and hostile as they had been at Belle Terre. She would be glad to bid this place *adieu.*

Finally she was ready. The gown of striped satin the shade of old gold shimmered in the candlelight, lending her a radiance all its own. Her hair was arranged in a smooth coil at the nape of her neck. Drawing a deep breath to settle her nerves, she thanked Minnie for her assistance and went downstairs.

Leon and Reid were waiting for her in the library. Once again she was struck by similarities to her first evening at Belle Terre. She wondered if Reid sensed it, too. Only this time it was Leon, not Etienne, who was resplendent in a silk coat embroidered with flowers and birds, gold waistcoat, and green silk breeches. Lace trimmed his immaculate white neckcloth and spilled over his wrists. Reid, as was his custom, dressed more conservatively in a dove gray jacket with breeches of the same shade. His single concession to the somber tones was a wine red brocade waistcoat. Upon her arrival, the pair ceased their desultory conversation and turned to greet her.

Christiane looked about the room expectantly, but saw no other guests. Leon set his sherry aside and came forward. "You must be wondering," he said, correctly interpreting her puzzled glance. "My neighbors, the Blanchards, will be unable to join us this evening. They sent their profound apologies, but their youngest has a fever and they don't want to leave him. They hoped you'd understand."

"But of course." Secretly she questioned whether such people even existed, or were merely a fabrication.

"Excellent." He offered her his arm. "My servants have just informed me dinner is ready."

Reid trailed behind as Leon escorted Christiane into the dining room. Leon seated her at his right, then, after indicating Reid was to occupy the chair to his left, took his place at the head of the table. Christiane noted that unlike Etienne, Leon preferred a more intimate seating arrangement rather than yards of polished mahogany between them. The meal began when a servant placed a steaming tureen of crayfish bisque on the table.

Christiane used a temporary lull in the conversation to ask a question. "You mentioned your brother . . . Gaston, I believe you called him. Am I correct in assuming he died at an early age?"

"Yes," Leon answered with a pained smile. "He suffered an unfortunate incident while we were abroad."

Christiane ignored the telltale tightening of Reid's jaw. "How tragic," she murmured sympathetically. "What happened?"

"You are very kind, but it is in the past. Please do not concern yourself."

She took a dainty taste of bisque. "I did not mean to pry, but only offer my sympathy. It must have been a trying time, especially since you were so far away—a stranger in a foreign land."

Leon broke off a piece of bread. "The situation called for drastic measures. I did what needed to be done."

Christiane cast a sidelong glance at Reid and noticed that he had given up all pretense of eating. "Ah, m'sieur," she crooned to Leon. "I see that you are a man who takes charge. A man who refuses to let adversity stand in his way."

"Yes, I suppose one could say that about me." Leon preened under her flattery. "You are very intuitive, *chérie.*"

She waited until after the servants removed the soup dishes before asking her next question. "Was your brother, Gaston, much the same as you, m'sieur?"

"Gaston?" Leon nearly spat the name in disgust. "He was nothing more than a buffoon, overly fond of drink and cards. If I hadn't intervened, he would have gambled away our legacy, our inheritance. Briarwood would belong to an interloper at this very moment."

"Briarwood is quite lovely," she said, keeping her tone noncommittal as she sliced a small morsel of the succulent roast. "What a grave injustice it would have been to lose your home."

"Yes, I thought so, too," Leon said agreeably. "That's why I did everything possible to keep it from falling into the hands of a stranger."

Christiane widened her eyes with interest. "Exactly what did you do, m'sieur, to save your home?"

"Methods not meant for gentle ears, *ma chère*." Leon's expression grew remote, closed.

"You do not seem overly fond of your brother." Reid spoke for the first time. "Or am I mistaken?"

Leon's heavy lids lowered fractionally. "No, we weren't close, but then we were only half brothers. We shared the same father, but had different mothers. Perhaps that explains why Father chose Gaston as his principal heir."

It had become blatantly apparent to Christiane that Leon had despised his older brother. Losing the deed to Briarwood in a game of chance must have driven Leon into a killing rage, providing ample motive for a heinous act. Now to find proof. "Your brother's actions were reprehensible," she commiserated, calling on all her acting skills to hide her true feelings.

"My brother was a weakling. A fool!" Leon reached for his wineglass, drained it, then collected his composure. "Enough said on the subject. It's considered bad luck to speak ill of the dead."

A wicked smile played across her lips as she leaned closer. "I would not have thought you were superstitious, m'sieur."

The corners of Leon's mouth turned down in displeasure. "You will soon learn that many in and around New

Orleans are superstitious," he replied. "Blame it on the voodoo practices brought here by slaves imported from the Indies."

The sound of breaking glass drew the diners' attention to the doorway. A crystal decanter lay shattered amidst a river of spilled wine. Rollo, his wizened face puckered in distress, was stooped over, frantically picking up shards of broken glass.

Furious, Leon tossed his napkin aside, climbed to his feet, and with quick strides traversed the room. "You clumsy dolt." He towered over the hapless servant. "Now see what you've done. That was one of the finest wines in my cellar. I ought to have you flogged."

"Sorry, master. Don't know what come over me." Rollo swallowed nervously, but kept on picking up splinters of glass. "The bottle just slip from my hands. Jest gettin' ole."

"Minnie!" Leon bellowed. "Fetch a mop and help Rollo clean up this mess before it stains the floorboards." He straightened his jacket with a tug, then, calmer, addressed his guests. "Fortunately there is another bottle downstairs. If you'll excuse me, I'll get it myself, since I can't trust anyone else with a simple task."

When they were alone, Christiane leaned forward and dropped her voice to a whisper. "Don't you find it odd how Rollo reacts every time he sees you?"

"And how is that?" he asked, frowning.

"You make him jittery, agitated." Gnawing her lower lip thoughtfully, she studied Rollo's bent form, but the servant kept his eyes on his task. "Do you think he might recognize you?"

Reid, too, studied the stooped figure. "Can't say I remember ever seeing the man before."

"Could it have been in Spain?" Christiane felt a flutter of excitement at the prospect.

"I suppose it's possible." Reid absently twirled the stem of his wineglass. "However, there were a lot of people in the casino that night. I can't say I specifically recall seeing him."

When Leon returned moments later triumphantly brandishing a bottle of wine, he seemed elated to find his guests sharing a morose silence. Taking his place once again at the head of the table, he resumed his role of host, relating anecdotes about the city's unique customs and colorful history. When the last of the dinner dishes had been cleared, he invited Reid to join him in the library for brandy and cigars.

Christiane wanted time to sort through some of the information she had just gleaned. In spite of Reid's having no recollection of him in Spain, she couldn't shake the notion that Rollo held the key to the mystery. If not, why did the man act so strangely in Reid's presence? Upon their arrival at Briarwood, she had noticed a dirt path leading to a series of whitewashed outbuildings and to the slave cabins beyond. Rather than retiring to the drawing room, she decided to search for the servant instead.

Outside, the night wafted about her, weaving its sultry Southern magic. A silver crescent of a moon played hide-and-seek among clouds scudding across an indigo sky. The sweet fragrance of night-blooming jasmine lingered in the air like a woman's perfume. *A night for lovers.* The notion skittered through her mind, took hold. She imagined herself and Reid, hand in hand, wandering down a path leading toward the meandering river. Imagined him gathering her in his arms . . . and kissing her.

There's no room in my life for someone like you.

Dreams, nothing but pretty dreams. A tear rolled down her cheek, and she brushed it away with a trembling hand. In spite of her resolve, doubts crept in. Lost in a tangle of longing and despair, she nearly collided with the stoop-shouldered figure emerging from a lower-level storage room.

"Rollo . . . ?" she managed when she found her voice. "You startled me."

"S-sorry, ma'am." He hugged a teakwood case to his thin chest, ready to bolt at the slightest provocation.

"Please don't run off." She gave him a reassuring smile. "It's a beautiful night, and after such a wonderful meal I felt the need for a little exercise. Tell me, Rollo, have you been with M'sieur du Beaupre for very long?"

"Yes, ma'am." He nodded vigorously. "Been with his family most of my life."

He edged away, but she forestalled his retreat by falling into step with him. "How interesting. Have you always served as M'sieur Leon's personal servant?"

"No, ma'am. Afore that I tended his brother."

Lightly placing a forefinger against her cheek, she pretended to consider the matter. "Ah, you must be referring to Gaston? Were the two brothers much alike?"

Rollo avoided her gaze. "No, ma'am. Different as day and night."

Leon had been deliberately vague about the details. Christiane's mind sifted through various ways of asking the servant whether he had accompanied his master to Spain without arousing the man's suspicions. She didn't want to appear overeager and frighten the man off.

"Sorry, ma'am," he apologized. "M'sieur Leon be wantin' his fine cigars. He gets mean if he's kept waitin' too long." Rollo scurried away.

Frustrated by her lack of success, she kicked a stone in her path. A childish act, she knew, but it made her feel better. Her instincts screamed that Rollo had recognized Reid as the man accused of killing Gaston even if his master didn't. What prevented him from sharing this information with Leon? So far Leon had been too taken with her to pay more than perfunctory attention to Reid. But that could soon end. She must convince Reid to leave not only Briarwood but New Orleans. His house of cards was about to collapse.

The evening seemed to stretch interminably, but finally it was time to bid their host good night and retire to the privacy of their individual bedrooms. Christiane's robe drifted around her as she paced back and forth. Sounds from the distant bayou carried through the open window. Now that night had fallen, the swampland seemed alive with the cries of birds and nocturnal animals. The hoarse call of a bull alligator reverberated through the darkness, adding to her unrest.

She continued to pace barefooted, waiting for the household to fall asleep before making her move. Leon du Beaupre reminded her of one of the alligators she had seen lazing in the bayou, patient, lightning quick. Deadly. He was the sort to allow his victim a false sense of complacency before snapping his massive jaws closed, trapping, then demolishing.

Assured at last that everyone was asleep, she tiptoed out of her room, down the hallway and to the room assigned to Reid. Since there were no locks on any of the rooms, she slowly eased inside and quietly closed the door behind her.

Within seconds she found her arm pinned behind her back and the blade of a knife pressed against her throat. She froze, too terrified to protest. Just as suddenly she was released.

"You!" Reid whispered. "What are you doing sneaking about at this hour? I could have hurt you."

"You did, you idiot!" she snapped, furious with him. "You nearly broke my arm."

"I was more worried that I might have slit your throat." At odd variance with his gruff words, Reid ran gentle fingers over the spot where his knife had touched.

She jerked away, tossing her hair over her shoulder, and rubbed her arm. They regarded each other in silence. He was wearing only the dove gray breeches he had worn at dinner. His broad chest gleamed like polished teak. In the dim light filtering through the slats of the blinds, he looked primitive, dangerous. The quintessential warrior.

"I came to warn you," she said at last. "I'm almost certain Rollo suspects who you really are."

Reid raked a hand through his tawny locks. "Then why hasn't he voiced his suspicions to Leon?"

"Who's to say he won't?" She posed the question paramount to both of them. "Once he's certain, he'll tell his master and you'll be returned to prison—or worse. Coming here was folly. We can't remain at Briarwood."

Folding his arms across his bare chest, he considered what she had just told him, then nodded his consent. "Very well. Be ready to leave first thing tomorrow morning."

"*Bon.*" She heaved a sigh of relief. "I am relieved to find that you possess some sense after all."

"I needed to see Briarwood." Turning his back on her, he walked to the window, staring bleakly at the darkened landscape. "All I know is that I can't let this man get away with murdering his own brother."

She went to stand next to him. He looked so unhappy, so tortured, she wanted to reach out and soothe his pain— but she refrained. "Why does it matter so?"

His shoulders rose and fell. "Maybe I need to understand

why one brother could kill another. My brother Chase gave his life to save mine. Then he died in my arms."

"So this is the burden you carry," she murmured.

"A team of horses bolted, overturning the carriage they were pulling and dragging it behind. It happened just as the two of us came out of an alley. If Chase hadn't shoved me out of the way, I would have been the one trampled to death. Instead . . ."

"Reid, it was an accident, a horrible accident. But what has it to do with the du Beaupre brothers?"

"Nothing . . . everything." He released a weary sigh. "Brothers share a special bond. I only know I can't walk away while Leon gets away with murder."

Surrendering to impulse, she slipped her arms around his waist and rested her cheek against his scarred back. Her heart bled for him. He was such a fine, decent man, immersed in his own private hell. She wished there were something she could say to dissuade him from his mission, but his mind was made up. Further argument would be futile. He was desperately trying to assuage the guilt that he had lived while his brother had died. In some convoluted way, seeking justice for Gaston's murder would fulfill that need.

Her eyes bright with unshed tears, her throat clogged with emotion, Christiane didn't trust herself to speak.

I love you, Reid Alexander. Love you with all my heart.

Every fiber of her being hummed with the knowledge, but she didn't speak the words aloud. Turning, she left him to his brooding.

With his bedroom door ajar, Leon du Beaupre had an excellent vantage spot. He had observed Christiane's clandestine visit to her husband's bedroom. She hadn't seemed particularly happy or pleased upon returning to her own room a short time later. There had been none of the telltale signs of a satisfactory coupling.

He had been relieved to learn that theirs hadn't been a love match, but rather a marriage of convenience. He rubbed his hands together gleefully. That suited his purposes perfectly. He intended to marry Christiane after an appropriate period of mourning. The last thing he wanted was a grieving widow, weeping and wailing over the demise of her dearly departed.

Christiane Delacroix would be the ideal mistress for Briarwood—and mother of the dynasty he planned to found.

Naturally he would insist on her fidelity. Soon she would be too busy raising a family and running a household to complain about his frequent visits to New Orleans. Like many Creole gentlemen, he'd keep a beautiful quadroon mistress in a little house near the docks.

He smiled in the dark as he slid between the sheets. He was looking forward to bedding the French countess. Having glimpsed her passion and strong will, he eagerly anticipated molding them to fit his needs. She would present a challenge—and no one enjoyed a challenge more than he. It was time he devised a plan to rid himself of the only obstacle in the way: her husband.

Just before succumbing to sleep, he wondered why Pierre LeClerc was taking so long to answer his inquiry regarding the future Madame du Beaupre.

Chapter
Twenty-two

The morning after their return to New Orleans, Dulcie's shrill scream splintered the quiet.

Bedroom doors flew open as the occupants streamed out. Reid was the first to reach the courtyard, followed by Christiane. Jean-Claude, leaning heavily on the railing, brought up the rear.

Babbling incoherently, Dulcie pointed to an object at her feet.

Christiane stared down at the item that had precipitated such a commotion. A black crow lay on the doorstep, its body limp, its head bent at an odd angle.

Jean-Claude peered down at it in distaste. "Tsk, tsk. All this fuss over a dead crow?"

Dulcie let out a loud wail and clutched her apron to her ample bosom. "Somethin' bad gonna happen. Somethin' bad gonna happen soon."

Christiane patted her on the back. "There, there, Dulcie, calm yourself."

The rotund housekeeper fanned herself with her apron. "Ain't jest a dead bird. No way, nohow."

Reid and Christiane exchanged worried glances. "Dulcie," Reid said sternly, "what are you trying to tell us? What do you know that we don't?"

Dulcie's lower lip trembled like a toddler's, an incongruous sight in a woman her size. "It's evil . . . black magic."

"Sheer and utter nonsense." Jean-Claude shook his head in disgust. "The bird simply flew against the building and broke its neck."

Dulcie's gaze flitted nervously from Christiane to Reid. "Someone out to get you."

Christiane studied the object thoughtfully, then shifted her troubled gaze to Reid. "It looks as though there's something stuffed in the bird's mouth."

Reid hunkered next to it for a closer inspection. Using his thumb and index finger as forceps, he extracted a small scrap of paper from its beak. Christiane read the crudely scrawled note from over his shoulder.

"Well," Jean-Claude prompted. "What does it say?"

"Nothing," Reid replied, getting to his feet. "It merely has my name written on it."

"It bad, real bad." Dulcie rocked back and forth. "Trouble comin'."

"What's all this carryin' on about?" Rosie O'Banion's matter-of-fact tone sliced through the tension. Amid all the commotion, no one had noticed her approach. Mouthwatering smells of spicy cinnamon and fresh-baked bread wafted from a wicker basket slung over one arm. "Don't tell me," she drawled, "ye all came down to greet me seein' as this is me last day carin' fer the count."

Reid indicated the small limp form at his feet. "Someone sent a gift with my name attached."

Rosie's eyes widened. "Jesus, Mary, and Joseph," she muttered, making a hasty sign of the cross. "A voodoo warning."

Jean-Claude scratched his head, his shaggy white brows knitted in puzzlement. "Why would anyone . . . ?"

"Mr. Delacroix must have made himself a powerful enemy." Rosie shifted the basket from one arm to the other. "Someone who wishes him ill luck."

"I nearly steps on it." Dulcie sniffed.

Christiane linked her arm through her grandfather's. "Why don't we all go upstairs and enjoy the wonderful treat Rosie has brought us. Perhaps Dulcie will brew us a pot of her special coffee to go along with it."

As she herded everyone toward the stairs, Christiane cast a final look over her shoulder in time to see Reid gingerly pick the bird up by the feet and disappear around the corner of the building.

They were all gathered around the dining room table enjoying sweet rolls and café au lait when Reid returned grim-faced. Jean-Claude fixed him with a penetrating stare. "Do you have any idea who might have sent that disgusting object?"

Reid poured himself a cup of coffee, studiously avoiding meeting Jean-Claude's eyes. "Not really, but I plan to do some investigating. Probably nothing more than a prank of sorts."

Jean Claude's scowl darkened. "Well, whoever it was has a perverse sense of humor."

"Sad to say, many blacks here in New Orleans practice voodoo," Rosie said around mouthfuls of pastry.

Christiane sipped her coffee, but left the sweet roll untouched. "Voodoo was also popular in St. Domingue."

Jean-Claude rested both hands atop his silver-handled walking cane. "In one of our conversations, Polly . . . that is, Mrs. Wakefield," he corrected, "mentioned that during the Galvez administration, the importation of slaves from Martinique was strictly prohibited. The governor believed them steeped in the pagan practice. Unfortunately, however, the practice seems to have already taken root."

Rosie helped herself to another sweet roll. "To this very day, the importation of slaves from the West Indies is strictly forbidden. But who would wish harm to people the likes of you?"

"And why?"

Jean-Claude's question hung suspended. Christiane and Reid avoided looking at each other. Christiane's attention was suddenly consumed by stirring more cream into her coffee, Reid's with brushing crumbs from his jacket. Christiane wondered if Reid felt the same impending sense of urgency.

Like time slipping through an hourglass.

Mama Joe's Coffeehouse came alive after midnight. Reid viewed the scene from his vantage point at a table in the far corner. Attired in the latest fashions, young Creole gentlemen circulated among the tables, boasting to friends of their winnings that evening at various gambling halls, or soliciting sympathy for their losses. Still others discussed the beautiful quadroons and possible liaisons with them, a custom practically universal among Creoles. Reid watched and listened, but maintained a comfortable distance. He felt far removed from such frivolous pursuits, older, wiser beyond his years.

He leaned back in his chair and stretched his long legs in front of him with ankles crossed. Perhaps Christiane was right after all. Maybe it would be best if he left New Orleans while he still could. All this time and he was no closer to proving Leon had killed Gaston. Maybe he had set himself upon an impossible task. What had Christiane termed it? A fool's errand?

But what gnawed at him most of all was the fact that if his true identity was disclosed Christiane must also pay a penalty. Her reputation would be irreparably damaged. Society did not look kindly upon a woman residing openly with a man without benefit of matrimony. She might also face legal censure for sheltering a fugitive from the law. God, what a woman his countess had turned out to be: generous, loving, passionate. A woman to dream about. To die for. She gave everything, asking nothing in return. And he couldn't even begin to tell her how he felt.

Reid barely glanced up when an attendant refilled his cup and moved on. The kindest thing he could do would be to persuade her to leave Louisiana. Her grandfather had sufficiently regained his health and was well enough to travel. Reid knew he would never forgive himself if anything happened to her. Christiane would be better off without him. She'd be free to start life anew, meet a man worthy of her, marry, raise a family.

The mere thought of her in the arms of another caused him pain. His gray eyes turned bleak, stark. He'd promised himself he'd stay away from her and, since the night on the gallery, he had succeeded. God help him, though, it hadn't been easy.

"Mind if I join you?"

Swiveling his head, Reid looked into a narrow face with dark, heavy-lidded eyes that lent the man a perpetually sleepy appearance. "I don't believe we've met."

"I am Gerard Rousseau." Without waiting for an invitation, the man sat opposite the table from Reid. Crossing his long legs, he signaled the attendant for a cup of coffee. "I understand you've been asking questions about an acquaintance of mine," he said without preamble.

Assuming a studied casualness, Reid leaned back in his chair and regarded the man curiously. "And just who is this 'acquaintance'?"

"Leon du Beaupre." The name dropped like a stone in a still pool. Rousseau's coffee arrived, but went untouched. "Perhaps I could be of some assistance. Precisely what do you wish to learn?"

Reid gave a diffident shrug. "I'm curious as to what kind of man he is. How his friends and acquaintances regard his character."

"What have you learned thus far?"

Actually Reid had uncovered quite a few interesting facts. He had quickly learned that the enmity between the two brothers was an acknowledged fact in New Orleans. Animosity had flared anew when their father had died, leaving Gaston his sole heir. People expressed surprise at their proposed trip to Spain. Most important, he had discovered that Leon's hot, vicious temper was legendary.

Impatient for an answer, Gerard Rousseau drummed his fingers against the tabletop.

Reid decided to proceed with caution. "I've learned that du Beaupre has a mean temper, along with a talent for exacting revenge for slights both real or imagined."

"True." Rousseau's drooping lids shuttered his expression. "Anything else?"

Reid idly circled the rim of his cup with an index finger. "I'm also interested in du Beaupre's background. I'm told his brother was killed under rather strange circumstances during a trip abroad."

"That is also correct." Rousseau dipped his head in acknowledgment. "Gaston was murdered while visiting Spain."

"I received the distinct impression that the pair weren't particularly close. That they were rivals."

"Sometimes it is that way with brothers," Rousseau replied.

Leon observed the Creole from across the table. Though the man attempted to appear insouciant, something in his manner aroused suspicion. He sensed an underlying tension, a certain watchfulness. Reid decided to test the Creole's loyalties, to gamble on a long shot. "Some whisper Leon might be responsible for his brother's untimely demise."

Rousseau sprang to his feet. With a single swipe of his arm, he sent coffee cups flying. Coffee spewed on startled patrons and pooled on the floor. "How dare you slander my friend's reputation?" he accused loudly. "What gives you the right to pry into his personal life? Impugn his character?"

"I merely repeated gossip." Reid kept his tone conciliatory, his voice level. He was aware that silence had befallen the coffeehouse as all eyes turned to observe the confrontation. "I'm simply trying to find out what the man is like."

"You have insulted my friend. I demand an apology."

"And you . . . can go to straight to hell."

Rousseau whipped his leather gloves from the table and slapped Reid smartly across one cheek. "I challenge you to a duel. Tomorrow at dawn in St. Anthony's Square."

Belatedly Reid realized he had swallowed the bait. According to local custom, he must now face Gerard Rousseau on a field of honor. Quarrels in New Orleans never resulted in fisticuffs. An unwritten law absolutely forbade the striking of a blow. The man who forgot found himself ostracized from polite society.

"Very well, Rousseau, we meet at dawn."

Turning on his heel, Gerard Rousseau stalked off in triumph.

Christiane was awakened before daybreak by someone pounding at the front door. Since the hour was still too early for Dulcie, Christiane threw on a wrapper and, not bothering with a candle, groped her way downstairs. She flung the door open and found a lad of ten or twelve, bleary-eyed and shivering in the predawn dampness.

"Miss Wakefield tol' me bring it." He handed her a single sheet of parchment.

Christiane's hands trembled as she fumbled to light a candle. Hurriedly she scanned the brief message. The words danced on the page in front of her.

"Oh, my God." She gasped in dismay, scarcely able to comprehend its contents.

The boy yawned. "Miss Wakefield say she be bringin' up the carriage for y'all."

Christiane barely heard him as she raced upstairs. The premonition of danger that had haunted her all week had come to fruition. Long-standing habit led her straight for her grandfather.

He drew himself up on one elbow as she burst into his room. "Christiane, *ma petite*, what is it?"

"R-Reid," she stammered, wild-eyed. "Reid's about to fight a duel at St. Anthony's Square."

Jean-Claude took charge, reverting to the autocratic, decisive Comte de Varennes, a man accustomed to having orders obeyed without question. "Get dressed at once. I'll meet you in the courtyard."

Christiane hastened to follow his instructions. She quickly donned the first gown she found in the armoire, tossing a dark woolen cape over her shoulders and pulling up the hood as she ran to meet her grandfather. Jean-Claude was already downstairs waiting.

Polly's carriage rolled to a stop just as they exited the gate leading from the courtyard onto the Calle Real. Polly peered at them through the darkness. "Hurry," she urged. "It'll soon be light."

As soon as Christiane and Jean-Claude scrambled aboard, the carriage headed toward Plaza de Armes.

"How did you find out about the duel?" Christiane asked, reaching out to clutch Polly's arm.

Polly patted her hand reassuringly. "One of my servants heard the news through a friend and rushed to tell me."

"When did this happen?" Christiane struggled to understand the events leading up to this dreadful situation.

"Apparently this occurred last night when Etienne questioned Leon du Beaupre's reputation. A friend of Leon's took offense and issued the challenge."

Christiane pressed trembling fingers against her bloodless lips. *Dieu! Is this the way Reid's quest for justice was to end. In a senseless duel . . . ?*

Jean-Claude rested his folded hands atop his walking cane. "Who is Etienne's opponent?"

"Gerard Rousseau." Polly's round face wore a troubled expression. "Rousseau is a *maître d'armes* who operates a fencing academy in Exchange Alley."

"A fencing master . . . ?" Christiane felt a sinking sensation. What did Reid know about the *colchemarde*, the rapier? By his own admission, he was a gambler, a rogue who played with games of chance and not with deadly weapons.

"Dueling is a barbaric practice," Polly agreed. "Governor Miró personally deplores the custom. In his *"Bando de*

Buen Gobierno," he announced that he would rigorously enforce the regulations against dueling. But not even the highest officials pay any heed. Although heavy penalties are provided, they are rarely inflicted. Men engage in the sport for the most venial reasons imaginable."

By the time they arrived at the cleared area in the middle of St. Anthony's Square, which was located directly behind Saint Louis Church, a crowd had already gathered. A small knot of men huddled at one end of the field. Reid stood silhouetted against dark sky at the opposite end. The church formed a dark shape in the background, but its silent admonition went unheeded by those hungry for the thrill of spilled blood.

Christiane clambered from the carriage before it came to a complete stop. Clutching her skirts high to keep from falling, she ran to the spot where Reid stood alone and unattended.

"Just what do you hope to accomplish by this . . . ?" She flung out a hand, gesturing wildly. How had Reid allowed himself to be drawn into such a position? How could he have been so stupid? Fear for his safety, his life, transformed itself into fury. Fury was an emotion Christiane felt capable of handling. Fear, on the other hand, paralyzed her body, numbed her mind.

"I didn't expect to see you here. Go, Christiane, while there's still time."

Her hands balled into fists at her sides. "You surely did not think I would stay away, did you?"

He sighed in defeat. "I hoped you wouldn't find out."

"I think you have taken leave of your senses," she charged furiously. She pointed in the direction of the men across the field. "This Gerard Rousseau is a fencing master. What chance do you stand against such a man?"

"Do not concern yourself." His jaw hardened, his gray

eyes assuming the hardness of flint in the stingy predawn light. "I will do whatever needs to be done."

"This is madness! Insanity! Just turn your back and walk before it's too late." What could she say, what could she do, to make him change his mind? she wondered frantically.

"You do not understand, *ma petite*. Etienne has no choice," Jean-Claude spoke with cold finality. "A man's honor is at stake."

"What honor is it to lose your life in a matter of little consequence?" she questioned bitterly.

Jean-Claude ignored his granddaughter's ranting and addressed Reid. "What did you do to cause this man to challenge you?"

Reid's eyes cut across the field. "I insulted his friend."

Christiane's gaze followed his to Leon du Beaupre, who observed their heated exchange from a distance. He acknowledged them with a complacent smile, then swung back to his cronies. For a split second, Christiane felt that she had glimpsed into the soul of a blackguard. A soul without pity—without remorse.

"Have you chosen weapons?" Jean-Claude asked Reid.

Polly, who had been standing somewhat apart, spoke up, "Has anyone informed you that according to code duello, the challenged person has the choice of weapons?"

"No." Reid rubbed his jaw thoughtfully. "I assumed I would have to use a rapier. Sad to say, my skill is no match for that of a master swordsman."

Jean-Claude clapped Reid on the back. "Then you have the right to select an appropriate weapon, one that puts you on equal terms with your adversary."

The sky was brightening at an alarming rate as the first crimson streaks stained the horizon, presaging dawn. A gaggle of officials approached with somber faces. "Are you ready to proceed with the duel, M'sieur Delacroix?"

Reid nodded. "I chose the pistol as my weapon at forty yards."

"A pistol?" The senior official lifted a bushy brow. "I was told . . . Never mind. I will procure whatever weapon you wish." The group retreated across the field to convey the information. Irate voices carried on the slight breeze, communicating the displeasure of Gerard Rousseau and his friends.

While the group waited for dueling pistols to be brought to the field, Jean-Claude spoke to Reid in low tones. "You do not have to kill your opponent," he instructed. "Merely shoot to wound."

"If you draw first blood, you will be considered the victor," Polly added helpfully.

Christiane resisted the urge to scream. Instead of counseling Reid against a foolhardy undertaking, her grandfather and Polly were actually abetting his cause. She drew Reid aside, determined one last time to reason with him. "Is there nothing I can do or say to dissuade you?"

"No," he said, a small smile hovering about his mouth. He studied her upturned face as though branding it into his memory. "It is enough to know you care."

Before she could divine his intent, he jerked her hard against his chest. He kissed her with savage passion, ravaging her mouth with his. Then, ending the kiss just as abruptly, he strode toward the center of the field.

Christiane watched him go, her knees weak, her heart hammering. Reid meant the world to her. She couldn't bear the thought of losing him.

Ever.

The official indicated Gerard Rousseau with a wave of his hand. "Who is here to act as this gentleman's second?"

Leon du Beaupre stepped forward, confident and smiling. "I am."

The official pointed toward Reid. "Who will act as second for M'sieur Delacroix?"

"I will." Jean-Claude slowly took his place at Reid's side. Simultaneously, Christiane and Polly smothered words of protest.

Emotion darkened the hue of Reid's eyes from silver to pewter as Jean-Claude joined him on the field of honor, clearly touched by the unexpected show of support.

Polly linked her arm through Christiane's. "Don't worry, dear. He'll be all right."

Christiane swallowed, not trusting herself to speak past the lump in her throat. Polly, she noticed, without her usual perky smile looked every day of her advanced years. Worry was etched on her brow and in the fine network of lines at the corners of her eyes. Christiane hugged her friend tightly, grateful for her presence.

"He's so handsome. So brave," Polly murmured.

"Handsome, *oui*, but more foolish than brave." Christiane's gaze never wavered from Reid's tall figure.

"Not Etienne, dear," Polly corrected absently. "I was referring to your grandfather."

The group of spectators had steadily grown. Women also flocked to the event, avid to witness bloodshed and subsequent suffering. People took up positions along the sidelines careful to avoid the possible path of a stray bullet.

Rousseau and Reid selected dueling pistols from a velvet-lined box, then waited while they were loaded with shot. Next to the slender Creole who had challenged him, Reid cut a dashing figure. Taller, more muscular, he possessed the battered face and scarred body of a battle-worn knight. He had never seemed so dear. Christiane deeply regretted that she had never told him she loved him. Now it might be too late.

The two opponents faced each other, weapons at their

sides, across a measured distance of forty yards. They were instructed to raise the pistols and fire after the count of four. Christiane stiffened until her body felt so taut it could have snapped in half like a twig. She couldn't breathe, didn't blink. All her attention was focused on the man she loved.

"One, two, three, four," the official intoned. "Fire!"

A single shot rang out, sending a covey of pigeons scattering. Christiane recoiled at the sound. Catching her lower lip between her teeth, she waited for the smoke to clear. Her knees nearly buckled in relief to find Reid standing unscathed. The fencing master, though expert with a rapier, was less skilled with a firearm. He had pulled the trigger prematurely, the shot going wide of its target.

Now it was Reid's turn to aim and fire. He took his time, making Rousseau quiver with dread. Calm and deliberate, Reid pointed the dueling pistol and gently squeezed the trigger. His shot rang true. Rousseau doubled over in agony, cradling his bleeding right arm and sobbing. "He broke my arm," he wailed in disbelief. "The bastard broke my dueling arm."

The official summoned a doctor to the scene. After examining the wound, the physician suggested the duelists retire from the field. Blood staining the pristine cuff of his shirt, Rousseau quickly agreed, though Leon du Beaupre didn't appear pleased with the decision. An angry exchange of words followed the men from St. Anthony's Square.

Christiane's first impulse was to throw herself into Reid's arms and weep with relief. She needed the solid feel of him to reassure herself that he was alive, uninjured. She took a tentative step forward, then hesitated. Something in Reid's expression warned her that her demonstration of affection would be unwelcome. An abyss seemed to widen between them, a chasm too wide, too deep, to traverse. She craved intimacy; he courted distance. Weighted under crushing disappointment, she stood rooted to the spot, watching as he approached his trio of supporters with leaden steps.

Reid extended his hand to Jean-Claude who clasped it firmly. "*Merci,* M'sieur le Comte, for generously acting as my second. It meant a great deal knowing you were there if I faltered."

"Nonsense, my son." Jean-Claude cleared his throat. "What else could I have done. After all, you're family."

Christiane and Reid swapped guilty looks, but Polly and Jean-Claude were too immersed in each other to notice.

Chapter Twenty-three

Preparations were in full swing for a masquerade ball scheduled to take place that evening. Polly insisted they all attend. She was determined to introduce Jean-Claude to New Orleans society. And once the widow's mind was made up, there was no dissuading her. Even Reid, who had been reluctant at first, had acquiesced under her steady barrage of coaxing and cajoling.

In spite of her best efforts, Christiane had failed to capture her friend's lighthearted spirits. She had spent the entire day trying to ignore the premonition of encroaching disaster that hovered over her like a dark cloud—a feeling not dissimilar to the one that plagued her the eve the slaves stormed Belle Terre. She tried to blame her gloom on the spate of rainy days that turned the streets of the city into a morass, but with only partial success.

"Missus," Dulcie called from downstairs. "They done bring the costumes."

By the time Christiane joined her in the drawing room, Dulcie was already busy unpacking a large box that had just arrived by special courier from a costumer Polly had recommended. "Oh, missus." Dulcie held up a filmy white concoction. "This must be whut Miss Polly calls your Greek goddess outfit."

Christiane regarded it with a raised brow. The garment was simple, and deceptively revealing, designed to drape and cling to her soft curves. Polly had vigorously overridden her objections, claiming she had seen the same type of costume worn by the nobility in Europe the previous spring.

Jean-Claude sauntered into the room. He had grown so much stronger of late that he rarely relied on his walking cane. "What's all this fuss I heard about costumes arriving?"

Dulcie reached into the box, removed a folded linen square banded in royal blue and gold, and held it up. "What kind of costume is this supposed to be?" she asked, shaking her head in bewilderment. "Look like a fancy bedsheet, or maybe a tablecloth."

Christiane giggled, then, seeing her grandfather's frown, tried to school her features into sterner lines, but failed. "That must be your costume, *Grand-père*."

Still shaking her head, Dulcie looked from the costume to the count. "You gonna wear a bedsheet to that fancy party?"

Assuming a dignified air, Jean-Claude adjusted his neckcloth. "I'll have you know, madame, that I'm going to the masquerade ball as a Roman senator."

"All you needs is a mattress an' you can go disguised as a bed," Dulcie muttered, unconvinced.

Christiane's bubble of laughter was so infectious even Jean-Claude had to smile. At first neither noticed the change in Dulcie's manner until she stepped away from the box, hands pressed against her mouth.

"Dulcie?" Christiane asked, seeing the servant's expression. "Are you all right? Are you ill?"

Shaking visibly, Dulcie pointed at the box in which the costumes had arrived. Jean-Claude strode forward, dipped his hand inside, and pulled out a mound of wax. The item was black in color and approximately twelve inches long. Staring at the object in stark terror, Dulcie found her voice at last and let out a scream that reached to the rafters.

At the sound, Reid, who was just returning home, bounded across the courtyard and up the stairs. "What is it?" he demanded. "Is anyone hurt?"

"This is a bad sign, real bad sign," Dulcie babbled. "Somepin' bad gonna happen. Someone gonna die."

Reid and Christiane gathered around Jean-Claude to examine the item in question while Dulcie maintained a safe distance. Upon closer inspection, they were able to discern it to be a black candle crudely shaped in the form of a man.

"First a dead bird, now this." Reid took the candle from Jean-Claude. "Exactly where did you find it, Dulcie?"

"It be layin' with yer costume." Dulcie stared at Reid accusingly, clearly certain the warning was directed at him.

"Surely not more of this voodoo nonsense?" Jean-Claude scoffed, but his voice lacked conviction.

"Voodoo real. Powerful magic," Dulcie insisted with a stubborn nod that sent her tignon wobbling. Reaching inside the bodice of her dress, she pulled out a small pouch of red flannel fastened about her neck with a string. "I wear gris-gris to ward off evil spirits. You wants I get you gris-gris?"

"That won't be necessary, Dulcie," Christiane said firmly.

"I refuse to listen to any more of this foolishness." Jean-Claude spoke with a trace of asperity.

"Someone bought you a curse. Watch yo'self tonight, Mr. Reid." Gathering up the costumes, she hurried from the room.

Reid watched her leave with a frown. Someone was trying to frighten him, but who? Was Leon du Beaupre the instigator? he wondered. But why would Leon warn him? That wasn't the man's style. He was the type who liked to strike without warning. To catch his opponent off guard.

"I've never heard of such foolery," Jean-Claude said in disgust, turning to Reid and Christiane. "Surely you don't take this nonsense seriously?"

"Christiane and I happened to witness one of their ceremonies while in St. Domingue," Reid explained carefully. "Its followers are quite devout in their beliefs."

Christiane sank down on the settee and stared down at her folded hands. She wished she could speak to Reid in private about the matter. Plead with him to leave before it was too late. Convince him time was running out.

Jean-Claude lowered himself on the settee next to his granddaughter. "Well, then, we'll just have to put our heads together. All we have to do is find out who had access to the box of costumes, and our riddle will be solved."

Reid stared down at the roughly crafted effigy. "I'm going to visit the costumer. See what I can learn."

As she watched him leave, Christiane bit her lower lip to keep from calling him back. Every minute they shared was precious. She wanted him safe at her side where she could see him, touch him, protect him. Despair that she could do none of these things weighed on her spirit.

Jean-Claude wrapped his arm around her. "I can see you love him, *ma petite*. I pray whatever problems exist between you and Etienne can be resolved."

With a half sob, she buried her head against his shoulder. But strangely enough the comfort she usually experienced in her grandfather's embrace was lacking. All she felt was a profound sense of loss as Reid drifted farther and farther away.

Christiane paused on the threshold of the drawing room to admire Reid, who appeared dashing as a medieval English lord. He wore a fur-trimmed coat over a moss green velvet tunic, and hose that conformed to his long, muscular legs.

"You look magnificent, milord," she said softly.

His stormy gray gaze heated as it wandered over her slender figure revealingly outlined by the gossamer-fine weave. Narrow gold ribbons crisscrossed under her breasts and twined through her hair, which had been left to tumble down her back in soft ringlets. "And you . . ." He smiled winningly. "I find words inadequate."

"Aren't we a pair?" She laughed, though secretly pleased at his flattery. "I can hardly wait to see the costume Polly selected for herself. She refused to tell me what she was wearing."

Reid's smile broadened. "Knowing Polly, she probably wants to impress your grandfather."

"Ah," she said, moving farther into the room. "So I'm not the only one who's noticed a blossoming romance."

"They're two wonderful people. I couldn't be happier for them."

"I feel the same way. Only . . ."

"Only . . . ?" he said, waiting patiently for her explanation.

"The longer we remain in New Orleans, the fonder

they'll become. It will make their ultimate separation difficult."

"I'm not sure I understand what you're referring to. Why will they have to be separated?"

"We can't let this charade of ours continue indefinitely. *Grand-père* is stronger now. I'll soon have to tell him the truth. He'll be furious and will probably insist we go someplace where no one knows that I lived with a man who is not my husband."

"If you want me to leave, tell me."

"*Non,*" she denied vehemently, catching his arm as though she could forcibly prevent him from going. "I want you to remain here as long as it takes to prove Leon du Beaupre killed Gaston. It's just that I hate deceiving *Grand-père.*"

He slowly traced a finger along the line of her jaw. "A guilty conscience is a heavy burden, isn't it, Countess?"

"*Oui.*" Her thoughts scattered beneath the light touch. "The longer we perpetuate the lie, the more harm it will do."

He tilted her face up to his. "Never fear. I won't let you shoulder the blame alone. I promise to be at your side when you tell your grandfather."

She ran the tip of her tongue over her bottom lip. "I never meant to carry things this far."

"I never intended a lot of things," he admitted, gazing deep into her eyes. "Least of all what happened between us."

The love she tried to contain flamed hotter, brighter, threatened to burn out of control. "You never asked— or took—anything that I was unwilling to give freely and wholeheartedly."

For a long moment their eyes locked, seemingly trying to read secrets locked in each other's hearts, their very souls. Reid dipped his head, and his mouth brushed hers, spark to tinder. Her lips parting in eager anticipation, Christiane raised on tiptoe, leaning into the kiss. His mouth moved over hers with deliberate slowness, savoring, seducing in lazy increments.

Beguiled by this sensory assault, she wrapped her arms around his neck, subtly moving against him, wanting, yearning, for more. His tongue stole inside her mouth, lightly tracing the satiny moist lining, the sharp ridges of her teeth, then engaging her tongue in a playful foray.

Splaying one hand at the small of her back, using the other to cup her buttocks, he pulled her tighter, shifting his weight so she fit snugly against his aroused manhood. She wriggled against him and purred, a throaty, contented sound that was nearly his undoing.

"Harrumph!"

Startled, they broke apart. Jean-Claude stood framed in the doorway. The lively sparkle in his eyes was at distinct odds with his guise of sagacious Roman statesman. "I hate to interrupt, children, but there will be time after the ball for such pursuits. We don't want to keep Polly waiting."

Due to the recent inclement weather, it had been previously decided that they would meet Polly at the ballroom. The streets were awash in mud ankle-deep, making travel by carriage slow and perilous at best. Christiane wore pattens made of wood, leather, and metal to protect her slippers as they made their way painstakingly down the banquette. Inured to mud and water, guests in a wide array of clever and elaborate costumes swarmed the ballroom.

Polly spotted them immediately. "You must put on your masks," she chided. "Masks must stay on until midnight."

The newly arrived trio dutifully followed her instructions. "You make an enchanting milkmaid, *ma chère.*" Jean-

Claude took her arm and escorted her toward the dance floor while Polly giggled coquettishly.

Reid waited while Christiane removed the dark cloak protecting her Grecian gown and the pattens from her feet. "Shall we?" He offered his arm.

They took their places just as a contredanse was beginning, moving through the prescribed set of figures. As soon as the set ended, a gentleman dressed as King Henry VIII claimed Christiane for his partner. A row of seats ran the entire length of the ballroom, behind which stretched a three-foot-wide space where young Creole gentlemen waited to claim dance partners. Christiane proved in constant demand, and much to her chagrin caught only occasional glimpses of Reid from across the room. As the evening wore on, she was besieged by the need to look over her shoulder. Try as she might, she couldn't rid herself of the sensation of being watched.

The masquerade ball had assumed a strange, dreamlike atmosphere. Identities hidden behind masks, no one was who they seemed. Glancing around, she couldn't help but notice the inordinate number of male guests dressed in military costumes. There was something vaguely familiar about a figure in a devil's costume, but she couldn't quite put her finger on it. Several times a man dressed as Sir Walter Raleigh jostled her. From his murmured apology, she recognized the voice as belonging to none other than Leon du Beaupre. She was grateful he hadn't pressed her to be his dance partner. It would have been difficult to refuse without creating a scene. From time to time she caught sight of Polly and her grandfather, who seemed inseparable. She wished the same were true of her and Reid. She would feel more at ease if he were at her side.

It was nearly midnight before they were reunited. "I wish we could leave now," she whispered.

He placed his hand at her waist and leaned forward to be heard above the clamor of the crowd. "As soon as the unmasking takes place, I'll find your grandfather and tell him you are suffering a headache."

It would be no fabrication, she thought, feeling tension build at the base of her neck. She was eager to leave the overcrowded, noisy atmosphere behind.

Leon in the guise of Sir Walter Raleigh pushed his way toward the front of the room, mounted a dais, and held up his arms, signaling silence. The noise abated gradually and an expectant hush fell over the crowd. "Lords and ladies, saints and satyrs, distinguished guests, I have a delicious surprise planned as this evening's entertainment."

A wave of anticipation rippled through the ballroom. The man grinned broadly and waited until he had regained everyone's attention.

All her instincts screaming a warning, she clutched Reid's arm. Behind her mask, her eyes darted about wildly, searching for a possible escape route. But the possibility of a hasty departure seemed unlikely. They were securely hemmed in by a tight crush of people waiting for the promised entertainment.

"I thought," Leon continued, a dazzling smile appearing beneath his mask, "what better place than a masquerade ball to rip away the facade of a man pretending to be someone he's not. A man who feigns honor, but has none. Someone who has moved about this city, been welcomed into our homes . . ."

Christiane could barely hear Leon's words above the roaring in her ears.

"A man, dear guests," Leon continued, his honey-smooth voice oozing triumph, "who has killed in cold blood."

Beside her, she felt Reid's body grow taut, rigid. She darted a frantic glance over her shoulder and found they were surrounded by a ring of masked men in soldier's uniforms. Genuine uniforms, she realized with a sinking sensation, not costumes, as she had originally thought.

Leon pointed at Reid, a cunning smile curling his handsome mouth. "The *immigré* from St. Domingue known as Etienne Delacroix is really Reid Alexander, the man convicted of the murder of my brother, Gaston du Beaupre. Seize him!"

The soldiers closed in, roughly grabbing Reid, pinning his arms behind his back while he struggled. Another stepped forward and ripped off his mask so everyone could plainly see his desperation.

"Non," she cried, imploring the startled guests. "Reid Alexander is innocent. He killed no one. It was Leon du Beaupre who killed his own brother."

"Silence!" Leon roared. "Do not listen to the ravings of a besotted woman—a woman who is not even this man's wife."

Shock and outrage rippled through the throng. Jean-Claude, with Polly close behind, shoved his way to Christiane's side. "Granddaughter, are these charges true?" he demanded.

"Reid is innocent of murdering Gaston du Beaupre." She pleaded for her grandfather's understanding. "That is all that matters."

"Does the term 'family honor' mean nothing to you?"

"Do not blame her. None of this is her fault." Reid strained to break free from his captors. "I coerced her into helping me."

"Coerced?" Jean-Claude appeared ready if need be to take the younger man apart with his bare hands to salvage his granddaughter's virtue. "Coerced in what manner? I demand an explanation!"

Hands clenched, Christiane turned on her grandfather,

all fire and passion. "You speak of honor, *Grand-père*. Reid saved my life. If not for him, I would have perished in St. Domingue. Granting him time to prove his innocence seemed a small favor to give in return."

They regarded each other in heavy silence, both having forgotten the crowd of onlookers; then Jean-Claude's shoulders slumped in defeat. "I did not know. . . ."

Sensing the sympathy of the crowd slipping away, Leon loudly interrupted. "Ladies and gentlemen, I have still more entertainment planned for this evening." He motioned for quiet before continuing. "There is a special guest I'd like to introduce."

The slender man garbed in a red velvet devil costume who Christiane had noticed observing her from the sidelines took his place on the dais next to Leon. "I, too, would like to end a charade." Reaching up, the man removed the devil's mask and casually tossed it aside to reveal arctic blue eyes glittering with malice.

The room swirled about her as Christiane stared into the face of her worst nightmare. Stunned, horrified, she barely heard the babble of voices. The room tilted, dimmed, then slowly came into focus.

Etienne smiled diabolically from the dais, reveling in her obvious distress. "*I*, dear people, am Etienne Delacroix, newly arrived from St. Domingue. I come to claim my faithless wife, the lovely Christiane, who together with Reid Alexander, my former overseer, stole a fortune in jewels and left me to the mercy of savages."

Impossible! The word echoed over and over in her brain. *Etienne alive? How could this be?* She had seen the machete plunge into his chest, watched him crumple onto the stairs, blood seeping from his wound.

Jean-Claude gasped. "Granddaughter, tell me these are all lies!"

Christiane opened her mouth but couldn't speak. She felt as though she were sinking in a quagmire of despair and treachery.

"Surely there has been some mistake." Polly's face was creased with worry.

Gloating with triumph, Leon and Etienne left the dais. The crowd parted to let them through. Smug and self-righteous, they took their places on either side of Reid and Christiane. Etienne removed the mask Christiane still wore and carelessly tossed it aside. Catching her chin, he pinched it between thumb and forefinger.

"Take your slimy hands off her, you bastard." Reid surged forward but was restrained by his captors.

Etienne ignored the outburst. "So, *chérie*, we meet again. Only this time," he warned silkily, "I will not let you get away as easily."

Reid's gaze locked contemptuously on Etienne. "I should have known you were too evil to die, Delacroix."

Etienne abruptly released Christiane and backhanded Reid so viciously that he staggered against the soldiers holding him.

"Stop!" Christiane quickly slipped between the two before Etienne could inflict any more punishment. "Leave him be. Haven't you done enough already?"

Leon motioned to the soldiers. "Haul him away. The governor said he's to be aboard the next ship bound for Hispaniola."

As the soldiers dragged a struggling Reid from the ballroom, he twisted around for a final appeal. His eyes found Jean-Claude's. "Promise you'll protect her. Don't let her leave with Delacroix. He plans to kill her."

"I suggest you slap manacles on him," Etienne advised. "He managed to avoid justice once. He's slippery as an eel."

"Non!" Christiane lunged after them, but Etienne's long fingers biting into her arm stopped her.

"Shall we go, *chérie?*" He dropped his voice to a whisper. "We have some unfinished business between us."

"Grand-père . . ." she entreated shamelessly as Etienne dragged her away. "Don't let them send Reid back to prison. He's innocent. Promise you'll help him."

Now I understand," the Hairy girl said, straightening along humps once more drawn up, gripped her...

similar to go around," Hairy girl said. Its voice so a...

"We have some unfinished business between us."

Tingling...... She struggled a moment in her plu...

snapped him away..."

ope as the eye could see, as far as it may stop...

Chapter
Twenty-four

"Do you really think he intends to kill her?"

Hands behind his back, Jean-Claude nervously paced in front of the fireplace in the drawing room as he considered his answer to Polly's question. "After the events of this evening, I don't know what to believe."

Jean-Claude and Polly had been up all night discussing the strange turn of events. Both had been stunned and shaken by the revelations that had been made at the stroke of midnight. In spite of the allegations, neither believed that the man they now knew as Reid Alexander could be guilty of murder. What worried them the most were Reid's pleas on behalf of Christiane's safety.

"And those eyes . . . Frigid as ice." Polly shivered. "Poor Christiane, she seemed in a state of shock at finding her husband still alive. Why would Delacroix want her dead?"

"Perhaps it was a gross exaggeration." Jean-Claude's tone lacked conviction.

"But what if it wasn't?"

Polly's question hung in the air.

Eyes downcast, Jean-Claude continued his agitated pacing. "What exactly did he charge?"

"My dear, please, we've been over this ground before. Hearing it repeated only upsets you."

Jean-Claude paused in front of her, anxiety etched across his patrician features. "Let's see." He began enumerating Christiane's transgressions. "She is a faithless wife who absconded with a fortune in jewels, leaving her husband to the mercy of savages while she took off with the overseer of his plantation. That might be construed as ample motive for wanting her dead. Delacroix has been publicly humiliated. He doesn't want to be viewed as the cuckolded husband every time he steps foot in public."

"No," Polly concurred. "He's much too proud to tolerate that in a wife. I fear for her well-being. Etienne Delacroix did not impress me as considerate or kind."

Jean-Claude let out a ragged breath, then massaged the bridge of his nose between thumb and forefinger. *"Non,* definitely not considerate or kind. Cold, unfeeling, perhaps even cruel, but definitely not kind."

"I noticed the way he touched her." Polly shuddered at the memory. "He has hurtful hands. His touch will leave bruises."

"Damn!" Jean-Claude slammed his fist against the mantel. "I feel so useless. I read the fear—and resignation—in her eyes as Delacroix led her off. Yet here I sit bemoaning her fate like a feeble old man."

Polly went to his side and put her arm around him. "Don't be so harsh on yourself. There is little you can do. No matter how we despise the man, he is her husband and well within his rights."

"If I were younger, more of a man, I'd have beaten him

to within an inch of his life." He glanced down at hands that were gnarled and speckled with age. "I've grown too frail to protect my only grandchild from a fiend."

"The years take their toll, dear," she reminded him gently. "No one, not even you, is exempt from the ravages of time."

"You're right as always, my sweet." Sliding an arm around her waist, he hugged her to him. "I couldn't help but feel touched at the selfless way Reid tried to protect her."

Polly rested her head against his shoulder. "And she him. The entire time Delacroix was leading her away she kept insisting on Reid's innocence."

"I can still hear Reid begging me to protect her as the soldiers hauled him away."

"They truly love each other, but with all the obstacles in their path, I doubt if they've ever admitted their feelings. How sad for both of them."

"I only wish there were some way we could help them. The longer she's with Delacroix the greater her danger. If Reid were here, he would give her the protection she deserves. That boy wouldn't let any harm come to her."

"If only there were some way to convince the magistrate that Reid is truly innocent of the charges against him. That Leon, not he, killed Gaston. Then with Reid's release from prison, he would find Christiane and protect her from the monster she married."

They pondered this in silence, knowing full well the enormity of the task, the hopelessness.

Polly spoke at last, diving into the gloomy void. "Where do you think Delacroix's taken her?"

Jean-Claude rubbed a hand wearily across his jaw. "He and du Beaupre seem to be two of a kind. My guess would be that he's taken her to Briarwood."

A lengthy silence spun out once again. From all accounts Briarwood was remote, isolated. Servants would be instructed to ignore any cries of distress. The thought of his grand-daughter alone and frightened increased Jean-Claude's grow-ing sense of urgency. "I can't let anything happen to her," he said softly, almost to himself.

Polly and Jean-Claude broke apart and turned as the drawing room door was thrown wide. Dulcie rushed in, her tignon askew in her haste. "I heards the news. Know it's early, but thought mebbe there was sompin' I could do to help."

"That's very thoughtful of you, Dulcie," Polly said, "but I don't know if anyone can help."

Dulcie whipped off her woolen shawl. "Sure sorry about Mister and Missus; they's good people. I knowed trouble was brewin' minute I found that dead bird on the doorstep. Then when we found that black candle . . ."

"How did you hear so quickly? It's barely light outside."

"Hmph!" She sniffed. "Any house servant worth his salt know what goes on. Don't let nothin' gets by 'im. No sirree." Out of habit she went about the room, plumping pillows on the settee, refolding a knit throw. "A good servant know how the master like his eggs, how many times he use the chamber pot, how he likes his underwear folded."

Jean-Claude crossed the room and slumped wearily into a chair. "Dulcie, could you please bring us a pot of tea? We've spent the entire night discussing the situation."

"Sure thing. I brings you some biscuits and honey along with it." Dulcie paused on the threshold. A frown pleated her brow. "In all the commotion, I nearly forgets to tell you a funny thing I heard last night. Someone tol' me they sees the du Beaupre slave, Rollo, slinking around out front same mornin' the dead bird done come. What you make o' that?" Not waiting for a reply, she waddled off.

A speculative gleam lit Jean-Claude's dark eyes with hope. "A personal servant such as Rollo must have accompanied his master on the trip abroad."

"You don't suppose . . . ?" Polly asked.

"I couldn't help but notice the strange way the man behaved when he met Reid the day he delivered the invitation to Briarwood."

Now it was Polly's turn to pace. Absently she twirled the diamond solitaire she habitually wore. "In the meantime, we still need to rescue Christiane. Considering the hatred on Delacroix's face when he looked at her, I fear we don't have much time."

"It's worth a try." Jean-Claude rose to his feet. "I need to locate Rollo."

"If only Reid were here . . ." Polly murmured. Then a smile spread slowly across her face, as bright as sunshine after a storm. "I have an idea . . . ."

Etienne eyed Christiane dispassionately as she huddled in the far corner of the du Beaupre carriage. They had been traveling for hours, the journey even slower than usual over roads muddy after recent rains. Leon had chosen to proceed on horseback, and the men had agreed to rendezvous at Briarwood. Christiane had no idea of the hour. It seemed ages ago since Etienne had dragged her from the ballroom. They had stopped at her town house only long enough to retrieve what remained of the jewelry, not even allowing her time to pack her belongings or change out of the costume she wore.

The shades were drawn over the carriage windows, prohibiting her from seeing out, preventing anyone from seeing in. At Etienne's direction, the doors of the carriage had been bolted from the outside should she feel an uncontrollable impulse to leap from the moving vehicle. Her cheek still bore livid proof of Etienne's displeasure at discovering that the magnificent diamond necklace—once his mother's prize possession—had been disassembled. The blazing heat of his anger had cooled into smoldering rage. Christiane knew, however, that it could rekindle with the least amount of provocation.

Shifting uneasily under his cold-eyed appraisal, she tugged her cloak more closely around her shoulders. If Etienne had planned to make her feel trapped or confined in such close quarters, he had succeeded. Adding to her misery was the fact that each revolution of the carriage wheels carried her farther and farther from Reid. The memory of him being dragged off by armed soldiers was incredibly painful. Seeing him stripped of dignity had torn at her heart, leaving it feeling wounded and bleeding. He was doomed to spend the remainder of his life paying for a crime he didn't commit, to toil at hard labor under a grueling sun until the day he died. How tragic, how unjust for a truly fine man. In comparison, her problems seemed of little consequence.

"The slave revolt in St. Domingue seems to have left no lasting effect on you, *chérie,*" Etienne observed dryly. "You appear unchanged."

She studied him warily. "The same could be said of you, m'sieur."

He let out a harsh bark of laughter. "You're not very observant, are you?" he asked, indicating his left arm. "It's a miracle I survived the attack at Belle Terre. My left arm was damaged during the assault. The surgeon at Le Cap told me certain nerves had been severed, that it's unlikely I'll ever regain full use."

"I'm sorry," she murmured, unsure what response he expected from her.

"Liar!" he snapped. *"Au contraire, chérie,* you are not the least bit sorry."

At his vicious tone, she pressed back into the cushions and bit back a sharp retort.

He regained his composure. "Luckily for me, I always had the reflexes of a cat—and nine lives as well. Thanks to specially prescribed exercises, I've succeeded in strengthening the right one—in case you get any foolish ideas."

She swept him with a disdainful glance. "You and M'sieur du Beaupre have already thought of every eventuality should I try to flee."

"I admire a man with a devious mind," he said with a wicked grin. "The locks on the carriage door were Leon's idea. They'll be removed once we reach Briarwood. In the meantime, *chérie,* they'll prevent you from doing anything rash."

"What is going to prevent me from leaving once we reach Briarwood?" she was goaded to ask.

His pale eyes sparkled with malevolence. "Wait until you see the quarters we have prepared. Fit for a countess."

Fear trickled down her spine, chilling her to the marrow. She tried to keep the tremor from her voice as she asked the question paramount in her mind. "What do you intend to do with me?"

"You do realize, don't you, that I can't allow you to live?"

The total lack of inflection in his voice made his threat all the more menacing. Christiane felt as though turned to marble. She was going to die by his hand. The last thing she would see would be his ghostly blue eyes alight with satisfaction as he robbed the breath from her body, wrung the life from her soul. Gradually her initial terror leached away, replaced by a profound sadness. There were so many things she hadn't done.

So many things left unsaid.

If she could do things over again, she would tell Reid she loved him. She despised herself for being a coward. Although the words sang in her heart, she never had the courage to say them aloud. She keenly regretted that, along with the fact that his face wouldn't be the last thing she saw every night, and the first thing each morning.

Yawning broadly, Etienne stretched his long legs, crossing them at the ankles. "Seeing you dressed as a Greek goddess reminds me of our wedding night. You look . . . virginal. Are you?" he asked bitterly. "Or did that bastard rob me of the privilege of being your first?"

She stared fixedly ahead, tight-lipped, but didn't reply.

"So," he said with a sneer. "I have my answer. Where did he first take you, Countess? On the forest floor like an animal in heat?"

Again she refrained from answering, unwilling to give him ammunition to despoil an experience that had enriched and altered her life forever.

"Did he find you unresponsive as a block of ice?" Etienne studied her behind lowered eyelids. "Was he able to perform, *chérie*? Or did you wilt his manhood as you did mine?"

"He didn't find me lacking as you did, m'sieur," she fired back.

Only after the words were out did she realize she had made a tactical blunder. What if Etienne should decide to try to force himself on her one last time? In doing so, he would succeed in slaying not only her body but her spirit as well. The notion of his rutting body pounding hers filled her with revulsion, sickened her. Without Hera's potion to render him impotent, she would be powerless to prevent his unwanted advances.

He glowered at her from across the carriage. Even in the meager light of a single carriage lamp, she could detect his flushed skin, the hard set of his mouth, and sensed waves of fury cresting higher and higher. She watched with a mixture of fascination and trepidation as he slowly regained control.

"I'm not interested in bedding you, but du Beaupre is," he informed her in a clipped voice. "I warned him of your lack of passion; however after private tutoring by murdering scum, perhaps you've become more adept at pleasing a man. My Creole friend stated that he likes a challenge. I may just consider his request, provided he lets me watch."

She stared at him aghast. "You're sick. Perverted."

"*Oui.*" He laughed with genuine humor. Propping his legs on the seat next to her, he closed his eyes and went to sleep.

Though Christiane's limbs felt weighted with lassitude, sleep eluded her. Worry and fear kept rest at bay.

Eerie fingers of light stretched across the horizon as the carriage rolled to a halt on the shell drive in front of Briarwood. Rubbing sleep from his eyes, Etienne roused himself from a deep slumber, waiting patiently while the bolt was removed from the carriage door. Metal scraped against metal, and the door swung open to reveal Leon's swarthy face.

"Welcome to Briarwood, Madame Delacroix," he said, holding out his hand. "I see that on this visit you have brought your husband, and not your lover." He chuckled at his own humor.

Glaring at him, she ignored the hand he extended and scrambled unassisted from the carriage. Etienne followed close behind. She cast a hopeful look about, but the yard appeared deserted at this early hour. In the house beyond, only a single room was illuminated. The driver kept his eyes trained straight ahead, and at a given signal from Leon, drove off without a backward glance. No help was likely from any quarter. She had only herself to rely on if she wished to survive. Flanked by Etienne on one side and Leon on the other, she was escorted up the stone steps, across the wide porch, and into the entrance hall.

"You must be exhausted after your long journey," Leon said, acting the role of host. "I trust you will find your accommodations quite comfortable. I had one of my servants bring refreshments to a room I had specially prepared for your visit."

"How very thoughtful, m'sieur," she replied stiffly. "However, I'm not a bit tired and would prefer to remain downstairs." She veered in the direction of the drawing room, only to have Leon grab her arm. She tried to pull free, but to no avail.

Etienne captured her other arm. "Oh, no, you don't," he said, firmly steering her toward the stairway.

She balked, planting both feet firmly on the first step, and caught hold of the newel post. She should have staged a similar dissent in New Orleans when Etienne had forced her into the du Beaupre carriage, but she had been too numb with shock to protest—a fact she bitterly regretted. "I'm not going anywhere unless it's back to New Orleans."

"So our guest needs a little persuading, does she?" Before she could divine his intent, Leon wrenched her arm behind her back, jerking her wrist between her shoulder blades and sending excruciating pain radiating to her shoulder. The agony was so intense it made her knees weak and tears spring to her eyes.

"Change your mind, *petite?*" Leon purred silkily. "Have you decided to cooperate like a good little houseguest?"

All she could do was gasp her assent.

"Now march. Up the stairs, quickly. Don't dawdle."

Not relinquishing the tight grip on her arm, Leon forced her ahead of him. Pain coursing through her, she concentrated on taking them slowly, one step at a time. On the second-floor landing, he urged her down the hallway past the bedrooms to a craftily concealed door behind which a steep flight of stairs wound from cellar to attic for use primarily by the house servants wishing to be unobtrusive. "Don't stop now. Up you go, all the way to the attic."

Etienne smirked at her stricken expression. "We thought you might enjoy some privacy in which to contemplate your transgressions. And time in which to anticipate the pleasures to come. After a few days—or perhaps a week or two—of solitude, you'll be much more compliant."

"Never," she managed through gritted teeth.

Leon opened a sturdy wood door at the top of the stairs and thrust her inside. With a shove, he sent her sprawling to the dusty floor. "I'm a patient man, *petite.*"

"Call if you need anything, *chérie,*" Etienne said on a laugh. "In fact, call until your throat is hoarse. No one will come to your rescue."

The door swung shut. Christiane's last shred of hope vanished with the sound of a lock being snapped shut.

Her arm throbbing, she raised herself into a sitting position. Gradually her eyes adjusted to the gloom. Narrow slats of gray light shone between boards nailed over a recessed dormer window. In the far corner of her prison, she heard the scampering of mice. Pushing to her feet, she stood in the center of the small attic room and gazed around. The tiny room smelled musty and stale. A straw pallet with a threadbare blanket lay in a corner. Next to it sat a jug of water and a loaf of bread. A chipped chamber pot was the only other item in her tiny cell. Trying to allay her steadily encroaching panic, she moved like a sleepwalker toward the solitary source of light. Using all her strength, she tugged at the boards, knowing even as she did that they would refuse to give beneath her prying fingers.

Trapped. Just like Reid, she, too, was a prisoner. She wiped at the tears streaming down her face, leaving smudges of dirt in their path. After a while fatigue blessedly overcame her. Curling onto her side on the lumpy pallet, she closed her eyes.

Chapter
Twenty-five

The moon hovered above the treetops like a broken silver medallion lying on black canvas. Reid used the stingy light to guide the mare along the narrow road that bordered the bayou. Spending nearly twenty-four hours in a small, dank cell had given Reid ample opportunity to reflect on his life. Given the chance, he would do many things differently. But first and foremost, he would tell Christiane that he loved her. He had hoarded that precious declaration like a miser's gold. He had never told her how she filled his heart. That she was the bright half of his soul.

He prayed it wouldn't be too late. Feeling as he did, he knew that if either Delacroix or du Beaupre harmed her in any way he would have to kill them.

Abruptly a harsh bellow, full and blunt, came from the swamp, startling both horse and rider. From his previous visit, Reid recognized the cry as that of a bull alligator. He finally succeeded in calming the skittish animal.

As he urged the mare ahead, his thoughts drifted back to his escape from the old Spanish prison hours earlier. His rescue had come from a totally unexpected source. Who could have imagined the crafty mind lurking behind a guileless, genial expression? Yet gray-haired, dimpled Polly Wakefield had managed to engineer his release. Remembering, Reid still marveled at her audacious feat. If he hadn't witnessed it himself . . .

He had been dozing in his cell when the jangle of keys had awakened him. Opening his eyes, he had found Polly, a wicker hamper slung over one arm, accompanied by one of the prison guards.

"Here is your nephew, señora," the guard said, unlocking the door of the cell. "Visit as long as you'd like."

"*Gracias,* señor." Polly beamed brightly as she slipped inside. "I've brought you supper, dear. I've worried you weren't being properly nourished."

Reid scrambled to his feet, shaking the cobwebs of confusion from his brain. What would bring Polly to such a place at this hour of the night?

"Well, nephew, aren't you glad to see me?" she chided, a mischievous twinkle in her bright blue eyes. "Is this any way to greet your favorite aunt?"

"Polly, I'm just surprised. I thought at first I must be dreaming." Embarrassed to be seen with his wrists manacled and still wearing the ridiculous costume of the night before, he rubbed the stubble on his jaw. "Excuse my appearance, but I haven't been allowed to bathe or shave."

Not the least put off by his appearance, Polly raised on tiptoe and kissed his cheek. "Are they mistreating you, dear?"

"I've had worse," he said, shrugging off her sympathy. "Treatment here is more humane than in Spain. At least so far I haven't been beaten, and prisoners are fed regularly."

Polly set the basket on the cot. "I'm so relieved to hear that. Jean-Claude and I have been concerned about you."

Reid raised a brow inquiringly. "Polly, what *are* you doing here?"

She turned to him, hands clasped at her waist, her expression grave. "We need your help, dear."

"*We?*" he repeated.

"Jean-Claude and I," she elaborated.

Reid held his manacled wrists out for her inspection. "As much as I'd like to offer my services, I'm afraid I can be of little use," he said, his voice hard, bitter.

Polly rested a hand on his arm beseechingly. "We're terribly worried about Christiane's safety after seeing how that devil of a husband looked at her. We fear he intends her grievous harm. He's not the sort to forgive a woman who publicly humiliated him."

A muscle worked in Reid's jaw. "No, he's not."

"Then you'll help us."

"I'd cut out my heart for her."

Her blue eyes suspiciously moist, Polly gave him a wobbly smile. "I brought you some dinner, nephew." She lifted the cloth covering the basket, then nudged aside the loaf of bread and the mound of Dulcie's fried chicken.

Reid gaped in astonishment at the pistol, primed and ready, lying on the bottom of the hamper.

"Enjoy your dinner, dear. You'll need your strength for the task ahead." Polly perched happily on the edge of the cot. "No need to rush. Besides, it'll take a while for the sleeping potion I added to the guard's brandy to take effect."

"You what?" Reid asked when he finally found his voice.

"Shh . . ." She held a finger to her lips. "Sit down, dear. Eat."

Words deserted him. Sinking next to Polly on the cot,

Reid helped himself to a piece of chicken and sank his teeth into a drumstick.

Polly nodded her approval at seeing his appetite. "I also brought you a change of clothes. You'll find a horse saddled and ready in the stable two doors down."

"There's still one problem." He indicated the heavy iron bands at his wrists connected by a short length of chain.

"Jean-Claude and I tried to think of everything." She smiled sweetly. Reaching into her skirt pocket, she produced two keys. "The blacksmith who fashioned those odious locks was more than happy to supply this after a small reward."

An hour later, Reid had left New Orleans behind.

At last Briarwood came into sight. Predawn darkness cloaked the stately house in shadow and mystery. Reid guided the weary mare along the perimeter. In another hour or so, house servants would begin their daily chores, and a procession of field slaves would trek toward land cleared for indigo. But for now Briarwood slumbered. Reaching down, Reid patted the horse's neck. He had pushed the poor beast to its limit and wished he could reward her valiant effort with a brisk rubdown and a trough of hay.

Glancing toward the house again, he frowned. He had to believe Christiane was there unharmed. The authorities would grow suspicious if anything happened to her this soon after an entire ballroom of people had heard his warning. In all likelihood Etienne would bide his time, then choose a subtle method of disposing of his recalcitrant bride. In the meantime, though, where would he keep her?

Reid rubbed eyes gritty from lack of sleep. Knowing Christiane as he did, given a chance to escape she'd take it. No doubt Etienne realized this, too, and would take precautions to made certain she couldn't. He probably had her under lock and key at this very moment.

But where?

Reid mentally reviewed the layout of the house. A maze of storerooms was located along the lower level, with stone floors and walls thick enough to muffle cries for help. In the house itself, the bedrooms were on the second floor. The attic, with its neat row of dormer windows, occupied the uppermost floor. Etienne's perverse nature would be appeased by inflicting as much discomfort as possible. Reid suspected he'd find Christiane imprisoned either on the lower level or in the attic. Resting a hand on his hip, he felt the reassuring weight of the pistol tucked into the waistband of his pants.

Dismounting, he looped the reins over a low-hanging branch and made his way toward the house under cover of darkness. He'd begin his search of the storerooms, then systematically work his way through the house. His time was limited. He knew he had to hurry before it was light.

One by one, he tried each storeroom door, frustrated to find most of them locked. Apparently du Beaupre didn't trust his slaves not to steal from him. His frustration grew steadily as he felt time slipping away. Keeping his voice low, he called Christiane's name repeatedly, but heard no answering cry.

The darkness had already lightened from charcoal to slate when he decided to abandon his search of the lower level. He would try again later after gaining access to the storeroom keys. Reid stealthily crept up the stairs, cursing silently when a tread creaked under his weight. He froze, waiting, listening, but the house remained still.

A thought staggered him as he made his way down the long center hallway, past the bedrooms on either side.

What if Christiane shared a room with Etienne? How would he react if he found them together? Had Delacroix forced himself on her? Or worse yet, what if he had given her to du Beaupre? Scalding rage surged through him at the grim possibility.

Reid ruthlessly tamped down his unruly emotions, then resumed his quest. Quietly easing open a bedroom door, he peered inside. It took a moment in the gloom, but he eventually discerned the shape of a single form. Breathing a sigh of relief, he closed the door as silently as he had opened it. His relief was short-lived, replaced with the knowledge that he still hadn't found Christiane. There was still one level of the house he hadn't searched. Scarcely daring to hope, he moved down the hallway toward the narrow staircase concealed behind the false door that led to the attic.

He recalled from his previous visit that du Beaupre had boasted of the cleverly concealed passageway that ran from cellar to attic, allowing servants unobtrusive access during times when the house overflowed with guests. He had gone only as far as the second step when he felt something hard jab his ribs.

"Couldn't stay away, could you?" Etienne said in a hiss. "I warned the authorities you were slippery as an eel."

"What have you done with her, Delacroix?"

"I assume you're referring to my wife, and it's none of your damn business. Now," he ordered, "put your hands in the air where I can see them."

Reid did as he was told, realizing it was unwise to resist with the barrel of a gun pressed against his back.

"Turn around. Slowly."

Hands in the air, Reid did as instructed. Etienne, dressed in a silk dressing robe, stood at the foot of the stairs, the pistol in his right hand leveled at Reid's heart.

"While we weren't expecting company, your unexpected arrival presents an interesting wrinkle. I think we ought to inform our host he has an uninvited guest." He motioned with the gun for Reid to proceed him down the hallway toward the master bedroom.

He paused outside the door of du Beaupre's bedroom. "Leon," he shouted. "Get your Creole ass out of bed and welcome your visitor."

"Crazy Frenchman! You'd better have a good reason to wake me this early." Moments later the bedroom door swung open and Leon squinted into the hallway. His jaw dropped when he recognized Reid. "Well, well." He smirked. "What have we here?"

Etienne grinned broadly. "I thought depositing him on your doorstep would get the day off to a good start."

"Excellent!" Leon rubbed his hands together in anticipation. Stepping into the hallway, Leon subjected Reid to close scrutiny, then, reaching out, tugged the pistol from Reid's waist. "For the time being, I'll relieve you of your weapon. I doubt you'll have the opportunity to use it."

"Do you want to kill the bastard, or should I?" Etienne asked, clearly relishing his role.

Leon chuckled. "Don't be hasty, *mon ami*. Let's consider the situation from all angles before we do anything rash."

"Very well." Etienne nodded agreeably. "What do you propose we do with the intrepid M'sieur Alexander while we discuss his fate?"

"Ah." Leon snapped his fingers. "I know just the place. Then perhaps over a hearty breakfast, we can devise a plan whereby each of us will be rid of our personal nemeses once and for all."

The two men escorted Reid down the concealed staircase to the lower level, shoved him into one of the thick-walled cooling rooms, and locked the door behind him.

The sound of their laughter echoed after them. To vent his frustration, Reid pounded on the stout door. Just as he had imagined, the portal could have withstood a battering ram.

Desolation washed over him as he slowly sank to the floor and rested his head against the stone wall. With not one but two twisted minds scheming their demise, he and Christiane didn't stand a chance.

Children with tawny hair raced across an immense lawn. In her arms, she cuddled an infant with eyes the color of her own. A ruggedly handsome man approached from the direction of a broad, winding river, his gray eyes alight when they rested on her.

"Wake up, you faithless bitch. We've got a surprise waiting."

Reluctant to leave the pleasant dream, Christiane burrowed deeper into the straw pallet, only to find someone rudely jostling her awake. Being imprisoned in the stifling attic with little food and an abundance of anxiety had left her listless and lethargic. Fitful bouts of sleep provided her only escape. Shoving the hair out of her eyes, she pushed herself onto one elbow.

Light spilled through the partially opened door, glinting on the pistol Leon du Beaupre held negligently in one elegant hand. "What do you want?" she asked in a dull voice.

"Get on your feet." Not waiting for a response, he yanked her from the pallet.

Setting the gun aside, he withdrew a length of rope from his pocket and roughly bound her wrists behind her back.

"I find your hospitality sorely lacking, m'sieur," she said

scornfully, having been reduced to sarcasm as her sole weapon.

"Still the saucy wench, eh?" He tightened the knots with unnecessary force, smiling with satisfaction at her whimper of pain. "It's time a whore like you collects what she deserves."

His shove sent her stumbling across the dusty planks. "Your surprise awaits, madame. Don't tarry on the stairs."

Christiane scrambled down the narrow steps as quickly as possible with her arms restrained. She paused to catch her breath on the landing. She knew from experience that Leon's bedroom as well as a series of guest rooms spread from either side of a wide hallway. Having been locked in the small, dark room had dulled her concept of time. Was it only yesterday morning that the two men had marched her along that passage like a prized trophy?

"Not that way," Leon corrected as she started forward. "Do you foolishly mistake yourself for a guest?" he said with a sneer. "Even the servants' stairs are too good for a slut like you."

Vertigo engulfed her as she stared down the remaining stairs. A misstep would prove fatal. With no handrail to hold on to, it was a long fall to the bottom.

"No longer sure of yourself, *petite*?" He nudged her along. "Wise of you to realize that a single push would send you toppling down two flights of stairs. With your arms bound behind your back, you'd be helpless to check your fall. Afterward we could claim you simply tripped— and broke your neck."

Christiane knew full well how easy it would be for them to insist her death was an accident. Without witnesses, there would be no way authorities could disprove their story.

"You're wasting time," he taunted. "Your husband doesn't like to be kept waiting."

To keep her lower lip from trembling, Christiane caught it between her teeth and bit down until she tasted blood. Cautiously, her back hugging the wall for safety, she edged down the steps.

"Actually," Leon continued conversationally, "a nasty fall is one of the methods we considered to end your misery, but something better came along."

"You're speaking in riddles."

"You'll find out all in due course."

Christiane released a shaky breath when they reached the bottom step leading into the storerooms. A shiver swept through her, as much from nerves as from the sudden coolness. Impatient now, Leon caught her arm and pulled her from the dim lower level into the bright sunlight beyond. Her foot snagged on the uneven floor, and she fell, landing with a force that drove the air from her lungs.

"On your feet, bitch."

Leon reached down and hauled her to her feet. Grabbing a fistful of her hair near the scalp, he twisted his fingers in it, causing her neck to arch in pained response. Tears sprang to her eyes and streamed down her cheeks. After she'd been locked away, the bright glare of the sun was blinding. Reflexively she squeezed her eyes shut to blunt the intensity.

She heard Etienne's voice through a haze. "Open your eyes, *petite*. It's time to bid your lover good-bye."

Blinking moisture from her eyes, she coaxed them apart and saw Reid's familiar figure silhouetted against a bright sky. "Reid . . ." The name broke from her lips.

He took half a step forward before Etienne stopped him. "Move again, Alexander, and she'll get the first bullet."

Her gaze slid from Reid to the gun in Etienne's hand.

Uncontrollable shivers racked her body. She knew with certainty they were both about to die.

"Let's head for the stable, shall we?" Leon suggested.

A gun aimed squarely between his shoulder blades, Reid led the way with Etienne close behind. Leon, his fingers still twined in Christiane's hair, forced her along in front of him. Ignoring her stinging scalp, she swept a glance over her surroundings, but not a soul was visible. No doubt Leon had ordered the servants away on errands. Leon and Etienne wouldn't risk witnesses to their misdeeds.

"You'll never get away with this," she said, summoning a small measure of bravado. "My grandfather will insist upon a full investigation. Everyone heard Reid warn that Etienne would kill me."

Etienne shot her a smug look over his shoulder. "The old man can hardly dispute our story of a lovers' quarrel. Your hotheaded paramour is about to fly into a jealous rage when you refuse to run off with him and choose to remain with me, your newly reunited husband, instead."

Leon supplied the remainder of the details. "Alexander shoots you in a fit of jealousy, then turns the gun on himself, putting a tragic end to your sordid affair."

Without turning around, Reid knew Leon prodded Christiane to follow close behind. His heart had leaped with joy at seeing her virtually unscathed. True, her gown was torn, her face smudged with grime, her hair disheveled, but passion still flickered in her expressive dark eyes. It pained him to see the callous treatment she received from her captors. But if he didn't act—and quickly—that exquisite spirit would be extinguished forever.

He was the first to enter the shadowy interior of the stable. He continued to walk slowly, calmly, past the row of stalls toward a tack room at the back. With seeming disinterest, his gaze roamed about. Then he spied what he was looking for.

In a lightning-quick move, he grabbed a bridle from a peg on the wall and whipped it across Etienne's face. Leather cracked across flesh and cartilage, sending blood spurting from a nasty gash across the bridge of the Frenchman's nose. Before Etienne could do more than howl with pain, Reid followed the attack with a solid punch to his jaw, then another to his midsection. Etienne crumpled to the floor, his form inert as a sack of feed.

Flinging Christiane atop Etienne, Leon reached for the pistol tucked into the waistband of his pants. Not giving him an opportunity to fire, Reid fell on him. The pistol dropped to the earthen floor with a thud and disappeared beneath a mound of straw. Reid swung his fist, but Leon dodged to the right and received only a glancing blow. Both men assumed a crouched position, circling each other like gladiators in an arena. Leon lunged first. Reid feinted, bending as he did so to scoop up the bridle he had used to strike Etienne. Holding the bridle by the browband, he flicked his wrist. The reins snapped like the crack of a whip.

Seeing the bridle his enemy held with casual authority, Leon's eyes darted about, frantically seeking a weapon of sorts. He slowly inched backward. "Only one of us will leave here alive."

"Then you'd better seek peace with your maker." Reid sent the reins lashing across du Beaupre's knuckles.

"Damn you, Alexander." Leon flexed fingers where red welts were beginning to appear. "Why couldn't you just stay out of my life?"

Reid circled him, his eyes never leaving Leon's. "Why did you do it, du Beaupre? Why did you kill your own brother?"

"I'm surprised you ask." He let out derisive laughter. "Gaston was a fool. He had no right gambling away something that should have been mine."

The reins lashed out again, but Leon dodged out of their range. He snatched a pitchfork with long, wickedly curved tines that had been carelessly left against one of the far stalls. "Now we'll see who's the victor." Brandishing it with short, threatening jabs, he forced Reid to retreat.

"I still don't understand," Reid said, playing for time. "Gaston was your own flesh and blood."

"He was a buffoon," Leon said with a snarl.

Raising the pitchfork above his head like a javelin, Leon took aim and hurled it straight at Reid. The tool ripped through the sleeve of Reid's shirt, pinning him to the wall. Blood streamed from a gouge in his upper arm. With a grunt of pain, Reid twisted around and jerked the pitchfork free. When he turned again, Leon was rooting through the straw, searching for the pistol he had dropped.

Reid heaved the pitchfork to one side. "Now we're even, du Beaupre. Just you and me."

Leon balled his fist and swung, but Reid ducked in time to avoid the blow. Using skills he had developed as a youth in the streets of London, Reid was in no hurry to end the fight. He had waited too long for such a moment.

With his left arm tucked close to his body, he struck with his right, catching Leon's jaw and snapping his head backward. He followed the blow up with another short jab, this time hearing the satisfying crunch of breaking cartilage. Blood gushed from du Beaupre's nose and dribbled down his chin.

"Damn you!" Leon swore. "You'll pay for this." From the corner of his eye, he spotted a shovel that had been used to muck out a stall. Reid noticed it, too, but it was out of his reach. Leon grabbed it greedily, a grin spreading across his features. "I'll smash your head in, you bastard. Beat you to a bloody pulp. Not even your lover will recognize you after I'm finished."

Using both hands, Leon swung the shovel. His right foot landed on a small clump of manure that had dropped from the blade. He struggled to regain his balance, his arms pinwheeling wildly. His feet scrambled for purchase on the stable floor, but landed in fresh straw at the edge of a stall, then slid from under him. He toppled backward, landing with a solid thud. An expression of bewilderment crept across his face as he lay unmoving.

Reid stood over him, legs braced for renewed battle. When Leon made no attempt to rise, Reid looked closer and saw the reason. Four thick metal tines protruded from the Creole's chest. Frothy blood bubbled at the corners of Leon's mouth as his lips parted in silent protest. More blood began to stain the front of his snowy white shirt and pool on the yellow straw beneath. As Reid watched, du Beaupre's breathing became increasingly labored.

Knowing the Creole's fate was sealed, Reid turned slowly, looking for Christiane and ready to settle the score with Etienne. But except for Leon, the stable was empty. Christiane and Etienne had vanished.

Propelled by a burning urgency, he raced from the stable toward the house, shouting her name. He ran through each of the rooms, searched the bedrooms, then climbed upstairs. The attic door stood ajar. Bending down, he picked a narrow gold ribbon from the dusty floor, mute evidence of her recent captivity.

"Damn!" He clutched the ribbon in his fist. Where could that devil have gone? They couldn't have traveled far. It was unlikely Etienne would have taken time to saddle and bridle a horse. Perhaps he found the mare Reid had left tied behind a clump of brush. The thought mobilized him, sending him from the house at a full run. But he found the mare exactly where he had left her.

Reid stood, considering his next move. The Mississippi lay to his back, the bayou in front. Without a boat, it would be impossible to navigate either waterway. A road wound through the bayou, ultimately leading to Baton Rouge to the north and New Orleans to the south. Without a horse, the waterways represented the most logical escape route. But which one, he wondered, river or bayou? Hadn't du Beaupre mentioned owning a small craft for use on the bayou? He scanned the shore, but saw no sign of such a craft. Had Etienne procured it for his escape? he wondered.

While he stood there in indecision, a small boat floated into view. The craft made from a hollowed cypress seemed to glide effortlessly over the brackish water. The pirogue, as it was called, was paddled by a wizened man with leathery skin and a bushy mustache. Hair black as a raven's wing peeped from beneath a wide-brimmed straw hat. It appeared to be the same fisherman he had glimpsed in the bayou during his initial visit.

Seeing Reid watching from the shore, the man grinned and gave him a friendly wave. "You lookin' to find som'on', I ask you, hein?"

Judging from the man's unique speech pattern, Reid guessed he must be one of the Acadians, or Cajuns, who had been driven out of Nova Scotia by the British and had settled in Louisiana. "Have you seen a man and a dark-haired woman in the bayou?"

The fisherman shoved back his straw hat and scratched his head. "Me, I see man who don't know how to paddle pirogue. He wit' dark-hair lady. She don' look happy, she."

"I've got to go after them. I need your boat."

"You wanna borrow Octave's pirogue, you?"

"Here, take my horse," Reid urged. "If I don't return your boat you can keep her."

With a wide smile, Octave agreed to the trade.

The instant the pirogue touched shore, Reid stepped into it and pushed off. Dipping the paddle into the water, he propelled the craft in the direction Octave had indicated. After a few minutes he fell into the natural rhythm. The little craft gracefully skimmed across waters spattered with pennywort and duckweed.

He spotted his prey after going less than two miles. To avoid detection, he kept to the reeds, allowing the sturdy pirogue to make a stealthy approach. Christiane sat rigidly erect and statue still in the center of the craft, her wrists still bound. He studied Etienne, puzzled by the man's awkward attempt to paddle. Then his confusion cleared as the reason for his halting progress became evident. Delacroix, he noted, had only limited use of one arm.

Gliding from behind the stand of reeds, he called out, "Delacroix, stop. You aren't going to get away."

Startled at the outcry, Etienne stood up, nearly overturning the pirogue. Reid watched in alarm as the boat rocked wildly, ready to dive in and rescue Christiane. Finally the craft steadied.

Christiane twisted around on the seat, her eyes wide with fear. "Reid," she shouted. "Be careful. He has a gun."

Even as she called out the warning, Etienne drew the weapon and fired. The shot missed its intended target. The loud report sent a pair of egrets fluttering skyward with flapping wings. Reid dug his paddle into the water, and the pirogue shot forward.

Etienne saw him coming, raised his paddle, and swung. The abrupt movement caused the pirogue to overturn, flipping both him and Christiane into the weed-choked water. Leaning over the side of his craft, Reid caught Christiane by the hair as she sputtered to the surface. Drawing from a combination of skill and luck, he managed to pull her into his pirogue without upsetting it. Glancing up, he saw Etienne wading through waist-deep water toward firmer ground. Reid squatted on the bottom of the little boat, untied Christiane's wrists, then pulled her into his arms.

"Are you all right?" he asked anxiously, smoothing wet tendrils of hair away from her face. "If anything had happened to you . . ."

She gave him a tremulous smile. "No matter how much you protest, Reid Alexander, you'll always be my hero."

He swallowed a lump in his throat that felt the size of a grapefruit. "If I am, it's because you've made me a better man."

"I love you," she said, reaching up to touch his cheek.

He was about to reply when Etienne's anguished scream resounded through the bayou. They looked up to see him standing in water that was now only hip-deep. A snake about three feet in length with a triangular black head and a series of wide brown bands around its thick body slithered away.

"It bit me," he cried in outrage. "The damn snake bit me."

"Hold still," Reid called out. "We're coming."

But Etienne refused to listen, trudging instead toward a small rise of cypress trees. Before he reached his destination, however, his knees folded, and he collapsed, slowly sinking below the surface.

As Reid and Christiane watched helplessly, an alligator slid from the bank. It drifted across the still water with remarkable speed toward the spot where Etienne had disappeared. Then the corrugated snout swung open. Catching Etienne's limp form between powerful jaws, the giant reptile gave a twisting motion and disappeared beneath the green, weed-choked waters.

Silently, Reid turned the pirogue in the direction of Briarwood.

Chapter
Twenty-six

Upon reaching the edge of the bayou, Reid lifted Christiane from the pirogue and held her in his arms. Words weren't necessary. It was enough to touch her, hold her, know she was safe. She wrapped her arms around his neck, murmuring words of love. He felt as though he held heaven in his arms. The moment should have been complete. Perfect.

But it wasn't.

Like a sharp blade ready to fall, a murder charge still hung over his head. Until he cleared his name, established his innocence, he had nothing to offer her. And with du Beaupre dead his chance was gone forever.

Raising her face to his, she traced his lips with her fingertip. "I love you," she said softly.

Reid's heart swelled with joy until it felt as though his chest would burst. "I love you, too." He brushed a kiss across her brow. "When I feared I would never see you again, what I regretted most was never having told you how I felt."

"Nothing will ever change my love for you," she vowed.

"Whatever happened to my practical little countess?" he asked with a wry smile. "Falling in love with an accused murderer is far from sensible."

"You have taught me to listen to my heart."

"Ah, Christiane . . ." He claimed her mouth in a kiss that spoke of pent-up longing and hinted of desperation. Then he drew back and set her on her feet.

Hand in hand, they walked toward the house.

Halfway across the wide expanse of lawn, they were met by a small contingent of soldiers. Christiane's hand tightened in his, but she held her head high, her step unfaltering. Reid was never prouder—or loved her more—than he did at that moment.

"Señor Alexander?" the highest-ranking officer formally addressed Reid. "I am Captain Miguel Figaro. On behalf of Esteban Miró, governor of Louisiana, it is my duty to inform you that you have been exonerated in the death of Gaston du Beaupre."

Reid shook his head, certain he had misunderstood. "W-what?"

"The governor begs pardon for the grave injustice inflicted upon you."

With a shriek of joy, Christiane flung herself into his arms. Alternately laughing and crying, she rained kisses over his face. Reid wondered dazedly if this was all a dream, and whether he would soon wake and find himself back in chains.

The captain cleared his throat discreetly. "You have guests waiting back at the house. They were most anxious about your well being and will be greatly relieved that you are safe."

Reid barely heard him. The enormity of what had just happened finally penetrated. Picking Christiane up in his arms, he swung her around. Suddenly the future beamed bright as a newly minted coin.

He and Christiane were still smiling when they reached the house. Polly and Jean-Claude came out onto the porch to greet them.

Jean-Claude clapped Reid heartily on the back. "Congratulations, my boy."

Reid, his arm possessively around Christiane's waist, shook his head in bewilderment. "I don't understand. How did you learn the truth?"

Polly clucked her tongue when she saw Christiane. "You're dripping wet, dear. You'll catch your death. The news will wait until we get you into dry clothes."

With her customary efficiency, Polly whisked a protesting Christiane upstairs, where she had a hot bath and a fresh change of clothing waiting. She chattered on while Christiane hurriedly bathed and slipped into a gown of primrose yellow.

"Your grandfather was worried sick until the Acadian told him a man matching Reid's description had gone in pursuit of a couple in a pirogue. I told him Reid wouldn't let anything happen to you. And I was right," she added smugly.

Leaving her hair to dry in loose curls about her shoulders, Christiane hastened downstairs with Polly close on her heels, eager to hear all the details.

The story unfolded with everyone gathered in the drawing room. It seemed Jean-Claude's suspicions had been aroused from the beginning by Leon du Beaupre's servant, Rollo. The morning after Reid's arrest, Dulcie's innocent remarks about servants being privy to everything involving their masters caused him to seek out the man for questioning.

"Rollo, poor man, hasn't much longer to live," Polly explained, picking up the tale. "He knew Leon killed his brother. He had heard them argue; then when Leon left, he found Gaston dead. He was afraid to speak up sooner for fear of retribution, but doesn't want to die with a guilty conscience.

"Rollo is the one who left the voodoo warnings. He recognized you at once and tried to scare you away before Leon had you returned to prison."

Captain Figaro regarded Reid somberly. "Leon du Beaupre was still alive, though mortally wounded, when we first arrived. He admitted killing his brother and stealing the deed."

"The slave Rollo also supplied the names of various people who witnessed the faro game," one of his lieutenants volunteered. "They should be able to testify that you won the deed to Briarwood honestly."

Captain Figaro rose to his feet and adjusted the brim of his hat. "I have some training in the law. After certain formalities are attended to, the deed to Briarwood will revert to you. Now, if you will excuse us, señor, we must return to the city."

As soon as the soldiers had departed, Christiane left Reid's side and went to her grandfather. "I am so sorry for deceiving you into thinking Reid was my husband." She rested her hand lightly against his chest. "I hope now that you know our reasons you will understand and forgive."

Jean-Claude smiled at her fondly. "My dear child, do you take me for a fool? I've known almost since the beginning that this man wasn't Etienne Delacroix."

"But how . . . ?" Reid asked, coming to stand behind her.

Jean-Claude squeezed her hand reassuringly. "I remember Reid picking me up in his arms and carrying me from that dreadful hospital, all the while as gentle with me as if I were a newborn babe. That was definitely not the act of a man who would refuse shelter to his bride's only kin."

Reid placed both hands on Christiane's shoulders and met the older man's gaze. "With your permission, sir, I'd like to beg your granddaughter's hand in marriage. I promise to love and honor her all the days of my life."

Jean-Claude cleared his throat. "Nothing would please me more."

In a chair by the fireplace, Polly sniffed loudly and dabbed her eyes with a lacy handkerchief.

Christiane turned to Reid, her heart in her eyes. "You're determined to make a respectable woman out of me?"

Cupping her face between his hands, he gazed deep into her eyes. "I want to declare my love before a priest and in front of family and friends. I want to sign my name next to yours in the church register. I want to grow old with you."

Laughter borne of sheer happiness bubbled from her lips. Raising herself on tiptoe, she draped her arms around his neck. "Did you once say seven was your lucky number?"

He grinned down at her. "Hmm. I believe we once had that discussion aboard ship."

Unmindful of anyone looking on, she playfully nipped his ear with her teeth. "If you want four boys and three girls, m'sieur, we should plan a short engagement."

His kiss sealed their bargain.

Put a Little Romance in Your Life With
Fern Michaels

__**Dear Emily**	0-8217-5676-1	$6.99US/$8.50CAN
__**Sara's Song**	0-8217-5856-X	$6.99US/$8.50CAN
__**Wish List**	0-8217-5228-6	$6.99US/$7.99CAN
__**Vegas Rich**	0-8217-5594-3	$6.99US/$8.50CAN
__**Vegas Heat**	0-8217-5758-X	$6.99US/$8.50CAN
__**Vegas Sunrise**	1-55817-5983-3	$6.99US/$8.50CAN
__**Whitefire**	0-8217-5638-9	$6.99US/$8.50CAN

Call toll free **1-888-345-BOOK** to order by phone or use this coupon to order by mail.

Name_____

Address_____

City _____ State _____Zip_____

Please send me the books I have checked above.

I am enclosing	$_____
Plus postage and handling*	$_____
Sales tax (in New York and Tennessee)	$_____
Total amount enclosed	$_____

*Add $2.50 for the first book and $.50 for each additional book.

Send check or money order (no cash or CODs) to:

Kensington Publishing Corp., 850 Third Avenue, New York, NY 10022

Prices and Numbers subject to change without notice.

All orders subject to availability.

Check out our website at **www.kensingtonbooks.com**